OUT OF THE GOLD

THE HUNTE FAMILY SERIES
BOOK THREE

ARELL RIVERS

OUT OF THE GOLD
Book 3 in **THE HUNTE FAMILY SERIES**
ARELL RIVERS
Copyright ©2020 Tarnished Halo Publishing LLC
Published by Tarnished Halo Publishing LLC
2020 Edition

ISBN digital: 978-0-9980316-6-8
ISBN print: 978-0-9980316-7-5

Editing: Trenda Lundin, It's Your Story Content Editing

Emily A. Lawrence, www.lawrenceediting.com

Proofreading: Angel Nyx, https://www.facebook.com/ProfreadingBayouQueen

Roxanne Blouin

Cover design: Dar Albert, Wicked Smart Designs, www.wickedsmartdesigns.com

Synopsis: Jennifer of Romance Rehab, www.romancerehab.com

For my father-in-law Joel Gutterman

May your soul now rest in peace

MELODY

His damn thighs are so thick.

Squinting, I focus on each individual stitch I sew. Who thought this was a good idea? Oh crap, I did. His inner thigh twitches and I maneuver so my needle doesn't nick him. Or his stupid black boxer briefs.

He clears his throat. "If you want to touch my junk, you could ask nicely. I'd let you, you know."

A chuckle from his personal assistant, Thomas Berg, approves his inappropriate remark.

From my position on my knees, I pull the needle through the thick material and bite back the retort dying to spill from my mouth. Ignoring the broad shoulders and six-pack abs on full display, I redouble my efforts to sew him into the spandex as fast as possible with this tricky stitch.

Actors are an entitled lot. And the man I'm sewing into the costume, Chase Wright, is the typical Hollywood pretty boy who happened to grow up in my Chicago neighborhood. Even though he's five years older than me and we never attended school together or met before now, I know his real name. And his sister. Any relation to her is *no* friend of mine.

He wiggles his knees. "At least we shot the rest of the movie in regular clothes already. But it looks like this freaking superhero part is going to take forever." His complaint lodges above my head. "Longer than filming the last two movies combined."

Closing my eyes, I ignore his words and let him settle down before continuing my painstaking work. It wasn't my idea to change the costume. Judith Harris, my boss on our HBO TV show, took over the lead costume designer position for the movie when the original designer was in a fatal car accident a few months before filming was to start. Judith wanted to make her own mark on the trilogy, so she created this ingenious—although not fast and easy—new design for this costume. Since filming was to take place during our show's hiatus, Judith invited both me and my coworker, Helene Parker, to join her here. My first movie. I'll be damned if some over-entitled *movie star* ruins this for me.

My gaze skims over the work I just did. A functional and decorative DNA stitch was a design touch bandied about during our creative process, but was discarded as too difficult. On my own time, I took it upon myself to research and develop what I call the "Manipul8 Stitch," which looks like a stylized infinity symbol filled with horizontal lines. It was included in my prototype for the costume I submitted to become the lead's dresser. Helene also tried out, but she used a simple running stitch in her design. My creativity was rewarded, even if the "reward" comes with Chase attached. Whatever. Now my résumé boasts my addition to the costume.

I earned this all on my own. It's *my* work. My lungs expand to their fullest. No one can claim I got this job because of my father.

"So, Chase, once we wrap here in a couple of weeks, you need to get back to the States to jump on the publicity for *I Was Made for Her*. The red carpet for it is in a month, and we need to get you a new tux. Who do you want to wear?" The PA consults his clipboard, clicking his pen.

The clicks pound like nails on a chalkboard. I inhale.

"I wore Tom Ford last time. How about Versace? I'm feeling more traditional. Must be all this Italian air."

I roll my eyes and abandon the tricky Manipul8 Stitches in favor of a running stitch since his boots will cover this bottom part. How fucking tall is this guy anyway? It's like his legs go on forever. Deftly, I tie off the thread. Before I can start on his other leg, though, I need to check that everything fits this one without any problems.

I pose my instruction to the movie star. "Can you bend your left leg, please?"

His leg bends and flexes a few times. The unsewn material on the interior of his right leg flaps with the movement, but the left one looks good moving with him. My hands skim over his leg, double-checking the costume—ignoring his hard muscles—all the while his conversation with Thomas continues. Names of hairstylists and jewelers roll off his tongue.

When we wrap, *I'm* going back to my condo in New York City to begin prepping for the upcoming season of *Ladies of the Abbey*. I've walked the Emmy red carpet a couple of times, and we won last year. A small smile plays over my face. Our costumes have improved over the three years I've been working there, and I feel confident we'll get another nod again this year. And win.

Chase does a deep knee bend. "Can you tell me again why I have to actually be *sewn* into these leggings rather than put them on like pants?"

My eyes trace the intricate helixes embossed on the outside of his spandex-covered leg—the look I imitated on his inner thigh. The design is fantastic. His question, not. "Because Judith created this new design so it wouldn't be as hot for you, and so you'll be able to use the restroom without having to make it a big production."

He rakes his hand over his perfectly ruffled almost black hair, rubbing the undercut at the nape of his neck. "Guess I can't argue those reasons," he grouses.

Finished checking my handiwork, I haul myself upright and stretch—*I'm* the one who's been laboring over it for the past hour, not *him*. On stiff legs, I shake them as I traverse the trailer to grab a bottle of spring water. "This first time should be the longest it takes." I cross my fingers while downing the water.

"Hope you're right."

No matter what, it isn't easy to sew someone *into* a garment—he's not a mannequin. But the result will give *me* props. *Eyes on the prize, Melody.* Taking one last swallow of water, I toss the empty bottle into the recycle bin and return to Chase. Shaking out my hands, I ask, "Ready for your right leg?"

Chase kicks, and the material flutters again. "Yeah."

I wait a fraction of a minute for Judith to appear, but when she doesn't, I get down on the pillow at his knees. Stretching the spandex around his upper right thigh, I begin the process all over again. Concentrating so as to avoid his *junk*.

The phone rings and Thomas addresses Chase. "It's Sam."

"Great." He takes the phone from his PA and greets Sam Kirkland, his legendary agent. Even though I focus on my needlework, it's impossible for me not to eavesdrop on his conversation. I am, after all, right below his cell phone, and the conversation is on speaker.

"There's a new movie I just heard about. A rom-com. Set to start filming late next year."

Chase's leg tightens. What's that about? I wait for him to relax before continuing my task.

"Any leading ladies interested yet?"

His agent replies, "I've heard various names. Julia. Emily. Ashley. Gwen. Marlo. No one in particular, but you'd look good against all of them. Want me to submit your name for the role? Pay is great, with the same perks as usual."

Beneath my hand, Chase's leg tenses again. I drag the needle away and flex my fingers. His tenor voice continues, "Who else is up for the lead?"

"The usuals. Plus"—Chase's body stills as he taps his left thigh while waiting for his agent to continue—"a few younger guys. But you're the one with the star power."

Chase releases an exhale, which sounds more like a sigh to me. "Sure. Should be interesting. Send me what you have so I can take a look." He disconnects and tosses his phone back to Thomas.

After a few moments, his leg relaxes and I return to my stitching, trying to puzzle out his body's reaction to the new movie. Discarding such a useless endeavor, I do my best to ignore the rest of his conversation with Thomas, which consists of the upcoming red carpet for his last movie. From the corner of my eye, I catch his PA taking lots of notes. Must be challenging being the right-hand to one of Hollywood's leading men.

Ha! Leading *boy*, more like it. When not on a set, Chase is well-documented as being off partying with some starlet or another. Or out with his posse of other actors, all of whom probably are up for this movie his agent pitched.

Of course, there's the obligatory gym sessions he has to make in order to maintain his physique. Which is pretty damn good. Not an ounce of fat on him, that's for sure. Matches what's on the inside, from what I can see. Nothing under the hood.

A lifetime of living with my dad has taught me all the smoke and mirrors Hollywood employs. Even though he's a rock star and my mom's his accountant, I've met too many actors to count. Some of them are nice, but the vast majority have been either empty-headed, insecure, or too full of themselves. No matter what, they've all wanted to get to know me as an access point to my family—and what the last name "Hunte" can do for them.

Like Grant.

Slamming my eyes shut, I silence the voices in my head. I'm *not* thinking about my ex-boyfriend ever again. Except to reiterate my vow. Never, ever get involved with anyone in the business. Period.

Chase continues barking orders to Thomas. Now he's directing him to get more special fizzy water only available at some high-end boutique here in Amalfi. The PA exits the trailer five minutes later, presumably in search of the specialty water.

Using both of my hands, I turn Chase's body a little bit to the side for better access.

The door to the trailer opens again, footsteps announcing someone's walked up the steps. Geez, Grand Central much?

"Looking like Doctor Manipul8, man." Mark Ivan walks up the

aisle, his very distinctive baritone with slight Russian accent caressing the words.

No such thing as privacy on a movie set. I glance at the newcomer, noticing he's already in his villain costume. Giving him a dispassionate appraisal, I nod—Helene did a good job. He looks camera ready.

I pull back when Chase bends his knees. "More like a One."

The two fist-bump. I concentrate on sewing the tricky area around Chase's knee. They discuss the scene they're about to film and laugh at Mark's role as the villain. Mark makes fun of the superhero costume Chase is wearing. Like the two kids they are. Pretty boys. Actors. No, worse—*movie stars.*

When Chase's legs move again, I grab them to still the movement. I'm now at his mid-calf and the end is in sight. I tune out their conversation and focus, switching to the running stitch below the boot line. Finally, I'm done. Raking my eyes over both of his legs, I admit they look damn good and allow the exultation of the moment to wash over me.

Blowing air out of my mouth, I rise to my feet. At five-foot-seven, I'm still seven inches shorter than Chase, but standing upright again is revitalizing. Not to mention it's demeaning to be on my knees in front of him.

I clap twice, catching the attention of both of the boys in the trailer. "I think I'm done with your pants. Take a walk around and tell me how they feel."

Chase's hand slashes through his hair. "About time." His audience gives a hoot of laughter. Jerks.

I stifle the urge to seize one of the knitting needles holding up my bun and lodge it at Chase's throat. I can see the headline from here— "Crazed Costumer Kills Doctor Manipul8 over Leggings."

Dropping my hands to my sides, I grit out, "Just do it." Obviously unused to being challenged, the spoiled actor quirks his eyebrow, and I mumble, "Please." I force my hands to remain open at my sides. And my breakfast to remain in my stomach.

Mark shoves Chase, causing the desired effect, if not the manner.

Chase takes a few tentative barefoot steps, bends down from his knees, and jumps. I watch his every movement for any signs of the stitches not holding, but everything looks good. "How do they feel?"

"Weird. But the leggings aren't pulling or anything."

"Good. You'll get used to how the suit feels in no time." I'll also get used to sewing him into it. Wonder which one of us gets across the finish line first?

Mark adds, "Yeah, Doc. Gotta wear the getup or you're not a superhero."

"Douche."

Mark punches his shoulder.

Chase gives him the finger.

He walks around the trailer for a few minutes and I study his movements. Pride at my handiwork grows as the costume looks good. Next up, I have to get Chase into the upper-body part of the costume, a bodysuit made of a heavier spandex-rubber material than the pants. I walk over to the closet where two exact replicas of the bodysuit hang, running my hand over the black material. A gold stylized "8" is located over the heart. Defined six-pack abs plus an Adonis belt are the main feature of this design. Have to give props to Judith—her design really is awesome and the weight of the material is deceptively light. It'll look fantastic on camera.

"Okay, here's the next part of your costume." I give him the wicking undershirt our shopper picked up. Once he's in it, I shake the bodysuit, which snaps at the crotch. Not the most conventional outfit for a man, but super-practical.

Chase looks at the bodysuit with wide eyes. "You have to be shitting me."

Mark stifles a snort, mutters a goodbye, and hightails it out of the trailer.

"This better be worth it," he gripes.

What a primadonna. I shake the bodysuit. Again.

His jaw clenches as he snatches it from my hands, puts it down to the floor and lifts his foot.

My eyebrows reach my hairline. "What are you doing? You put it on over your head."

He gives me a dirty look as his foot goes through the bodysuit's opening and lands on the floor with a thud. "I've been dressing myself for thirty years. I think I know how to do it by now." He places his other foot through the opening and yanks it up. His body contorts in all sorts of ways as the material makes its way toward his arms.

When the bodysuit gets stuck mid-abdomen, I shove aside my annoyance and help the thirty-year-old baby. I'm not being altruistic, but how this costume looks will affect how Judith views me.

He grunts as it gets caught again around his arms. I take my time and settle the material over the rest of his body with care. I don't want to rip this, as it took over forty man-hours to create. Due to time constraints, we only have one other for the shoot.

When the material is situated over his upper-half and spandex abs are in place, I motion for him to snap it beneath his crotch. His lip curls downward.

What a baby. "For heaven's sake, just do it."

"This outfit is so much different from what I had before." He motions up and down his body.

His whining is the last straw. "You're getting paid a shit-ton. Do your job and stop complaining."

He scowls. "Says the woman in street clothes."

He steps apart and reaches down, causing me to turn my head. When I hear the telltale third snap, I return my gaze and check out the effect. My God, he is a masterpiece. Shoving this errant reaction away, I give a critical eye to the superhero ensemble before me. You can't see the snaps at all. They're obscured by the bulge. The very pronounced bulge. Yay, Judith, way to stroke his oversized ego.

Satisfied with the costume so far—and ignoring a weird flutter in my gut—I turn my attention to the last remaining pieces. All that's left are his boots, which he shouldn't complain about. Well, and the mask, which can wait till last. I hand him a pair of socks and the black boots, and point to the chair. Stiffly, he maneuvers to it and sits down with extreme care. Soon after, he's wearing the footwear.

I offer him the mask—a gold affair that covers up his eyes and nose. He takes it from me and secures it in place, then turns his azure eyes on me. Despite all I know about Charles Wainwright, which is Chase's real name, I swallow. He has been transformed into the graphic novel character.

Piercing blue eyes.

Tousled black hair.

That damn cleft in his chin.

Body chiseled as if by Michelangelo.

I stifle my reaction. Filming in Florence with all the artist's masterpieces before we arrived here must've gotten to me. I shake my head. "Why don't you stand up and walk around to get a feel for the full costume?"

He places his hands on his knees and rises. His *bare* hands. Shoot. I forgot the gloves. While Chase walks around, I head over to my bag. Holding out the gloves, I say, "Almost forgot these."

He glances at my hand and takes the gloves but doesn't put them on. Whacking the side of his leg with them, he paces through the trailer.

"Does anything pinch?"

"No. It's okay." He stops. "Not as heavy as the one before."

His observation warms my heart. "I'm happy to hear that. It was designed to be as comfortable as possible."

He nods and starts to do a few yoga poses, getting used to moving in the costume. I focus on his whole body at first, then zero in on his legs to make sure the Manipul8 Stitches are holding. Everything looks good. Although . . . an unusual bump has formed around his knee.

With a furrowed brow, I watch Chase go through several standing poses, but the bump grows. "Stop for a sec. I think something's wrong by your right knee."

Face turned downward, he bends both of his knees. I walk to him and run my hand over the back of his leg and knee, feeling an air bubble. Relief streams through me. "It's only air. Take off your boot and let me see what I can do about it."

"Really? You couldn't have caught this before?" He plops down into the chair—if another issue with his costume existed, it would appear after *this* tantrum—and rips off his boot.

Placing my hands on my hips, I stare at him with disgust. "It looked fine before. Now stand up."

He does and I run my hand down his leg, starting mid-thigh. Ah. Here's where it started. I work the air out of the costume to the background music of Chase's annoyed noises. Whatever.

"There. It's all fixed now."

"Better be." He sits down and puts his footwear back on. A knock on the trailer door grabs both of our attention. Chase slips on the gloves, which I turn to check their fit. Giving him the all clear, he yells, "Come on in!"

His co-star and love interest in the movie, Jessa Mendes, bounds into the trailer. "Chasey, darling, are you almost . . ." Before she can finish her question, he stands. "Christ. You look hot enough to eat in that suit." She licks her lips and I turn my head so they can't see my repulsed expression. Not that they'd care. Why do I?

She approaches him, placing her hand on the "8" over his heart. "Holy Moly, Chasey. You look every inch a superhero. More so than ever before."

The two talk in low murmurs, and I head toward my three-tiered design suitcase, snagging another bottle of spring water along the way. My job here is done, until filming is over today. Tossing my scissors and sewing supplies into the top compartment, I close everything up.

In spite of Chase, I'm proud of the work I did in here today. Two more weeks of this, maybe less, and I'll be free of him. The delight welling up in me for executing Judith's design can't be dampened by his behavior.

Finishing up the bottle, I toss it into recycling and roll my suitcase under the table for later, then pick up my essentials tote. Passing them, I say, "I'll let the director know you're ready, Chase."

His gloved hand clamps around my wrist. "I think the costume will do."

At the contact, a tremor ripples up my arm. What the hell? My gaze drops to his glove and travels up to his blue eyes. I dip my head in acknowledgment.

When he releases me, I ignore the odd disappointment in my chest and leave the two actors. Free of the trailer, I inhale the fresh, beautiful Amalfi air. Well, to be fair, we're located somewhere above Amalfi, looking down on the Tyrrhenian Sea. The tiny village with quaint storefronts and lots of open land is perfect for this part of the movie.

I pluck my sunglasses out of my essentials tote—needles, thread, scissors, stitching tape, and other doodads at the ready. Let's hope I don't need any of them for today's filming. Or ever.

As I head toward the set, my cell phone rings. Digging into the tote, I grab the phone and a smile crosses my face. "Daddy!"

"Hey, Princess. How's the Italian coast treating my baby?"

Even though we're not Facetiming, I do a three-sixty. "It's gorgeous here. I mean, I loved Florence and Rome, but the Amalfi Coast is sort of magical."

"I know what you mean." After pleasantries, he says, "I got some news."

I quirk my eyebrow. "What's up"

"We're making great strides on the movie about Hunte. Since Hollywood released *Bohemian Rhapsody* and *Rocketman*, everyone's saying it's perfect timing. We've already started auditions for actors to play us." He chuckles. "Can you believe several actors want to play me?"

I turn and head toward the set. "I'm sure a lot of guys wish they could *be* you, rather than simply get the role."

"You're too good for my ego. Your mother doesn't say such nice things to me." He grunts. "Ouch! That woman hit me!"

I laugh at their antics. Married for nearly a quarter of a century, every time I see them, they are more in love than before. "I'm happy for you."

Chase and Jessa pass by me on their way to the set. Guess they didn't need me to let the director Ned Nobleman—whom everyone calls Noble—know he was ready. I slow my steps.

"I want to be happy for you, too, Princess. How would you like to be the *lead* costume designer for the movie?"

My feet stop moving as if they were immersed in cement. My head shakes from side to side.

When I don't respond, he asks, "What do you think?"

I lick my dry lips. "I appreciate the offer, Daddy, I really do, but"—I rack my brain for a positive spin—"I'm sure you'll be filming when I'm back on the television show." There. He can't argue with that.

"Honey, I'm an executive producer. We can work around your schedule, no problem."

Rats. Ahead, several people surround Chase, slapping him on the back. Guess the costume is a hit. I should get there. Which means I need to end this conversation.

Gulping Italian air, I screw up my courage and say, "Daddy, I'm excited for you and the band. I think your movie is going to be amazing. But I don't think I'd be a good fit."

He interrupts, "That's not true—"

Judith motions for me to join them on the set. I don't want to admit this, especially to my dad, but time's up. "Actually, I can't do it for you. Everyone would think I got the job due to nepotism, and you know how hard I've been working. I have to make it by myself, and if I took your offer, I'd be going backward. I earned my job on *Ladies of the Abbey* by my hard work in school"—despite what the press release said—"and because of that, I'm here on *Doctor Manipul8.*"

"I guess I can understand," he grumbles.

"I will gladly walk the red carpet with you at the premiere. I will be your biggest cheerleader. I promise! But I can't take the job."

Judith waves at me again. I walk briskly toward her.

"I can understand your logic. Your mother said you wouldn't take it either."

I chuckle at how disgruntled he sounds. "Wise woman." I'm close to the set. "Oh, and, Daddy, please don't say anything to me about the movie at all. I want to experience it with the rest of the moviegoers, okay?"

He sighs. "Sure thing, Princess. My lips are sealed."

I smile. "Thanks. Now, I have to get on set. I love you. Give Mom a big kiss from me."

I disconnect the call, put my phone on silent, and toss Daddy's movie out of my head. Now, I'm all about *Doctor Manipul8*.

Even if that means Chase.

MELODY

Noble yells, "Action!"

Chase and Jessa walk down the cobblestone street, his head swiveling from side to side as if he's looking for something. Which he is supposed to be doing—a jewel encased in a material called Aurumite, a special gold-like metal both he and his archenemy played by Mark are searching for. With each step, Chase seems more comfortable in the costume, which probably was Noble's purpose for filming this part today.

Light catches the inside of Chase's leg. The Manipul8 Stitches are subtle but enhance the costume. A satisfied smile crosses my lips.

"CUT!"

The actors surround Noble.

With a break in the action, my gaze steers to the only female cameraperson, my best friend in the whole world, Sophia Jenkins. She and I grew up together, but it was dumb luck we both ended up on *Doctor Manipul8*. Spending so much time with her has been a huge part of why I'm having such a great time on set. I wink at the tall, lanky woman with a brunette pixie cut, and she waves before focusing her attention on an impromptu meeting.

After watching her with the crew for a moment, I grab my Burt's

Bees lip balm from my essentials tote. Hard to say how much longer we'll be at it today, but I'm proud of how everything's gone so far. Before they started shooting, Chase received a huge round of applause from everyone for his full Doctor Manipul8 getup.

We did a good job. *I* did a good job.

"I like that smile." Sitting next to me, Judith wears an identical expression on her face.

"He looks good. Great design."

Without turning her head, my boss adds, "Great execution."

Her praise seeps into my bones. It's rare and always to be savored.

She clears her throat and looks from me to Helene, who sits on her other side. "So, I was talking with Noble before, and he's very impressed with everything we've done here. He pulled me aside just now to compliment us on the revisions to the superhero costumes. Did you know he's going to be directing a new trilogy?"

Helene's shoulder-length frizzy red bob shakes while my eyebrows rise. "No, I hadn't heard."

Judith nods. "He asked me to interview to be the lead costume designer for them." She turns her head to me. "That's why I wasn't able to get into Chase's trailer while you were sewing him into the costume earlier."

Now that I understand where she was before, my heart rate accelerates. With excitement for Judith, who deserves this opportunity to shine. With questions as to what this possible move might mean for the TV show—and my career. "Wow. That's amazing." I clear my throat. "I'm sure you're going to get the job. Look at what you did here on *Doctor Manipul8*."

Helene pipes up. "You've worked your butt off at HBO for years, Judith. Now on this movie. It's your time." She flicks her eyes to me. "I agree with Melody. You're going to be a shoo-in."

Judith sits straighter. "I really appreciate all the hard work you've both put into this movie. Not to mention what you do on *Ladies of the Abbey*."

Noble claps and the actors take their places. Out of the side of her mouth, Judith whispers, "If I get this job, my position on the show will be open."

This is happening so fast. I had expected Judith to get some movie offers, which represents the pinnacle of our industry. Movies open so many new doors, including the possibility of an Oscar to add to her Emmys. Selfishly, I hoped she would stick around the show for a few more years so I would get more time to learn from her. While I'm loving being in Italy, my experience here has taught me that I prefer the family atmosphere of working in TV rather than the team aspect of movies.

This thought leads to my next one. If Judith leaves the show, who will replace her? I remove the knitting needles from my bun and fluff my hair. After graduating *magna cum laude* from NYU with a degree in costume design, I landed my job there three years ago. I worked hard for the opportunity, no matter the press release announcing my addition to the show had the headline "Legendary Rock Star Braxton Hunte's Daughter Joins HBO Costume Design Team." However, I'm the one who arrives early and leaves later than anyone else. I've learned a lot from Judith—am I ready to step into her heels?

Glancing at my "rival," Helene, her squared shoulders and jut of her chin seem to show she is. Over the past fifteen years, she's been working her way up in HBO with other shows.

Yet, I'm the one who thinks outside the box to include unusual details. Working with other professionals on set, I help create the illusion viewers demand, like fun fringe on the bottom of the lead's knapsack—while Helene stays well within the lines with expected holes in jeans. My embellishments are the ones fans tweet about all the time. Hell, yes, I'm ready!

The assistant director yells, "Quiet on the set!"

Placing my hair back into a ponytail, I recreate my bun and secure it with the knitting needles. My motivation to show Judith exactly what I can do here on set is renewed. I have the remainder of the movie shoot to prove myself. With that thought, I rededicate my energy to giving more than one hundred and ten percent. I glance at Helene again, who plays with her earring. *Game on.*

The scene restarts. The two actors walk down the street, discussing the research done by Troy Oro, Chase's character, that involved revising people's DNA to eradicate diseases.

Chase doesn't tell Jessa this, as it already was in the first movie, but one of Troy's experiments went terribly wrong. Or right, I guess, depending on how you look at it. He's now able to touch the top of a person's head and rearrange their DNA—for good or ill. When he does this, CGI effects will make the gold stylized "8" over his heart glow.

As they walk down the sidewalk, Chase talks with his hands, gesturing toward a group of people ahead. One of the minor actors steps forward, pushing a curly-headed boy ahead of him. "Doctor Mainupul8, my son's been diagnosed with a rare cancer. We've heard" —the actor looks behind him and all the extras nod—"you can cure him." He pushes the child forward. "Please."

Chase extends his hand toward the kid and ruffles his curly hair. "Let me see what I can do."

Chase's glove-covered hands land on top of the child's head, and he strikes a pose in front of the green screen that he holds for a full minute. When he tries to pull back, though, the Velcro securing the glove appears caught in the child actor's hair.

"OWWWWWW!!!! MOOOOOOMMMMMYYYYY!!!!!!!"

I'm out of my seat and onto the set within seconds, essentials tote swinging behind me, racing to the wardrobe malfunction. Sophia's wide eyes meet mine. Before I reach the actors, Chase tries to remove the gloves but only succeeds in getting the Velcro more tangled in the boy's hair. Jessa works the buckle, and that, too, only makes matters worse.

"Wait! Wait! Let me do this," I scream as I approach the throng of actors.

Brushing aside all hands but Chase's, which is ensconced in the child's curls, I order, "Stop moving, both of you."

I take a deep breath and assess the situation. The strip of Velcro holding the glove in place around Chase's wrist somehow got loose. A bunch of curls are wrapped around the buckle and now enmeshed in the Velcro. Great. The best course of action is for me to remove the glove from Chase's hand, and then remove the Velcro from the hair. Or cut it out—but I'm sure the actor wouldn't appreciate that. Nor would the hair department.

"Okay, I'm going to get you out of the glove, Chase."

My eyes dart to him, and he's scowling. I bury my mother's admonition to lose the scowl before his face remains like that forever, and focus on removing the flap from the decorative buckle. Once that's done, I open up the glove and Chase slides his hand out, rubbing his wrist.

"Some fucking great costume," he mutters. "Not like I'll ever have to put my hands on another actor's head. That's the whole damn movie. Get it fixed." He rips his hand out of the other glove and throws it onto a table. With that, he storms off the set, pushing by Judith and Helene.

I resume my efforts on the child's hair. Jerk. *He* was the one who put the gloves on. I double-checked them, but obviously not good enough.

My musings are interrupted when the child actor screams again. "Ouch! This hurts!!"

His mother, who has been on set as required by law, rubs his back and tries to comfort him. I catch her gaze and she offers a wan smile. At least one person is sort of on my side.

After minutes of wrestling with the child's curls, I hold the offending glove high over my head, free and clear.

Sophia and some of her friends on the camera crew clap. The hair people swoop down and begin to fix the damage done to their creation. I exhale and close my eyes.

"Guess we didn't think this part through." Judith's voice floats to my ears. "Can I see it?"

I pass her the glove, grab the other one Chase left, and we walk off the set. Judith turns the offensive glove in various directions. "The Velcro should've stayed on the glove. What happened?"

I shake my head. "I think it was the buckle that got caught first, allowing the Velcro to adhere to his hair. It never occurred to me this could be a remote possibility."

Helene adds her two cents, "Better change it up. I don't think Chase would want to be afraid his gloves will do that every time he does the DNA trick."

Judith undoes and re-secures the glove. "This looks fine, but Helene has a point. Because Chase must lay his hands on everyone's head, we can't chance this happening again."

I bite the inside of my lip. "We could use a different material and have the glove go under the arm of the costume instead of over it. No buckles. Since Noble has to digitally enhance the gloves anyway, it might not make too big of a difference." I think about the fabrics I have in his trailer. "We could use a black cotton material."

"Cotton? Not against the body suit," Judith muses. "I do like your idea about having it go underneath the sleeves. And no buckles."

"What about silk?" Helene offers.

Shoot. That's a good idea. Why didn't I think of it?

Judith considers her suggestion. "Silk. That could work. Black silk. Matte, not shiny."

I consider the fabrics I have, discarding them all.

Helene pipes up, "I have the perfect thing. It's in my bag, in Mark's trailer."

Noble approaches.

Judith rushes us away, "Go make a prototype. I'll stall for time." She braces to face the unhappy director.

Without even an inhale, Helene and I race off the set. "Bring me your material while I prepare a pattern in Chase's trailer." We part and, panting, I rip open the door and rush up the stairs.

Chase lounges in a chair, flipping his mask. "You better get my gloves fixed pronto. I hate delays for stupid shit."

I see red. "This isn't stupid. How were we to know the buckle would wrap around someone's hair? I've worked with gloves before, you know, and they've been fine. Maybe it was the idiot who put them on." I'm so angry I don't care about my use of the slur.

"Or maybe it was the *idiot* who double-checked the fastenings."

I suck in my breath. Not having time for his obnoxious comments, I force a calm voice. "We're going to remake the gloves out of a different material." I rip open my three-tiered design suitcase and toss pieces of fabric aside, grabbing some muslin.

"Here." I point to the table now covered by the material, the rubber band around my wrist catching my attention. I flick it, allowing the tiny sting to absorb my negative energy like my mother taught me so long ago. "Set your hand down. I'm going to make a quick pattern."

Chase's brow forms a deep V. "Really? Starting that now? Couldn't have thought of this before?"

I pluck the rubber band twice more.

CHASE

Melody snaps the stupid rubber band around her wrist two times and repeats, "Put your hand here. *Please.*"

Her last word sounds more like Noble's orders —*please* get this done in one take so we can all go to lunch—rather than a polite request. Despite that, I plunk my hand down on the cloth. She traces an outline, twice, with a Sharpie, repeating the same process for my other hand.

Pacing inside the trailer, I head over to the fridge and grab one of my waters to calm my nerves. I'm renowned for never getting upset on a shoot. Directors always comment about how even-tempered I am, and how much they enjoy working with me. I'm not a diva.

Then why am I running on empty for this movie?

When we were in Florence, it wasn't bad. Everything went pretty well, with the usual hiccups. Something changed with the salt air, ever since we arrived in Amalfi. Maybe it's the realization I'm wearing a stupid superhero costume again, no matter how well designed this one is. Perhaps it's the two hours it takes for me to get into said costume.

Yeah. That must be it. I've never had so much attention paid to my wardrobe before.

Placing the blame for my surly attitude squarely on the learning curve for my new costume, I twist the bottle open. A burst of fizz soaks into my soul, and I take a sip. The water flows down my throat, leaving inner peace in its wake. All I need to do is adjust to this new normal. Besides, it's only another couple of weeks of filming, and this trial will be over.

"There. Try these on." She shoves a couple of slips of material at me.

While I was finishing up a bottle of my water, she made a proto-type for the new gloves. I take the hastily made garments from her and slide my hands into them.

She turns them in all different directions. "How do they feel?"

I form fists, then release them and wiggle my fingers. I count to five before replying, "They're good."

The door to my trailer opens and her colleague enters. Helene's older than Melody and doesn't put me on the defensive like she does. Perhaps I can ask to have my dresser switched? Walking over to us, she examines the muslin gloves on my hands and whispers something in Melody's ear.

She nods at her co-worker then moves each one of my fingers. "I agree," she addresses me. "I think these will work." Melody points to the ends of the gloves that finish partway up my arm. "I made them this length so your bodysuit will easily cover them."

Whatever. It's a smart design. I don't bother telling her that. "How long will it take you to make real ones?"

"About an hour."

"Okay. I want to get out of the bodysuit." After stripping out of the new gloves, I head to the back of the trailer and stand with my legs wide. Reaching down, I unsnap the material.

In the front, Helene holds out a black fabric. "Here, I found this silk. Judith agrees—should be perfect."

Melody responds, but I'm not interested so long as the gloves get fixed. I try to wiggle out of the bodysuit, but it gets caught across my upper body. Damn. Without a word, Melody appears at my side and helps me take it off. Freed, she returns to Helene while I toss the bodysuit on a table, throw the damp undershirt away, and leave the two women in the trailer to create gloves that should've been done correctly the first time.

A few steps from the trailer, Judith meets me. "So very sorry for what happened to you back there. We never considered the possibility the glove could become a liability for you."

"Thank you, Judith. I appreciate your words." Not like either of her assistants offered any such sympathies.

"How are the new gloves coming along?"

"Okay." I point toward the trailer. "Melody created a pattern and Helene dropped off the new fabric."

Her eyes follow the direction of my finger. "I'll make sure everything will work as you need it to."

Before she takes a step, I ask, "How about switching up Melody for Helene as my dresser?"

Judith grimaces for a split-second, then schools her features. "Did something happen between you and Melody?"

We grew up together in Chicago and, even though we never met there, she knows who I really am.

She's living her truth—being a costume designer.

Her beauty rubs me the wrong way.

No sooner do these thoughts enter my brain does my ingrained need to be seen as easygoing resurfaces, and I shrug. "I just feel more relaxed around Helene."

The lead costume designer sighs. "Normally, I would make the trade. It's only that Melody developed the stitch for the inside of your leggings and Helene doesn't know how to do it. I suppose—"

I close my eyes, searching for my inner Zen. Which I'm going to need a lot of to finish this shoot. "No, that's fine. I can deal for two weeks."

Judith inclines her head. "Thanks."

We part ways, and I return to the set, sitting down next to Mark and Jessa. "Did I miss anything?"

Jessa doesn't respond with words. Her eyes, however, descend over my naked torso as if it were her lips doing the traveling.

Mark finishes a sandwich. "Nah. Noble and Judith were talking about your glove for a long time. Since she left, he's been watching a replay of the aborted scene we just shot."

"Let's hope the new gloves work better than the original ones." I offer him my naked fist, which he bumps.

Jessa finds her voice. "So, it's our first night in Amalfi. Want to check out the nightlife? Heard about a club that's off the chain, and a bunch of us are going there tonight to check it out."

Although I have little desire to go out, I reply as expected and summon a smile. "Count me in."

Mark replies, "You know I'm there."

Jessa offers us both a beaming smile, yet my body doesn't react at all. It's the first time her gorgeous expression has failed to rouse my attention. Huh.

Before I can really dissect my last thought, Noble approaches us holding an iPad, and offers some constructive criticism about how to improve the scene. When the new gloves are finally ready.

Which better be soon.

My eyes return to the area of my trailer, but it remains empty. I kick my booted foot.

When Noble pulls Jessa aside, Mark places his hand on my bare forearm. "How's it feel to be Doctor Manipul8—in full regalia—for the final movie?"

"Weird," I answer. "Sad. I'm going to miss it, but not all the hoopla over the suit." I gesture to my bottom half.

"I can imagine. Is the suit as awful as it looks?"

"Actually, no. There's a lot more breathing room than the other two times, which is good. How's yours?"

Mark bends down and picks a cup off the ground, the smell of coffee wafting up to my nostrils. Wish I liked the stuff, but I'm one of the few freaks who doesn't. "Well, since it's my first time in it, I don't have anything to compare it to. I have to say, I'm much more comfortable than I had feared I would be. Hope they can fix your gloves the way Judith said."

"Me too. By the way, I want to compliment you on your portrayal of Mr. A so far. You almost had me fooled that you were on my side."

He smiles, a prosthetic golden tooth on full display. "Thanks, man. Playing the villain is so much fun. I love luring people into a false sense that I'm doing good." He sips from his cup and plunks it back down on the ground.

I sigh. "Yeah, I hear you. I'd love to play the villain, you know?"

Mark grabs my cheeks and squeezes. "With a pretty boy face like this one, no one would ever believe you." He lets go of my face and gestures to his own. "You need some battle scars, like me."

I scoff. "They were drawn on you by Tina." Gotta tip my hat to the makeup artist, though. She did a great job.

He smirks. "Yeah, well, stick to your lane, buddy. Leave us ugly friends some roles, okay?"

I push his shoulder. "Sometimes I want to get out of this box I'm in, you know. Sam called earlier and wants to put my name in for another rom-com."

Mark winces. "Well, you make good bank with them, that's for sure. My agent called about a few roles he wants me to try for—all villains."

"We should switch." Even though my suggestion was made with a lighthearted tone, the idea tugs at my heart. I love acting. I love everything about my craft. Lately, though, I've been wanting *more*. Like the rush of a live audience—the remembered feelings from when I was in school. I guess losing a couple of movie roles to younger guys lately has put me in a reflective mood.

Next to me, Mark picks up his coffee again. "You know the studios wouldn't go for that. We've both been pigeonholed." He tips the cup to his lips.

He's right. As much as spreading my acting wings appeals, I know the powers that be wouldn't like it. Besides, I draw a great payday with what I'm doing. Why rock the boat? Dismissing my stupid fantasy, I reply, "Guess you're right."

Judith arrives on set, holding the new gloves out for Noble's inspection. Melody and Helene trail behind her. I open and close my fist, watching as they examine the new addition to my wardrobe.

"Looks like they got a replacement," Mark notes.

"Yeah." I stand. "I better make sure these fit and won't get stuck in anyone else's hair."

"Good luck," he calls as I stride over to the trio holding the last piece of my wardrobe.

"How's it looking?"

Noble holds out one black glove to me. "Here, try this on."

I take the silk and slide it on my right hand and up my forearm. "Fits like a glove."

Noble smiles at my obvious pun, while Judith plays with the material. "Looks good," she notes.

"Something's missing," Melody pipes up.

Of course she finds something wrong. Can't she ever leave well enough alone?

Before I can even open my mouth, she grabs my right arm and twists so my palm is facing upward, then moves so it's facing downward.

"You're right," Judith muses.

Melody snaps. "An eight!"

Noble joins the conversation. "Good catch. On the palm. CGI can make it glow gold when he's performing his DNA transformations."

A patch won't be that effective unless . . . I rush in, "Two patches. Palm and top of my hand for both gloves. That way, everything can be captured easier on film."

"I like the sound of that." Noble pats my shoulder. "Good thinking. Yes. On both sides." He looks at Judith. "Do you have any patches you can use?"

Helene responds, "I do. They're sort of small, but they'll be perfect."

Judith whispers in Helene's ear, who then scampers away.

I move all of my fingers, grudgingly impressed that Melody created the gloves in such a short time. Of course, if the design had been perfect from the beginning, none of this would've been necessary. My annoyance returns. I remove the glove, drop it on the table next to Judith, and return to my chair next to Mark.

"How's it working out?"

"They're making a few more adjustments."

He nods and, using his coffee cup, points in the general direction of the camera crew. "Have you talked with that one?"

I search through the group, and my eyes land on the only woman. "Ah. Sophia."

"Yeah." He sips his coffee. "Know her? Care to introduce a guy?"

I'm surprised he's asking about her, considering she's not his usual blond-haired beauty. "Honestly, dude, I don't really know her all that well. Joe Connelly introduced us at the beginning of the shoot, but she wasn't on set during the last two movies."

"Then we have something in common." He crushes the cup and heads toward the garbage can across the way. Melody reappears with my bodysuit, a new undershirt, the gloves, and mask. She passes the new gloves to Judith. Together, they bring them to Noble. After a brief discussion, he motions me over.

"Here you go, Doctor Manipul8." Noble winks at me. "Try these on."

I take the scraps of material out of his hands and examine them. The eights do finish them perfectly. Not how they were portrayed in the graphic novels, or in our prior movies, but a good workaround. Plus they look good with the revised costume. *Too bad this wasn't thought through before filming started.*

Melody plucks the material from me and slides them over my hands, making minor adjustments. The meticulous woman—her attention to detail too late in my book—checks out the gloves from every angle before holding them up for the others to see.

Noble examines every inch of the new gloves. "They look great. Good job, Judith." He looks at the team surrounding him. "And Melody, Helene," he adds, then claps. "All right, let's get this shoot back on track. I'm glad I only scheduled this one scene today. Chase, get back into the top half of your costume." Noble turns his back on us and yells for everyone to resume their places.

Off to the side, Melody helps me back into the bodysuit, while hair and makeup do quick touch-ups on the others. When I'm in the suit again, they rush over to me. At least this part is minimal, given my costume. Especially now, with my mask back in place.

Noble calls for action, and we redo the scene. A father steps out of the pack of extras, pushing his son ahead of him. "Doctor Manipul8, my son's been diagnosed with a rare cancer. We've heard"—he looks behind him and all the extras nod—"you can cure him." He pushes the child forward. "Please."

I reach out and tousle the kid's curly hair. "Let me see what I can do." I switch my hands to lay on top of his head, closing my eyes, and hold the position for a full minute so the CGI folks can do their thing. All the while praying there's not a repeat of what happened before.

I open my eyes, drop my hands—thank God nothing caught—and look at the father. "Go. Take him home. He needs to rest so his DNA makes the necessary changes." I step back and the child fake swoons. The father catches him and picks him up.

"Thank you, Doctor Manipul8. I am forever in your debt." He turns and carries the child toward the throng of people watching the superhero miracle.

Jessa claps. "That was very impressive, Troy, I mean Doctor Manipul8. Are you sure you healed him?"

"I am. I felt it."

She places her hand on my chest, her Botoxed lips begging to be kissed. We hold the position for another moment for maximum sexual tension effect, before she murmurs, "Come on, let's get you back to the lab."

We continue our walk and I turn my head to the right, locking eyes with Mark. He squints and ducks behind a building. I blink as if I wasn't sure I just saw him. Then I shake my head, acting like there was no way it was him.

Grabbing Jessa's hand, I kiss her palm. "I'm so glad you're on my team." We take a few steps.

"AND CUT!"

Noble jumps up, clapping. "That was great, guys!" He motions for the father and son to join us and gives us more notes about how to make tweaks to the scene. We run through it another five times before he's satisfied.

Once we're done, I remove the mask. The tiny additional amount of fresh air on my face feels wonderful. "Thank God we didn't have any more wardrobe malfunctions."

Mark takes my mask from me. "Amen." He slaps it against his thigh. Raising his voice, he yells, "Party tonight at eight to celebrate my boy, Doctor Manipul8!" A round of cheers sound their approval.

The start time tonight is due to our very early call time tomorrow. "We're going to really enjoy this town, Chase." He hands me back the mask as we enter the lot where our trailers are parked. "See you there."

Holding up my gloved hands in mock surrender, I reply, "Can't wait."

Jessa turns to me, wrapping her arms around my neck. "You did great out there today, Chasey." She kisses me, her collagen-enhanced lips moving against mine.

We've enjoyed each other's bodies previously but, for some reason, I'm not into her at the moment. My solitary goal is to get out of this stupid outfit. I pull back. "Thanks, Jessa. I really need to get out of this." I motion to the costume. "I'll meet up with you tonight at the party, okay?"

"Definitely. It'll be a blast." She kisses me again, then leaves in a swirl of heavy floral fragrance.

Thomas ushers me into my trailer, praising me for the scene and giving me tomorrow's lines to review.

"Thanks," I say, skimming over the scenes we'll be laying down. "Will you be joining us tonight at the party?"

"Wouldn't miss it. Heard all the ladies from the crew will be there."

I laugh and clap him on the back. "Like your priorities, man. Have anything else for me tonight?"

My PA consults his clipboard—all the while clicking his pen—and shakes his head. "The rest can wait till tomorrow. See you later." He turns to leave.

"Catch you then."

Finally, it's time to get out of this superhero costume. Lucky me.

From deeper inside the trailer, a woman's voice directs, "Take off your boots and socks, then unsnap the bodysuit. I'll get you out of the costume as quickly as I can."

I close my eyes. Melody's voice alone makes me vibrate with annoyance. We would've been done an hour earlier if not for the glove snafu. Swallowing my opinions in exchange for expediency, I take off my footwear and do the undignified unsnapping. Gathering the material from underneath, I drag it upward, getting caught around my torso. Again.

Her hands land on my upper pecs. "Here, let me help you. We need to preserve this bodysuit."

I fucking hate this feeling of helplessness.

Finally we manage to get me out of the rubber material for the second time today, and I rip off the soaking wet undershirt. Melody takes it from my hands, balls it up and tosses it into the garbage. Good place for it.

Picking up a pair of scissors, she swishes them open and closed. Advancing toward me, she says, "Now for the leggings."

Despite myself, I recoil at someone advancing at me with a pair of scissors. Layering my hands over my package, I stand taller. "Watch that."

She opens and closes the scissors again. "Don't worry. Not interested. I only want to get you out of these leggings so I can go about with the rest of my night."

Her sharp words wound my pride. "That's not what other women say."

"I'm not like other women."

Damn straight. She's nothing at all like any of the other women I know. "Couldn't agree with you more." I widen my stance. "Get to it."

She cuts the material up the hems until mid-thighs. "There. You should be able to rip the rest by yourself." She stands and heads over to her suitcase.

Grateful for the extra air hitting my legs, I tear the material the rest of the way, pull the wrecked leggings off and toss them into the garbage. "Freedom." Standing in nothing but black boxer briefs given to me as part of the costume, I move my hips and savor the air caressing my almost naked body.

Without looking at me, Melody says, "I'm done for today. I'll be here at six in the morning to sew you back into the suit."

My elation slides downward. Thirteen more days of shooting.

With this tyrant.

CHASE

Mark yells, "Three, two, one!" In response, a bunch of us down our shots.

Exchanging the empty shot glass for a scotch—given the call time, this will be the only one I'm allowing myself . . . thankfully—I leave the little huddle and head toward the back of the club. Bars line one side, but the center dance floor is the main attraction. People cluster in curtain-lined alcoves with plush sofas throughout the rest of the dimly lit space. A DJ plays great tunes. Case in point, an Ozzy Martinez hit blasts through the speakers.

Across the room, long, blond hair diverts my attention. My body twitches at the sight of the unknown woman. Standing with her back to me, she gathers the lustrous locks into a ponytail. No! Such fantastic hair shouldn't be mistreated like that. My feet start in her direction, with every intention of grabbing the silky mane and instructing her to keep it down. So I can wrap it around my fist as our naked bodies enjoy each other.

She turns.

All momentum in my body freezes, my cheek heating as if someone had slapped it. Seriously? Melody. My *dresser*? No fucking way.

Disgusted at the vignette I conjured over *her*, I turn on my heel and stalk toward the sofas. She can go drape her freaking hair over every other man in this club for all I care. Before I realize it, I've approached an alcove occupied by locals and a few Italian women giggle. I clench my drink, struggling to retain my composure as the room closes in on me.

After more than a decade in the business, how did I make such a rookie mistake? It's all *her* fault.

Hiding my annoyance at myself behind a smile, I hold up my glass. "*Signorinas!*"

On the sofa, two of the women separate and pat the cushion. "Sit with us, *Signor Wright?*" The way the brunette says my name, with her thick Italian accent, is adorable. But not adorable enough that I'd take her up on her offer. I cast about for someone to save me, and locate Thomas standing near the bar. Our eyes lock.

"Thank you so much for your kind offer." Taking my time, I focus on each woman, watching my PA approach in my peripheral vision. I take two more slow, small steps toward the sofa.

Before I reach them, a male hand lands on my arm. Thank God. "Excuse me, Chase. Sorry to interrupt, but I need to speak with you."

Halting, I offer the women an apologetic look. "I'm so sorry. Another time, *sì?*"

One of the ladies pulls out a cell phone. After shooting a death glare to Thomas, she holds it up to me, now wearing a pleading expression. "A photo first?"

Please, anything to get away from these women. Narrowing my eyes at my PA like my acting teachers taught me shows annoyance, I retrieve the phone and offer it to him. "Would you mind?"

"Of course not," he replies. I think her evil eye had its intended consequence.

I take a seat between the two Italian women, wrapping my arms around both of them. Thomas snaps three quick shots and, after kissing both of their cheeks, I leave with my assistant.

"Thank God you were here," I mutter.

He chuckles. "Always. How did you get yourself into that situation anyway? That's so unlike you."

I shake my head. "I know. I wasn't thinking." I was thinking about my annoying dresser. All because she has hair like spun gold, the likes of which I haven't seen before. She certainly doesn't wear it like that when she's with me—it's always been hidden in a bun.

Thomas leads us toward an alcove with a few people from the set. When we approach, Thomas hooks his finger toward the dance floor and they make a show of getting up and heading there. Being the star of the movie does have some perks.

Sinking into the now empty sofa next to my PA, I swallow a big sip of my scotch. The burn trails all the way to my stomach. I refuse to let my face reveal my thoughts about the loathsome drink, which is what all the A-lister men are expected to drink nowadays. Too bad I prefer a nice glass of pinot noir. How did things come to this?

I rub my forehead. "I do appreciate the save, Thomas. I'll pay more attention in the future."

He tips his glass to his lips. "Thought they were going to flay me alive."

I chuckle and place my glass down on a table. Leaning back into the cushions, I watch the dancers enjoy themselves.

Jessa sidles up to us. "Hey, Chasey, want to dance with me?" She wiggles her ample backside.

While Jessa's hot, I'm still not feeling her. Even though I love dancing and would like to get out on the dance floor, I decline. She gives me a pouty face and tosses her rather brassy blond hair over her shoulder, which only cements my decision. "Sorry, Jessa. Not tonight."

She leans over to me, placing her surgically enhanced tits in my line of vision. "We can do horizontal dancing, if you'd prefer." Her hands snake around the back of my neck.

Placing my hands on her wrists, I stop her from completing the clench. "Maybe another night."

"Fine. Your loss." Jessa kisses my lips, straightens, and heads to the dance floor.

I glance at Thomas, whose head swivels from side to side. "What are you looking for?"

"Chase Wright. What have you done with him? I swear I just heard you turn Jessa Mendes down."

His antics give me pause. "I'm not." I search for the words. "In the mood."

"Dude. You're *always* in the mood for Jessa."

Crap. I have been off lately. A flash of blond ponytail captures my attention for a split second, and I force my attention to my PA. "It's nothing, really. I have a very early call time and only want to unwind for a while before getting some rest."

He quirks his lips to the side.

I add, "It's a big day of shooting tomorrow."

He holds his hands up, as if in surrender. "Can I get anything for you?"

"Nah, I'm good." We both check out the dance floor, and soon he's wiggling in his seat. "Go out there and have fun. I'll probably join you once I finish my drink." I swirl the scotch.

"Don't have to tell me twice."

Thomas drains his glass and, with one more appraising look at me, heads toward some crew members. Alone, I will my whirling brain to quiet, even in the loud club. From my vantage point, I check out the dance floor. Everyone from the mother of the child actor I "cured" today to many of the other actors and crew are out there. Jessa's in the middle, dancing with a small group, including Mark. The song changes to "Taboo" by Cole Manchester, and I let the sultry beat flow through me.

As I take another sip of the required drink, Judith sits down next to me. "Chase, I'm glad to catch you alone. I'm so sorry about what happened today. I believe the new gloves probably will work out even better."

I finger the rim of my glass. Not wanting to stoke any ill feelings, I reply, "Yeah, I think the new ones will be good."

She sips a glass of red wine, forcing me to swallow my desire to rip it out of her hands. *Any* red would be better than scotch.

Judith continues, "The costume fits you perfectly, Chase. It really did transform you into the superhero, that's for sure." She lets out a small laugh.

She deserves to know how I feel about all the thought that went into her design, even if I didn't show it earlier. "Thanks to your innovations. I do appreciate all the effort you put into making it more, uhm, accessible than the last one."

A self-congratulatory smile steals across her face. "Thank you. We wanted to do something different. I worked a long time designing the costume to make it easier for you. The whole team did."

She sips her wine again, and I swallow my own saliva. "By the way, I hope you can get along with Melody. She really is a wonderful person. Is there something I can do to smooth things over between you two?"

At the mention of the woman with the golden hair, my body tenses. I can't let my distaste for everything my dresser represents— my own childhood and living her dream—show. "She's fine."

A woman from accounting approaches and catches Judith's attention. Happy not to probe the subject further, I stand up. Leaving my remaining scotch on the side table, I excuse myself and head toward the dance floor. Maybe some physical exertion will do me good.

Before I even hit the actual dance floor, a couple of women from makeup and hair surround me, gyrating. Smiling, I twirl them around and away from my body. I'm not interested in hooking up tonight. I only want to blow off some steam.

The music changes, blaring "Your Kiss Destroys Me," Hunte's first Number One. A yell goes through the crowd as fists pump into the air.

About halfway through the song, one of the ladies in the crew places her hand to my ear and says, "That's Melody's father's band, you know."

"Yeah."

Hard growing up in Chicago without knowing about all of its famous citizens—and their families, even if we never met. I grab the woman by the hand and spin her, my mind bouncing back to my almost-forgotten audition for the upcoming movie about Hunte's rise, fall, and rise again to success. Sam touted it as the best role of the year. Maybe Melody can be of some use after all? She might be able to give me the inside scoop about the movie. Possibly even talk me up to her father?

The music changes to a Daughtry anthem. With everyone else, I roll my hips and clap with the beat. I dance with Janie from set design, and the song ends with us laughing and high-fiving each other.

After a few more songs, I need a break and make my way toward a sofa—an *empty* one, preferably. "Looking good out there," Joe, the camera operator, says as I sit down.

"Thanks." I wipe sweat off my brow. "It's been a while since I danced like that."

"Can I get you something to drink?"

"I'd love some water. I'm parched."

He nods and heads over to the bar. A second later, Mark plops down next to me. "Hey," I fist bump him. "Great music."

"Sure is." He holds out his glass as if to toast and realizes I'm drinkless.

"Joe's getting me a water. Need to get hydrated and not drunk, considering my call time," I grumble.

Mark swallows his scotch. Is he drinking it like I do, because it's expected? He diverts my wandering thoughts by noting, "Being the lead can suck sometimes."

"Being a human pincushion before the sun rises sucks more," my voice drips with resentment. Joe drops off my glass of water and before he can say a word, he's pulled away by another cameraman.

With his eyes on Joe and the guys, Mark says, "If it's any consolation, your costume did rock."

After I swallow half of my water, I reply, "Thanks. Be glad you don't have to be sewed into yours."

The bastard smirks, his eyes roving around the room. And stop. Under his breath, he mutters, "There she is."

I follow his line of vision to the back wall. Melody and Sophia are there, talking between themselves. "She . . . who?"

As if holding the precious Aurumite our characters desperately seek, he replies, "Sophia."

For some inexplicable reason, relief pours over me. "Ah. The camerawoman."

Without moving his eyes, he brings his scotch to his lips. "She's talking with your dresser."

My gaze travels to Sophia's companion. I run my fingers through my hair, wondering if hers is as silky as it appears. "Yeah. That's her."

"Think they're friends?"

"How should I know? We're not. Friends, that is. She sews me into my outfit, fucks up my gloves, and that's about it. We don't chit-chat like little girls, braiding our hair."

Mark slants me a dirty look, then his eyes return to the two women. "They look like they're friends."

To shut him up, I glance at the duo again. Their body language is relaxed between them. "Yeah. Guess so." I grab my glass of water, wishing it were a pinot, and finish it. Glancing at the clock, my eyes widen. "Shit. It's already ten. I better get back to my room so I can get at least a little shut-eye before I have to head to the gym at four, and then to wardrobe."

Against my will, my eyes stray back to Melody and Sophia. *She* can get more sleep than me since I'd bet my left nut she doesn't work out. Huffing, I stand.

"Wait, dude." Mark scrambles to his feet. "You're introducing me."

"Huh?"

"I want to talk with Sophia, and you're my wingman. You told me today that you've met her."

"Since when did you need help talking with a woman?"

He finishes his scotch and deposits the empty glass on the table. "I don't. But it's smoother when someone else does it. And you're right here." He slaps me on the back. "C'mon."

With slow feet, I follow him to the women. Before we get too close, though, Mark hangs back so I'll be the first one to approach them. "You owe me, asshole."

"Got your back, Doc, you know that. It's your turn now."

Sighing, I lead us to the women. "Hey, Melody. Sophia." Real original, but it gets the job done.

Melody licks her lips and tilts her head, as if trying to figure out where some annoying buzzing is coming from. She plays with her earring for a moment, then pulls, sending her big gold hoop swinging. For her part, Sophia's gaze runs up and down us like we're something stuck to the bottom of her wedge sandals. Mark has a long way to go with this one.

I'm shoved from behind. Before I can say something else, Sophia's no-nonsense voice cuts through the awkwardness. "Hi, Char—Chase."

Ignoring her near-slip to my real name—damn Melody for telling her—I introduce Mark, who opens with a comment about the club. He tries to make small talk about Amalfi, but the ladies barely engage. Doesn't look like this is going to work out for him.

Tired of listening to the stilted conversation over the loud music, I decide a retreat is the best offense. "It was nice seeing you, but I have an early call time." My eyes land on Melody's amber-hued ones, which show no reaction at all. I mirror her expression. "See you at six."

I wrap my arm around Mark's neck and haul him away from the two women. For the first time I wonder if the next two weeks will be the biggest battle of wills I've ever encountered.

My chest puffs. I've never met a role—or woman—I couldn't conquer.

MELODY

"C'mon, Mel. We just got to Amalfi and everyone is going to be out at the club."

In only my bra and panties, I sit and trace the design on the bedspread. It's pretty. Nothing like the harsh designs we've used here, but perhaps I could replicate it in *Ladies of the Abbey*?

Sophia snaps her fingers in front of my face. "That's it. We're going." She opens my closet, zipping through the hangers there.

"I don't want to go. I'm beat."

"Too bad." She pulls out a dress and then replaces it back on the rod.

"Honestly, Sophia, I don't have it in me." I drop my hands on my thighs. "The whole glove situation—"

"Was an honest mistake. Could've happened to anyone. Stop beating yourself up over it." She walks toward me. "Here. Put these on." She plops a pair of black capris and a purple sleeveless top onto my lap.

"I don't want to."

Sophia sits next to me, plucking at her maxi dress with an unusual paisley print, and tapping her wedge-sandaled foot. "Exactly why you're going. You need to get out of your head, see some people. Have a few drinks."

Only my best friend since first grade would dare challenge me like this, but I still have an ace in the hole. My head pops up. "I have an early call tomorrow. Noble wants Chase ready by eight, which means I'll need to be sewing him into that damn costume by six." Why did I think a movie was a good idea? Certainly not for my sleep, that's for sure.

"Fine. One drink. We'll get you back here by ten, I promise. Should be enough snooze time for you."

I remove the knitting needles from my hair and let it fall loose around my mid-back. Playing with a needle, I don't respond.

My best friend steals it out of my hands and hoists me to standing. "We're going. You know who is going to be there? Judith, that's who. If she gets the lead costume designer position for Noble's next trilogy, her job on your TV show will be up for grabs. For God's sake, Helene will be right next to her tonight, sucking up as usual."

It's not Judith's name that lights a fire under me. It's Helene's. She doesn't suck up, *per se*, rather never misses a chance to extol her long history in the industry. "She's not so bad."

"But not so good, either. Plus, you don't want *Charles* gossiping about how you're holed up in your hotel room because you're too embarrassed to show your face after the whole 'glove fiasco.'" She makes air quotes to emphasize her point.

I take a deep inhale. Looking at the clothes Sophia selected and place them on the bed, I say, "I need to take a shower."

A satisfied smile overtakes Sophia's face. She makes a hurry-up motion and I dash into the bathroom. Turning on the shower, I let the water warm up and check the mirror. Oh boy, I look like crap. I need to put on a ton of makeup to hide the circles under my eyes and add color to my face. I agreed to go out tonight? Before I change my mind, though, Sophia's words about Chase's possible snarky comments come to the fore and I strip out of my underwear.

My mind leaps from the glove fiasco to Chase standing there so stupid sexy in his Doctor Manipul8 costume. *He's Lindsay's brother.* I scrub my skin harder than required.

Showered, I wrap a towel around my body and apply makeup, doing a good job of hiding those circles. Blush and bronzer make me look human again. Satisfied, I head into an empty room. Sophia left a note on top of my clothes, telling me she's waiting in her room for me.

I get dressed and select a pair of wedge sandals to match hers. Bold gold hoop earrings and bangles complete my outfit. I'll start the evening with my hair down, but I grab a ponytail holder should I decide to put it up later. Checking out the floor-length mirror one last time, I select a small purple clutch and leave to pick up Sophia.

As we walk through Amalfi's winding streets, Sophia broaches the proverbial elephant in the room. "So, Charles looked like he was in rare form today."

"I call him Chase. That's who he's become. Although knowing his real name and being related to Lindsay doesn't gain him any points in my book."

Sophia and I had the displeasure of going to school with Chase's younger sister, who was the biggest "mean girl" of all time. Made the movie of the same name look like a fluffy comedy.

Because I've kept in all the day's problems, I use this opening to lodge my gripes. "Having to sew him into that costume was so demeaning. I mean, I was on my *knees* in front of him, for God's sake. He barely acknowledged me other than to complain about how long it was taking me to get him ready. When the glove incident happened, well . . ."

"He looked pissed. I rechecked my camera before deleting the footage."

"You can say that again. He made it seem like I had planned for it to happen." I reflect on what he said in the trailer. "Or, at least I was totally incompetent for not thinking the buckle and Velcro would be an issue."

Sophia makes an unladylike noise. "That sucks. Did you remind him it was Judith's design?"

I fiddle with the rubber band around my wrist. "No. The whole design team signed off on the costume. Honestly, I was as shocked as anyone when it got caught."

We take a few more steps and make a left turn. "To make matters worse, using silk for the replacements was Helene's idea."

"Ouch. That sucks." We take a few more steps, then Sophia points. "There it is." She lays her hands on my shoulders. "Forget everything that happened today on set. You're Melody Hunte, Badass Costume Designer."

"Assistant."

"Whatevs." She chucks her fist under my chin and together, we walk into the club. A long bar is set along one wall, seating alcoves on the opposite side, and a pretty packed dance floor in the middle. The lights are low and the DJ spins Top Forty hits, with a cool laser light show. Immediately, I relax into the chill vibe.

Screwing up my courage, I say, "I'll get my one and only drink. What would you like? A Cosmo?" Both of our favorite beverage.

She gives me the thumbs up then motions toward the dance floor. "I see some ladies from set design. I'll be out there with them."

Parting, I head toward the bar and wait my turn. This place reminds me of the clubs Grant used to play when we were dating. His band was good, but not as good as he thought they were. I shake my head to rid it of those miserable college memories and place my order with the bartender. Two Cosmos in hand, I make my way to the dance floor and hold out Sophia's to her. After clinking, I take a long sip, allowing the beverage to slide down my throat, leaving relaxation in its wake. Maybe Sophia was right—this is what I needed after the shitty day I had.

We dance for a full set, ending with a song by my dad's band. Everyone on set knows I'm his daughter, and they point to me when it comes on. I smile and dance, harder than to any other song.

I'm super proud of what he's accomplished, as very few musicians from the eighties still are rocking, and on top of today's charts. He's the best man I've ever met and treats my mother like a queen. For her part, she never abandoned her own dream in subservience of his. She changed it somewhat once she realized being a partner at an accounting firm was no longer her goal. Instead, she's the band's accountant. And she does a great job. That's the type of relationship I want. Based on love and mutual respect.

However, the movie about Hunte is just that—*his* movie. I can't be any part of it if I'm ever to hold my head up high in costume design. No. It's his gig.

I look around the club—*this* is my gig. For now. Judith may be headed to the movies, but I hope to be her replacement on the TV show if she does.

My Cosmo long finished, I lift my hair off the back of my neck to cool down. Sophia looks tired too, so I tilt my head toward the sofas on the side of the room. She approaches me. "Mel, I'll get us some waters and meet you over there."

I sit, waving my hand in front of my overheated face, then put my hair into a ponytail. Shortly, Sophia appears and plunks two cups of ice water onto the table, condensation forming on the outside of the glasses. Instead of drinking mine right away, I hold it against my cheek. "Ahhh."

"I hear you," she says, lifting the material of her dress away from her chest and blowing downward.

I catch sight of Chase on the dance floor with some people from the crew. "Don't look, but Chicago's at three o'clock."

"Well, there goes a great club," Sophia quips. "Guess they'll let anyone in."

We giggle and I take a long swallow of water. "I'm glad you made me come out, Sophia. I didn't know how much I needed this release."

"It's what best friends are for."

"Especially when we don't get to hang that often anymore, now that you're working in movies and I'm usually in New York."

We clink our glasses. She asks, "So, any of these fine men catch your attention?"

A lump forms in my stomach. Ever since my relationship crashed with my one and only boyfriend, I've been wary of men. They only want one thing from me, and it's *not* my body. It's a connection to my dad. "Nah."

Sophia sips and rests the cup on her knee. "Come on, there has to be someone who catches your eye."

I cross my legs. "Really, no one."

I never told *anyone* what happened with Grant, but Sophia knows what I went through back in Chicago. Even though she didn't accompany me to NYU, and we drifted apart until reconnecting on set, maybe it's time to share. I dip my toe. "You know I have a hard time judging people."

"Hasn't changed since high school?"

"Nope. If anything"—I take another drink of water mainly to stall —"my original thoughts have been solidified."

"Talk to me, girlfriend."

I gaze into her brown eyes, which are filled with sympathy. Shared experiences. Somewhat. Her father isn't an international rock star, though. Nor have people used her for her parents' connections. "Just like when we were growing up, I can't ever seem to distinguish between people who like me for me, and those who . . . don't."

"Oh, honey. I was hoping college would've helped you out with this. You're an amazing woman. You're not even twenty-five, and you're an assistant costume designer on an HBO show. Now you're working on a major motion picture. How many other women can boast that?"

I roll my eyes.

She continues, "Certainly not Lindsay."

I laugh at her mention of Chase's bitch of a sister. This is why Sophia and I get along so well. We share a sense of humor that got us through growing up. Neither of our childhoods was terrible, although disparate. Her family is super awesome—her dad's a bus driver and her mom's a receptionist at an urgent care center. Bonus—they're still together, like my folks. The fact she went to school on a scholarship never entered into our friendship at all. It was our schoolmates who sucked.

Catching my breath, I say, "Thanks, I needed that."

"Is there anyone here you'd like to get to know better?"

"I've got you. I'm good." My knee knocks into hers.

She smiles. "Yeah, but you can't live on Sophia alone." Her attention wanders as one of the actors with a minor role walks by. Without turning to face me, she continues, "You never know when I might become indisposed."

She does have a point. I can't keep relying on her for my social life here on set. Well, it'll be ending in a few weeks, so I can hole up in my hotel room alone if need be. "In that case, I'm sure I can find a special gelato to keep me occupied."

She swings her foot, strumming her fingers out of time to the music. Even growing up around me couldn't instill some rhythm into her. "C'mon, Mel. There must be one guy who turns your head."

Her words make me tense up. At first, I was too ashamed to tell anyone why Grant and I broke up. It served as proof that I'm only good for what my dad could do for him. As time went on, the shame morphed into a type of phobia, one I'm not about to get over any time soon. But I have to try. That is, if I ever want to have any sort of relationship like my parents. I sigh.

"I've never had much luck on that front."

She shoulder butts me. "Well, who has? All we can do is keep trying."

Keep trying. How about never started? "Yeah, guess you're right. No one has really caught my eye, though."

"I could be persuaded to check out that guy." She tilts her chin toward the back sofas, where Chase and Thomas are talking.

Discarding the asshole movie star, I give her a sideways glance. "You mean Thomas? Chase's PA?"

"He's not hard on the eyes."

He's kinda cute, in a nerdy sort of way, which is Sophia's catnip. He's always so serious when he's around Chase. He has to be competent, though, since he's able to handle that over-privileged actor.

"You do know he works for Chase, right? He's in the trailer all the time when I'm getting him into costume. Maybe I could put in a good word for you."

Sophia's brown eyes light up. "Thanks. It's hard for me always being with the camera guys, you know? *You* get all the access."

Access. Guess that's a word for it.

"Okay, I've spilled my guts. Your turn." She focuses all of her attention on me.

I play with the hem of my shirt. "I've been so busy with wardrobe, I really haven't noticed anyone." She gives me an incredulous look. I cross my heart, like we used to do as kids. "I'm serious."

Next to me, Sophia sets her glass down on the table. "All right. But promise me you'll keep your eyes peeled while we're here. It's so romantic in Amalfi, and we both need men in our lives to bring out the full Monty, as it were."

We both giggle at her awful mixed-metaphor. When an Imagine Dragons song comes on, we return to the dance floor. After dancing like maniacs to a few more songs, we find ourselves holding up a wall, since all the sofas are now taken.

"I've had a great time with you tonight. But I'm getting tired and you know I have to get up at some ungodly hour tomorrow. I need to head out. Are you coming with?"

Sophia looks around the room, and her eyes fixate on the dance floor where Thomas dances with Tina from makeup. She deflates.

I place my hand on her arm. "Tomorrow, I'll somehow get Thomas and you together."

"Promise?" she whispers.

I hold up my little finger. "Pinky swear."

Her lips tip upward and she links her finger with mine. "Pinky swear," she repeats.

Movement from off to my right catches my eye. Chase and Mark cross the room, and everyone parts to let them through. Seriously? No wonder he acts so entitled. "Look at that." I point my chin toward the two men.

Sophia follows my line of sight.

I pluck the rubber band on my wrist. "They need to be treated like they're normal people. Sure, it's their faces on the posters for the movie, but without us, where would they be?"

The men laugh at something being said and continue walking

across the room. Everywhere they go, people let them pass as if they were some sort of royalty.

"You have a point. Chase is just an asshole older brother, and Mark's the biggest player there is."

The actors keep coming our way. I whisper, "What the hell? It seems like they're heading to us. Why?"

"Dunno. Maybe Chase wants to talk with you about his costume?"

I consider her words for a moment. "Doubt it. Besides, we have two hours together in the morning to discuss it," I whisper back.

Stopping right in front of us, Chase says, "Hey, Melody. Sophia."

Oh for goodness' sake. What do these two want? I tilt my head upward, lick my suddenly parched lips, and fiddle with my hoop earrings. Sophia gives the men the once-over, but not in a good way. Hint, much?

When they remain in front of us, Sophia mutters, "Hi, Char —Chase."

Chase offers us his megawatt smile, which causes an unwanted thrill to race through my body. In disgust, I focus on the floor. His voice enters the awkward breach. "Sophia, this is Mark Ivan. Melody, I believe you've already met Mark."

As if we both don't know who his co-star is. Mark launches into a commentary on how nice the club is. Then he jumps into a soliloquy about Amalfi. Gotta hand it to him, he is a one-man show—neither Sophia nor I need to do much more than nod. Chase is quiet, too. For once.

After a while of Mark's rambling, Chase shakes his head. "It was nice seeing you, but I have an early call time." His piercing blue eyes land on me, but I school my features to remain neutral. "See you at six." He grabs Mark and the two leave us.

I watch the pair as they exit the club. "Well, that was weird," I remark.

"Totally," she replies. "What do you think that was about?"

"No clue. But they're actors. Who knows what motivates them?"

"You're certainly right about that, Mel. Other than what the writers tell them." We both giggle. "Are you ready to head back?"

"Yeah." We say our goodbyes to our friends and retrace our steps to our hotel. Given the small size of the town and its hotel capacity, everyone in the movie is scattered in various locations. Sophia and I are in a delightful spot right across from the water. We walk along the marina on our way back.

As we tread through the cobblestone sidewalks, Sophia muses, "Why would they come over to us like that, Mel? What was Mark's deal talking about Amalfi?"

"As I said, I have no idea. But who cares? We don't have to be friends with them, we only have to work with them. And pray the Doctor Manipul8 costume holds up for the rest of the shoot."

"Amen, sister."

I'm also praying that any wayward tingles the man inside the suit evoked were merely the result of a Cosmo on an empty stomach.

CHASE

I stand still while my fastidious dresser sews me into the Doctor Manipul8 leggings. Damn, this is a long, slow process. And for the first time in days, we're the only two people in my trailer.

Picking up my phone, I click on social media accounts but nothing catches my eye. Huffing out a sigh, I toss the phone onto the sofa.

I look down at the woman on her knees, who's concentrating on my left knee. I count the ceiling tiles. Even though it's a smooth ceiling.

The silence is killing me.

Mocking me.

Making me wish for things I don't have. *Can't* have. I rake my hand through my hair. Unable to move, I weigh the possibility of jumping out of my skin. I glance down again. Maybe she can do me a solid with her dad? "So tell me. What was it like growing up as Braxton Hunte's daughter?"

Her needle pauses inches away from my knee for a few moments, then continues her stitch. Without looking up, she replies, "He was a great dad."

Wanting to fill the dead air as well as possibly get intel for the

Hunte movie, I press, "Was he around a lot? Or was he out with his band mostly?"

Her expressive eyes flick to mine. I thought they were straight-up hazel, but they actually are a much deeper amber, rimmed with browns and greens. Her tits push out as if she inhaled deeply.

Why did I notice them?

"Actually, he tried to schedule his concerts around my school vacations so I could go with him on tours. It was a very exciting life, being able to see all different cities as a kid."

She focuses her attention on sewing the leggings, mouth clamped shut. Her childhood certainly was charmed—especially compared to my absentee parents. Several stitches later, she claps her hands together and vaults to her feet. "Please walk around so I can check the fit."

"K." Suddenly lighter, I take a few steps. Crossing the trailer twice, I try to ignore the odd feeling of flapping material on my right leg. Shit. The left one feels looser than usual near my crotch. "Melody, I'm not sure this fits me as tightly up by my, ah, junk."

Frowning, she nods and examines my gait. "You're right." She motions for me to return to my spot.

Standing with my legs on either side of her pillow, she falls to her knees and undoes a few of her stitches near my most sensitive area. I hold my breath as the scissors come near my dick, releasing it only when she puts them down. Soon, she motions for me to walk around again.

I do. The legging is right now. "Feels good."

My pronouncement interrupts her mid-stretch. Dropping her arms, she replies, "Great. I agree. Give me a minute to get the circulation going, and I'll tackle your right leg."

"Sounds good." I do a couple of deep knee bends. With still just us two in here, I bring up an innocuous subject to steer our conversation back toward enlisting her help with her father. "So, which was your favorite city that Hunte visited?"

She smiles, a twinkle I never noticed before lighting up her eyes, causing my breath to still. "I actually enjoyed visiting almost every place. My favorite, though, was New York City. One of the reasons I went to college there."

My thoughts drift to my few trips to the Big Apple. "I love New York City, too. Although I haven't spent all that much time there."

"You should definitely visit. There are so many great restaurants, plus the theater district is amazing, of course."

Her two choices to extol are like punches to my gut. Restaurants mean food, which is something I'm not allowed to enjoy unless it's broiled fish or chicken. God, if I didn't have to maintain this ridiculously low body fat, I'd be all over the pasta in Italy. And that's nothing compared with New York City's theater. A twinge of longing lands in my heart, which I erase by running my hands up and down my legs.

Knowing I left her hanging, I reply, "I'll put it on my list."

She makes eye contact with me, causing a zing to zap. *What the?* Before I can process the reactions racing through my body, she cracks her knuckles in an impressive show of dexterity. "Okay, I'm ready if you are."

I kick my legs to eradicate the zinging and zapping, and return to my spot next to the pillow on the floor. She sinks to her knees and for a fleeting moment, I picture her doing something very different in that position. Her next words erase that pleasant image. "Okay, Mr. Movie Star. Let's get this done."

Silence descends again. I *hate* that nickname with a passion. I may *be* a movie star—the leading actor here and in all the films in recent memory—but I'm much more than that. Dammit, I am a classically trained actor. The empty air reminds me I'd like to do something with that training.

To shift my thoughts, I pick up the thread of our conversation from before. "I bet all the kids envied the traveling you were able to do."

She laughs, but it rings hollow. "Hardly. I was singled out as a target by the school's mean girls." She pauses. "Too many kids wanted to get close to me so they could either meet my dad, or use him for his connections."

"Shit. I didn't realize."

Her lips purse and she continues sewing the leggings. The mood in the trailer dives.

Maybe because I'm somewhat responsible for the cooler vibe—or maybe it's how she shared a part of her childhood with me—I offer a piece of myself I usually keep private. "If it makes a difference, my parents were always working. They're partners at a major Chicago law firm, and they prioritized their careers over my sister and me. You know Lindsay, right?"

In a clipped tone, she replies, "I do." She continues the stitches.

Wanting to defend my folks, I continue, "I mean, they weren't bad parents. It's just that they were mainly absent. They did get us nannies, though."

Her hands bend my knee. "I didn't have a nanny. Mom was—still is —Hunte's tour accountant, so she worked from home. As I mentioned, my dad's schedule revolved around mine growing up."

"I can't imagine having both parents around that much." I chuckle. "Did they get in your way as you grew up?"

Melody's hand drops from my leg and she fiddles with the rubber band around her wrist. "No, they didn't. I loved having them around."

They were her support system. Huh. So different from how my sister and I grew up. Although I should have paid more attention to, essentially, raising her. Melody grabs the material around the bottom of my knee, and I concentrate on her stitching rather than go down that rabbit hole. Again.

Her obvious love for her parents gives me the opening I need. "I hear a movie about Hunte is in the works."

She nods. "Yes, my dad's very excited. I told him I was going to cheer him on from afar. I don't want to have anything to do with the film except to support him and walk the red carpet."

Given the fact she mentioned kids tried to use her to get to her father, this response shouldn't surprise me. It also shuts down my line of inquiry. Crap.

The door opens. Whoever it is, I'm grateful for the relief from this awkward conversation with the intriguing girl on her knees. Thomas bounds into the trailer.

"Hey, Chase."

Relief buzzes throughout my body at my PA's welcome intrusion. "Hey. What's cooking?"

He drops his bag on the sofa. "Got some stuff to go over with you. Is now a good time?"

Thank God. I'll take his frivolous questions over the prolonged silences and stilted conversation—not to mention the unwanted lure —Melody provides. "Sure is." I point down. "Looks like we have half a leg."

"I'll talk fast."

The woman on her knees mumbles something unintelligible. Ignoring her, I say, "What's up?"

Thomas starts, "What are your plans for tonight? Do you need me to arrange any—" His eyes dart to Melody.

I roll my eyes, "Any*one*?"

He licks his lips and Melody tightens the material around my leg. "Well, yeah."

In a teasing tone, I reply, "I'm good."

He expels the air in his lungs and shoots me a dirty look. I make the "what?" motion, and he juts his chin toward Melody. I raise my shoulders.

"May I ask what you're doing tonight? Do I need to set anything up with the press?"

"Nah. Mark and I are hitting the hotel bar."

"That's it?"

I grin. "Sorry to disappoint. Filming's been brutal, and we're both running on empty. We decided to go out for a quick drink and hit the sack early."

He clicks his pen and scribbles something down on his clipboard. "Tomorrow's a free day, you know. Do you have plans for that?"

"I've been invited to go to Positano."

"Yeah, a bunch of us are heading over there."

The thought of being able to finally sleep in makes me feel better than I have since we got to Amalfi. I'll have to work out, of course, but at least it won't be until eight rather than four in the morning. "I'm looking forward to it."

"Me too. I've heard the beach is to die for, and the women are"—he darts a look at Melody—"Italian."

"Lame, man. The women are fucking hot," I correct him.

He waves his pen. "Yeah, well. True." A few more clicks follow his scribbles. "Well, it promises to be a good day tomorrow. Are you joining us, Melody?"

The woman working on my leggings pauses for a moment. "I don't think so."

Her words give me a sense of relief. No, not relief. I refuse to name the emotion.

Thomas picks up the chatter. "We're meeting at ten at the docks if you change your mind." He turns to me. "Now, Chase, I have it from Tina in makeup that Susan from Noble's office mentioned a new project that Stephen Janus is going to be starting soon."

I sort through the barrage of names, then focus my attention back on my personal assistant. "What's Stephen up to?"

Thomas's face lights up with knowledge he has good gossip. He rubs his tight abdomen—although it's not as tight as mine. Nor fueled with so much clean eating. I grimace.

"Mr. Janus picked up a script for a brand-new sci-fi epic. Rumor mill has it the movies will be better than *Star Wars* and *Star Trek* combined."

My eyebrows rise. "That's some boasting going on." I chuckle.

"Right? But if anyone can live up to the hype, it's him. Want me to contact Sam to get your name put in for the lead? I can see you now in some futuristic outfit, green screening against an army of bad guys." He grins.

All air whooshes out of my body.

At my leg, Melody's needle pulls back.

MELODY

At Thomas's sci-fi suggestion, Chase's body goes rigid. I yank my needle away from his leg to avoid pricking him.

The muscles in his body relax, one by one, until he's his normal self again. This is the second time he's reacted this way. The first time was about a rom-com movie role, if I remember correctly. What's up with that?

Why do I care? He's just a movie star. A body to showcase our design work.

Besides, he got me to spill my secrets about growing up. Even if I managed to leave his sister's name off the "Mean Girls" description I gave earlier.

"Why don't you see what you can find out about the movie first?" Chase instructs his PA.

Thomas clicks his stupid pen again and writes the order down. Chase should call Sam himself. What a pampered jerk. Annoyed at myself as well as irritated at the leading man, I mutter, "Doesn't seem to me you're too interested in the role."

While I'm talking, Thomas makes a show out of picking up his stuff and heads out of the trailer. I focus my attention on Chase's freakishly long legs. Damn him.

"See you on set," Chase calls to his PA. The door closes. Chase directs his attention down to me. "What did you say? I didn't hear you over Thomas's rustling."

Clenching my jaw, I reply, "I said you don't seem into the sci-fi movie." I go to finish another complicated Manipul8 Stitch.

His leg flexes.

My needle misses its mark. "Shit!"

He bends down. "What happened?"

"You shuffled, Mr. Movie Star." With deliberate movements, I rip out the stitch.

"Oh. I didn't mean to ruin your work."

He sounds sincere. I glance up at him, and his expression seems contrite, despite his tight leg muscles. Annoyed with myself for treating him poorly—even actors deserve to be acknowledged as human—I sit on my heels. "That was on me. I apologize."

He places his hand on my shoulder for a brief moment, causing me to be the one who stiffens. His stance returns to normal. Keeping my own counsel, I focus on the stitches.

"Listen, you hit a nerve. Thomas did, too." He rubs his forehead. "And I would appreciate it if you don't refer to me as 'Movie Star' from now on."

"Why?" The word escapes my mouth before I can stop it.

"I may play roles in film, but I'm not simply a movie star." He clears his throat. "I actually graduated from Yale's drama school. My favorite courses were about Shakespeare."

I mull over his words. "They were?"

He nods. His posture relaxes slightly.

I consider his shocking words. "I have to say I'm not overly surprised. I've been watching you on set here, and you're clearly well-prepared. You know your stuff, and I'm not only talking about your lines. You got the blocking, and an awareness of the other actors on set with you."

"Thank you. I did a lot of acting on stage in school. Some of my best work, if you ask me."

I pull the material around his calf. "What was your favorite role?"

He pauses. "I think my favorite play was *Hamlet*. As for musicals—"

I remember the fuss he caused when he played Fiddler in high school. Of course, I was only in middle school at the time, but Lindsay never shut up about it. "I had forgotten you sing."

"I'm all right. No Braxton Hunte, but I can put over a tune."

I smile at his use of my dad's name. "Few have his talent."

"That's true." He rubs his palms together. "As for my favorite musical, it was *Aida*. Not as popular as many others, but I loved the storyline. Elton John's score rocked it."

"He's nice," I say as I tie off the bottom of his right leg. "There. I think you're done. Take a spin."

He complies and I study his lithe body movements. I intertwine my fingers and pulse them to get the circulation going. "How's that feel?"

"Good."

On my feet, I pass him the gloves while continuing to work out the kinks from my own hands. Chase's admissions are softening my opinion of him. I make quick work of getting him into the rest of his costume and soon I'm back on the set, sitting next to Judith and Helene.

Noble calls for quiet and the actors begin the scene. Chase's love of the theater replays in my head, which explains why he tenses whenever a new movie role is proposed. I slip my hand into my essentials tote and find my cell. While the scene is being filmed, I click on *Backstage*, a Broadway-based site that lists auditions for all the shows. For my own edification, of course.

When shooting finally ends, I trudge back to the trailer. All I want to do is some yoga followed by a long, hot bath. But first, I get to rip Chase out of the superhero costume. I open the door to silence. Must've beaten Chase here—he's probably with someone in the cast. Probably Jessa.

When I get into the main part of the trailer, the bathroom door opens and Chase walks out, his bodysuit unsnapped. Startled, I blurt, "You're here."

His blue eyes laugh at me. "Who were you expecting? Christian Bale?"

"Ha-ha. Very funny. I thought you were, ah, visiting with someone."

He reaches down and starts to pull up the bodysuit. I rush to his side and help rid him of the spandex. Success means I hold the body-suit while he strips off the wet undershirt.

He takes aim and tosses the damp shirt into the garbage. "Two points!"

"You're in a good mood."

"It was a fun day on the set." He sits and removes his boots, tossing the socks into the garbage as well.

I go into the top level of my design suitcase and pick up a pair of scissors, opening and closing them. He flinches once.

While I focus my efforts on cutting him out of the leggings, I debate telling him about the open auditions I happened to notice on *Backstage*. With his left leg cut open, I move over to the right.

Should I tell him? They *were* announced for anyone to see. I glance at his strikingly handsome face, the cleft in his chin seeming more pronounced. I swallow. "You know, I saw something that might interest you."

His right leg cut open to mid-thigh, he takes over and rips the material off his body. "What's that?"

I ball up the ruined leggings while he heads to the back of the trailer. "I'll show you when you come out."

He disappears into the bathroom and I pick up my cell, pulling up *Backstage*. Within a few minutes, he comes out wearing a pair of shorts and a T-shirt. His cologne—a light grassy smell—is inviting.

I search my scent inventory. "That's Tom Ford, but I can't place the line."

"Grey Vitiver." He runs his fingers through his hair, effortlessly styling it into a messy look.

"That's right," I muse. Shaking my head, I hold my cell up to him. "Thought of you when I saw this."

He takes my phone from me. "*Hamlet 2.0?*"

A tingling sweeps up the back of my neck and across my face. I force myself to pack up my design suitcase, making careful note to put everything back in the right spot. Why did I show him my cell? With each quiet moment that passes, I heap more criticism on myself. When he remains silent, I walk over to him, intending to rip my phone out of his hands. His expression stops me cold.

Longing.

Desire.

Futility.

He settles on a mask of indifference and returns my phone. "Thanks. I don't think Broadway is ready for all this." He waves at his body.

If I hadn't seen his first few emotions, I would leave him alone with his cologne. But it's too late. I saw them. "It might be interesting for you to diversify your résumé."

"Leading men don't diversify."

"I thought you might be interested—"

"Listen, I appreciate your thoughtfulness. I'm not . . . interested." He sits to put his cross trainers on, resting his hands on his knees. "You know, you're a quite talented costume designer."

His change of topic gives me whiplash. Followed by a nagging feeling of insincerity. I pull the knitting needles out of my hair. "Uhm, thank you," I reply, equally insincere.

"I mean it. I've been watching you, considering I don't have much else to do while you're sewing me into that damn suit. I've never seen stitches like them before."

In the off-chance Chase means what he says, I reply, "That's because I invented them." I redo my bun.

His eyebrows express his surprise. "Wow. That's cool."

Re-securing my knitting needles, I warm to the topic. "Judith explored it during pre-production, but everyone dismissed the idea as too complicated. I spent the better part of a couple of weeks coming up with the stitch. When I showed it to my boss, she seemed impressed." I clear the *Backstage* tab from my cell phone and toss it into my tote.

"She has a good eye."

His praise would make me feel on top of the world but for the brittle actor mask settled over his face. I tilt my chin. "What are you playing at?"

Chase stands. "I'm not playing. I'm telling you the truth. I've never seen someone as skilled with a needle as you are."

I squint. "Really? Not around too many costume designers, are you?"

He straightens to his full height. "I've been in countless movies. So, yes, I've met my fair share of designers. Geez"—he collects his wallet from a drawer—"I was just trying to give you a compliment."

Maybe I misread him? Closing my eyes, I rub my thumb over the tip of my knitting needle. "Sorry. I didn't mean to come off as rude. I get a lot of condescending remarks about my chosen career."

His face softens. "Then you're not hanging around the right people. You're very talented. Don't let anyone say otherwise." He motions for me to lead us out of the trailer.

Biting my lip, I twirl on my heel and place my hand on his forearm. His very masculine, very strong forearm. "I really appreciate your compliment. I, I'm happy you like the superhero costume. And thanks for reminding me that 'people'"—I make the sign of air quotes —"don't really count."

He reaches toward a piece of my hair that's fallen out of my bun but before making contact, draws back. "I'll tell you what one of my acting teachers told me when I was at Yale. It's a quote from Albert Einstein. 'Great spirits have always encountered violent opposition from mediocre minds.'"

"So are you saying I'm a great spirit?"

He taps his thigh with his pinky. "It's also important to remember not to let someone's opinion of you go to your head."

"Who said that?"

He chuckles. "Me." He turns me around and pushes me forward. "Now let's go."

CHASE

Mark brings his scotch over to my wine glass. "May Doctor Manipul8 live on at least as long as Ant-Man!"

His words wring a chuckle from my mouth. "Seriously." We clink and I savor the pinot noir as it glides down my throat.

Sitting at a corner table in the back of the restaurant bar, we don't attract attention. Being left alone in public is a unique—and very welcome—experience. Maybe I should hang out more in small Italian towns? I settle into the cushions.

Mark asks, "So, are you joining us in Positano tomorrow?"

"I've been invited. I was thinking of staying in my room and sleeping, though."

He makes a face. "Seriously? Get out to the Amalfi Coast much?"

"I've been here once before." I run my finger down the stem of my wine glass. "I could fly out here anytime I choose."

"True." He places his glass down on the table. "But like those married couples without kids who don't have sex on the kitchen floor, would you really be in Italy but for this movie?"

"You have a point." While I've had sex on many a kitchen floor, I don't hop into a plane and fly across the country—let alone cross the ocean—too often. If ever. "Although, granite floors are fucking cold and uncomfortable."

He fist bumps me. "Good one, Doc."

Our waitress stops by. After eye-fucking both my drinking buddy and me, she licks her lips. "Can I get you anything else?"

Too easy. I glance at Mark, who clearly shares my opinion. "Nah, we're good for now," I reply. "We'll call you over if we need something."

"I'm at your beck and call."

Mark watches as she heads toward a different table. "Think her approach works around here often?"

I savor my fermented grapes. "Wasn't doing it for me."

"Me neither." He picks up his glass. "What's happening to us? We should've been all over her."

"We're not getting old, if that's what you're thinking."

"I know *I'm* not. I can only take your word for yourself." He swallows more of his drink. "Being on set proves I'm still in the game. Sophia's running me in circles."

"Still hung up on her?"

"I like to think of it as politely pursuing."

I reach for the popcorn on the table, but instead of pulling the bowl toward me I toss it onto an empty table. Remove temptation. "It's been a few days now. Must be some sort of record for you."

"Hey, she passed me a soda yesterday at lunch."

I stifle a chuckle. "That good, huh?"

He uses his glass to point at me. "Well, what about you? I haven't seen you with anyone on set either."

A vision of the golden beauty on her knees sewing me into the superhero costume pops into my mind. I force it to blank. "I've been focused on memorizing my lines and working out. No time to meet anyone other than Jessa, and I've already tapped that."

"The sex scenes you two did back in Florence were smoking."

I take another swallow. "Well, most of my relationships end on a positive note. Probably because neither one of us is too invested. The women usually are trying to see what I can do for their careers, and I simply enjoy her body until someone else turns my head."

"Harsh."

I rock my head to the side and back. "Nah, not harsh. Just realistic. I've seen my parents, who are like comfortable partners. Who needs a relationship when that's all there is to look forward to?"

Mark taps his glass. "Well, have you seen the Manchesters around lately? They're the epitome of love and marriage." He traces a design on the tablecloth. "I'd like a slice of that for myself."

My hand lands on my forehead. I've seen the rock star Cole and his wife Rose out and about, and they do dote on each other. "Exception, not rule. I bet you want the white picket fence, too?"

"Now don't go all pussy on me. I was only saying I'd like to have someone who cares about me."

Would I like that? Nah. I've been pampered enough by the various women in my life, even though I'm not the profligate womanizer tabloids like to portray. I refer to myself as a serial casual monogamist. "I wish you well."

"You know, I invited Sophia to join us in Positano tomorrow."

Can't he let her go? "I hope she comes, for your sake."

"Me too. During filming, I wanted to ask you if your dresser could put in a good word, but we kept getting sidetracked with shooting."

"Damn work," I quip.

"Ain't that the truth. So what's the scoop on her?"

My eyebrows come together. "Her who?"

"Melody Hunte, of course."

There she is again. No matter how hard I try to push her away, she keeps popping back into my consciousness. I shrug. "She sews me into the damn costume." I take a sip of my wine. "Really talented at it, though. She created the stitch herself."

His glass arrests on its way to his mouth. "I would've thought Judith made all decisions regarding the design."

"Yeah, so did I. But she told me the design team didn't think it would be either noticeable or worth the time and effort. She took it upon herself to create the stitch."

"Impressive."

I lean back in the booth, needing to bury this topic. "At least there haven't been any more malfunctions since my glove got caught in that kid's hair."

"Yeah. That was something. The design team got it fixed pretty damn quick, though."

"True." With the benefit of time, my rage over the delay in filming doesn't return. I've developed an appreciation of how fast Melody was able to whip up a new pair of gloves from scratch. My mind returns to a subject that's glommed onto me lately.

Giving Mark an assessing glance, I clear my throat. "Do you ever miss it?"

"Miss what?" His index finger circles the rim of his glass.

"Your life before you became *the* Mark Ivan?"

"Deep, man." He knocks back the remainder of his scotch. "To answer your question, not really. I grew up in Russia, which my parents fled when I was twelve. We came to the United States with little more than the clothes on our backs. I learned English by watching cartoons, and later sitcoms. I was fat and acne-prone, and since I didn't speak the language, I was bullied in school."

"Sorry, Mark. I didn't know."

"That's okay. I don't hide my past, but I don't broadcast it either. Plus, everything changed when Mom gave me a bottle of ProActiv for Christmas when I was fourteen. My face cleared up, and then I took an interest in how I looked. I joined a gym and dropped the weight. That helped."

"That's quite the story. Was that when you got into acting?"

He nods. "I fell into it, actually. My high school was putting on a play requiring a Soviet character. Since I was one of the few kids in school from Moscow, they approached me. I took the role."

"So your background informed your first role."

He chuckles. "You could say that. Of course, it was the villain of the play. Guess it did sort of set me up for my career."

"Pretty cool. And look at you now. You're killing it as Mr. A—he's more evil than Lex Luthor, but the way you portrayed him at the beginning showed a real empathy."

"Thanks. I always try to inject some humanity into the bad guys. Makes it seem much more real. No one is all good or all bad."

"Truth." I finish my pinot noir. I want to drink another glass, but I'm keenly aware of the requirements for my body on the set. Instead, I ask, "Do you keep the boy you were alive in your dealings today?"

"Who are you, Dr. Phil?"

I wave my hand. No need to go any deeper. He wouldn't be interested in hearing my sorry tale of woe. I'm not like him—I didn't suffer like he did growing up. So what if the kid I was has been lost? He was stupid, anyway. Into classical music and psychology and bees, for God's sake. The man I am today is much more interesting, playing amazing characters in the movies. With sexy actresses dripping off my arm.

So what if I miss the excitement of performing live on stage?

My thoughts stray to *Hamlet 2.0.* Shaking my head, I punch Mark in the shoulder. Fuck my diet. "Let's get another round."

MELODY

Knocking on my door makes me turn over and throw the blankets over my head. It's my first day off in weeks, and I want to spend it right here with my pillows. I'm exhausted.

The knocking doesn't stop. Instead, my best friend's voice sails through the door. "Open up, Mel! I know you're in there."

Throwing the blankets off my body, I get up and unlock the door. I don't bother opening it and am back in bed before the Sophia whirlwind makes her way into my room. I burrow back into my cocoon. "What are you doing here?"

My bestie jumps on the bed. "Kidnapping you!"

My body undulates. "Are you nuts? It's our only day off from this shoot!"

"Yep. And you're coming with a bunch of us to Positano today." The bed bounces again.

"Thomas mentioned that to Chase yesterday." I flip my hand. "You go. I have a hot date with my bed."

"If I thought for a moment you wouldn't be alone," she taps the comforter, "I'd totally leave you here. But I know you mean to sleep away the day, Mel, and I refuse to allow that."

I roll my eyes. "Aren't you tired? Don't you need sleep?"

"Yes, I'm exhausted. I spent a couple of hours last night working on my camera skills improvement class project. But today we're *free*. We're in *Italy*. I won't allow you to hide in here."

While she was doing her project, I was getting Chase Wright out of his superhero costume. And for the first time, we actually talked. He almost turned into a real human being. *Almost* being the operative word. I flip my head on the pillow.

Sophia yanks the blankets to my waist. "We're meeting everyone down at the docks for the ten o'clock ferry. I've never been to Positano—and neither have you—so you better get going. I'm off to check the cameras I had set up last night, and I'll be back in an hour to get you." As she moves from the bed, she steals the blankets clear off me. Walking out of my room, she leaves the door wide open.

Why did I think working together with my bestie would be a good thing?

Because she's my oldest and dearest friend.

Crap.

I clamber out of bed, close the door, and trudge into the bathroom. One hour later on the dot, Sophia returns to my room. "I like your outfit. Boho chic."

My shower lifted the cobwebs, and now I'm actually excited to be a tourist. I twirl around in my loose dress, a score I picked up in the Village in New York City. "Thanks."

"Grab your purse and let's go. I can't wait to see who all is going to be with us today."

Translation—Chase's PA better be on that ferry.

We link arms and head down to the water, passing a sign listing nearby towns. "Ravello," I remark. "Sounds pretty."

"Oh, I've heard that's the most romantic town in all of Italy." She fans her face. "I wish we were going to film there."

"The sign says it's only six point seven kilometers from here. We should visit."

"I agree. But I don't want to go alone. We can double-date there. Thomas and me, and you and . . ." Her voice trails off.

"Judith? Janie?"

"You're hopeless!" She shakes her head. "We need to find you a man. That'll be my mission for today."

"Good luck with that."

Her shoulder contacts mine. "Don't count me out." She points to the dock, where a bunch of people are waiting. "Oh look, Thomas is here!"

As she tugs me forward, my gaze scans the group, noting Thomas. And Mark. And Chase. Tina's there too.

We purchase our ferry tickets and approach the group. "Hey, Sophia," Joe calls. She smiles at the camera operator and drags me along to chat with him, flirting with Thomas as we pass. He gives us both a quick nod.

Soon the ferry docks and we all scramble in, jockeying for the best seats. I end up next to Chase so that Sophia can be closer to his PA— who seems to be more interested in the fantastic makeup artist Tina than my bestie. Mark pushes his way over to us and squishes in next to Sophia. The boat leaves the dock and we head toward Positano.

"Have you ever been here before?"

I do a double-take when I realize Chase is talking to me. "Um, no. I haven't. Have you?"

He nods. "Once. Did you bring your suntan lotion?"

I point to my oversized purse.

He holds out his hand. When I tilt my head, he explains, "Give it to me. Your nose is already turning red."

Embarrassed by his comment, I whip the suntan lotion out of my bag and squeeze it onto my palms. Turning my back to him, I watch the shoreline as I spread the white lotion over my face.

Next to me, Chase chuckles. I glance at his perfectly tanned face. Of course it's perfect. Just like the rest of him. Not a freckle or hair out of place, even as the wind attacks all of us on the boat.

Sophia reaches over and shakes my arm. "Look, there's Positano!"

She points and the town comes into focus. Built on a steep hill, white houses dot the countryside, leading upward to the sky. My breath catches. "It's beautiful."

"Sure is," Thomas agrees. He nudges Tina. "I bet Positano has a great beach."

She giggles at him.

Leaning forward, I gaze into my bestie's eyes. "We can explore all the little alleyways."

"Yeah," she answers without too much interest.

Mark pokes his head forward. "I've been to Positano a few times. I'd be glad to show you ladies around."

He seems interested in Sophia. I rub my eyebrow while catching her profile. She's giving him a speculative look. Interesting.

"I'll join you," Chase adds.

Why can't he squire Jessa? I reply, "I'm sure a bunch of us will explore together."

My statement is proven correct. While Thomas and Tina head off to the beach right in front of the dock—much to Sophia's dismay—the rest of the group decides to investigate the town. We wander through small alleys filled to the brim with boutiques, restaurants, and little stalls with handmade goods.

I enter a store, crammed with unique clothing. The dresses call to me. Pulling a particular hot pink one off the rack, I hold it up to my body in front of a full-length mirror.

"The color looks amazing with your hair," Sophia notes.

"Thanks." I examine the craftsmanship. "It's made really well." I flip it to the bottom and check inside. "They even did great anchoring stitches on the inner hem." Impressed, I drape the dress over my arm.

Sophia flips through a rack of dresses. "What do you think of this one?"

I wrinkle my nose. "Nah. The neckline isn't right for you." Selecting a violet dress, I hold it up for her inspection.

"Oh. That's gorgeous!" She snatches it from my hands. "Let's go try them on."

We find ourselves in two tiny dressing rooms in the back. My elbows bump the walls. Slipping out of the tiny room, I stand in front of the full-length mirror and examine the fit from every angle. Sophia joins me.

"Looks good, Sophia," a masculine voice with a slight Russian accent opines.

My bestie twirls around. "Oh, Mark. I didn't see you there."

He saunters in, Chase behind him. Mark pokes him in the stomach. "Oof! Oh, uhm, Melody, yours is nice, too."

I roll my eyes and—in spite of the *movie star*'s comment—decide to purchase it. Because *I* like the dress. "I'm going to take it. Sophia, how about you?"

Mark responds, "She is."

I raise an eyebrow at her and she shrugs. Under her breath, she admits, "I do like it." We return to the dressing room and change back into our own clothes. Before we leave the tiny dressing area, she pulls me aside.

"What do you think Mark's doing here?"

"If I had to hazard a guess, I'd say he likes you."

Her shoulders raise. "Really?"

I laugh. "Guess you were too absorbed with the other's PA to notice."

"Well, maybe. I'm sure the guys are long gone by now, anyway. Why don't we pay for our new dresses and grab a bite to eat? Then the beach is calling my name."

We approach the grinning shopkeeper who says our nice *uomini* already took care of it. What men? We exchange puzzled glances and exit the boutique where Mark and Chase wait for us.

While Sophia chats with Mark, I study Chase. "Thanks for the dress. You didn't have to do that."

He rubs his nose. "It was nothing. And the dress looked very nice on you."

Mark diverts my thoughts by pointing toward a building. "The rest of the group went into that pizzeria."

Walking into the *ristorante*, we place our orders and meander to the back where open-air seating is dotted with lush trees. I inhale the beautiful scent of citrus. "This place is amazing."

"It really is," Sophia replies.

We join a half-empty table—Mark sits next to Sophia, then me with Chase to my right—and enjoy the best pizza ever. Which is saying a lot, considering this *is* Italy.

Jessa sidles up to Chase and kisses his cheek. "I'm hitting the beach. Anyone want to join me?" She preens, her perky breasts nearly poking Chase's eye out. Everyone decides to join her, probably to see what floss bikini she'll be sporting.

Because I want to rest and catch the sun, I agree. I'm definitely *not* spurred on to see Jessa's body on display, however. We take turns using the bathrooms as a dressing room, and I toss my boho dress back over my bathing suit. Soon we're all heading toward the beach.

Mark walks next to Sophia, so I give them their privacy. He seems like a nice guy, but he's an actor, which means he's more about himself than anything else. He probably sees her as a means to a better camera angle in the movie.

I stop moving. That was a very unfair thought. Sophia's an amazing woman and perhaps he sees that. Although . . . he is surrounded by beautiful women all the time. Not to mention he's not known for having any long-term relationships.

When we reach the beach, we walk past an outdoor gym. Chase perks up. "Challenge you to a circuit, Mr. A." He punches Mark in the arm.

"You're on, Doc!"

The two of them go into the open-air gym and start to show off. I mean, jump on the various pull-up bars, fly machines, and other equipment. A bunch of the crew cheers them on, while Sophia and I set up chairs on the beach. A couple of pleasure boats sail by, adding to the perfect afternoon.

I point to the fluffy white clouds. "Thanks for making me come today. Positano has been wonderful."

"What are besties for?"

I settle into the chair, ignoring when Chase and Mark abandon their workouts and rush into the water like the little boys they are. Instead, I slather on more suntan lotion and recline. The sun soothes my nerves, relaxing me like before we arrived in Italy.

After a while, Sophia checks her watch. "We should be getting our stuff together pretty soon. We all agreed to catch the six o'clock ferry back to Amalfi."

Sighing, my body absorbs the fact our trip is coming to an end. But it really rejuvenated me for the last stretch of filming. I stand and shake the sand from my towel. At my actions, Mark comes over and starts to chat up Sophia.

"I'm going to hit the restroom before we leave." The two of them wave at me, so I sling my bag over my shoulder and leave them be.

Once my personal business is finished, now wearing my dress once more, I step onto the walkway. Instead of heading toward the beach and the ferry, I go in the opposite direction. A cathedral up ahead had caught my attention, and I haven't had a chance to visit it. Before I reach the door, my cell phone rings.

Fishing it out of my tote, my dad's face smiles at me. I press the FaceTime button. "Hi, Daddy!"

"Hi, Princess," he replies, his face somber.

My nerves skitter to a halt. "What's wrong?"

"It's your brother. An unknown assailant attacked him, and he's in the hospital out in the Hamptons. I'm on tour in Arkansas and can't get to him. Sara wanted to go, but, as you know, their relationship's almost non-existent."

My hand covers my mouth. His use of mom's proper name shows how off-kilter he is. "Oh, no. Will King—is he—"

"The doctor said he's going to be fine."

The air surges out of my body. Like my mom, I don't have much of a relationship with my half-brother, but I know the distance between my dad and his firstborn has only brought him pain. "I'm glad."

"Your mother and I sent him flowers. We included your name on the card."

"Thanks. I'm sorry you can't get out to see him."

"Yeah. I talked with my agent about canceling the tour and rescheduling, but it would be a nightmare. Especially since it's a shortened tour already."

I trace his sad features. "I'm sure King will understand."

"I don't know. We've been going through a very rough patch lately."

"If I know you, you'll figure out a way to make things right with him."

"Thanks, Princess." His amber eyes—identical to mine—survey my surroundings. "Where are you?"

"Oh. Well, today was a rare day off and a bunch of us went to Positano to explore. It's a beautiful town."

He smiles. "Yes. Your mother and I liked it there. Basically, we liked everywhere in Italy."

We both laugh. "I was about to explore the cathedral here."

"Then I'll let you go. Enjoy."

"Thanks, Daddy. And I appreciate your telling me about King. Please keep me posted."

"Will do, Princess." The screen goes blank.

I turn and lean on the railing, not really seeing the houses in front of me, or the beach slightly below. My mind floats back to the few times King visited while I was growing up.

"Hey, Melody!" Chase jogs up to me.

Startled, I clear my mind. "Oh. Chase?"

"We're getting ready to head back to the ferry. Sophia yelled, but you didn't hear her, so I volunteered to get you."

"I was lost in my own thoughts," I muse. I turn and glance at the cathedral. "Do you think I have time to pop my head in there?"

Chase bites his lip. "I'm sure you have a few minutes."

"Okay, thanks." Leaving him standing on the walkway, I hotfoot it to the door. Inside, beauty and serenity sink into my soul. I walk around the perimeter, amazed at the craftsmanship that went into the creation of the marble frescos, statues, and reliefs.

The altar is a marvel of intricately carved wood and shiny gold leaf. Behind, the stained-glass windows enhance the reverence within. I wander over to one of the tables filled with lit red candles and pick up a long match. Striking it, I light one for King.

"Dear Lord, please be with King as he heals after his attack. Please let the cops catch who did this to him. And please help Daddy to reconcile him into our family. Amen."

A tenor voice repeats, "Amen."

Clutching my heart, I whirl around. Chase stands behind me. "I didn't realize you came inside."

His eyes are filled with questions. "I gave you a couple of minutes, but when you didn't come back out, I came in to find you." Shaking his head, he looks around. "It's ethereal in here."

"It is." Leaving him, I stop at the donations box and drop some euros into it. Chase does the same.

We emerge from the cathedral, and it takes a few moments for my eyesight to acclimate back to the sun's rays. A bunch of people from the movie are boarding the ferry.

"Oh, no!" I grip my purse. "We have to run. The ferry's boarding."

Chase's hand lands on my arm. "No. Wait. We'll never make it back in time. We can catch the next one."

"*I* can make it." I snatch my arm back from his tense grip and make a run for it.

We race down the walkway and pass the beach. The ferry's horn sounds. I place my hands by my mouth and shout, "Wait!"

The ferry ignores me. I halt as it pulls away, Sophia waving her arms at me. Panting, I curse, "Crap!"

Stopping behind me, Chase says, "Like I said up there, we'll catch the next one." The jerk isn't even breathing hard.

My hands drop to my knees and I bend over, sucking in great gulps of fresh Italian air. He rubs my back. "Breathe."

"No." I pant. "Shit." I wheeze and force my head up to look at him. "Sherlock."

His arms come up as if in surrender. "I was only trying to help." He steps backward.

Now I feel like the jerk. I bring myself up to standing, my breathing still labored but not the desperate gulps of a few moments ago. "I'm sorry, Chase. That was awful of me. You only came to get me from the cathedral so all of this could've been avoided."

"Hey, what's the worst thing that happened? We get an extra hour in Positano?" He smiles, the cleft in his chin enhancing his gorgeous face.

"Well, when you put it like that." I flick the rubber band around my wrist. I need to make amends to this man who has been nice to me. "Want to get a gelato? There has to be at least twenty gelaterias nearby."

"Sure, let's go." He loops his arm around my shoulders and we head off in the direction of the shops.

We pick the third place we come across and head inside. It offers at least thirty different flavors—all homemade, of course—with cute little tables off to the right. I order a hazelnut and vanilla double cup, while Chase opts for one of his preferred fizzy waters—which they surprisingly offer.

I lead us to an empty table in the back, where he might not be recognized. He sits with his back toward the front in order to facilitate his anonymity. "No gelato?"

"It's not on my diet. And we're still filming."

"Man, that sucks." I dig my spoon into the deliciousness and bring it to his lips. "A taste would be all right?"

His eyes dart from the spoon to me and back again. "I wish. I already did a ton of damage with that slice of pizza earlier."

"But you worked it off at the beach gym."

"Well, let's not tempt fate." He takes a long swallow of his water.

"Would you like to leave?"

"Nah. Finish your gelato. For the both of us." He winks.

I laugh. And it hits me. This is the first sort-of real conversation I've had with the leading man since filming started.

Before I can assess how this makes me feel, he asks me a question. "So, who's King?"

My body tenses. He must've heard my prayer back in the cathedral. "Since I'm torturing you by bringing you in this gelateria, the least I can do is give you an explanation."

He taps the bottle onto the table.

"King is my half-brother. My dad's son with his first wife—he's eight years older than me. He used to come and visit us when I was a kid, but he stopped coming when he was a teen. My dad and he have a very rocky relationship and they've been on the outs recently." I shake my head, not knowing exactly what transpired. "Anyway, King was the victim of an attack. I was praying in the cathedral for his health and for the person who did it to be caught."

His tenor voice drops. "I hope your prayers are answered, Melody."

"Thank you." I scoop some more gelato onto my spoon. "Even though I don't really know him, I don't want anything bad to happen to him."

"I get it. My sister and I have gotten closer since we've been adults, but family dynamics can be a bitch to overcome."

My spoon stills in my gelato.

CHASE

The engaging woman across from me bites her lip. Then dips her spoon into her gelato again. "You mentioned before that your parents were too caught up in building their careers to pay much attention to you and your sister when you were growing up."

My fingers slice through my hair. "Yeah. And I was too busy hanging out with my friends to deal with her. So, I guess you could say, we both raised ourselves." Although Lindsay bore the brunt of it. I swallow the smothering guilt over my part in all her issues with my sparkling water. It was only due to fantastic emergency room doctors that she escaped death—twice.

"That kinda explains a lot."

I don't bother to decipher her comment but redirect our conversation. "That was ages ago. So tell me, where did you get your costume design experience? You certainly have a great eye for clothes." My eyes drop to the bag with her new dress. "Not to mention you can sew me into my leggings like a superhero."

Her cheeks pinken. "Thanks. I graduated from NYU with a degree in costume design."

"Great school."

She nods. "It is." She looks down. "I don't want to brag, but I graduated *magna cum laude*." Her voice takes on a harsher edge. "Even though I'm only turning twenty-five, I have a lot of experience behind me."

I cock my head. "I never said you didn't."

"Sorry. Must've been my chip." She swipes her shoulder a couple of times, causing me to smile. "I need to remind myself not everyone thinks I got my job on *Ladies of the Abbey*—and, hence, this one—because I'm Braxton Hunte's daughter."

My head pushes back. "Really? People say that?"

"You'd be surprised," she replies, the pink of her tongue licking the last of the gelato off her spoon.

Relief courses through me. I'm not sure what I'm more grateful for, though—the ice cream being gone, or her tongue being hidden again from view. I frown. *She's your dresser.* I push away from the table and grab her empty cup.

Tossing it into the trash, we walk side by side through Positano. As we travel through the little alleys, I study her patrician profile. Her nose and cheekbones beg for my touch, which causes me to scrub my hands on my thighs. She's not traditionally gorgeous, like Jessa, but has a true vitality about her. Nothing has been enhanced surgically. Our conversations are refreshing. Unique.

Her comments back in the gelateria run around my head. As we leave a jewelry boutique where she bought a bangle bracelet, I blurt, "You shouldn't wonder why you were hired, Melody. You're very talented and dedicated. Plus, you're a hard worker."

She stops like she hit a brick wall. Her hand flies to her bun and she removes the knitting needles, fluffing her silken hair. I bury my desire to touch the spun gold in my pockets.

"Thanks." She tilts her chin upward. "I know I am. I'm working very hard to prove it to everyone."

I smile at her confidence. "You've won my vote."

Her eyes shine. "Thank you, Chase." She pauses, giving me a speculative look. "Charles."

I freeze at her use of my real name. "No one calls me that anymore."

She bounces her bags of purchases against her leg. "Well, you're not Charles when you're on set. There, you're the movie st—actor—Chase Wright." She licks her lips. "But now, here with me, you're the real person underneath all that"—her free hand waves around—"stuff."

Her words lodge in the back of my throat. With difficulty, I swallow over the large lump. "You know, you may be right. With you, I'm more of myself than I've felt in ages." I shake my head. "I don't know why."

"Maybe 'cause we're two Chicagoans." She bumps her shoulder against my arm.

"That must be it," I lie. No, geography certainly isn't the reason why I'm so comfortable around this woman. She doesn't want anything from me—she already has a great career going for herself, tons of money thanks to her father, and with her looks, I can't imagine she's lacking for male attention.

Fists form as she flips her hair, once again halting my inclination to verify its softness. Her next words catch me off guard. "You mentioned before you like to perform on stage."

This is something I haven't shared with anyone. Ever. But I did with her. I try to make light of yesterday's confession. "When I was in college."

"But a bug like that can't be squashed," she persists.

I shrug. "It was good training."

"For Broadway." She fiddles with one of the knitting needles. "Sorry. You can tell me to shut up if I'm getting too much in your business."

The two words play on my lips, but I can't bring myself to say them. I sigh. "I've been thinking about the theater a lot lately."

She remains silent.

I take a few more steps. "Sam tells me I need to go where the money is."

"For him."

I slant her a glance. "That thought has crossed my mind." My hand lands on my forehead. "He's right, though. I need to bank as much as I can now, as I'm not sure when this gravy train will end."

"What do you mean? You're very sought after. I've heard—over-heard—your conversations with your agent. He's always proposing new roles."

"Yeah. Rom-coms. Or more like *Doctor Manipul8*."

She frowns. "Don't you like playing these types of characters? You're so good at them."

A reluctant smile tips my lips. "Thanks." We stop in front of a novelty shop, filled with all things Italy. Her eyes roam over the display. "Want to go inside?"

She tosses the knitting needle into her purse. "Do we have the time?"

I check my watch. "Yeah. This has to be our last stop, though."

She nods and I open the door for her. Following her in, I watch as she picks up unusual items, usually located on the bottom shelves. She shows me a pretty hand-painted spoon rest with the word "Positano" on it.

"I like it." I take it from her and am impressed with the craftsman-ship—it's not a typical souvenir. The scene is not of the water, but rather one of the small alleys, with a lemon tree next to a gelateria. Like where we just were. I return the ceramic to her.

"Me too." She brings it to the cash register.

While I keep my head down, Melody starts talking with the clerk. She's friendly.

And perceptive.

And talented.

And beautiful. I shake my head.

She returns to my side carrying the new bag. I reach out for all of her packages. "Here, let me take these for you."

"Nah, I've got it. I bought all of these, so I should have to carry them. Besides"—she gives me a sideways glance—"they're not heavy."

This independent streak is out of my depth. No woman ever refused my help before. "Are you sure?"

"Yup." We head toward the ferry. "So, Charles, if you don't mind my asking, what's the difference between acting on stage and in movies?"

What a question! "Well, in the movies, it can take hours to get maybe a minute's worth of usable footage. The cameras have to capture every angle, and the director has to be happy with it. On this set, there's quite a bit of green screen, as you know. That's definitely a learned skill."

"I bet. But you do make it look easy."

Her compliment warms my chest. "Thanks, Melody. Since this is my third round as Doctor Manipul8, I've learned how to deal with it." I scrape my palm over my stubble. "The learning curve was a bitch, though."

We exchange smiles. After a few moments, she prompts, "How's all this different from the stage?"

I rub my forehead. "On stage, there's no time for re-dos, so you really have to hit your mark on the first try. When you flub a line." I roll my eyes.

"What happens then?"

"Nothing good." I chuckle. "I remember this one time, we were doing . . . what was the play?" I remember the scene and snap my fingers. "Right! We were doing *The Tempest*, and the woman playing Miranda was supposed to say, 'Your tale, sir, would cure deafness.' Instead, she said, 'Your story, sir, would give me the remedy for,' and she stopped. Mute." I chuckle again.

Wide eyes filled with mirth, Melody asks, "What did you say?"

"Well, I was playing the lead, Prospero, and she was responding to my story. I have to admit, I tortured her a little. I said, 'hemorrhoids?'" Remembering the actress's horror, I throw back my head and laugh.

The woman next to me puts her hand in front of her mouth, hiding her giggle. "You're bad."

"She was so mad! She spent the rest of the run trying to get back at me."

"What did she do?"

"She tried to get me to flub my lines, but I was too prepared for that. So she resorted to tampering with my wardrobe. Her worst was shaving cream in my shoes." I chuckle.

"That one never gets old. Although"—she cocks her head—"she probably should've tried to mess with your hair." She reaches up and runs her fingers over my undercut, ending with shaking the top askew.

"Nice try." I rake my hands through my hair, catching sight of myself in a window. "Looks normal to me."

She checks me out. "The trials of having perfect hair. Guess you left your actress friend no other option but the shaving cream."

I grimace, remembering the squishy feeling against my feet. "It was pretty effective." We resume walking.

"So, you loved Shakespeare on stage but now are playing Doctor Manipul8. Is it the challenge of acting before a live audience that you miss?"

I shove my hands into my pockets. "That's part of it. The connection with the audience simply can't be replicated, especially here on these massive movie sets. There's a tension, a camaraderie, with other actors that's also missing. Don't get me wrong, I do enjoy the movies."

"While wishing you were on stage."

"Lately, yes." But I've only given her part of my reason. Sure, I do miss the adrenaline of live acting. Dare I share the more gnawing reason? I glance at her but can't bring myself to share such a deep secret. "It looks like you're living your dream to me."

She blinks. Clearing her throat, she replies, "I'm trying. That's all any of us can do, right?"

Am I trying? Instead of shutting down like I normally do when a subject gets too heavy, I find my mouth running away from me. "Some more than others."

Her expressive eyes peek at me from under her long lashes. "What's holding you back?"

I inhale and consider her question. She waits for me to reply but doesn't push. Lets me work out what I'm able to share. What I *dare* to share. For some reason, I think I can trust her. "Well, you see, I guess there are a couple of things. First, I've recently lost some roles to younger actors."

Her head pops up. "Really?"

"Yeah." Because I want to do something with my hands, I grab the bags away from her. "Two times in the past couple of months, studios went with an unknown over me."

"That sucks."

Like Russian dolls, I shove one bag into the other in an effort to assimilate her belief in my skill. "Actually, it only hurt my pride. I wasn't all that into the roles. However, the increased competition has shown me that, unless I change tracks, my career is definitely on the downswing." I switch the now one bag to my other hand. Before I can confess more, I bite my lip.

"Hence your renewed interest in the stage?"

"Sort of." I switch the light bags again. "Truth be told, my heart never truly left the stage. Movies don't really allow me to expand my acting chops." I shake my head. I'm not explaining myself.

"I get it," she murmurs. "You want longevity and meatier roles than what you've been doing in front of a green screen."

I'm a little shocked at her perception. "Yeah. Exactly."

"Then you should try out for Broadway, instead of the rom-coms Sam's throwing your way."

"Easier said than done." Movement to my right catches my eye. A line of reporters form along the side of the walkway toward the ferry. "Shit."

"What?" Melody's head swivels from side to side, stopping when she spies the paparazzi. "Oh, crap. I thought we'd be able to avoid them all day." She rummages in her purse for a moment and offers me a baseball cap.

"Thanks." I bring the bill down over my forehead. One of the reporters yells my name as our ferry makes its way toward the dock. "Our ferry's coming."

"Good."

Melody twirls around in front of me as if to shield me from the cameras, causing me to chuckle. "I doubt that'll put them off."

Her hazel gaze locks on mine. "Maybe they'll think they have the wrong guy." Her hand slides up, rasping against my stubble.

Everything in my body seizes. This glorious woman is trying to protect me from the paparazzi with her own body. Without command, my hands land around her waist, pulling her closer. "Now what?"

"Your hat's brim should cover us." Her warm breath tickles my lips.

I nod, and the bill taps her on her forehead. Behind us, the paparazzi scream my name. "Chase! Chase Wright, is that you?"

The ferry's horn blasts.

I don't react to either noise. Instead, my gaze drops to Melody's lips. Lush. I incline my head toward hers.

Her head tips upward. "Charles," she purrs.

In a husky murmur, I reply, "Yes."

"Chase!" The reporters shout from behind us. Gaining on us.

With strength I didn't know I possessed, I lock eyes with Melody. Clasping her hand, I order, "Run!"

We bolt toward the ferry, zigging and zagging around people. The ferry docks as we catapult near the front of the line, still being chased by a hearty group of reporters. Panting, I give them my back and wrap Melody in my arms, as the other passengers effectively cock block the reporters. "We made it."

Pressed together, her body shudders as she seeks air. I want to tip her head up and kiss her. I want to slow her breath with mine, then increase it with passion. I do neither. The salty air stings my lungs, allowing me a brief moment to savor her limbs wrapped around me. I press her head to my chest while my breathing evens out.

The ferry docks and we make our way onto the boat. Other passengers look in our direction, but I keep my head down and direct Melody to an empty side row. With my body facing away from the dock and the paparazzi, I sit. Expending some of my nervous energy, I bend down and stow her bag of purchases under my seat.

Melody stands above me, still trying to obscure my identity. "I think we lost them. I don't see them on board."

"I hope not," I reply. Her fingers worry her dress, so I capture them and tug her down into her seat. Her startled features meet mine. "Thank you." My voice sounds raspy.

An impish smirk overtakes her face. "Plenty of practice with my dad."

I didn't anticipate her response, although I should have. "I bet."

"Actually, it's kinda fun so long as it doesn't happen too often."

I rub my neck as the ferry's horn sounds and we leave Positano—without pesky reporters. "I think we're safe." I hope they didn't tip off their friends in Amalfi. "For now," I add.

Her smile gleams at me. Beckons. Whispers secret promises.

Was our almost kiss back there a ruse for the reporters, or something more? My whole body begs to know the answer.

Instead of asking the question, I swallow and bring my face toward hers. Her smile disappears, and her breathing accelerates, although not from exertion this time. A slight blush stains her cheekbones. And I have my answer.

It wasn't for the reporters.

MELODY

My brain turns to mush as Charles's gaze devours my lips. I can almost feel his lips caressing mine, bringing me to ecstasy with the simple joining. Without thought, my mouth opens and I lean slightly toward him. My pulse reignites in a faster and faster allegro tempo. Anticipating. Wanting. *Needing*.

He leans back.

My pulse stutters and, self-conscious, I reach for my knitting needles—only to realize they're in my purse. I'm out of my element here. With him. Charles. Chase. Whoever he is.

"People are looking at us," he whispers.

Understanding dawns. They were intruding on our private moment, one that was for no one but him and me. I sit up straighter. Struggling to regain my composure, I cast about for a topic of conversation. "I had a lovely time in Positano today, Charles."

He smiles, and my insides flip. The lowering sun glints off blue eyes that rival the color of the water we're on. "The last part was my favorite."

Is he flirting with me? This man who has been driving me crazy in his trailer twice daily? Tentatively, I reply, "Who knew Doctor Manipul8 likes to shop in little boutiques?"

He wiggles his eyebrows at me. "Maybe it's because his dresser has such good taste." He leans forward and whispers in my ear, "And I desperately want to know how she tastes, too."

Holy shit. This is for real.

We both collapse against our chairs, and he puts his arm around the back of mine. We watch the shoreline disappear while the ferry takes us toward our home away from home. His finger rubs my upper arm. Resting my head on his shoulder, I inhale the salty scent of the sea and the light grassy one of the man who's unexpectedly turning my world upside down.

About twenty minutes later, the ferry docks in Amalfi. Charles picks up my bags of Positano treasures and carries them for me, despite my telling him I could do it. This side of the man is much different from the one I've come to loathe in his trailer. With an agent who offers him roles he doesn't want, and a personal assistant who caters to his every perceived whim.

Charles grabs my hand as we walk down the gangplank, the brim of his hat downward. A bunch of other passengers crane their necks trying to catch a glimpse of the man the paparazzi were chasing, causing him to lengthen his stride. I extend my legs to match. Once we're away from the crowd, walking toward the main area of town, I say, "I think we're free of all of them."

"Hope so."

I expect him to drop my hand, but he doesn't. Instead, he brings us toward a line of restaurants on the waterfront. Confused as to his intentions, I hook my thumb backward. "My hotel is back the other way."

"I thought we'd get some dinner, if that's okay with you?"

Since I've only had pizza and gelato all day, my stomach screams its desire to be fed. Yet, I can get room service. "Uhm, yeah, sure. I could eat." I take another step. "But don't you want to be with your—" I search for the right word. Posse? Girlfriends? Lovers? I settle for the least offensive, considering the drastic turn of events over the past hour. "Friends?"

He stops in the middle of the sidewalk. "You're the only person I want to share time with."

"Really?" The word leaves my mouth before I can censor it.

He smiles and tucks some of my hair behind my ear, closing his eyes. "I really do."

"Oh, okay."

Hand-in-hand, we stroll past several restaurants looking for a menu that captures our attention. We decide on a small place a little off the beaten path, less touristy. Ascending to the second floor, we're shown to a window seat with a gorgeous panoramic view of the Tyrrhenian Sea.

I settle into my seat, placing the crisp white linen napkin onto my lap. "I've never eaten here."

"Me neither. Let's hope it's as good as it looks."

I let my eyes wander around the dining room, which is filled with native Italian speakers. "Well, if the clientele is any indication, I think we're in for a treat."

The waiter comes by and Charles orders a bottle of pinot noir. He licks his lips. "I hope you don't mind. I'm dying for a good pinot."

"Not at all. I'm always up for trying new things. I'm usually a Cosmo girl myself."

"Can you keep a secret?"

His words take me off guard. "I might be persuaded. After all, my lips are sealed about how much of a gentleman you are by carrying all my purchases." I don't remind him about his confession about the stage—or our almost kiss.

"I hate scotch. I'd rather have a good pinot noir any day, and twice on Sunday."

I scrunch back into my seat. "But I've seen you drinking scotch, like, all the time? In so many photos."

"Yup."

"Wow." I shake my head. "Even my dad always drinks his beloved Bud."

"He's a rock star."

The waiter sets our glasses down and offers Charles a taste. Once he approves it, both glasses are poured and we place our dinner orders.

Wanting more info about the intriguing man across from me, I return to our conversation. "What does being a rock star have to do with what you choose to drink?"

Charles sips his wine, an expression of pure joy crossing his face. "Rock stars are rebels." He takes another sip. "Actors are supposed to always be on the cutting edge of everything. You know, living the best life and all that bullshit."

I taste the wine and find it refreshing. When a breadbasket is placed on the table, I select a roll and dip it in some olive oil. "I promise not to let anyone know your true drink of choice."

His shoulders bob, like he's holding in a laugh. "You're a real trooper. If I had confessed this truth to you when you were sewing me into those damn leggings, I'm not so sure you wouldn't have outed me from the rooftops."

"I'm not that bad. Besides, I'm the one on her knees for nearly two hours. Cut a girl some slack."

"Now that you mention it, it's certainly a provocative position." He takes the smallest roll in the basket and rips it apart. His eyes skewer mine as his hand slips across to my plate and he dips the roll into my oil.

"Hey!" I swat at him, but he's too fast and the bread disappears into his mouth. Which is surrounded by those lips—holding untold promises. Are they soft? Hard? Would they mold perfectly against mine and turn my brain to mush? Or crash hard against me and work me into a frenzy? Electricity zips through my nerve endings, and I cross my legs to tamp down the feeling.

He smiles at me, his eyes dancing with mischief. "Gotta be faster than that, Goldie."

I manage a squeak. "Goldie?"

He dips his remaining scrap of bread in the oil on my plate. After swallowing, he wipes his hands on his napkin and reaches for my hair. Holding out a lock, he says, "I've never seen hair this color before. At first I thought it was just blond, but it really isn't. It's actually gold."

Lowering my eyes, I swipe my hair away from his grasp. "I'm sure you've seen this color before. It's the same as my dad's."

He chuckles. "Guess I never stared too hard at his hair."

Heat races up my throat. Not wanting him to see my embarrassment, I stand. "I need to use the restroom."

Charles nods at me, and I race down the stairs. Once inside the single bathroom, I turn the faucet on and let the cool water run into my cupped hands. Taking a deep breath, I splash my face, letting the water droplets slide down my throat. Why am I reacting to him like this?

I stare into the mirror and realization hits like a bolt of lightning. *No!* No. Freaking. Way. I am *not* falling for the leading man. My lips tingle and my lie falls away. "Shit." This can lead nowhere good. Even though I can't figure out how my family connections could help him in any way, I'm sure he's not interested in a costume designer like me. Not when he has beautiful starlets falling all over themselves to serve his every whim.

Not to mention Grant . . .

A knock brings me back to my altered reality. Reminding myself not to become the worst sort of cliché, I force my head up, straighten my shoulders, and brush past a gorgeous Italian woman standing on the other side of the door. Who would look great on Charles's arm—and probably in his bed. Desperately trying to banish the image, I return to my seat, where our meals have been served.

Charles smiles around a mouthful of food. "Sorry. Couldn't wait."

He looks so young and carefree, nothing like the authoritative guy I sew into a superhero suit daily. Returning my napkin to my lap, I pick up my fork. "No problem. Is it good?"

He nods. "Fuck yeah. This fish is so fresh. With all these herbs, it tastes amazing." His gaze strays to my oversized bowl. "Bet yours is fantastic."

Needing the distraction, I lick my lips and dig into my seafood stew. The delicate flavors dance along my taste buds. "This is the best thing I've ever tasted." I hold up a razor clam. "Want to taste?"

"Thought you'd never ask," he teases, leans forward, and opens his lips.

I put my fork into his mouth, only realizing what I've done when it's too late. Now we're sharing utensils? He pulls back, chewing. "You're right. It is good."

I look down at my fork, which was just in his mouth. Do I ask for another? Steal one off a neighboring table? Casually drop it onto the floor so the waiter brings me a new one? I inhale and dig into my dish again. As my mouth closes around the fork, I try to ignore the shiver of knowledge about where it was a second ago.

He sips his wine. "So tell me something, Goldie. What was it that drew you to costume design in the first place?"

His choice of topic relaxes me. I love design and can blabber on about it for ages. While removing a mussel from its shell, I reply, "It's the fantasy of it, you know? Creating a feeling through fabrics that translate to the screen. The challenge of figuring out what conveys the best visible support to bring the writer's words to life. Sometimes it's subtle—like the Manipul8 Stitch inside your leggings—while other times it's big, like a wedding dress." I shove more stew into my mouth to stop myself from waxing too poetic.

He places his fork on his empty plate. "I never thought about it in those terms. It was always what do I have to wear so I can get on with delivering my lines." He closes his eyes. "Now that you mention it, though, I can see exactly what you're saying. About how wardrobe enhances the overall presentation. I mean, I always knew it was important—hell, there are Oscars for it—but I never truly understood how vital until you put it in those terms." He reaches over and places his hand on top of mine. "Thank you."

After a long pause, I remove my hand from under his by taking another bite. "That was why when your glove problem happened, we were all frantic. Of course, there was no excuse for the buckle getting caught in the young actor's hair, but so much planning went into every piece of the design. When that one part went sideways, we had to rethink everything on the fly."

He nods. "I get it. Your solution is working well. No problems. Bonus—it looks good with the costume."

I sigh. "I am really sorry that happened."

"And I'm sorry for how I overreacted." His kissable lips tip upward. "But it's all fixed now. It really was the only problem we've had."

I rap on the table. "Knock on wood." I take one final swallow and place my fork down onto the nearly empty plate. "Enough about me. What got you into acting in the first place, Mr. Hotshot?" No more use of "Movie Star," even in jest. He's so much more.

He glances sideways. "Well, you know I was into acting back in Chicago. I got my first role in middle school."

"Emory Middle School?"

"Yeah." He rubs his forehead. "I fell into it by accident, sort of. I didn't set out to be in the drama club for acting. I was, ah, looking for a new identity." His cheek hollows like he's clenching it.

I cock my head. "What was wrong with your old identity?"

"He wasn't someone I wanted to be."

I sit back in my chair, mulling over his last statement. The waiter comes and clears our table, then asks if we want any dessert. I want to explore this conversation more with Charles, yet the server seems to linger forever. When neither one of us orders anything—him because of his crazy diet and me because I'm way too full—the disgruntled waiter finally leaves us alone. Only to reappear within moments with our bill.

My hand reaches for the check so I can calculate my portion. Charles is too fast and holds out his credit card, which the waiter spirits away.

"Charles. Let me pay half."

"No, Goldie. I never let a date pay for anything."

I blink. Date? "I appreciate that, but . . ." How can I say this?

He interrupts my thought. "I like you. I like spending time with you. And for some reason, I'm willing to share way too much about myself with you."

My heart rate accelerates. "Oh." I place my napkin on top of the table, for want of something to do. "I, uhm. Well, I'm enjoying our time together, too."

The waiter returns and Charles signs the receipt. Leaving it on the table, his face lights up as he gets to his feet. Walking behind me, he helps me stand then lets his hand slide down my arm until our fingers are intertwined. "Let me walk you back to your hotel."

"Okay." I don't even recognize my own fog-filled voice. I clear my throat. "I'd like that."

He squeezes my hand. The cleft in his chin winks at me, causing my stomach to flip. Once we're back on the nighttime street, he turns his head. "Which way?"

I point down the road, back toward the ferry. "My hotel is down there, on the right-hand side."

His blue eyes scan the horizon and land on my hotel. "Nice view."

"I like it. Although, I'm sure it doesn't compare with where you're staying."

He shrugs. "It's a hotel."

We walk in silence on the sidewalk, watching as tourists and Italians alike stop and gawk at my date. My *date*? My eyes stray down to our joined hands. "Do you always cause such a commotion?"

He rolls his eyes. "People are amazed that I walk on the street like a regular human being. I guess they think I live in a mansion filled with naked women who do my bidding at all times." He chuckles, but it sounds sad to me.

I slant him a glance. "I'm sure you have plenty of naked bunnies running around."

"Just like your father, right?"

I bark a laugh picturing my dad in the kitchen doing dishes, with a dishtowel thrown over his shoulder. "Not a bunny to be seen."

He throws his head back and joins me with laughter. This time, it's uninhibited. Real. "Thanks, Goldie. I needed that."

"That's what I'm here for." We take a few more steps, and his unusual statement back in the restaurant bubbles to the surface. "Can I ask you a question?"

"As long as it doesn't have to do with naked bunnies, sure."

I draw a cross over my heart. We're now in a secluded spot, so it's safe to broach the subject. I hope. "What did you mean when you said that as a kid, you weren't 'someone you wanted to be'?"

He stops and takes my free hand in his so we're connected by both our hands. "When I was growing up, I was into strange stuff."

What does he mean?

My face must betray my confusion, because he tucks my hair behind my ear. "Like bees."

Bees? "Oh."

Without smiling, he nods. "I was fascinated by them, and my father bought me a beehive. I had the whole suit and everything. Kids can be mean, though, and they picked on me for my hobby. That Halloween, I dressed up as a beekeeper and my costume was the talk of the town. That's when I learned it was better to play a character rather than be one."

His words make me sad for the little boy he was. For the person who had to escape from his interests to gain acceptance, back in the judgmental schooldays of Chicago. Where the mean girls—led by his sister—terrorized me and Sophia. Guess he wasn't immune back then, either. "I'm sorry you had to go through all that."

"It was a long time ago."

Wanting to lighten the mood I had caused, I quip, "Well, it looks like the little beekeeper has stung the world."

His lips tilt. "I try. Recently, though, all the stinging is coming from the needle of my wicked costume designer." He brings one of my hands up and kisses the back of my hand, then we resume walking toward my hotel, accompanied by a buzzing throughout my body.

We take the stairs. When we reach the reception landing, I turn to him. "Thank you so much for the escort. And dinner. And for a great time in Positano."

"I had the best time with you." His gaze strays to the elevator. "So much so, I don't want it to end. Would you mind if I see you to your room?"

My mind blanks. He wants to walk me to my room? No way would he want me for . . . or does he? He's older and sexy and probably gets sex at the drop of a hat. Yet I'm just me, not one of his play-things. No, he's being a gentleman—nothing more. Realizing he's awaiting my response, I shove these nonsense thoughts to the side and mutter, "Uhm, sure."

Despite all my concentrated efforts, my legs become more wobbly with each passing step to my room. Sophia's accurate teasing plays on repeat, as I haven't had a man anywhere near my room, condo—or anywhere close to my person—since Grant. By the time we arrive at my door, the hairs on my arms are standing straight up. In a shaky voice, I announce, "We're here."

He holds his hand out. When I don't move, he prompts, "The key?"

"Oh!" I remain still.

He wiggles his fingers.

Charles's childhood bees have taken up residence in my stomach. "Right." I fumble in my purse and retrieve my keycard, which he uses to open my door.

"After you." He sweeps his arm and bows.

As I stumble inside the room, my breathing comes in faster pants. What does he want from me in here? Besides my body. Oh God, will he kiss me? I close my eyes. No way. He can get sex anywhere, from a multitude of super-hot women. I drop my purse onto the bed as the door clicks shut.

Bracing myself, I turn to face the man in my room. He seems to have grown larger over the past minute. Yet, he looks as if he belongs here. He holds up my packages. "Okay if I put them here?" He motions to the table.

My head bobs. "Sure." I wish I could catch my breath. The items on the bedside table are messy, so I head over there to straighten them.

He frowns. "Hey, are you all right?"

I place a knickknack down. "Yeah. I'm good."

He looks around the room, his eyes landing on the chair. "Why don't you have a seat?"

I blurt, "Why are you being so nice to me?"

He takes two steps and is in front of me. "Because I find that I like you, Goldie. You're funny. You're smart. You're fantastic at your job"—he pounds his chest—"which only makes me look better."

I offer him a small smile.

He stares at my lips.

His head travels toward me, and my brain explodes with desire to feel his lips covering mine. We're all alone in here—no interruptions, no paparazzi. Nerves rise up, but slip away as his soft lips cover mine.

If this kiss is a mistake, it's the best one I've ever made.

My mind turns to mush and my limbs grow weak. I wrap my arms around him to stay upright. But I don't need to, because his sturdy arms encircle my body and brings it flush against his hard, muscular one. I want to purr like a kitten and rub my softness all over him. I settle for a moan.

He caresses my lips with his, asserting ever-increasing pressure, which heightens the pleasure rampaging through my body. His tongue traces the seam of my lips, begging for entrance. I open my mouth and he swoops in, sending shivers exploding in all directions.

Charles's hands drop to my butt, and suddenly I'm wrapping my legs around his torso and being transported across the room. The plush bedding welcomes my back as I'm deposited onto it. His shirt flies over his head.

I don't have time to revel in the hard planes of his absurdly defined torso when his mouth returns to mine and his tongue continues its exploration. He tugs my dress upward. "Lift your hips," he implores.

Without any thought, I comply and my dress sails over my head and lands on the floor. His eyes roam over my nearly naked body, bouncing over my bikini. A large hand lands on my boob. His finger dips inside the cup. It runs over my nipple.

"Oh!"

"Like that?"

My mouth opens, but nothing comes out. A thought that he's going too fast tries to catch my attention, but like a delicate stitch, it disappears when he pinches my nipple. Charles reaches behind me and undoes the ties. My bikini top soon joins my dress on the floor.

"So beautiful," he growls.

His mouth lowers, and his tongue flicks where his fingers just were, causing my body to ripple beneath him. Little bites on my rock-hard nipples cause my core to contract, followed by the laving of his tongue. He pulls back and smiles at me, his face flushed.

Maybe it's the overwhelming feelings flooding my body, or maybe it's the change in his coloring, but the thought I ignored a minute ago resurfaces. With friends. I need to tell him.

"Charles."

He kisses me again. "I love that you use my real name." His hand skims to the elastic at the top of my bikini bottom.

"Charles," I repeat with a bit more force.

Above me, he stills for a moment, then dips to kiss my neck.

I close my eyes and revel in the tingles exploding throughout my body. My excitement is short-lived, though, as that damn voice inside my head screams—*tell him, tell him, tell him.*

I suck in a breath.

Tell him, Tell Him, TELL HIM.

I blurt, "I'm a virgin."

CHASE

My hand tugs on the hair at the back of my head. It's as if virtual ice-cold water pours over me. A *virgin*? I take deep breaths to control my rampaging desire—is this my simple normal desire to plunge into her, or . . . an overwhelming need to be her first?

And only.

I push away from her body and toss her dress over her nearly-naked body. Grabbing my shirt off the floor, I glide it over my torso.

Melody needs to be with someone she loves for her first time. Or at least thinks she loves. No matter the fact that I'm falling hard for her. She's so unlike any other woman I've ever known. Beguiling. Bewitching. Beautiful.

"I should go," I murmur. Forcing myself to the door, I refuse to look back at the wanton, amazing *virgin* strewn across the bed. One glance and I'm afraid I'd be back on top of her.

I stand still while Melody sews me into the leggings. Her hands— so passionate last night—are too professional. Like a gnat, Thomas circles around us, clicking his damn pen, scribbling down my responses to his insipid questions. I want him to leave so I can be alone with Goldie.

How can a woman like her still be a virgin? I spent all last night unable to answer this question.

Thomas asks, "What do you think?"

Huh? I have no idea what he's talking about. "Uhm, okay?"

His eyebrows rise. "Really? You'll accept the invitation to go on the talk show?"

What? "No, wait a minute. What talk show?"

My PA sighs. With deliberate enunciation, he replies, "I said, the *Evening with Eddie* folks want to interview you the day after filming wraps here."

I close my eyes. "Oh, shit. No way. I won't be in any shape to do TV then. Tell Eddie I'll catch up with him later."

His pen clicks. "Already did."

I grumble, "Then why did you ask?"

"Because you told me to tell you about all invitations."

My eyelids slam shut. I'm all up in knots because of my dresser, but I shouldn't take it out on Thomas. He's a good guy. "You're right. I'm sorry, my mind was elsewhere." Entrancing hazel eyes meet mine. I need to get her alone.

I clear my throat. "So, Thomas, have I answered all your questions for now?"

He consults his clipboard. "Yeah, we're good, boss." *Click, click.* "I need to restock your fridge."

Which means he has to go to the store. "Go on. I'll be on set soon, so there's no rush."

"Will do." He bends down and says something to Melody I can't hear, and my blood pumps faster. What's this? Jealousy?

"Appreciate it, though," Melody responds to my PA. With a salute to me, he leaves us alone in the trailer.

Finally.

Melody rises to her feet. "Can you please walk to check out how the leggings fit?" Her voice sounds forced.

I bend my knees and pace throughout the trailer, not paying any attention to the fit. No. My mind is focused on the woman who sewed me into them.

"They look good. How do they feel?" She swipes a bottle of spring water.

Instead of responding, I open the fridge. "Would you like to try some of my specialty water? It's much better than regular."

She tips the bottle to her lips. Lips that were on mine last night. Lips attached to her sinful body—which no one has touched. But me. An unusual spark makes me stand taller.

"Thanks, but I don't like carbonation in my water. I'm a plain girl."

Talk to her, dude. "There's nothing about you that's plain, Goldie."

She puts the empty bottle into the recycle bin and stares at it. She whispers, "How do the leggings feel?"

I approach her. "Like they were sewn with care."

Her head tilts upward, hazel eyes widening when she realizes I'm right next to her. "Chase."

Not my given name. The air thickens. "I want to go out to dinner with you tonight." My breath seizes at the disbelief and dismay written all over her face.

"Last night . . ."

"I was shocked." I go to cup her chin, but she moves backward, out of my grasp. "I couldn't imagine someone as gorgeous and intriguing as you is still a virgin."

Her arms cross over her chest, in a clear effort to protect herself. From me. For the first time, I notice dark circles under her eyes, covered with concealer. "Well, I am."

The urge to be her first grabs me by the balls. "We'll take it slow." An unwanted thought crosses my mind. "That is, if—" I can't make myself complete the rest of the sentence. She *has* to have feelings for me, considering mine for her.

Her hands reach behind her head and out come the knitting

needles. Her spun gold hair tumbles over her shoulders. How can she be unaware of how enticing she is? Her broken whisper reaches my ears. "Please."

Her response breaks my dam. My naked arms reach out and bring her willing body against mine. "I think you're very special. I want to spend more time with you." I tap her forehead. "I need to know how your intriguing mind works."

Her voice is a squeak. "My mind's intriguing?"

I smile. "Very." I want to pull her closer and kiss the crap out of her. Remove her cute tank top and skirt from her gorgeous body. Discover the secret of how on earth the daughter of the *legendary* Braxton Hunte is still a virgin. However, I don't do any of that, heeding an overwhelming desire to make her comfortable with me.

The possibility of us.

She stares into my eyes. "I'd like to go to dinner with you."

How does she make me feel like I just won an Oscar by simply agreeing to go out with me? "Great." Because excitement ricochets throughout my body, I give her a brief kiss. Too brief. "By the way, the leggings feel fine."

"Good." Her breath wafts to my lips.

The trailer door opens and we jump apart like two kids caught hunting for birthday presents. Helene walks up the stairs. "Melody, Judith asked me to get you. She wants to talk with you about something. I'll finish up here with Chase."

Melody responds, "Oh, hey, Helene. Do you know what she wants to discuss?" She works the knitting needles back into her hair.

"I'm not sure."

While Melody's colleague is nice enough, *now* I have no desire to switch my dresser. "Melody, if you don't mind, can you talk with Judith after you help me into the bodysuit?" Not waiting for her response, I address her colleague. "Helene, please tell your boss she'll be there in a few minutes."

Helene has made her way over to Melody's designer suitcase thingy, which she left open when she got her scissors. "It's no big deal, Chase. I can finish up."

"No offense, but I'd rather keep to my established team." I pause. "You know us actors and our superstitions. Don't want to mess with my mojo before hitting the set."

Helene plays with the items in the top tray.

I raise my eyebrow, and she steps back.

Her hands return to her side. "Fine." She sighs. "I'll go let Judith know. Maybe I can help her out with whatever she needs." With that snide remark, Helene glides out of the trailer.

Within seconds, Melody's next to me, all business. After tossing me the undershirt, she shakes out the bodysuit. "Here. We have to hurry. I have no idea what Judith wants, but I know she doesn't like to be kept waiting."

Not wanting to impose more than I already have, I put the shirt on, slip into the gloves, and then work the bodysuit up my torso. Of course it gets stuck mid-chest. "Sorry. I'm going as quickly as I can."

Her hands land on my torso, causing my stomach to tighten. "We don't want you to ruin this. Let me help you."

Between the two of us, I'm suited up in no time. Once the snaps are done, I grab the socks and boots and head to the chair. "Go meet with Judith. I'll be on the set shortly. I'm fine here."

"Are you sure?"

Placing my left ankle on my right knee, I reply, "Yup." She takes a couple of steps and picks up her tote bag. Before she leaves, I say, "I'm looking forward to our date tonight."

Melody stops but doesn't turn to face me. "Me too." Then she scurries out of the trailer.

Finished with my costume, I walk around, confirming everything's in the right place. Today's lines sit on the table, which I pick up and review. Placing my mask on, I glance one last time in the mirror to confirm Doctor Manipul8 is ready for action.

∾

I watch Melody pour olive oil onto her plate and pick up a hunk of delicious looking bread. "So what did Judith want to talk with you about before the shoot today?"

"Oh, she wanted my opinion about a couple of new ideas for the extras to wear during the movie's climax." She pops the bread into her mouth.

"Not as urgent as Helene made it sound, huh?" Fisting my hands to keep them out of the breadbasket *and* off her body, I continue, "Heard a rumor Judith's up to be Noble's new lead costume designer for his next movies. If that happens, what will you do?"

Without hesitation, she replies, "I'll stay on the show." She bites into another piece of bread. "Don't get me wrong, working here on the movie is amazing, but my heart belongs with the television show."

"I get it. You've worked there for a few years now?"

"Three. They're my family-away-from-home, you know? We've become pretty tight here on the set, but it doesn't compare with working with people for ten months a year."

"I get it. Noble's decision will be made soon, I'm sure."

The waiter brings our appetizers, and I dig into my shrimp cock-tail, trying to ignore the meatballs on her plate. Maintaining such a low body fat sucks. When our meals are finished—she had a nice mahi mahi while I opted for broiled chicken, again—I ask, "What would you like to do after dinner? I was thinking we could either hit a club, or walk by the waterfront, or maybe go back to my room?" Please pick the last option.

"Oh." Her eyes dart around.

"Don't worry. I won't force you to do anything you don't want to do."

"Thanks." She plucks at the rubber band around her wrist. "A walk sounds nice."

I keep disappointment out of my voice. "Then a walk it is." Maybe we can discuss how on earth she's still untouched at twenty-four. Did something happen to her? My mind conjures up terrible possibilities. I need to ferret out the truth.

Outside, it's a beautiful night, with an array of stars filling up the inky sky. I wrap my arm around her shoulders.

"It's so gorgeous," she remarks.

"Yes, you are."

She stops and turns to face me. "Charles, seriously, what's going on here?" She motions between the two of us. "I'm all sorts of confused."

My eyes travel from the top of her head to her hands, settling on her mouth. "I really enjoy your company, Goldie. I like how feisty you are." I brush my lips against hers. "Not to mention your passion."

As if her response is dragged from the depth of her soul, she replies, "I like you, too."

My forehead collapses against hers. "I'm not some overeager high schooler. We'll take this slow, okay? Whatever you're comfortable with is good for me." As soon as the sentiment is in the air, I realize how true it is. Sex has always come easy for me. I don it like another role. But with Melody, it's all changed. I do want to know why she's made the decision not to indulge, although her innocence is an unexpected turn-on.

Her forehead rolls against mine. "You're used to so many women throwing themselves at you."

"None of them mattered. They were warm, willing bodies. You, however, are different. I've never known anyone quite like you, Goldie."

She pulls her head back, confusion written all across her face. "Do you mean it?"

"I do." I tuck some stray hair behind her ear. "Come on, let's go for the walk you requested."

"Okay."

Holding hands, we wander the Italian roads for a while, passing fountains and other tourists, eventually ending up inside her hotel room. With every step, her confidence seemed to increase, and she leads me over to the only place big enough in here for both of us to sit —her bed. Her hands land on my thigh, which causes my cock to stir. I give him a stern warning.

"Charles, I never thought I'd be feeling this way toward you, of all people."

"Why not me?"

"Oh, you know." She laughs. "You're *the* Chase Wright, tabloid fodder with zero body fat. No to mention the looks of a superhero."

I roll my eyes. "A happenstance of genetics, workouts, and lots of broiled chicken."

Her smile reaches her eyes. "Well, I guess that's true." She licks her lips and it's all I can do not to suck her tongue into my mouth. "Is this for real?"

"It is for me." I square my shoulders. "I sure as hell hope it's real for you."

"It is."

With one final glance at her gorgeous face, I squeeze her hand on top of my thigh. "I'd like to kiss you now."

"Please."

Her permission unleashes my desire, and I take her into my arms. As I kiss her lips, her cheeks, her neck, I keep reminding myself she's a virgin. With every encouraging response she offers, the reminder plays louder.

Like when I remove her shirt. Then her bra.

When I take her nipple into my mouth and suckle. When she rolls against me.

When she tosses my shirt to the floor. And lies back on the bed.

Putting all my weight on my forearm, I trace her upper body with my index finger. I ignore the pressure against my fly where my cock begs to join the party. Instead, I play with the zipper of her skirt. "May I?"

She nods and lifts her hips for me, and soon the fabric is on the floor. Her hand lands on my belt buckle. Placing my hands over hers, I shake my head. "Not tonight."

Her pout is replaced with a gasp when my fingers slide inside her panties. They swirl around her clit, and she gasps. When I enter her tight, wet center, her legs tighten around my hand, so I kiss her until she relaxes. Slightly.

Her fingernails dig into my back as she moans at the feelings I'm triggering inside her body. With one more stroke, she comes around my hand, her whole body going rigid as she pants out a scream. When she softens under me, I collapse onto the bed beside her, pushing her silky hair off her face.

Her finger graces my mouth. "I've never felt anything like that before."

I catch her finger between my lips and bite. She giggles. "That's just the beginning."

Her eyes drift downward, toward the bulge in my pants, and she licks her lips. Instead of letting worry overtake her, I draw her back to my mouth and kiss her, exploring every inch of her delicious body with curious fingers.

Later, when my own body screams for more, I pull back. "I think I better go."

The nearly-naked woman asks, "Why?"

"Because my heart"—I roll my hips to demonstrate I don't mean *that* organ—"can't take any more." I toss my shirt over my head. "Get some sleep, and I'll see you in my trailer in a few hours." I give her one last kiss then hightail it out of her room before I give in to the desire rampaging through my body.

Back in my room, I take a very cold shower and jerk one out. Someday—not sure when, 'cause I sure as hell won't pressure her—I'll be doing this with Melody. Until then, my right hand is my new best friend.

I throw the soaked undershirt into the trash. "Where would you like to go to dinner tonight?"

Melody pauses while hanging up the bodysuit, casting a furtive glance toward Thomas who's busy at the front of the trailer. She whispers, "I liked the place last night."

I nod. "It was good."

Up front, Thomas coughs. Directing my attention to my PA, I ask, "Are you okay?"

He blows his nose. "Yeah." Crinkling sounds as he unwraps a throat lozenge.

After a quick glance at Melody, I head into the bathroom and switch into my T-shirt and jeans. Buckling my belt, I head over to my PA. "Are you sure everything's all right? I heard a lot of coughing on set today."

"I think it's just a cold. Nothing to worry about. But, if you don't mind, I'm going to take off and lie down. You're all set in here for tomorrow, so nothing to worry about."

I clamp my hand on his shoulder. "Feel better, man."

He waves and exits the trailer, causing me to turn around and walk to where Melody's closing up her suitcase. "All alone."

She smiles, and her whole face lights up. For some reason, this "letting her lead" thing makes me feel like a better man. Her next words confirm it. "I like being alone with you, Charles."

I kiss her. Because I want to. And because I can.

When we separate, she whispers, "I enjoy going out to restaurants and all, but would it be okay if we had room service tonight?"

My heart skips a beat. My mind knows better than to think she means what my body desires. I place my hand onto my belt, in an effort to calm my overeager body. "Sounds nice." Because I can't help myself, I add, "Your place or mine?"

She pulls the knitting needles out of her hair and shakes. "How about yours? You've seen mine."

When she goes to put the needles back into her hair, I steal them. "Let's go."

She looks from my hands with her knitting needles in them and back up to me and smiles. Exiting the trailer, I don't grab her hand like I want to. When she wants everyone to know about our relation-ship—like I do—she'll take it. Until then, we walk toward my hotel side by side.

Helene walks by us. Coughing, she waves. "Something's in the air."

Melody replies, "I heard Thomas coughing before. I hope you're okay."

"I'm sure it's nothing." She points toward the street that leads to their hotel. "Are you going back?"

I bite back the retort that wants to escape.

Melody says, "Not yet. I, uhm, have to discuss something with Char—Chase. I'll see you tomorrow."

Helene appears oblivious to Goldie's word challenges, so we part ways with her and continue toward my hotel. Soon, we're in my room. The sight of the woman who's taking up a big place in my heart standing in here makes me want to bellow from the rooftops. Instead, I pick up the room service menu and pass it to her. "Want to order dinner for us?"

She shakes her head. "I'm not hungry yet."

I drop the menu onto the counter. Pointing to the living room area, I ask, "Talk?"

When she agrees, we sit side by side on the couches. Before I can stop myself, the pressing question I've been disregarding pops out of my mouth. "May I ask you why?"

She tilts her head. "Why what?"

"You're beautiful, smart, and funny. Why hasn't someone snagged your heart yet?" Not to mention your amazing body?

She sighs and tucks her leg under her thigh. "It's not what you think."

"What do I think?"

"That I'm frigid."

I chuckle. "Not a shot in hell on that one."

She grins, probably at the incredulous tone in my voice. "I've never told anyone this. Not even Sophia."

A heavy weight descends on my chest. "If you don't want to share, you don't have to."

Her damn tongue licks her pink lips again, causing me to remind my body to calm the fuck down. She blinks several times. "No. I want to. I want you to know."

Unable to sit next to her and not hold her when she's about to spill her guts to me, I bring her into my embrace. I whisper, "Are you sure?"

Her head bangs against my chest as she nods. After a pause, she begins, "I had a serious boyfriend when I was in college. I was a sophomore, and he was a senior. I thought the sun rose and set on Grant—that's his name. He was a musician, the lead singer and guitarist in a band, and I went to all his shows. He reminded me of my dad, I guess."

I don't interrupt, just stroke her hair, reveling in the light vanilla scent rising to my nose. She goes silent for a little while, then continues, "I thought I was in love with him. His lifestyle was one I knew and understood since birth, and we got along really well. He was a pretty big man on campus, and I was his girlfriend. It felt so . . . right."

What did this asshole do to her? I want to scream my question from the rooftop but bite my tongue instead.

She pulls back to look into my eyes. "Remember when I told you I was subjected to a lot of ridicule growing up?"

I do. "We all were, in one way or another."

"Right. Well, the people who weren't bullying me all wanted to get to know me for what my dad could do for them. His connections. His money."

Blood rushes through my system. "I'm sorry."

"Not your fault." Her chin climbs upward. "Anyway, I had Sophia. She was my lifesaver." She settles against my chest. "I told you that not for your pity, but so you'd understand a bit better."

She inhales deeply, and I continue smoothing her gold mane, giving her strength to finish her story. When she doesn't, I prompt, "So, Grant?"

"Yeah. Grant. The night I decided to go all the way with him, I went to his rehearsal room to tell him. I figured he'd be excited, and his performance would be off the chain. Well, when I got there, the door was open and I overheard what he and his bandmates were saying."

My hand stills. "Which was?"

"He was bragging how my dad would give the band everything

they need because he'd shackled himself to me. How he was taking it for the team so Hunte would promote them."

I tangle my hand in her long locks and push her head to my chest. In a muffled voice, she adds, "Like everyone else, he only wanted me for what my family could do for him."

She starts to cry, and I hold her tighter, each tear slamming into my system. "Shhh, Melody." I try to soothe her.

After a little while, her tears subside. In a small voice, she adds, "That was too much for me, Charles. I decided I didn't want anything to do with men, and focused on the one thing under my total control, which was my career."

My heart breaks for her pain. "So you graduated at the top of your class and landed your job with HBO."

"Even then, the press release announcing my hire only talked about how I was the daughter of *the* Braxton Hunte."

Her words blast apart inside me. I place my hands on her shoulders and disengage from her. Using my pointer finger, I tip her chin to force her to look at me. After a full minute, tear-filled hazel eyes lock onto mine.

"Listen to me, Melody. You are damn good at your job, which you earned through hard work. Being Braxton's daughter may have played into their hiring decision—so they could boast of their new hire—but you wouldn't have gotten the offer if you weren't qualified. And"—I wipe away a tear that rolls down her cheek—"you certainly wouldn't have kept the job more than a hot minute if you sucked."

Her chest rises and falls. "Thank you." She forces a sad smile. "I don't think anyone gets me like you do. Even though you didn't grow up in a famous household, you've been famous for nearly a decade. I appreciate the kind words."

My heart expands. "Only telling you the truth."

Her tear-stained lips cover mine. When she pulls back, she says, "I can't figure you out, though. What's your angle?"

"I'm not Grant. My angle is that I like you."

A beaming smile overtakes her face. "Right answer."

She kisses me again, and all I want to do is make her feel good.

Wipe away the assholes who have ruined her accomplishments. Or used her for their own ends. I deepen the kiss and she reciprocates with fervor.

I pull back. "Melody, I have absolutely no interest in anything your father can do for me."

"I believe you."

All the tension flows out of my body, and I can't stop myself from reaching for her shirt. "May I?"

She nods. Soon she's divested of all of her clothes. I bring her prone on the couch and place one of her legs onto the floor while the other one goes over my shoulder. I kiss her inner thighs, letting my hands run all over her body.

Memorizing.

Learning.

Adoring.

I play with her pussy, which is so wet for me. Her expressive face shows all of her emotions. Desire and lust top the list. "Trust me."

Wary, yet excited eyes follow my movements as I kiss between her thighs. My tongue encircles her clit, and she cries out. My fingers enter her core.

"Oh!"

There's much more where this came from, Goldie. I continue my ministrations on her body, savoring every single moan and movement of her hips. When she clenches, I give a full-out assault on her body, including pinching her nipples. She comes with a long scream, ending with a chant of my name.

Even without rounding home, tonight was the most profound sexual experience of my entire life.

So far.

MELODY

My phone rings, ripping me out of a delicious dream about Charles and his magical hands. Well, in the movie they're magic but on my body? No comparison. It's been eight hours since our amazing interlude in his hotel room last night, and I need more. Much more. My cell rings again.

With a smile, I fumble for the phone, and Judith's name appears. It's five o'clock. I don't have to be in Chase's trailer to start dressing him until ten. Sitting up, I answer, "What's wrong?"

Over the phone, my boss sneezes. She must've caught whatever bug's been going around the crew. *Another reason to stay with the actors.* Rather, only one actor.

Coughing, she says, "Sorry to call you so early, but Noble just called. He's down for the count with this bug. Filming is canceled for the next two days. If you're not sick, I suggest you leave this germ-infested town."

Excitement streaks through my body. Two whole days off! I school my features, even though she can't see me. "Oh, thanks for letting me know. I really hope you feel better soon."

"Thanks."

We disconnect and I flop back into my bed. My mind races with the possibilities of what Charles and I can do together with our new free days. Heart racing, I text him.

> Just got the news that we're free for two days. Everyone's sick.

While I await his response, I consider the various towns nearby. Didn't Sophia say Ravello is rumored to be the most romantic spot on the entire Amalfi Coast? I'm searching for hotels there when his response comes.

> Charles: Confirmed. Noble's down for the count. But we're not! Whatever shall we do, Goldie?

I squirm at the nickname he gave me. A sappy smile covers my face. After spending the past days and most of the *nights* with Charles, I know he's going to be my first. He doesn't want anything from me or my family. I'm ready.

> Heard good things about Ravello.

> *Charles: Then let's go. I'll have Thomas book us somewhere.*

I shake my head. When will my spoiled actor learn to do stuff on his own?

> No. I'll book us a room and a car. Text you again when I'm on my way over to yours.

Returning to my search, I select a secluded villa in what's called "the most romantic hotel on earth." Kinda cheesy, but the photos look fab. I race to take a shower and throw some clothes into my overnight bag. With any luck, I won't be needing any of them while we're there.

My face heats with the thought of spending the next forty-eight hours, naked, with Charles. When I have everything in order, I go down the hall to Sophia's room because she's my bestie and I want to share my news with her. The door opens a crack and a somewhat green Sophia appears. I step back, placing my fingers in a cross in front of my face.

"Oh no, not you, too?"

She holds up a tissue. "Yeah."

"Guess you've heard filming is canceled for the next two days."

She nods and blows her nose.

"I came over here to let you know I'm going away with Charles, to escape those germs you all are swapping."

Watery brown eyes meet mine. "Going away with as in 'going away with'?"

I swallow. "Yeah."

"If I didn't have the cooties, I'd be hugging all over you right now, Mel. I *knew* something was up between you. So happy you listened to me. Go." She waves her tissue. "Have fun for the both of us."

"I will." I blow her a kiss and return to my room, calling for a car service on my way. Within fifteen minutes, I'm loaded into the black car and we're on our way to pick up Charles. My *boyfriend*. He is my boyfriend, right? Considering what I'm planning, he sure as hell better be. I text him I'm on my way.

"There." I point to his hotel. "We have to pick someone up here, and then we're on our way to Ravello." Excitement strums through my body. The next two days are going to be epic.

Charles leans against the cement fence, a small bag at his feet. The driver makes a startled noise. In a strangled voice, he asks, "That's, I mean, isn't that Chase Wright?"

My eyes gobble him up. "Yeah," I reply on a sigh.

The car stops next to Charles, then the driver jumps out and grabs his bag. He ushers Charles into the car and stows his kit in the trunk. When he returns to the driver's seat, he chatters about all the Chase Wright movies he's seen and what a huge fan he is. For his part, Charles kisses the top of my hand. Then, he engages the driver for the twenty-minute drive.

Despite the crazy, corkscrew skinny road without guard rails, I manage to smile at the driver's reaction to Charles. After all, I'm used to my dad's fans treating him much the same way. He reacts exactly how Charles is. With respect. As if they're family. My opinion of my *boyfriend* goes up yet another notch.

When we pull into the hotel, I ask them both to remain in the car while I check us in. No need to get Charles noticed by anyone else. While people know my dad here, they don't associate me with him, so I slip in under the radar and get the key to our private villa.

The driver takes us to our room, then asks for photos, to which Charles graciously agrees. Once ensconced inside our room, I head for the balcony and fling open the French doors. I step outside and inhale the beauty that is the Amalfi Coast. We're high up, with an unobstructed view of the town and the water below us. Blue skies are filled with fluffy white clouds.

Charles steps behind me and whispers in my ear, "Perfect." He kisses my earlobe, then bites it.

A shiver of excitement races through me. I reach out and play with his hair. "The view is perfect."

"Not talking about the view." His hands come around my waist, and he settles my back against his front.

I melt into him. Tracing each of his fingers, I murmur, "I was thinking . . ."

He blows into my ear. "About?"

My shoulders wiggle against his torso. I blurt, "I can call you my boyfriend, right?"

He chuckles, a low, rumbling sound that courses through my body. "You'd better. I've been thinking of you as my girlfriend since Positano."

His words catch in my throat and I spin around in his arms. Positano's where I shared about King and we saw the cathedral and had gelato. Escaped the paparazzi. Almost kissed. Where I started to fall for the man beneath the actor. "I like the sound of that, boyfriend!"

I pull his face down to mine. Our lips meet, slide over the other's, molding. His tongue presses forward, and I open for him. We kiss like we haven't done this mere hours ago and can't get enough of each other.

His hands slide down to my hips and pulls me to him. His bulge grows against my midsection, due to our height difference. I want more. I want all of this man.

I can trust him. He's not after my dad's connections, he has his own.

He believes in my talent.

And I believe in him. He's the real deal.

Charles breaks our kiss, panting. He places his forehead against mine. "Give me a minute, Goldie."

"I don't want to." I squeeze my arms around the back of his neck.

His blue eyes darken and he tips his head back down to mine. Our kiss reignites.

Charles runs his hands up and down my back. My nipples harden beneath my bra. The sensation's still new to me, yet it's amazing. I rub my chest against his.

Charles breaks our kiss and stumbles back two steps. "I have to stop."

I repeat, "I don't want to."

His eyes pierce right to my soul. I have no doubts and need to tell him. "I want it to be you, Charles. Please, show me what I've been missing."

His palm runs across his perfect stubble. "Are you sure? You want to take this step with me?"

"I've never been more sure about anything. I trust you to make this wonderful for me. For us."

His chest expands. "I haven't wanted a woman as much as I want you. Ever. I promise you'll never regret choosing me."

When he doesn't move, I step forward and place my palm on his pecs, over his heart. It's pounding as much as mine is. My gaze travels upward. "I know."

Chase closes the gap between us, his mouth landing on mine again as his hands travel down my abdomen and pull my shirt free of my shorts. Holding the hem, he tugs on the material. Raising my arms, he skims it up and over my head and buries his mouth on my neck.

He gives me little love bites, which zing straight to my core. My hips pulse in time with them, and I moan.

He licks my neck where he bit me, and his lips curve upward. "Like that, huh?"

"I like everything you do to me."

He unclasps my frilly yellow bra and slides it off my arms, then drops to his knees in front of me. "How about this?"

His mouth attaches itself to one of my distended nipples and he sucks. We've already established how sensitive I am, but this time is different. We're not stopping. And the intensity is off the charts.

"Oh, that's so"—I suck in my breath when his free hand plays with my other nipple—"good."

He removes his mouth from my body. "Only good, huh? I'll have to see what I can do to earn a 'great.'" He redoubles his efforts. When he bites—he gets an A+ for this skill—my knees buckle, which earns a chuckle from him. "That's better."

My body's not my own. It's his to play with, and I like it. When he switches to my other breast and gives it the same treatment, I moan my approval. Clamping his head to my body, I run my fingers through his silky, perfectly maintained hair.

We remain locked like this until his hands move downward. To my waist. I watch him undo my gold metal belt and slide it through the loops. It clanks on the floor.

But I don't want to be naked when he's still fully clothed. He inches toward my fly. "No, wait."

Breathing hard, he drops his hands, which curve into fists on his thighs. "That's okay, Goldie. We can stop right now."

I shake my head. "No, Charles. I don't want to stop. But I don't want to be the only one not wearing any clothes."

I reach for the hem of his shirt, but he beats me to it. Pulling it upward from the back of his neck, the shirt's on the floor before I realize what's happening, and my hands land on his naked torso. "Oh."

His stomach tightens with my touch, but his smile tells me he likes it. He holds his arms out to the side. "Enjoy."

My gaze explores every inch of the sculpted masterpiece that is Charles Wainwright. I step forward and trace his six-pack with my lips, causing him to hiss. The sound is heady. When I get to the top of his V, I close my teeth.

"Yeah, someone's a quick learner."

I step back. "I did graduate *magna cum laude*, you know."

"Inspiring." He reaches out for me again and draws me deeper into the villa. "Let's go find the bedroom, all right?"

"Thought you'd never ask."

"We can do it on the balcony later." He winks.

My gaze darts back to the private balcony, noting the discarded clothes strewn there. I catch my bottom lip with my teeth. "You think we could do it out there?"

He laughs. "Yeah. I do. But not this time. Now I'm going to spend hours worshipping you in a soft bed."

I mouth the word "worshipping." I like that. "I'm all in."

We enter the bedroom, which boasts another huge window overlooking the same view. A king bed with white bedding and a chaise lounge are off to the side. Two closets. Another door leads to the bathroom, I presume.

"It's gorgeous in here."

He turns me to face him and stares into my eyes. "I only see you."

I'm lost. In him. In this moment. I've waited almost twenty-five years, and it's more than perfect. I'm ready.

He bends down and takes off his shoes, and I slip off my sandals. Now we're both barefoot and half-dressed. My hands go to the button at the top of my shorts, but he shoos them away. "No. Let me. Please."

I smile. "Since you asked so nicely."

He kisses me as he undoes my fly, and my shorts slip to the floor. For my part, I reach out and untie his shorts. He wore workout clothes, probably to be less recognizable. Shortly, they're on the floor next to mine.

Charles reaches out to my yellow thong. I don't usually wear them, but I planned ahead. "A thong? Are you trying to kill me?"

I giggle. "Maybe a little."

He bends down, wraps his fingers around the sides, and pulls. The scrap of material moves down my legs, leaving sensuous sparks in its wake. When he reaches my ankles, I lift one and then the other. Now, I'm naked.

Instead of standing back up like I expected him to, Charles kisses my legs where my thong traveled. He licks behind my knee, causing my stomach to clench. "Oh!"

He licks again. "Like that?"

"Yeah," I reply on an exhale. Who knew that was an erogenous zone? They've always only been knees.

He smiles against my skin. "Good to know."

Charles kisses his way back up the inside of my legs, which reminds me of how I sew him into the superhero costume. Despite being turned on, I giggle. Charles rears back. "What, pray tell, is so funny?"

I school my face. "It's not funny." Another giggle escapes.

He places his hand high up on the inside of my thigh. "I can see that."

I try to suppress my wayward mirth, watching as he walks his fingers higher. My last giggle dies as Charles traces my folds. "Oh!"

"Not laughing now?"

I shake my head. "I was thinking," I moan. "About," I moan again. "Sewing you into your costume."

"Oh." The pad of his finger passes over my clit and I squirm. "Certainly *not* funny." He leans forward and kisses right where his fingers are.

"God, that feels good."

"Charles, not God." He kisses my sex again. "Yet."

Liquid seeps out of my body, and I try to pull away. Charles stills me by placing his free hand on my butt. He removes his finger from my core and licks it. "Delicious."

"It's okay?"

It's his turn to laugh. "More than okay. I live to make you wet."

His words do something to my insides. Dirty, yet thrilling. "I aim to please."

Charles gets to his feet. "That you do, Goldie." He kisses my lips again, and I taste a slight tangy flavor.

I'm naked, but he isn't. I reach out to the waistband of his boxer briefs. His hand covers mine. "Not yet."

"But . . ."

"Shhh." He covers my lips with his again, kissing me deeply. I cling to his bare shoulders as he picks me up and deposits me onto the bed. "Wait here."

Like I'd leave.

He disappears into the bathroom and comes back, placing a small towel on the side table. Then, he opens his luggage and rummages around, putting a bunch of condom packets on top of the towel. He glances at me. "I was hoping."

I don't tell him about the pit stop I made in my hotel's convenience store, for the same item. "Good hope."

He kisses me. "There's no reason for either one of us to leave this bed for a long time."

"I like the sound of that." I get onto my knees and maneuver over to him. "I like the sound of a lot of things, and they all start and stop with you."

"Damn. You know how to stroke my ego."

My hand reaches out and covers his erection, still covered by his underwear. "I want to stroke something else."

"You'll get your turn, my little minx. I'm going first."

He pushes forward and I land on my back. Standing, he grabs my ankles and pulls them apart, sliding me toward the end of the bed. Leaving his arm across my stomach, he gets on his knees and kisses up my inner leg again. When he reaches my core—and I think he's going to go for the gusto—he starts over on my other leg.

Finally, finally, finally, he ends at my sex. I get on my elbows as he spreads me open with his fingers. Our eyes meet, then his flicker down my body. His nostrils flare, and he kisses me. Intimately. His tongue swipes over my clit, and a thrill races up my body. I lose the ability to hold myself up and collapse onto the comforter.

His chuckle greets me before he attacks me again. Concentrating on my clit, he forms all sorts of designs with his tongue, eliciting a loud moan from me.

"Charles, oh!"

At my exclamation, one of his fingers enters my body. In the spot he'll soon be the first man to breach. The feeling is indescribable. Tight, but so good. He licks my clit again—more like devours it, while his finger now moves in and out.

Like when I use my vibrator, a buzzing starts at my toes. However, unlike with the toy, the buzz detonates throughout my body like lightning. Charles coaxes my orgasm faster than a BOB ever could. The force of it makes my eyeballs roll back in my head. I scream as I arch and come for my boyfriend.

When I return to my body, he's standing and pulling the comforter back. He takes the folded towel and puts it down, then places his hands on his waistband.

"No."

He stills. "No?" He lets out a breath and closes his eyes. "All right."

I jump to standing and approach him. "I mean no, don't *you* do that. I want to."

"Oh." Relief crosses his face. "Fine by me." His arms drop to his sides.

"You're amazing, you know that?" I trace his muscles, which ripple at my touch. "Your body is so hard." At his laugh, I smile. "Well, you know that, huh?"

Screwing up my courage, I grab his boxer briefs and drag them down his long legs. Legs I've sewn into his leggings for days. That have just the right amount of hair. Masculine legs. I throw his underwear on the floor and stand up, my eyes riveted on his erection.

No way will he fit inside me.

"Believe me, I'll fit. And you'll howl in pleasure for me."

How does he know what I'm thinking? I reach toward his cock, which is huge and long and pointing straight out at me. He's hard and silky at the same time, with some liquid at the tip. Adding the rest of my fingers, I close them around him. And squeeze.

Charles sucks in his breath. His hips buck in time with my stroking. His cock expands even further.

Stepping back, he says, "No. Not now. This time is all about you." Physically, he turns me around and smacks my butt. "On the bed."

I give him a saucy look over my shoulder—at least I hope it's saucy —and do as he bids. The bed dips when his much larger frame joins mine. He situates me over the towel and rests his chin on his hand while tracing my nipple with his index finger.

"You're so beautiful, Goldie. I'm lucky to have you in my life. Please don't think I'm taking your gift to me for granted."

I touch the cleft of his chin. "I know you're not."

We kiss again, the familiar tingles gripping my body. His mouth moves from my lips, raining kisses down my throat and back up to my ear. "I'm proud to be your first."

Because I can't form proper words, I nod.

He nips my lobe and moves down to suckle my breasts. His hand slips between my thighs, and he, once again, plays with my sex. He inserts one finger into me and pumps. My hips move in time with it while his mouth retakes mine.

Down there, a second finger joins the first. I still pump my hips, but relish the fullness. Charles keeps distracting me with his mouth, which moves to my ear. "How does that feel?"

"Great," I breathe.

Scissoring his fingers, he lowers his head to my pebbled nipple and bites. "Now?"

The sensations rolling through my body dial up a notch. "Oh!"

Charles makes his way up my body again and kisses me. He removes his fingers from me, which disappear into his mouth. Holding them up in front of my face, he orders, "You're delicious. Taste yourself."

My gaze locks on his fingers and I open my mouth. Sucking, I taste. They're tangier than his lips were before, but not in an unpleasant way.

"See?"

I whisper, "I do."

He removes his fingers from my mouth and situates my body flat on the towel he had laid down. Reaching over, he grabs a foil packet from the side table and rolls on the condom.

It's now or never. Last chance to change my mind. My breathing spikes.

I focus on the most gorgeous naked man I've ever seen. Well, the only entirely naked man I've ever seen, but he's perfect. Honest. Trustworthy. Wonderful. I take a deep breath and spread my legs wider.

He braces his weight on his hands and kisses me again for a long while. He lowers his body and the tip of him comes into contact with my clit. A familiar zing rushes through my body.

I moan. "Yes, Charles. Yes!"

He smiles, but it's more of a pained smile. "I'm debating whether I should go slow or fast. I don't want to hurt you."

My head knows this will hurt, but my body doesn't care. "I trust you."

At my words, he groans. "Melody, you're perfect."

His tip pushes against my entrance, slowly. My body accepts him and adjusts to his intrusion. A very welcome intrusion. Above me, Charles clenches his jaw, and sweat covers his brow. My arms slip up his back, encouraging him to continue. Which he does.

He pushes inside further, moving with deliberate speed. The full feeling morphs into something more.

Raw.

I catch my breath and he stops moving. We remain locked like this for a few heartbeats.

His lips crash down on mine again, his tongue seeking and gaining entrance into my mouth. He pulls back. "I'm sorry." He pushes forward and seats himself deep within my body.

Blinding pain sears through me. Oh, shit. This hurts. Tears leak from my eyes and trail down the side of my face. Charles's tongue captures them.

"Sorry, so sorry," he repeats as I struggle to adjust to my new normal.

He's kissing me when the pain recedes a bit. Tentatively, my tongue reaches out and licks the seam of his lips. My fingers cup his stubbled jaw and the kiss deepens.

Pain and budding excitement war within my body. Charles's mouth retreats a fraction as I struggle to regain my composure. Inches away from me, he asks, "How are you doing, Goldie?"

My eyes meet his, his pupils so dilated that I can barely see any blue. We stare at each other even as our bodies are connected.

In that moment, I realize the pain has diminished quite a bit. I lift my head and kiss him. "I'm good." I move my hips a fraction. "I'm good."

His lids slam shut over his eyes. Without moving at all, his breathing increases. In a strangled voice, he whispers, "I need to move. I'll be gentle."

I brace myself for the renewed pain and squeeze my eyes shut. "Go ahead."

Instead of covering my lips again, his lips trace the shell of my ear. He plucks at my nipple, which causes a chain reaction within my body. A thrill reignites.

As if in slow motion, Charles pulls back and pushes forward within me.

The sensation is not at all unpleasant. He repeats it, and my first impression is confirmed. Slow and steady, he plunders my body as his lips return to mine. Tender kisses.

A restlessness grows within me. I want something . . . more. I'm not sure what I need. For the first time, I deepen our kiss, extending my tongue to his. In response, he kisses me as if I were the very air he breathed.

I find myself moving in time with his thrusts, picking up my leg and hooking it around his butt. My arms go around his midsection and I squeeze. His tempo accelerates, and his hand slides up and down my leg.

The only noises are our lovemaking. Our hips rustle the bed coverings. Panted breaths, coming faster and faster. Sweat beads across my forehead and down his back. He's driving into me now, harder than ever before, and my body craves his touch.

The shimmer of an orgasm builds from my toes, causing my breath to catch. Can this really be happening to me? I meet his next thrust and the shimmer grows into an excited tingle.

"Charles, yes. Oh, please!" I don't know what I'm begging for. I hope he does.

"I've got you." He rolls his hips in a way that obliterates all my remaining pain. I want what only he can give.

He pistons in and out of me, his teeth fastened to my nipple. When he bites, a shock runs throughout my entire system and explodes behind my eyes. I cry out something unintelligible. I think it was Charles or God or Yes or Please.

Above me, Charles goes still and roars, letting himself come inside of me. He thrusts twice more before collapsing on the bed next to me, breathing as if he ran a marathon. His arms wrap around my body, holding me close.

Our heart rates are off the charts, and I relish being wrapped around this man. The man I love. My realization I'm in love with Charles Wainwright doesn't even scare me. I simply tuck it into my heart and let the glow of our lovemaking bathe over me.

He kisses my forehead. "You okay, Goldie?"

I nod, unable to form coherent words.

CHASE

When my breathing returns to a somewhat normal pace, I kiss the forehead of the woman warming my bed and carefully pull out of her body. She winces when I slide out. "Sorry." I kiss her lips. "Let me get us cleaned up."

I pad into the bathroom and dispose of the condom. Grabbing a smaller towel, I run warm water over it and return to the bed. Melody's still splayed over the sheets, all tousled and gorgeous. Because I can—because I made her come no less than three times—I bend and lave my tongue over her nipple. A rush of air streams from her mouth.

Grinning at her, I reach between her legs and press the warm compress on her inner thighs, cleaning up the specks of blood, ending on her pussy.

"Mmmm. Feels so good."

Instead of responding with words, I kiss her hipbone and remove the small towel. "Lift your hips." She does and I remove the other blood-spattered towel. Balling the towels up together, I return to the bathroom and toss them under the sink.

Slipping back into the bed, I cover us with the sheet and encircle her into my arms. I run my fingertips up and down her naked skin.

So soft.

So unblemished.

Virgin. Well, not anymore. My lips tip upward.

She slowly blinks. "That was, wow. So much more than I had expected."

"It'll only get better." I kiss her shoulder. Although I'm not sure how. That was the best sex of my life.

She snuggles in my arms, causing my breath to hitch. "I can't imagine."

My hand drops to her boob, and I play with one of her sensitive nipples. "So, you're all right? I wasn't too rough with you?"

She tilts her head upward. "No, Charles, you were perfect. It was perfect."

Her amber eyes tell me she's telling the truth. Well, and her satisfied expression. Which is the only thing she's wearing. "I'm glad."

Glad? I'm more than glad. I haven't been with a virgin since I was in high school, and back then I didn't care about anything other than getting off. This time was so different.

The realization brings me up short. *She* is different. Special.

Her arms wrap around my neck and she kisses the middle of my pecs. "Can we do it again?"

I redirect her head to right under mine, resting my chin on its top. "I think you need a breather. You're going to be sore."

She moves her legs under the sheets. "I'm not," she protests.

"Always the overachiever, Miss *magna cum laude*, hmm?"

She pulls her head back and bats her eyelashes at me. A classic flirtatious move all actresses are taught. When she does it, though, it's without pretense. Like everything she does.

"I try."

I run my hands up and down her back, refitting her under my chin. "Let's try to catch a nap."

She sighs and replicates my movements by running her hands on my back. However, she doesn't stop and dips below my waist, grabbing my ass. When she squeezes, I hiss as my cock awakens.

I rumble, "No sleep?"

She shimmies up my body and places her lips at my ear. "No," she whispers.

With that, I flip her on top of my body and am rewarded by her delighted squeal. Pushing her gorgeous hair off her face, I French kiss her. She meets my every move, spurring our passions. I want to devour her whole! Instead, I nibble on her nipple.

She grimaces, then tries to cover up by bringing her lips to my ear. Despite my cock begging for more action, I hold my breath and give him a stern talking-to. Melody's sore. She needs a break. With slow movements, I twist so she lies next to me again.

"Hungry?"

She scowls. I raise my eyebrows.

She sighs.

Her index finger lands on her mouth. "You know, now that you mention it, I'm kinda ravenous."

"Seems to be a theme. Not that I mind one bit, though. Want to go somewhere? Explore the town?"

She glances out the window. "Nah, I don't want to leave this room. If that's all right with you?"

Because I can't help myself, I kiss her collarbone. "Perfectly. Let me get the room service menu." I hop out of bed and stride toward the desk, where I saw a menu. When I turn around to return to her, she's sitting up. The sheet lies at her waist.

She purses her lips and whistles.

I shake my head and dive back into the bed, causing it to bounce and her to giggle. I like the sound. A lot. Sharing the menu, we place our order.

Kissing each one of her fingers, I enjoy all the different sounds she makes. She's so responsive, so genuine. I find it hard to believe she's had a hard time with men. Although, the fact she's only ever been mine warms my soul. And something farther south.

"So tell me, have you given any more thought to the auditions in *Backstage*?"

My stomach flips and I drop her hand, banging my head against the pillow. "Well," I begin. "I did go on the site. And." I pause. Can I confess this to her? She's going to think it's stupid.

I'm stupid.

"And what?" She circles my nipple with her tongue, then gives it a tiny bite. She's a fast learner.

I clear my throat and glance into her eyes. They've taken on a deep greenish hue as they urge me to continue. I was wrong. She doesn't think any of this is stupid. "Well, ah, the Hamlet retelling does look sort of good."

She grabs my hand and kisses the tip of my index finger like I did to her before. "When are the auditions?" I remain silent, so she flicks me with her tongue, urging me to reply.

"I think now."

She hums. It's a pleasant sound. Would sound good wrapped around my cock. "Something could be worked out for you."

Her response does two things. First, drives all thoughts of a blowjob out of my sex-fueled brain. Second, revives any hope I had for even a remote possibility of auditioning.

She fills the silence. "I'm sure you could audition via Zoom."

I close my eyes. She's right. If I really wanted this role, I could make it happen. Am I ready? Good enough? "I'm sure all the auditions are already lined up."

"You won't know until you ask." She blinks. "That's what my mother always says."

"She's a wise woman."

"She is." Melody turns over and picks up my cell phone. "Here. Call Sam. Get this off your to-do list."

With two fingers, I take the phone. Can I do this? Will Sam even entertain my offbeat desire? "Oh, I don't know. This is sort of ridiculous, don't you think?" I drop the phone onto the bed.

She kisses down my nose. "No, I don't think wanting to see your dream come true is ridiculous at all. You told me before how much you loved doing Shakespeare when you were in drama school. You said the roles spoke to you."

Me and my damned stupid mouth. Why did I have to confess all this to her? I try to turn my head, but she forces me to face her. Her eyes bore into mine. They give me a strength I didn't know I possessed.

Maybe I don't.

In a weak voice, I reply, "Well, I did say that."

"Charles, I'm not going to make you call Sam. The decision is all yours. I want you to know I have faith in your acting abilities. I also know whenever I pursued something I really wanted, whether I succeeded or not, I didn't regret anything."

Her words hit home. Regret. If I don't jump on this chance right now, will I regret the missed opportunity? Will I always wonder *what if* I'd made this call?

Inhaling, I hold my phone again. I lick my nervous lips and glance at her. She gifts me with a glorious smile. I can do this. I press the button for Sam.

He answers on the second ring, albeit a bit groggy. "Hey, Chase. How's my Doctor Manipul8?"

I force a smile. "Doing well. Um, better than most of the people on the set out here. Some nasty bug is going around and Noble caught it. We're on a short break until everyone recovers. Luckily, I'm one of the few healthy ones."

"Hope you left all the sickies and are gallivanting somewhere like Lake Como with George."

George and Amal Clooney, and their twins, are a great family. Melody would love them. I could schedule something with them. She pokes my ribs, bringing me back to the reason for my call. "Actually, I did get out of Amalfi, but only by about a half-hour."

"That's good anyway. So, what can I do for you?"

It's now or never. He's going to laugh at me and tell me I'm crazy. But at least I tried. I look at Melody, who plays with the end of the blanket, trying to give me space.

"Chase?"

"I'm here." I clear my throat. "Well, the reason for my call is because I heard about a role I'm interested in."

"Oh? Cool. Which one? I'll place a call."

"For *Hamlet 2.0.*"

Silence.

Silence.

Silence.

"Uhm, you do know that's a straight acting role, right? No CGI. No laugh track." He pauses. "On *Broadway.*" He utters the last like a curse.

At least he didn't laugh in my face. "Yeah."

"And the role you're interested in is . . . ?"

Here goes. "The villain. Claude."

"Geez, really?"

I shrug my naked shoulder. Because he can't see me, I reply, "I've always loved that play."

Silence.

Silence.

Silence.

"Well, let me see what's going on for it." I wait while he checks the schedule. "Looks like they're almost done with auditions. Last day is tomorrow. Listen, if you want to do some Shakespeare, let me put feelers out. I did hear about a new movie based on *The Tempest.* It's a light-hearted look at it, like *Pretty Woman* was. You'd be great in that."

"No."

"C'mon, Chase. *Hamlet,* really? On Broadway? Seriously? Leave this one for the real hard-nosed actors. Keep in your lane."

His words spur me on. I won't have a regret if the producers refuse to let me audition. If, however, Sam prevents me from even trying, well . . . In a much firmer voice, I state, "I said I want to audition for *Hamlet 2.0.* Can you please call the producers and see if they'll fit me in via Zoom or something?"

Melody's hand lands on my bicep.

In a strained voice, Sam replies, "Fine. Give me ten and I'll call you back." He disconnects the line without another word.

I took my first step toward changing my career. *Hamlet* has always been my favorite play. My drama teacher told me I was the best Prince of Denmark he'd ever seen. So what if the first director I ever auditioned for took one look at me and hooked me up with Sam. I connected with that play.

I want the role.

"Thank you. For giving me the courage to make that call."

Melody kisses me. "It was all on you. I only helped jump-start the dialing."

"You're so beautiful. And smart."

The woman next to me smiles, her eyes glowing. "Well, you're amazing." Her hand slips underneath the sheets, and she wraps it around my cock. "*Really* amazing."

My body clenches at her touch. "Did I create a monster?"

"A very sweet one," she quips.

The ringing of my cell phone breaks the spell between us. Sam's name appears on the screen, and I suck in my breath. I hit the speak-erphone. "Hey."

"All right, here's the deal. They can fit you in tomorrow. Last audi-tion's at four thirty. The problem? They don't want to see it by video. If you really want this role, you need to get to New York City."

At least I tried. "Well, thanks."

Sam continues, "Listen, if you really want to pursue Shakespeare—"

Melody grabs the phone out of my hand and puts it on mute. "You can do it, Charles. It's a quick flight from Rome to JFK. We can go, audition, and fly back the next day, before we start shooting again."

"Goldie, that's insane," I whisper, even though we're on mute.

She folds her arms across her bare chest, pushing her boobs upward. "Then I guess you don't really want to take your shot."

Her words land directly on my heart. And squeeze. "Fuck." I fumble with the phone and take it off mute.

"Chase? Chase? Did we lose our connection?"

"Sorry about that, Sam. No, we're all good. I'll take it."

"Wait, what? What did you just say?"

"I. Said. I. Will. Take. The. Audition." My gaze jumps to Melody, who's grinning like the Cheshire Cat. "I'll be there."

"Are you sure? How are you going to get there?"

"Don't worry about that. Call them back and hold my spot. Send me the sides I'll need to prepare."

"This is crazy."

"No. It isn't." I run my fingers over Melody's arm and slide toward her impressive boobs. "I'll look for them in my email. Thanks, Sam."

I disconnect the call and toss the phone onto the nightstand, then dive onto the woman in my bed. I'm strumming her nipples when a knock sounds. I break away and fling my arm over my forehead. "Shit."

Melody giggles. "Looks like our food is here. I'll get it." She rustles out of the bed. Heading to the closet, she pulls a plush white bathrobe out and encases her naked body in it.

While she's attending to our meal, I worry about the audition tomorrow. In New York City, for God's sake. I must be as crazy as Sam accused me of being. Who flies halfway around the world for a half-hour audition? I'm groaning when Melody returns into the bedroom and drops the clothes we left on the balcony onto a chair.

"We're all set up to eat on the balcony. The food smells delicious." She stops directly over me and tugs on my arm, which flops like spaghetti. "I'm so proud of you."

"What did I do?"

"You took the first step toward your new chapter."

I look up at her, all tousled and gorgeous. Warmth spreads throughout my body. "You're too good for me."

"I like to think we're good for each other. Now come. Get up. I want to eat." She turns around and heads out of the room.

Damn. Bossy. A smile spreads across my lips. I like it.

Hopping out of bed, I grab my shorts and put them on, commando. I meet her on the balcony as she takes off the silver domes, revealing a pasta carbonara for her and broiled bronzini for me. Freaking diet. I take my place at the table.

"Wine?"

She holds up a bottle of chianti. It's not pinot noir, but I have enjoyed this vino while we've been here in Italy. When I incline my head, she pours us both glasses and holds hers up. I join her.

"To new experiences," she says, a beautiful blush staining her cheeks.

"To enjoying every single second."

After sipping the wine, we dig into our meals. I enjoy the fish, but not as vocally as she devours the pasta. I can't stop myself. I reach over to her plate and spear some spaghetti and bring it to my lips. When I pop it into my mouth, I understand her moaning. "Damn, that's good."

"Next time order your own," she grumbles, a smile on her face.

When we're both satisfied—at least as to food—we return into the living area of the villa. Melody pulls out her phone. "We need to make reservations for the flight."

"I can have Thomas do that," I reply, placing my hand on top of hers.

She gives me a quizzical expression. "Really? I want to do this for you."

Warmed by her response, I incline my head. "Thanks."

She pecks at her phone and says, "Okay. Got it. Best I can do is a flight out tomorrow from Rome at ten twenty-five that lands at JFK at two fifteen."

It'll be tight, but I'll make the audition. I give her the go-ahead.

Her attention returns to her phone. "Return flight leaves at nine forty-five and lands back in Rome right after noon on Saturday. Not even time to get jetlagged."

My stomach dips. "But we'll be shooting on Saturday." My hopes for this audition plummet.

"Not without Doctor Manipul8. You can tell Noble you're stuck in Lake Como and will be on set by two. He was the one who canceled shooting for two days—he won't have a leg to stand on to yell at you."

"You make a good point."

"Of course I do." She holds her hand out. "I need your passport."

At her request, I head into the bedroom and rummage through my bag. Retrieving the document, I turn it over to her. After a few minutes, she lays her phone down. "Done."

"Thanks. I'm so sorry we had to cut our mini vacation short. We haven't even explored Ravello yet."

"There's still time tonight. I do think we need to get some sleep, though, as the helicopter leaves at six thirty so we can make it to Rome for our flight."

Her words sink in. "We? Our?"

"Yes, silly. I'm not letting you fly there and back alone. You'll need someone with you to give you moral support."

The fact she booked herself with me on my flight doesn't irritate me at all. In fact, it makes me feel warm. Hopeful. Positive. Like I can conquer the world—or at least this audition. "Thanks. It means so much to me."

She stands and unties her robe, letting it hang open. "Think we should go to bed? You know, for our early wake-up call?" She slips the terrycloth off one shoulder.

I stand up as well and discard my shorts, thoughts about my audition forgotten for now. "Oh, I seem to recall you were interested in learning about balcony sex."

Her voice rises a full octave. "Really?"

I take one step toward her and grab the end of the robe. "Yes, really." I pull and it ends up in my hands. For every one step I take, she retreats one, until her back is against the French doors. Her breath comes in pants.

Even though I'm all in for another round, I need to make sure she's okay. "Are you up for this?"

She nods, her eyes trained on my lips, then dip lower. That's all it takes.

"Right answer, Goldie."

MELODY

The blades of the helicopter whir and we rise from the helipad in Ravello. I suck in my breath at the magnificent landscape below. Small towns, windy roads and the water look beautiful from the air. "It's so gorgeous." I glance over at Charles.

"Yes, you are."

His repeated compliment lodges in my heart. He's been nothing less than wonderful with me. We made love twice yesterday and, even with the flash pain of the first time, it turned wonderful. He treated me with such care, always concerned about how I was feeling. Plus the balcony! Given our secluded villa, I knew no one would see us—still, it was a thrill.

Not to mention, his body is like the most perfect sculpture. Michelangelo be damned. Not an ounce of body fat on him, with the most defined muscles I've ever seen. Yet his body isn't what drew me to him. It's his vulnerability. He's been typecast in a particular role, and now he's taking the difficult steps to change that. Because he wants more. I glance over at him and smile.

He leans over and kisses my nose, one of the only spots on my face available to him, given the huge headsets we're wearing to block out the noise. "This was a great idea, Goldie. Much better than taking a car through those streets."

"Thanks. I was looking for the fastest way to Rome."

He nudges my shoulder. "Wanted to keep me in bed longer?"

His smile is almost boyish. I'm sure mine is pretty soppy. I've got it bad. "Not at all. I wanted you to get as much shut-eye as possible."

He laughs and returns his gaze to the papers on his lap. The lines he needs to memorize, internalize, and recite during his audition. I let him study, while enjoying the changing scenery below us.

Soon, we land at the heliport and are transported to the terminal. We arrive in the first class lounge with plenty of time, so we find a quiet spot in a corner. I grab the papers from his hands. "Why don't you give it a rest for a little bit."

Stormy blue eyes meet mine. He doesn't have to say a word, as those eyes convey all his feelings. Guess that's why he's such a good actor. Why he'll grow into a spectacular one, given the proper roles. This part sounds like it's a good platform to start.

"I need to nail this." He tries to take the papers away from me, but I hold them against my chest. However, I do understand his desire to know the words inside and out. "How about I quiz you?"

One eyebrow rises. "As in I give you my audition?"

I nod. "Yeah. Let's see where you're at." I make a big deal out of placing the papers in front of me.

His Adam's apple bobs. "I'm not ready yet," he admits.

"I bet you're in a much better spot than you think. Give it a shot. Consider it a sort of litmus test."

He huffs a breath. "Fine. All right. But if you're going to make me do this, right now, before I'm ready, you're going to have to do something for me."

His challenge stirs my competitive side. "You got it, big guy. What?"

A wolfish smile overtakes his face. "I'll tell you when I'm done. It'll give me something to look forward to."

I *know* this is going to be something I'll regret. Or really, really enjoy. "Fine."

He squeezes his hands together and closes his eyes. I let him prepare for this practice however he likes. His eyes open and I swear, he's a different person. More serious. Intense. Before he even opens his mouth, he's already sucked me into the vortex of Hamlet's world.

When he speaks, I'm transported. Not to the Hamlet of Shakespeare's time, but rather to a painful place in today's gritty world. I trail the lines as he performs the soliloquy with a couple of missteps, before stumbling to a halt.

I wait for him to continue, but he doesn't. Glancing up, his palm is on his forehead, eyes squeezed shut.

"It doesn't matter to me," I prompt.

"Right." He clears his throat and launches back into the role. When he's done, I clap. "Charles, that was fantastic. I mean it. You're well on your way to acing this audition."

He rubs his temple. "I can't do this. What was I thinking? Let's cancel our flights and return to the coast."

I touch his arm. "Stop."

He freezes.

"You can do this, Charles. You've only had this script for a few hours. You have about twelve hours ahead to get all the words memorized." I return the script back to him. "Don't abandon your dreams now."

He takes the papers from me and places them on the seat next to him. "This is hard."

"I have faith in you."

He places his hands on his knees, and I mirror his posture. "You're right. I can do this. I have to." He grabs the script. "Do you know what you can do for me?"

I bite my lip. "Get you a piece of fruit?"

"Well, yes, but that's not what I was thinking." His eyes sweep over my body, and he holds his hand out. "I want something of yours to hold on to during my audition. An anchor, of sorts."

My mind turns to mush. He wants a piece of me with him, in there? I could give him my earring. Or the bracelet I picked up in Positano. Before I can suggest either one, he continues, "Your thong."

"My what?" I squeak.

His head bobs. "I need it now, to help me finish memorizing these lines."

"Now?"

"Bathroom's over there. Unless you'd like me to get it myself." He reaches for my body.

I jump out of my chair and rush away from him. I have zero doubts he'd at least try to remove them from my person right here, right now.

Five minutes later, I walk out of the ladies' room, sans panties under my skirt. The sensation's odd. Instead of returning to Charles, who's deep into studying, I select a banana, an apple, and some grapes for him, as well as a Styrofoam cup of coffee for myself. When I offer him the fruit, our flight is announced.

Motioning toward the door, I say, "That's us."

"First things first. Hand 'em over." He holds out his palm.

I look around, but no one's paying us any attention. I pull my thong out of my purse and ball up the material. "Here."

He opens his fist and takes in the green wisp of material. Bringing it to his nose, he inhales.

"Don't," I admonish, smacking his hand away from his face.

He laughs and steals a kiss. "That was worth the hell I'm about to go through."

"Yeah, well, it better be." I step back as he picks up the overnight bag containing both of our things. Even though we're not staying even one night, we're going to need a change of clothes. "Let's go." Without checking to see if he's following me, I head out of the lounge. Sans panties.

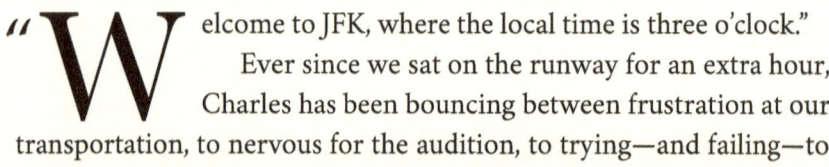

"**W**elcome to JFK, where the local time is three o'clock." Ever since we sat on the runway for an extra hour, Charles has been bouncing between frustration at our transportation, to nervous for the audition, to trying—and failing—to flirt with me. "We're here. You'll make it by your audition time, no problem at all. Let's go."

With only one carry-on, we're off the plane, through customs with our Global Entry passes, and in a taxi in no time. Charles offers the driver an extra hundred dollars to get us to the address in midtown by four. I take this opportunity to try to pass some calmness into my boyfriend's demeanor.

"Let the driver do his job, Charles. We're already in New York City. Your audition's in ninety minutes. You'll be great."

With effort, he pulls his glare away from the man behind the steering wheel and faces me. "Thank you, Goldie. I don't know what I would've done if you weren't here with me."

"Probably thrown yourself out of the helicopter over the Amalfi Coast."

He smiles. It's a genuine look that transforms his face. "Probably."

"Want to run your script one last time?"

He shakes his head. "Nah. I'm good. I have it memorized and I'd like to let everything soak in."

I slide across the seat and nuzzle into his warm, hard body. I try to distract him by drawing circles on his chest, loving the sensation of his heart beating.

The taxi stops at four on the dot. "We're here," the driver says.

"Well done." Charles reaches for his wallet as I get out onto the sidewalk of the bustling city. People dash by us as rush hour approaches, which is nearly ten at night according to our body clocks. "Want me to wait with you?"

"Nah. But I'm not ready to go inside yet. Let's walk around the block."

Knowing he needs to get rid of some pent-up energy, we walk around in the city I now call home. The vibe, which is so different from Italy, soaks into my bones. "I've missed this place," I admit.

"I like it here, too."

I stop as it hits me. I don't know where he lives now. "Where's your home?"

"LA."

I nod. If our relationship's going to continue, we'll have to nail down our living situations. Well, if he gets this role, he'll be in New York City. Smiling, we approach the main entrance to the building.

I touch his forearm. "Want company now?"

"No, I'm good. I have to do this by myself."

His reaction stings, but I get it. He needs to prove himself—to himself. "I'll text you my address, which isn't too far from here. Come over when you're done."

"Thanks."

I stretch onto my tippy-toes and kiss his cheek. "Break a leg, Charles."

"I will." He takes a few steps toward the front of the building, then turns around. He bellows, "You're the best, Goldie!"

I kiss my hand and blow my good wishes toward him. "Knock 'em dead!"

He disappears into the building. *You can do it*. Clutching our overnight bag, I hail a cab and arrive at my Upper Eastside townhouse ten minutes later. I give the doorman a hug, tell him that Chase Wright will soon be arriving, and go into my apartment.

The atmosphere in here's stale since I haven't been here in a month. I turn on the air and grab the only item in my fridge, which is a lonely bottle of water. When Charles gets back, we'll have a couple hours before heading back to JFK, so I order a food delivery. Chinese. Not something you get in Italy.

I wander around, touching my things. My dad's piano takes center stage, although my lessons ended miserably when I was eight. Discarded instruments likewise have turned into decorations—a violin, flute, and even a pair of drumsticks. In my bedroom, I fluff my floral comforter, images of what Charles and I might do in here soon dancing around my mind.

Sighing, I return to the living room and stretch out on my couch. Still being *sans* panties reminds me of where they are right now. Even though it's late in Amalfi, I'm too wound up to catch a catnap. I Face-Time my parents.

"Melody, we didn't expect to hear from you for another couple of weeks. How are you? Is everything okay?"

"Hi, Mom. Yes, I'm good."

I twirl a lock of my hair. "How's King?"

Mom bites her bottom lip. "He was pretty bad there for a while, but he's doing better now. He's dating a woman from his show."

I smile. Something we have in common. "That's nice."

Mom's eyes search the screen. "Where are you?"

"I'm actually home. For only a couple of hours. Charles had an audition come up in New York City, so we flew in this afternoon and we're leaving in a couple of hours."

"Charles?"

"Yes." She doesn't know about my boyfriend, and I'm dying to clue her in. "You know of Charles. I grew up with him."

Mom's eyebrows furrow. "Do you mean Chase Wright?"

My head bobs. "Yeah. But I call him Charles. Chase is his stage name."

"You're dating him?"

I swallow. "Yeah. It's new, but he's my boyfriend. I think you and Daddy will really like him."

She peers into the phone's camera. "Isn't he the older brother to that awful Lindsay Wainwright?"

At the mention of my childhood nemesis, I wince. "Well, you can't pick your family."

Her eyes widen a fraction before returning to her usual demeanor. "Tell me about him. Does he treat you right?"

"He's wonderful!" My mind replays how he treated me yesterday in bed, but I don't share that info. Not something I'll ever tell her. "He's a great actor and we're here in New York so he can audition for a role in a modern-day Hamlet on Broadway."

She digests my words. "Doesn't he usually play the pretty boys? Isn't he Doctor Manipul8?"

"Well, yes, he's the main character on the movie we're filming. But he has a deep desire to do live work."

"That's a good ambition."

"Right? I helped him prepare on the flight over. He's going to nail the audition, I know it."

"Princess, is that you?" My dad's voice floats through the air, and his head pops onto the screen with Mom.

"Hi, Daddy." I giggle. "Yes, it's me."

"How is Italy?"

I indulge him, giving a description of the places I've visited. "And the food. Oh, the food!"

He nods. "Like we told you before you left, we love Italy. So different from here, in a good way."

My parents gaze into each other's eyes, and I get the distinct impression they're recalling their own memories of Italy. For the first time in my life, I understand their look. Love and memories. And shared experiences. All the stuff I'm starting with Charles. Although, thinking about my parents in this way is disconcerting.

"How's the movie treating you, Princess?"

My dad's welcome question takes us off on a discussion about the set, costumes, and the trials and tribulations of the nasty bug we're currently dealing with. "Hopefully, we'll be filming again tomorrow afternoon."

Mom notes, "I bet Charles is anxious to finish up shooting."

My dad turns to her. "Who?"

I giggle. "I'm dating someone from the movie."

"Who?" He repeats, and Mom fills him in. Then he returns his attention to me. "I'd like to speak with this Charles."

"He's at an audition right now." My eyes dart to my clock. "He should be getting here any moment, so I guess I'd better go."

"Princess, I want to meet him, even over the phone."

Mom cuts him off. "She'll introduce us when the time is right." Thank God for my mother.

"Yeah, Daddy, I'll do that later. Right now, I better go. It's been great seeing you. I'll be back in touch soon." Before they can reply, I click off.

Whew. I love my parents, but I'm not ready to introduce Charles to them yet. My dad can be intimidating when he wants to be. Plus, I want to keep my boyfriend all to myself for a while longer.

I walk to the cabinet and pull out plates when a knock announces dinner's arrived.

CHASE

Exhaustion roils through me. Not from jet lag, but from the audition. It's like someone ripped my heart out, wrung it dry, and tried to put it back in without a jump-start. The taxi stops in front of a brick building two blocks from Central Park on the Upper East Side, and I double-check the address Melody texted me. Yup.

Sweet.

I lug my tired body out of the taxi and walk toward the front door, where a doorman opens it for me.

"Mr. Wright, so delighted to have you at The Mission. Miss Hunte's expecting you."

"Thanks."

Behind me, the doorman stops someone with a food delivery. My stomach rumbles, reminding me I haven't eaten a decent meal since Ravello. At least our meal last night was delicious. Both the hotel's food and the even more scrumptious morsel in bed.

"For Hunte, six-zero-nine."

My footsteps stop, and I spin toward the deliveryman. "For Melody Hunte?" When the delivery guy nods, I pull my wallet out of my back pocket and pay him, taking the bag. Sniffing its contents,

Chinese aromas tickle my nose. Leave it to Melody to select a cuisine we haven't had since stepping foot in Italy.

And to anticipate my needs.

I take the elevator to the sixth floor and stand outside her door for a few moments, gathering my thoughts. What should I tell her about the audition?

About how the three-person panel were ready to leave before I opened my mouth?

About how they tried to hide their eye rolling when I walked in?

About how their body language changed as I gave my audition? Well, somewhat.

The smell of the food in my hand diverts my thoughts. "Fuck it," I mutter. "Just wing it and eat." I knock on the door.

Melody flings the door wide, holding her wallet. Her mouth drops open when she realizes it's me, holding the delivery bag. "Expecting someone else?"

"Charles." She flings her body at me, causing me to stumble backward before gaining purchase of her body. Food in one hand and her in the other, I step into her apartment and kick the door shut.

She leans back but doesn't disengage from my body. "How'd it go?"

"I'll tell you all about it if you feed me."

She giggles, and my body perks up. How can she give me energy when I swore I was down for the count? She drops her legs, which dangle until I bend down and she regains her footing. Not one to miss out on a chance like this, I steal a kiss from her more than willing lips.

When her stomach rumbles, I pull back. "Food. We both need food."

"I was setting the table." She kisses my mouth once more and leads me into the kitchen. Not a table, but an oversized granite-covered island with two placemats. "I'll finish with this if you'll please take out the food."

"Sounds like a plan," I tease, smacking her ass, which elicits a cute squeal.

Shortly, my chopsticks rest on the side of the plate. "That was the best General Tso's shrimp I've ever had." I rub my now full stomach.

"Yeah, they're the best around here. My orange-flavored beef was great, too." She drops her chopsticks onto her plate.

Now that my physical hunger has been satisfied, my natural curiosity about all things Melody rises. Standing, I head into her living room, picking up various framed photos. The one of her father holding her high up in the air catches my eye. The sheer joy on her face is contagious. I doubt I've ever felt this way about my parents. "Oh my God, you were so cute. How old are you here? Four?"

She peers at the photo in my hand. "Yeah, about that. We had just returned from an extended tour, and Mom caught the shot." She smiles at me. "It's one of my favorites."

"I can see why. You were an adorable kid, Goldie." I wink at her, and color rises to her cheeks. I fucking love that.

She gets on her tippy toes and pecks my lips. "Thanks."

I return the photo to the shelf and continue my exploration. Requisite romance novels on the shelf. Flat-screen TV. Off to the corner, a sewing machine is set up, together with plenty of bolts of fabric and other sewing stuff. Skipping that area of her condo, which is more about work than anything else, I head over to another part with lots of musical instruments. Tapping the ivories of the piano, I ask, "Do you play?"

She waves her arm. "Nah. Failed miserably at all of those." Walking over to the flute, she picks it up. "Except this one. I did enjoy playing flute for a while. That is, until I found my true passion. Sewing."

I nod and walk over to the instrument that originally caught my eye. Picking up the violin, I let my fingers roam over the strings, plucking a couple of notes. "I bet your father was disappointed."

She laughs. "You could say that. Neither I nor my brother sing or play anything."

As I test the bow on the violin, I ask, "Have you heard an update about King?"

"Mom said he's out of the hospital and recovering."

"Great news." Satisfied with the sounds coming out of the violin, without thought I begin playing a song I've had memorized for ages. She snaps in time with the rhythm. Finished, I close my eyes and start in on another. When it ends, clapping forces my eyelids open. Melody's grinning from ear to ear. "Wow, Charles, You're very talented."

Her honest words of praise lodge inside my chest, which are so infrequently heard in this part of my private world. Usually, if I play for anyone, they either mock my choice of instrument or immediately change the subject. It's my turn to blush.

Placing the violin back on its place of pride, I reply, "Thanks. I don't really play much. Just those few songs."

"Seriously, you're super good. Acting, playing violin, singing. The trifecta!"

"Not exactly." I grab her by the hips. "But I can make you sing." I plant kisses on her neck, to her excited squirming.

"No way, Charles. You haven't told me how the audition went."

My body screams its desire to forget the undignified experience and turn to a much more pleasurable way to pass the time. I run my tongue around the delicate shell of her ear. She pushes against my chest.

"Stop it. I want to hear all about how they loved on you."

"Like how you're going to love on me." I close my teeth around her ear.

"No! I mean it, Charles!"

"All right." I sigh. I'm not going to let her off the hook this easily. "How about a little tit for tat."

She sucks in her breath and crosses her arms over her chest, obscuring her glorious boobs. "A what?"

I try to stifle my smile, but with rather mixed results. I lean forward so my lips are next to her ear. "I'll tell you something about the audition, if you give me a little of what I want." If I wasn't standing right next to her, I might have missed the shudder that screamed up her spine. But I am. And I didn't. I kiss the erogenous zone behind her ear.

"Oh." She rolls her hips into mine. "I guess that's fair." She twines her fingers behind my neck. "So tell me, what happened when you walked into the room?"

Because I'm feeling magnanimous, I answer her. "There were three people behind a long table, and a chair up on the stage. Nothing unusual. I hit my mark and introduced myself. To which they said, and I quote, 'Aren't you filming some superhero movie in Italy?'"

Her amber eyes darken before her long lashes cover her eyes from my view. Slender hands move downward, and she intertwines her fingers with mine. She whispers, "What did you say?"

I lick my lips. "I told them that, yes, we're filming, but I felt a calling to audition for the part. That *Hamlet*'s my favorite of all of Shakespeare's plays, and I love their updated concept. And I'd do the role justice."

She nods. "That's perfect! Then what?"

I pull her to me. "That's my tat. Where's your tit?"

She giggles and struggles for a moment, then stills. "Well, I guess that's only fair."

She wriggles out of my embrace and tosses her shirt off her body and over her head. Nice. My hand reaches out and plays with her bra. When she gasps, I reach behind her and unclasp it. Skimming down her shoulders, I remove the offending material from her body while my lips seek her nipples, which have pebbled due to my touch. She's so responsive.

"Okay, your turn."

From my position with her nipple in my mouth, our gazes meet. I suck. She inhales. "No, no more. It's your turn." She disentangles herself from my embrace.

Sighing, I stand and shove my hands into my pockets. "They said since I was there, I should go ahead. Not the most encouraging start to an audition, but at least they didn't throw me out on my ass. None of the three laughed, which was a positive."

"They had to know how important this was to you. You did, after all, fly halfway around the world to audition."

I bounce from one foot to the other. "Yeah."

Reaching for her body again, she jumps back, wiggling her finger at me. "Oh, no. I need more than that."

"You're a hard taskmaster."

She laughs. "You have no idea, mister. Now continue."

I shrug. "Well, not much more to tell you. I ran through my lines—"

"Did you mess any up?"

Shaking my head, I reply, "Nope. Nailed them all."

Her face lights up. "I'm so happy for you, Charles!"

"Happy enough to strip out of that skirt for me?"

"You're incorrigible!" With a smile, she unzips the side. "You mean like this?"

My breathing hitches. "That's a good start."

She runs the zipper up and down, teasing me with glimpses of her naked hip. I reach into my pocket and produce her thong. "Missing something?"

She swipes her panties from me and changes the subject. "You know, I think I want to see more of you first." Her hands land on my shirt and she pulls it out of my khakis, making quick work of undoing the buttons. I forgot she's a costume designer and adept at getting clothes on, and off, people. "There. Now we're both half-naked."

"That we are. Come here." I guide her to my body and kiss her as if I'll never have the chance again. My cock stirs against my own zipper, and I hold our groins together.

She moans, a sexy sound that encourages me to press for more. I slide the zipper down again, slipping the material over her legs. Without breaking our kiss, she kicks the skirt to the side. Melody turns her head and holds her breath, taking a step back from my aching body. Totally naked for me.

"When did they say you'd hear back?"

A rushing sound whooshes through my brain at her gorgeous body, bared for me. "Huh?"

She twirls in front of me, stepping out of her shoes. "Did they give you a date of when you'll hear back from them?"

"Soon. Whatever that means." I extend my arm in a valiant effort to grab her and reel her to my body, but she ducks.

Swinging her index finger at me, she asks, "How do you feel about your audition."

That question makes me stop my pursuit of the naked woman in front of me. When I called Sam on my way over here, he didn't ask me this question. I query my excited body. "I did the best I could. I was proud for not flubbing any lines. I really put my heart and soul into it."

"So, no regrets whether you get the part or not?"

"Well, if I don't get it, I'll definitely be bummed. But no. I did everything I could possibly do to show them my skill." This is the truth. I gave the audition my all and don't have any regrets. "I need to thank you. You helped me so much with this process. In fact, if it weren't for you, I wouldn't have made this insane journey."

She plays with the ends of her blond hair. "I like to think of it as I helped you see what was right in front of you."

"Speaking of, I see something I definitely want standing right in front of me." I lick my lips.

Melody closes the gap between us, unbuckling my belt and pulling my pants and underwear down my legs. As I kick them away, she drops to her knees in front of me, like when she's sewing me into my leggings. Only this time, her hand surrounds my swelling erection.

"Melody, you don't have to do this."

"I want to, Charles. I want to experience everything with you. Only you." She runs her fingers around my shaft with a light touch.

"Have you ever done this before?"

Eyes downcast, she shakes her head. "Teach me."

Her plea lands on my ears laced with a slight insecurity, which causes lust to shoot through my body. I swallow. Placing my hand over hers, I show her how I like to be touched. Together, we rub my length, ending with a twist at the base. We press down on the tip and trace my shaft downward. Over and over with increasing pressure.

"I want to taste you."

God, what this woman does to me. I release my cock to her tender mercies. She opens her mouth and swallows it nearly whole.

"Whoa!"

Sputtering and choking, she separates her tonsils from my manhood. "This looks so easy in porn!"

I can't help it. Laughter bubbles up and out of my mouth. "First off, those ladies have a lot more experience than you do. Second, it's filmed so any possible issues are cut from the final. And third, what the hell were you doing watching porn?"

She sits on her heels. "I wanted to learn how to—" Her sentence remains unfinished.

I touch the top of her head and let my hand remain on her crown for a few beats before dropping down to her chin. I tip it upward and her eyes meet mine. "You don't have to watch porn, Goldie. I'm right here and more than willing to experiment with you. Although the thought of you and porn makes me feel all naughty inside."

"I wanted to make you all naughty outside, too."

"Oh, you will. I promise. Now, why don't you put your lips to good use. Lick up and down my cock while keeping your hand here." I indicate the base.

She opens her mouth again and inserts my erection much more slowly this time. Gah, her mouth feels warm and wet and wondrous.

"You can play with my balls if you'd like." Before she reaches them, I warn, "Lightly."

She does. Her tongue traces circles around my shaft. Up and over the tip, while her hand applies a light pressure at my base. I place my hand over hers, guiding her to apply the pressure needed to drive me crazy.

Confidence growing, she hits the right speed and strength. My hand finds its way into her hair as my hips buck against her mouth. "You're a quick learner."

Her eyes flick to mine, satisfaction at my praise evident. My body gets wound tighter and tighter under her ministrations. My hips push with an increasing speed down her throat.

"I'm getting close. Let me pull out." Having her swallow my come is too much for me to ask.

Instead of listening to me like she's done this entire time, she redoubles her efforts. Her tongue swipes across my length and she hollows her cheeks and sucks hard.

In short pants, I huff, "Melody. Don't." Pant. "Come." Pant. "Mouth."

Ignoring my pleas, she continues working my straining cock with her lips and tongue and hands. My balls retract and a flash of energy ripples through my body as I explode in her mouth with a loud roar.

On her knees, Melody takes everything I give her and swallows. With a satisfied smirk, she kisses the tip of my softening cock.

Her actions almost bring me down to my knees with her. Instead, I drag her up my body, bury my face in her hair, and breathe in. She wraps her arms around my naked torso and holds on tight.

When my heart rate declines somewhat, I murmur, "You were amazing."

She squeezes me. In an uncertain voice, she replies, "You liked it?"

Pulling back, I gaze into her deep amber eyes. Her hesitant question tugs at my heart, making me fall deeper under her thrall. "Yes, you didn't know what to do at first, but after I showed you, you caught on fast. Like, really fast. You did things to me no woman ever has. Ever. I think that qualifies as amazing."

Her shoulders straighten. "You taste much better than I thought. A little tangy. I like it." She licks her lips.

My stomach flips. What the hell? Ignoring my body's reaction to her sultry words, I quip, "What am I going to do with you, Goldie?"

She winks. "Everything."

My hand skims over her body, seeking her pussy. Before I reach my destination, an unknown ringtone fills the room. She jumps back from my body.

"Oh! That's my timer. We have to get going to the airport now. The car service will be downstairs in five minutes."

"Fuck!"

"No time for that, Charles."

MELODY

I take my seat on the plane as Chase stows the measly piece of luggage we brought from Ravello some fifteen hours ago. I'm still on a high from giving my first blow job. Although, truth be told, I am a bit frustrated as well. We'll be back in Ravello in a *mere* ten hours. I can wait. I sigh.

Chase takes his seat on the aisle, where he can stretch out his long legs, even here in first class. The flight attendant is all over him like shoulder pads in the eighties, though. Seriously? Doesn't she have any pride?

Smiling like a lunatic, she asks him, "Would you like a glass of champagne?"

He turns to me. "Want one, darling?"

Even though I know he used the term of endearment for show, I can't stop my heart from skipping. Offering a saccharine smile to the flight attendant, I bat my eyelashes and reply, "I'd love that, Chase."

Chase. Using his stage name sounds so odd, but it was the right move for this moment. His eyes widen, then he turns back to the flight attendant and holds up two fingers. When she walks off, a now-fake smile plastered on her face, we both laugh.

"Chase?"

"Felt right, honey. My very own actor."

He rolls his eyes. "You don't need to lay it on so thick."

I lean over and kiss his cheek. "Actually, I've seen my mother do that with my dad to some of his overenthusiastic fans a lot. It's fun."

He runs the back of his hand down my cheek. "Tell me about your parents. I don't know them at all, despite having grown up in the same neighborhood."

His request warms my heart. "Actually, when I spoke with them before you got to my condo, I might have told them about you."

"You did? All good, I hope."

I nod. "Yeah. I told them I was in New York, traveling with you, for your audition. Mom knows who you are. My dad, well, he"—my voice trails off to barely audible—"wants to meet you."

He cups his ear. "Huh? I didn't hear that last part."

I clear my throat. "My dad was being a father, you know? He wants to meet you," I repeat, louder this time. "I told him he will, when the time is right."

Charles's eyelids slam over his blue eyes.

"That's okay, right? You do want to meet them, don't you?"

He opens his eyes, a softness there I've never seen before. "Yes," he says. "That'd be nice."

Our conversation is cut short when the flight attendant returns with our bubbly. Charles clinks his glass to mine. "Here's to a short ride back to Italy."

The champagne slides down my throat, leaving effervesce in its wake. Together with Charles's admission he wants to meet my family, my decision to trust my gut that he's a good guy is solidified. The plane takes off.

"So, tell me more about them." At my quizzical look, he continues, "Your parents."

"They're very much in love, still. I've caught them giving silly looks to each other all the time. I used to be embarrassed by their expressions and stolen kisses, but now I'm grateful. They've shown me what love looks like. They both work really, really hard, but never forget to take time out for each other." I explain how my mother turned the band's finances around when she first started working for Hunte. Concluding, I say, "Even when I was young, they'd go away for date weekends every so often."

"Sounds like a wonderful way to grow up."

Something in his tone prompts me to ask, "What was it like growing up in the Wainwright household? Both of your parents are high-powered lawyers."

He takes a swig of the champagne. "Yeah. They both valued their careers above everything else. Including their children. Now don't get me wrong. Lindsay and I never lacked for anything money could buy as we grew up."

I digest what he's telling me. "Sounds a little lonely. Especially since you and your sister are five years apart. Basically, you both were only children. Sort of like King and me. Although, you both were in the same household."

He pulls on the end of my hair. "What were you like growing up? I can picture you as this wild tomboy, causing havoc everywhere you went."

"Not exactly. I wasn't a tomboy, that's for sure. I was, well, just a regular girl. Or at least I wanted to be. Regular, that is."

"I can't imagine you being anything except extraordinary. Were you the ringleader of the cool chicks?"

His teasing tone doesn't register, as his words lodge in the center of my chest. "No, I didn't belong to that clique."

He cocks his head. "Were you involved with costume design back then?"

"Yeah. I was in the artistic crew. Sophia and I both were."

"Well, that I can believe. I didn't realize Sophia's from Chicago, too."

I smile. "Yup. She's my oldest friend. I was so excited to find out she was in the camera crew for the movie. We haven't had much time to hang out since graduating high school. Nothing beats being around each other every day."

"I get it. I met Mark on the set of my first movie, so I was happy to see him cast as the villain here."

"I could tell you were friends before filming *Doctor Manipul8*."

Chase yawns. "So, tell me a Melody story from when you were oh, say, ten." He tweaks my nose.

"Let's see . . ." When I was ten, his sister—who I thought was a good friend at the time—threw my dad in my face. I know Charles was seeking a fun memory, but this one wants to come out. I do modify it, for his sake. "That was the age when I first learned the world my parents had created for me wasn't how everyone viewed it."

His hand lands on mine. I entwine our fingers and continue, "To make a long story short"—and avoid any references to his sister—"I found out others thought I was getting preferential treatment because my dad's a rock star."

He squeezes my hand. "I'm so sorry."

"Ever since, I've had a very hard time trusting my gut as to whether someone likes me for me, or for what my dad can do for them and their careers."

"That's terrible, Melody. It doesn't matter what others say about you." He taps my heart. "It's what's inside here that counts. Everyone else be damned."

I give him a small smile. "I'm getting there. Thanks to you, Charles."

My free hand grabs at my ever-present rubber band. "Tell me about this," he raises our linked hands.

Inhaling, I remember when my mother first gave one to me. Helplessness, anger and frustration swell deep within. "To do so, we need to go back to when I was ten again. After a week of coming home from school crying, my mother gave me my first rubber band."

He nods for me to continue. "Anyway, Mom told me bullies torment others because they're hiding something in themselves. She said whenever I was feeling ambushed, I should snap it and let the hurt absorb all my anger."

His blue eyes soften, as does his voice. "Sounds like a wise woman."

"She is," I reply, nodding. "Anyway, whenever I'm annoyed or mad, I pluck it as a reminder to channel my negative energy and live to fight another day."

"Wow. I'm glad this has helped you throughout the years. Although," he snaps it and the sting seems weaker somehow. "I seem to remember you flicking it around me."

"You probably deserved it," I quip.

He winks. "Then I better do my best to avoid the dreaded rubber band snap."

"I'd say you're doing a mighty fine job." I give him a kiss, which ends when he yawns again.

"Please excuse me, Goldie. It's the hour, not the company, I swear."

I open the plastic bag with a blanket and pillow in it and cover us both up. "Why don't you get some sleep? You've had a very hard day."

He wraps his arm around my shoulders. "So have you, sweetheart." He directs my head to his pecs and closes his eyes.

I can't sleep, despite the fact the lights have dimmed and we're flying over thirty thousand feet above the earth. Verifying he's out, I whisper, "Your sister was the ringleader of the mean girls at school, Charles. She made my life a living hell growing up."

With that confession off my chest, I close my eyes and drift off into dreamland.

My core clenches with want. My swollen nipples are strummed, causing desire to streak directly to my core. My hips roll against the air. A second zing between my legs brings my eyes wide-open.

And I'm looking directly into passion-laden blues.

"Charles," I murmur.

His lips tick upward as his fingers play with my nipple beneath my bra. "Yes," he mouths.

A low moan escapes my lips. I try to push his hands away from my body, but he only brings me closer. Kissing my lips in that way of his, the one that makes me forget everything and everyone around me—including my own name—I trail my hands into his hair.

He pulls away, breathing hard. "Go into the bathroom and don't lock it."

I blink. Slowly. Is he actually proposing what I think he is? "You don't mean . . ."

He returns my breasts into the cups and inches the blanket away from my body. "Oh, but I do. Now go."

He's wearing a devious smile, which only serves to spur me on. Biting my bottom lip, I toss the blanket onto his lap and stand in the darkened cabin. Snores greet my ears. I glance over to where the flight attendants sit, and they're either talking among themselves or otherwise occupied.

On unsteady steps, I walk over to the lavatory and slip inside. I can't believe I'm going to get into the Mile High Club! Whoever would've thought me, a virgin until a few days ago, would ever be so daring?

Grinning, I rip my clothes off my body. Banging my elbow against the wall, I toss my shirt over my head. Damn. When he gets in here, how much room are we going to have? How will this even be possible?

I fold all my clothes and lay them on top of the tank. Ignoring the practicalities, I remember the way his fingers were just playing my body. He'll make it work. Somehow.

The doorknob turns and Charles enters the tiny room. His eyes widen at me, standing naked before him. "Well, well, well. Fancy meeting you here."

He clicks the door shut and locks it. The lights pop on. My eyes land on the huge bulge in his pants, topped by an open button. I reach out for him and unzip. His hand slides into his pocket and he retrieves a foil wrapper, then kicks off his pants and underwear.

I can't help myself but launch my naked body at his bottom-half bare one, kissing his lips and sharing his breath. The packet rips open and he pulls back slightly to roll the condom down his length. Damn. I need to do that next time.

While he's doing that, I unbutton his shirt and explore his sculpted torso. He turns me around so I face the mirror.

Inserting a finger into my body, he rumbles, "We have to be quiet. Think you can do that for me, Goldie?"

"Yes," I hiss, modulating my voice lower than the scream I want to let out.

"So wet for me. Have you been like this since your condo?" He rubs my clit with his thumb as he inserts a second finger into me.

"Yeah," I manage to get out. Between the taboo of doing this on the plane, the requirement that we keep quiet, what he did to me out in the seat just before, and the possibility of being caught, my body vibrates with excitement.

He circles my clit with more force. "My poor, poor baby. What you've been suffering with."

I push back against his hand. "Please."

Against the back of my head, his lips form a smile. "Since you asked so nicely." He lifts my right leg so it's on top of the closed toilet seat. In the mirror, I watch his left hand tweak my nipples again. He removes his fingers from my sex and positions himself at my entrance.

Before he pushes in, his fingers return into my body. "Are you ready for me?"

"God, yes," I half-yell, then catch myself. In a lower voice, I whisper-shout, "Please."

He removes his fingers and licks, then holds them up to my mouth. As soon as I suck on them, he plunges into me. My whole body lights up with want. Watching him thrust into me in the mirror, his shirt flapping with his every movement deep inside of me, I can't imagine anything ever being more erotic.

Then he removes his fingers from my mouth and plays with my clit again.

It's too much.

I've been primed since I gave him the blowjob. My core tightens, and I clench all around him while my body explodes. I open my mouth to scream, but he covers it with his hand—which still smells of me.

He thrusts twice more, then stills. He lets out a low grunt as he spills inside me.

When I come back to my senses, Charles holds my back to his front as if his every breath depended on it. "Each time is better than the last," he whispers in my ear, then nips the lobe.

I shudder at his words, savoring the feel of his body deep in mine.

Soon, way too soon, he eases out and removes the condom. Wetting paper towels, I help him clean up, and he returns the favor for me. I fling my arms around his neck.

"That was spectacular." I kiss him.

Tracing my bottom lip with his tongue, he replies, "That it was." His lip ticks upward. "Sorry it was so quick."

"No complaints here." I trace his mouth with my index finger. "Guess we have to get dressed, huh?"

He gives me a wolfish grin that would make every female's panties drop from age ten to ninety. My breath sucks in. "Since I'm halfway there," he raises his arms, indicating his open button-down shirt, "I'll go first. Follow me back to our seats when you're ready." He buttons his shirt.

My eyes follow his movements as he drags his pants up his long legs. Tucking himself into his fly, he zips up. Still ass naked, I grab his hand.

"Charles."

"Melody."

My heart overflows with love. "Can I trust you?"

His thumb rubs over the back of my hand. He leans in and kisses me. "Yes." He kisses me once more and slips out of the restroom.

I sigh and collapse against the small stretch of wall. My heart pounds with desire. Want. Hope.

As I reach for my clothes, I whisper to the airplane gods, "I do."

CHASE

The pilot announces we'll be arriving in Rome within minutes. I've been holding Melody's hand ever since she returned from the bathroom, so I bring it up to my lips. "Ready to go back to Amalfi?"

"It's like we never left," she quips, winking at me.

As soon as we land, I turn on my phone to a bunch of missed texts from Mark, Thomas, Jessa, Lindsay, and Noble. I open Noble's and my breath catches. "No filming until Monday."

"Yeah, just read Judith's text." She bites her bottom lip. "Whatever bug everyone else has, they better keep it to themselves."

"That's true." I glance out the window as we taxi toward the airport. The thought of getting on a helicopter right now to return us to the Amalfi Coast makes my stomach turn sour. "Want to take a slow route back to Ravello?"

Melody's eyes light up. "I like the sound of that. I'm sick of traveling by air, truth be told."

A girl after my own heart. "Twenty hours on a plane in twenty-five hours is enough." We both laugh. "How about I rent a car and drive us back? We'll take our time and enjoy. No rush."

"Sounds wonderful to me, Charles."

The way she says my *real* name makes me want to bare more of my soul to her. I did play violin in front of her and she didn't laugh. It's been so long since I've touched base with the real Charles, though, I'm afraid I don't know who he is anymore. With Melody, I want to try.

We're out in the Italian countryside, passing small villages on our way to the Amalfi Coast. Melody's quiet. I glance over to make sure she's awake, and her amber eyes greet mine. "Enjoying the ride?"

"I am. Such a beautiful country."

"It is. No wonder it's produced so many wonderful artists." I purse my lips. No one knows I was an art history minor in college. Well, that's not true. My fellow acting students knew and mocked my interest in the masterpieces. Ones I've had the pleasure of seeing in person. During this trip alone, I've seen Michelangelo, da Vinci, Botticelli, and my favorite Raphael. I'm living my secret dream.

"I don't know too much about art," she confesses. "I do enjoy going to museums, though. So many gorgeous paintings. They take my breath away."

Perhaps I can dip my toe? "Yes, the museums here boast originals. In the towns they were created."

She doesn't laugh in my face. In fact, her gaze wanders, then returns to me. "I know. I spent hours looking at *The David* in Florence. Although," she licks her lips, "now that I've seen you, I think Michelangelo used the wrong model."

I chuckle. "No, I don't hold a candle to *The David.*"

She wiggles her eyebrows, her gaze firmly on my crotch. "Don't sell yourself short."

I bring her hand over for a kiss. Releasing her, words fall out of my mouth. "I was an art history minor in college, actually. I learned all about the masters. Whenever I'm on set, I always make it a point to go to a museum to check out their collections. I'd be more than happy to take you on a museum tour while we're here."

When my confession is over, I clench my jaw. Did I reveal too much? Will she think I'm a pussy? Why did I share this part of me?

"I think that is so cool. You're a regular renaissance man." Her lips bus my cheek.

Her praise seeps into all my pores. She doesn't think my studies were ridiculous, like my parents did. Although, now that I can buy and sell their life savings many times over, they're more forgiving. At least they approve of my choice of career, especially since they can show me off to their friends.

"I'm not too sure a renaissance man would be playing a superhero."

She rubs her finger over my cheek, getting rid of her lipstick. "Oh, I don't know. Maybe not Doctor Manipul8, but a Shakespearean one."

At her oblique mention of my audition, I tense. I've done a damn good job of putting it out of my mind. I want that role so bad I can taste it. It's not up to me, though. "Well, we'll see about that."

Her stomach rumbles and she places her arm over it. "Excuse me."

I chuckle. "Better feed my woman. You're going to need your strength for later." I wiggle my eyebrows, and her complexion pinkens. So cute.

I'm falling for this woman.

Hard.

Soon we enter a small town where I park. Placing a cap on my head for a disguise, I guide her toward the nearest restaurant. It has an overly large carved mahogany door that's wide-open. The odors of fresh garlic, tomatoes, and lemons dance across my nose.

"Look good, Goldie?"

"It looks beyond fabulous. My mouth is already watering."

Wrapping my arm around her, we walk to the hostess stand and are escorted to a seat right by oversized windows overlooking the town square and its fountain. She leaves us with menus, written in Italian. I flip it over, but the wine list also is in Italian.

I toss my menu on the table. "Can you read any of this?"

She shakes her head and puts her menu down as well. "We'll just have to wing it."

Our server comes and says something in Italian. Clearing my

throat, I respond for both of us. "My girlfriend and I don't speak Italian. Do you speak English?"

"Ah, welcome, welcome. I don't, ah, speak English so well. Cush take you over for me. Drink?" He mimes as if he were drinking from a glass.

"We'll take a bottle of your best pinot noir."

"Pinot noir, *sì*. I will go to get it for you both."

He leaves and Melody grins at me. "He's cute."

I pretend to be affronted. "Hey. You're not supposed to comment about another guy to your boyfriend."

She giggles. "Not as hot as you, of course." She bats her eyelashes at me. Then giggles some more, ending with a snort. "Oh my God. I'm so embarrassed."

"Karma. Such a wonderful bitch."

She gives me the evil eye. Or, rather, tries to, but it's way too adorable to be effective. A new server, Cush, interrupts us. He presents a bottle, which I taste. Damn. That's good. When I nod, he pours two glasses.

"Your prior server, Angelo, asked me to help him here, since I am more familiar with English." He looks from me to Melody, then his eyes swing back to my face. Shit. Guess he recognized me. In a dramatic fashion, he places his hand over his heart. "Signor Wright, we are so honored you selected our restaurant."

I pull off my cap and toss it onto an empty chair. No need for it now. "*Prego*, Cush."

He beams at my use of his name and fiddles with his notebook. "What can I offer for your dining pleasure?"

Melody jumps in, diverting his attention. "I'd like some pasta. With a red sauce. And some meat." She eyes me up and down, and my body responds to her unspoken offer.

The waiter scribbles on his pad and turns to me. Feeling reckless, I say, "I'll have a pizza. With lots of cheese and . . . broiled chicken." I stifle a grimace.

"Spaghetti and pizza, I will bring right out." He heads off toward the kitchen.

I look out the window to check out the town square, where several people have gathered. A small group turns some plastic buckets upside down and they begin dancing and banging on the makeshift drums. We watch as the group does intricate steps.

"I'm surprised to see such a routine out here, away from the city."

"I was thinking the same thing. Maybe it's a festival?"

A few minutes later, the group disperses as quickly as they started. Their enthusiasm was contagious. I find myself tapping my foot to the music playing in the restaurant. "Want to dance?"

Melody turns her head from right to left. She leans forward. "Hate to break it to you, big guy. There's no dance floor."

"Who needs one?" I stand and hold out my hand. "Dance with me, Goldie."

Slowly, she takes my hand. I lead her through some simple dance moves around empty tables.

"Where did you learn how to dance like this?"

I dip her low. "I've always loved to dance." I bring her back upright and resume the proper dance hold. "But I had some formal training for a movie I did a few years ago."

"Nice."

Our waiter stands to the side, watching us enjoy ourselves. I lean to her ear. "I think dinner's almost here. We can pick this up later. Naked."

"You." She taps my chest.

We return to our chairs and our meals are delivered a minute later. I pour her another glass of wine, but ask for water for myself since I'm driving. Picking up a slice of pizza, I take a huge bite while she tastes her dinner.

"Oh my, this is totally delicious!"

"My pizza rocks, too." I hold out my slice toward her. "Wanna taste?"

She leans forward and opens her mouth, then closes it on my pizza. My cock takes note. Adjusting my lower half, I ask, "Am I right?"

She swallows. "Yes, that is awesome. Here." She twirls some pasta around her fork and holds it out for me.

I accept the proffered sample and wash it down with the remainder of my wine. "That's fantastic. Not heavy like I expected."

We devour the rest of our meals, enjoying simply being with each other. With her, I'm a regular guy. I don't have to play any role. She's helped me get back in touch with who I am. Who I'm afraid to let be seen.

Dishes cleared, she kisses my lips, her tongue licking mine. "You're not at all what I had expected, you know."

My eyebrow lifts. "Really? What did you expect?"

"More like the guy you were at first. Arrogant. Cocky. Annoying."

"Ouch. You wound me, *madam*."

She smiles. "You've made a lot of progress."

"Hmmm. I don't think I ever was those things. I think you were mistaken. I've always been a sweet, loveable kitty cat."

"Kitty cat?" She rolls her eyes. "Yeah, that's you all right." She finishes her wine. "I like the real Charles, thank you very much. The art minor. The hard-hitting actor. The violin player."

At her description of me—the *real* me—I recoil against my seat, even though she echoes my earlier thoughts. I remove some crumbs from our table. "How about we keep this our dirty little secret?"

"I can understand wanting to keep a part of yourself private. Hell, I've had a front-row seat to how my dad's handled being in the public eye." She lowers her voice. "There's a difference between privacy and hiding."

Like a whip, my response is fast and surgical. "I haven't been hiding." I smooth out my eyebrows. "I don't like to advertise who I really am. Doesn't go with my reputation, you know." I rise. "Are you ready to head back?"

"Charles, I didn't mean anything—"

I motion for her to stand and soften the tone of my voice. "I know. Let's get going. We still have a drive before we get to Ravello." To take the sting out of my outburst, I kiss her full on the mouth until she clings to my shoulders.

I wrap my arm around her waist while Cush thanks us for enjoying his restaurant. I sign a menu and take photos with him and the entire wait staff. Leaving a pile of euros on the table, I escort Melody to the car and resume our ride.

My phone rings. "It's Thomas." I look at Melody. "Should I answer it?"

"Yeah, he might have something important to tell you."

Taking her advice, I press the button for the car's Bluetooth to link the call. "Hey, how are you feeling?"

"I'm doing better. A lot better than some, that's for sure. How are you?"

"Good. I managed to escape the dreaded bug and got the hell out of Dodge." I place my hand on Melody's knee. "Is everything still in order?"

"Yeah, boss. Even with this little break, nothing got all wonky. Except—"

Thomas does love his theatrics. Perhaps I should encourage him to get in the acting game? But for now, I call his tease. "What happened?"

"I haven't seen Tina at all."

I chuckle at the mention of the set makeup artist who caught his eye. Under my hand, Melody moves her leg and emits a long sigh.

"Sorry, dude. Was she sick?"

"No. Can you believe it? She's like you, she has the constitution of an elephant. No, wait, that came out wrong. She's not an elephant at all. Neither are you. You know what I mean."

I let his word salad continue for a little bit. "I got you. Well, I think it's good she didn't get sick. Did she stay on set?"

"No. I heard she went to visit Naples with Joe. The camera operator."

"Ouch. Sorry, dude."

Melody whispers, "Ask him if he's heard how Sophia's feeling."

Thomas's voice comes over through the car's speakers. "Hey, are you alone? I didn't mean to interrupt something—"

I glance at Melody, who shakes her head. I evade. "Have you heard how Sophia is doing?" Then add, "And Mark?"

"They're both better, from what I've heard. Sophia got it real bad, though. I saw her walking into a local grocery store a couple of hours ago, and she looked like death warmed over. She has to have lost five pounds. I wanted to go over and talk with her but couldn't get my own body moving."

Melody nods, and I ask about Mark again.

"Oh, he's probably the best of all of us. He was back on solid foods yesterday."

"That's a little bit of positive news anyway."

"And Melody. No one's seen her at all. She must have it worse than Sophia."

At the mention of Melody's name, I squeeze her knee. In response, she opens her legs a little bit. No longer interested in gossip from the set, I try to wrap things up with my PA. "Guess we'll find out soon. Noble texted that we'll resume filming on Monday. I have a feeling we're going to be doing very late night shoots."

"Yeah. I know he's going to want to get the shoot back on track. You better get all the rest you can now."

"Good advice, T. Well, I better go. See you on Monday."

When the line is disconnected, I glance at my girlfriend. She's holding her phone. "I feel badly for Sophia. Especially since Thomas talked about Tina." She taps her phone.

I cock my head.

Melody sighs. "You didn't hear this from me, but Sophia has a little crush on your PA."

Understanding seeps into my bones. "Very interesting. Seems Mark may have something to say about that."

"I had a hunch." She holds up her phone. "Do you mind if I call her to check in?"

"Not at all."

On speaker, her best friend picks up on the third ring. Her voice is painfully scratchy. After Melody asks about her health, Sophia gives her a rundown. Geez, she still isn't ready for prime time.

"I'm so sorry, Sophia."

The sound of her blowing her nose fills the car. "I'll be okay before we start shooting again. I hope. Now tell me all about Doctor Manip-ul8. Has he performed any superhero tricks on you?"

Melody giggles, and the lighthearted sound makes my heart swell. Well, that in addition to the fact she's shared our relationship with her friend. She glances at me, her smile wicked. "Oh, he sure did."

To punctuate her point, I slip my hand up to the juncture of her thighs, keeping my eyes trained on the road. She swallows a surprised exclamation.

"Good for you. I'm so happy. At least one of us is having fun. And not sick."

"More than having fun."

At her words, I press my palm against her pussy and she clamps her legs together, trapping my hand. "That we are," I add.

"Oh my God. Charles, is that you?"

"In the flesh." I move my hand in a small circle.

"We're enjoying the Italian countryside," Melody squeaks.

Sophia coughs, then sneezes. "I think that's my cue to let you two lovebirds go. I'm so happy for you. Both." She clicks off.

"Sophia seems nice."

"She is. She's one of the only people on earth who I trust. Implicit-ly." She opens her legs a fraction. "You're another."

MELODY

We finally arrive at our villa in Ravello at six o'clock. We're both beat from all the traveling, Charles especially so. "I know it's early, but we should really hit the hay. We've traveled so much and our bodies need to unwind."

The smile he gives me is downright . . . *dirty*. I've never known a smile to be dirty before.

He drops our overnight bag to the floor, unbuttoning his shirt. "I think that's an excellent idea."

"You're incorrigible. I meant to *sleep*." I dash into the bathroom, locking the door behind me.

Even though I want to experience another round with him, my body really does need to recover. After seeing to my needs, I strip off my travel clothes and wrap myself in the white terrycloth robe. With caution, I open the door.

Charles isn't in the bedroom. Huh. Walking into the main part of the suite, I check out the empty balcony. Where he introduced me to balcony sex. My body hums to life. *Maybe I'm not so tired after all.*

Coming back into the villa, I walk around the sofa and stop. Charles is passed out. I study him in his sleep. My goodness, he is classically gorgeous. His Roman nose is straight and in the right proportion to his face. His cheekbones are pronounced but not so much as to make him appear skeletal. And that cleft in his chin is something Lucifer himself would covet.

My gaze travels downward, over his exposed abs. He left his shirt on, but unbuttoned. Same for his pants. In repose, he's downright scrumptious. Chest rising and falling as he sleeps. I memorize every inch of this man.

My man.

I am safe with him. He sees me for me, recognizing my costume design talents. I'm not Braxton Hunte's daughter with him. I'm Melody. My own woman. Someone he values for what I, myself, bring to the table.

My heart expands at the certainty he's the real deal. Not after me for what my dad can do for his career, or for what he thinks my money and connections—actually, Daddy's—can buy. Charles doesn't need any of that from me, as he's already set in his career. Even if he wants to take it in a different direction.

No, he doesn't *need* me.

He *wants* me.

Just as I want him for his true, renaissance self.

My eyes eat him up from head to toe. As much as I want to be with him again, he's exhausted. I am too, really. Should I wake him up to bring him into bed? Shaking my head, I pick up a blanket and drape it over his prone form, kissing his forehead. And tiptoe back into the bedroom. Tossing off the bathrobe, I slide, naked, into the bed and fall fast asleep before my head hits the pillow.

A flutter on my chest makes me turn.

A low rumble warms my body.

A nip against my nipple wakes me up.

An oversized naked man lies next to me in bed, the sheet draped low over his hips. He bites me again.

"Charles!"

He places his index finger against my lips. "Shhh." Moving his hands to my shoulders, he brings me flush against his body, tucking my head under his chin.

We remain like this for a while. The only thing that moves is his growing erection against my abdomen. Sliding my hand between us, I close around his girth and squeeze like he taught me to do in my condo earlier today. Or was that yesterday? Everything's a blur.

"Now, Goldie. I thought you were tired."

I move my hand up and down his shaft, and his breath catches. "Sleep is overrated."

Charles turns onto his back, pulling me on top of him and proceeds to kiss every thought out of my head. Panting, he breaks from me and grabs a condom from the side table.

I steal the packet from him. "Let me. I've always wanted to do this."

His chuckle rolls through me, then he spreads his arms wide. "I'm all yours."

A thrill at his words races through my body. I open the packet and pull the latex out. It's coated in a lubricant, but not too sticky. Concentrating, I pinch the top of the condom. Before covering his erection, though, I stick my tongue out and lick the pre-cum off.

"Need a clean surface," I explain.

He groans but doesn't try to take over.

I position the condom over him and roll it down his length, like how I practiced on a cucumber after watching a demonstration on You Tube years ago. Not even Sophia knows I did this. Too embarrassing. Definitely worth the practice, as it's a perfect fit.

"Better than a cucumber," I murmur.

He laughs loudly, his cock moving in my hand. "I would hope so."

Ignoring his comment, I situate myself over him. Leaning forward, I kiss him and let our tongues dance. Without breaking the kiss, I position his hardness straight up and sink down on him. I moan. He's so deep.

"Damn, Goldie." He thrusts his hips up once. "You feel so fucking good."

"Back at ya."

He lets me set the pace. Deep thrusts followed by shallow ones, fast then slow. I try out different rhythms, enjoying every last one.

Charles's left hand clamps on the back of my head while the other goes to my hip, guiding me in his preferred pattern. He's so big, but my body accommodates him like we were made for each other.

Maybe we were.

His hand slides from my hip to my clit and he rubs in a circular fashion. On his third pass, without warning, I explode. Splintering in his arms, I shout my completion. He continues to pump into me and roars my name. I collapse onto his hard body, melting around him.

I rest my chin on his chest, looking into his deep blue eyes while he brushes the hair away from my forehead. "You're amazing." He guides my face to him and kisses me while maneuvering me to his side.

I grin at his praise. However unfounded. "No." I kiss both of his cheeks. "You're the amazing one."

"Let's call it a draw." He wraps his arms around my body and kisses me senseless.

Two hours and my first sexual encounter in a shower later, we're dressed and standing on the balcony. His fingers play with my hair. "Want to explore?"

"Explore what?" I turn and wrap my arms around his neck.

"Ravello," he responds. "Although I'm not opposed to exploring other things." He squeezes my butt. "I think we should give your body a little breather."

Muscles I've never used before scream at me to explore the town. I drop my cheek to his pecs. "My brain is willing, but my body says otherwise."

He chuckles and slaps my right butt cheek. "Later, I promise." Taking my hand, we walk out of our cocoon and into the village.

We spend the next few hours walking aimlessly, trying on silly hats and modeling fun clothes. I've never laughed so much in all my life. Charles has a dry sense of humor, which keeps me in stitches.

"No more," I plead. "That visual is too much!"

He chuckles and wraps his arm around my shoulder. "Fine. No more talk about flubbed lines." He squeezes me to his side.

We pass a garden and he stops. "Let's go in." He motions toward the open gate.

As we enter the almost deserted space, the smell of roses hits me in the face as if I walked through a haze of perfume. I take a deep inhale. "It smells wonderful in here."

"It does," Charles says as he walks to a cluster of rose bushes. He picks a gorgeous, yellow bud and tucks it behind my ear.

I kiss his stubbled cheek. "Thank you."

He inclines his head toward an empty bench under what has to be a century-old tree. I go to sit next to him, but his hands encircle my waist and he pulls me onto his lap. Instead of struggling, I lean my head onto his shoulder and swing my foot. "I understand why everyone says this town is so romantic."

"I know what you mean. We're high above the water, so we have a perfect view out to all the boats. Yet, here we are, sitting in our own secluded paradise."

Noise from down the street catches my attention and I look back. A bridal party walks our way, no doubt for photos. What a perfect place for a wedding. I sigh.

His tenor voice whispers in my ear, "Looks like we should give up our slice of heaven to the newlyweds."

I lift my head and gaze at my boyfriend for a long moment before reaching forward and kissing him. The shock of our lips coming together still steals my breath. "Okay."

When I stand, I offer him my hand. As we head toward the gate, the wedding party enters. Charles ducks his head downward, causing my heart to reach out to him. I know how difficult it is to be recognized, given my lifetime as being Braxton Hunte's daughter. I point toward some bushes, gesticulating with abandon. Anything to divert their attention from the man at my side.

We're almost to the gate when one of the groomsmen says, "Hey! No way! Guys, it's Chase Wright!" Everyone in the party stops and turns our way. Guess this is an American celebration, given their accents.

Next to me, Charles stiffens. With practiced ease, he releases his pent-up breath and schools his expression to one of welcome. He waves. "Hi, everyone. Congratulations on your wedding. You remind me of my sister. You make a beautiful bride."

The dark-haired woman in an elegant white gown with sequins that catch the Italian sun turns a shade of red when she's singled out. So unlike Lindsay, who loves being the center of attention. Their photographer circles us, making me feel like a hunted deer. I can only imagine how Charles is feeling.

"We wish you all the happiness," I pipe up. "We'll leave you to your photos."

Before we can take another step, the groom appears at Charles's side and whispers something to him. Although I can't hear him, the subtle change in my boyfriend's demeanor tells me he's going to take some pictures with them. So much for a relaxing day in Ravello.

Charles turns to me. "I've agreed to add 'a little something' to their wedding album. I hope you're not mad at me."

My eyebrows rise. Guess he's used to this and, while not exactly thrilled, he's taking it in stride. I return the favor. "Take as long as you need." He bends down and kisses me, then joins the wedding party.

I wander over to the bench we previously occupied and watch him work the wedding party. He takes photos with everyone, not just the newlyweds. From the looks on their faces, they are beyond thrilled. A small smile plays around my lips. He's given them a memory to enhance their wedding, set in such a romantic place. Charles is a good man.

When he starts to sign whatever they've given him, I rise and go to the gate. Finished signing, he poses for one last photo, kisses the bride's cheek, and walks toward me. With measured steps, we leave the wedding party and turn left. Instead of going into any more stores, we head over to the low rock wall overlooking the water.

To break the silence, I rub the back of his shoulder. "Hey, you did a great thing back there."

He expels a long breath. Slanting me a sideways glance, he confesses, "I'm sorry I had to leave you alone like that."

"You were worried about me?"

He kicks a little pebble and it bounces off the wall. "Other ladies have lost their minds when I had to interact with my fans."

What sort of women has he been with in the past? "That's nuts, Charles. Being with your fans is a part of your job. My dad taught me that from a very early age."

He bends down. "He did?" His knuckles scrape the ground and he retrieves a small rock.

"Yes. I know how important your fans are to your career. You don't have to explain that to me. I'll never begrudge you any time spent with them." His whole body relaxes as if he was bracing for a much different response from me. However, I can't allow him to get away scot-free. "I know you'll make it up to me in other ways."

He throws his head back and laughs, then tosses the rock over the wall. We lean over and watch as it descends into the water, far below us.

"What 'other ways' were you thinking about, Goldie?"

A variety of possibilities come to mind, all beginning and ending with us naked. I lick my lips. "I'm sure you'll think of something creative."

"I can be damn imaginative when spurred on." He grabs my hand. "Let's get back to the room, where I can test out some of my creativity."

We begin the climb up the hill to our villa. Charles has been nothing but up-front with me, and I trust him. He was scared to tell me about his interactions with fans, but he did. He was even more nervous to share his love of classical music and violin, yet he did that too. Since he compared the bride with his sister, the need to share another piece of my reality with him becomes overwhelming.

I lick my dry lips and start in reverse. "After everything that went down with Grant the mistrust I had for people grew." He nods and I gather the strength to continue. "If you haven't noticed, it takes a lot to get to know me, the real me. I mean, I'm friendly with everyone, but no one really gets to know me all that well."

He kisses the top of my forehead. "I'm honored to be one of the few people you let in."

"You should be," I tease to break the tension. "But the truth is that after Grant, no guy could get close to me. I went out on a couple of dates here and there, but nothing ever got too serious. Until . . ."

"Me."

My breathing stutters. "Charles, I'm scared because I've never been in a relationship like ours." I'm able to take a deep breath. "The more time we spend together, the more I'm convinced you're the real deal."

"Goldie, I'm flattered you feel that way. If I could go back in time and change what Grant did to you, I would. No one, especially you, deserved to be treated as a pawn for what your family could do for him. That's so wrong."

"Thanks."

We keep walking up the hill toward our hotel, now passing by houses that have flowers in window boxes. "Relationships in show business can be tricky things," Charles points out.

"They can be done, you know. I do know people in the business who have successful marriages. The media likes to portray them as if they were unicorns, but it doesn't have to be that way."

He rubs his forehead. "I also know a couple of good marriages. Not many, but the ones who are real are true inspirations."

"Hope my parents are on your list."

"Definitely. Rock and roll at your fingertips, and two parents who supported you."

I smile. "That part of growing up was the best." I shake the tingles out of my limbs. "Not everyone got the memo, though."

He pounds his fist into his cupped hand. "Who needs a lesson, besides Grant?"

I slant him a look. I need to tell him Sophia and I dubbed his sister the main ringleader of the "Mean Girls" crew. *Please don't let this come between us.*

When I don't reply, he places his hands on my shoulders. "Talk to me."

I can't look at his face. Blinking to the side, I confess. "Remember when I told you about the kids who made it their job to be, well, bullies?" That's an understatement. I force my head up. "The ring-leader was your sister," I mumble.

His cheek indents to match the cleft on his chin. "Excuse me."

"You didn't know me back then. I know you're not responsible for your sister's actions."

His fingers dig into my shoulders. When I grimace, he lets me go. "Lindsay was the baby of the family, which isn't an excuse. She's been going through some stuff for years now." He slams his mouth shut and turns toward the hotel.

I follow him up the road and grab his hand, causing him to stop. "Hey. I didn't tell you to drive a wedge between us. I wanted to come clean to you, that's it." I bite my lip. "I haven't been that little girl in a long time."

The war crossing his face is heartrending. "I apologize for what my sister put you through."

His *mea culpa* is appreciated, although he wasn't responsible for his sister. "You're not your sister's keeper."

Charles's hand lands on the back of his neck, and his elbow moves up and down. "There's stuff I'm sure you don't know about Lindsay, and I'm not at liberty to divulge. Just know I feel awful for what she did to you." His arm freefalls to his side.

A twinge of pity for her runs through me. Not for the first time, I skirt my hatred of his sister and puzzle what crawled up her butt and made her so nasty. Whatever. She was a royal bitch to me growing up. Nonetheless, I appreciate his explanation, and his remorse on her account. Reaching for the knitting needles in my hair only to realize I left them on the dresser, I voice, "Thank you."

We continue the schlep toward the hotel, each deep in our thoughts. I spend the time burying, again, the feelings of inadequacy and pain his sister caused me growing up. When she's back in her box, I want to lighten the dark mood I caused. I slant a glance at my boyfriend, who's now eyeing me up and down like I'm a perfect couture gown. Looks like we're on the same page.

"You're definitely right about one thing. You're not a child anymore." He rubs his palms together. "Not with those tits and ass."

I cross my arms across my "tits." Yup, same page. "Really? You're going with that?"

He licks his lips. "Yep."

"Well, you better use some of that Doctor Manipul8 superhero mojo if you want any more of this T and A." I twirl and swivel my hips. His wolfish laugh lets me breathe easier in the certainty our relationship is back on track.

He grabs me around the waist and tosses me in the air as if I weighed less than a feather. Catching me, he puts me down and places his hands on top of my head like in the movie. He releases me and steps back.

I shake my head. "I think you lost your mojo. I'm still affronted by your crude description of my body." I manage to say this without laughing.

"Then maybe I need to make more crude descriptions, naked, in bed. I bet you'll *love* them then."

As he speaks, I walk backward toward the hotel. Shaking my head, I yell, "Oh no you don't! Keep your distance, Doctor Perverted! Besides, you'll have to catch me first!"

I turn and race toward our villa, Charles hard on my heels.

CHASE

Considering it's 4:00 a.m., I'm the only one in this gym, which is smaller than the one at my hotel but still service-able. Jumping onto the exercise bike, I pedal away the calo-ries I've been eating. Can't have a flabby superhero. Earbuds in, I feel the burn and push through. When I've done thirty minutes, I hop over to the free weights and start in on the arm exercises my trainer gave me a week ago.

Despite my best efforts to stay focused, my mind wanders to the woman who has invaded my life and turned it inside out, in a good way. To the woman I left sleeping—naked—in my bed.

Melody's teaching me by example of how to live your own truth. If not for her, I would've never flown halfway around the world to audi-tion for the Broadway play. It was a good audition. I nailed the lines, made appropriate eye contact, and did everything I've been taught. God. I really want that part.

But I don't have any control over whether they cast me. Their demeanor certainly wasn't encouraging. I sigh as I begin my last set of cross-body curls.

Huffing with exertion, I put the weights into their cradle and pick up some kettle bells. Sam thinks I'm nuts for wanting to change the direction of my career, but he's not me. This is what I want. Not another stupid rom-com. Not even the movie about Hunte that I auditioned for before filming for *Doctor Manipul8* began.

Shit. The Hunte movie. Maybe I should talk with Melody about my audition? Before the thought flits through my head, I'm already nullifying it. She distinctly told me how she is not involved with it at all. If I'm on the short list to play her father, I'll tell her. No use bringing up a what-if with her now. Besides, I should hear from the Broadway show first.

Dropping the kettle bells, I begin my final exercise, the dreaded burpees. I quiet my mind and get to work on the buggers. The sooner I complete these hundred, the sooner I can get back to the room. And wake up sleeping beauty.

Finally finished, I grab a cup and fill it with cucumber water. I glance at the TV and grimace as my face is plastered all over the screen as being a "wedding crasher." The bride and groom gave details about meeting me yesterday and shared some of the photos. I run a towel over my sweaty forehead and toss it into the basket. At least it was positive press.

At ten after five, I arrive at our villa. We need to get a move on if we're going to be in my trailer at seven to sew me into my suit. My lips quirk at how much more fun the chore is going to be. When I enter the bedroom, Melody's not in bed and the shower's running. A grin touches my lips. We definitely have enough time for what I have in mind.

A languid Melody drapes her hand on my leg as I drive us back to the lot. We managed to gather our stuff and get into the rental car by six thirty, after an amazing round in the shower. Where we got very dirty before we got clean.

I rub my finger over my lips. "So, are you looking forward to sewing me into my superhero costume today, Goldie?"

She blushes. I love that she blushes for me. "I think it may be more enjoyable than ever before, especially since I now know exactly what you've got going on underneath."

My voice drops an octave. "Only for you." Truer words have never been spoken.

On my thigh, she traces various shapes. After a few minutes where I have to concentrate on navigating the windy, narrow Italian roads down toward Amalfi, her head pops up.

"Charles," she begins.

"Hmmm?" A bus ahead honked, which I've learned means he's coming toward me and there's not enough room for both of us on the road. I apply the brakes and he passes. From now on, I'm leaving the driving here to those experienced with the crazy rules of the road.

"Charles," she repeats.

I spare her a quick glance, then return my concentration on my drive. "Yes?"

"I've been thinking."

At these three words, my stomach tightens. Nothing good ever follows this statement out of a woman's mouth. Has she been using me? Wanted to get rid of her virginity with someone who's a notorious player? My breath catches.

She continues, "I'd like to keep our relationship a secret."

My brow furrows. How could I have misread her so thoroughly? I was a means to an end, nothing more.

Before I can formulate a response, she blurts, "It's just that, I'm, well, in so deep with you and I don't want anyone to spoil what we have. I also don't want to get the reputation I'm with you to further my career." She retracts her hand. "I also don't want to diminish how others see you. You're like a god on set. I don't want the fact that you're with a lowly assistant costume designer and be dragged down." She turns her head and faces the passenger side window.

All of my insecurities evaporate. Her main concern is for *me*. She's worried about what others will think of *me* for being with her. My whole body relaxes. "Goldie, the fact *you* chose to be with *me* will make me the envy of everyone on set."

Her head whips around to me. "You're wrong. Believe me."

"I don't." I'd reach out and grab her hand, but I need to keep my concentration on the road and both hands on the wheel. Another bus honks, and I pull over to the side. The road is so narrow, and we're on such a tight swerve, that he can't make it without backing up a few times. While we're stopped, I face her.

"Listen to me. I'm damn proud you chose me. You're sweet, talented, funny, and I've seen every man from cast to crew giving you speculative looks. Eager looks." I push her long locks away from her face, which I asked her to wear down until we get to the set. "But you chose me."

"Charles." She breathes my name a split-second before her lips land on mine.

The rumbling of the bus as it passes breaks us apart. "God, you're wonderful." With effort, I turn away from her and resume our drive back to Amalfi.

"Still, I'd like to keep our relationship a secret. I really don't want to give anyone the idea I'm trying to sleep my way to the top. After having my dad's name brought up all the time, that's all I need."

Her words cut right to my core. "I'll do anything you ask, Goldie. I don't want to make this harder for you." I make another corkscrew turn. "But, I do want to proudly walk with you on my arm soon."

In a quiet voice, she replies, "Thanks."

I hate having to hide our relationship, but I understand. All her life, she's been touted as the daughter of Braxton Hunte, rather than as a very talented woman in her own right. I can give her this. For now.

Melody interrupts my thoughts. "Thomas said no one has seen me since they all got sick, and they thought I had a bad time of it. Why don't we go with that? I'll simply tell them I was down and out, too."

I weigh her words. "Sounds like a good plan." We approach the town. "Should I drop you off at your hotel?"

"It's already after seven, and we need to get you sewn in. How about you drop me off down the road from your trailer and I'll walk the rest of the way."

I nod, unhappy but understanding her decision. "I'll bring our luggage into my trailer and stow it with your wardrobe kit."

"Sounds like a plan."

I maneuver to a stop in a quiet alley and she turns to leave. I clamp down on her shoulder. "Oh, no. You're not getting away from me that easily."

Spurred on by our first parting in days—even if it's only minutes—I bring her back to me and kiss her one last time. When we break apart, she's panting. So am I.

Her hand lands on my cheek. "I'll see you in a few." Then she's gone.

I clutch the steering wheel for a long moment, and then pull away, leaving her trailing behind the car. A few minutes later, I park next to my trailer, my hand landing on the warm seat she just vacated. Closing my eyes, I breathe in her vanilla scent.

Forcing my eyes open, I get out of the car and collect our bags. I reach my trailer and am about to pull out my key but realize someone's already inside. So it begins.

I open the door and walk up the steps. "Chase, you made it."

"Hey, Thomas." I place our bag next to her work suitcase. "How are you feeling?"

"Much better. I'm about at ninety percent. You never got it?"

I shake my head. "Getting away from everything felt good, though. I feel like a new man." Not a lie.

My PA checks me up and down. "You look good, man. Better than I've seen you look in a long time."

Instead of responding, I slap him on the back. Opening the refrigerator, I grab one of my favorite specialty waters.

The trailer door opens and my heart begins to thump like an audio mixer was creating the score. Melody bounds up the steps, sees I'm not alone, and drops her head.

"Hi, Melody," Thomas says. "How are you feeling?"

She fidgets with her purse strap. "I think I'm almost back to one normal-ish. How about you?" Melody gives me the side-eye as she passes to get to her design suitcase.

"Not quite that good but getting better," Thomas responds.

"Some bug, huh?" She offers me a pair of black boxer briefs.

I busy myself by leaving for the bathroom. If Thomas weren't here, I'd demand she settle me into these. With pleasant thoughts about how such a feat might go, I reenter the main area in only the underwear. When my eyes land on her, my cock stirs.

Corkscrew turns with buses coming straight at me.

Sheer vertical drops into the water without any guardrails.

Wrinkles.

I try to think of anything to divert my body's reaction to being so near to my woman when I'm barely wearing any clothes. Thomas accomplishes this feat without even trying when he says, "So, Chase, we have a lot of ground to cover." My libido dies.

While Thomas goes over post-shoot plans, Melody starts sewing my left leg into the costume. The questions continue, and I know I have to involve Melody in the decision-making.

"Let's recap. I've got you down for the fitting with Versace the week after we wrap here. That'll give them enough time to make any needed alterations before the red carpet. Hair appointment for the morning of. Plus, you'll be at all the pre-parties except for the two the weekend after this shoot." He clicks his pen. "Where are you going after Amalfi?"

Put on the spot like this, I reply without thought. "Chicago. I haven't been home to visit my folks for a while and want to check in."

He nods and scribbles it down on his notepad. I lock eyes with Melody and she does a slow blink at me. Resisting the urge to pull out the damn knitting needles keeping her hair back in that austere bun, I return my attention to my PA.

"I'll make your reservations for Chicago. Will you be staying with your parents?"

Two problems arise. First, they have to be reservations for two. And second, what will our sleeping arrangements be while we're there? "That's okay. I'll make the reservations."

The color on his face is replaced with a greenish hue. Is he going into relapse? In a strangled voice, he says, "Are you sure? I mean, I always do your travel." He clicks his pen several times.

Melody's hand wraps around my calf. "Sorry to interrupt, but, Chase"—she pauses at the use of my stage name, which sounds weird from her lips now—"could you please move your leg. I want to be sure it's all set."

Thank God for her. Focusing all my attention on the task at hand, I shake my leg and walk around. Pride at her competence grows. "Feels great."

"I think I'm getting the hang of this," she replies, running her hands up and down my inner leg, paying special attention to the spot behind my knee. Gah.

"I think you are."

Her eyelashes flutter. "You know, the thought of going home after this shoot sounds like a good one, Thomas. My parents keep my room and a guest one ready at all times."

Thank you, Melody. Giving my leg one more shake, I look at my clueless PA. "Good idea. I think I'll stay with my parents, so there's really no need for you to worry about my trip to Chicago." After which, I'll have to go to LA and she'll be back in NYC gearing up for the HBO show. Hiding my disappointment, I instruct him to get me all set for my trip west for the damned red carpet.

Melody makes a show of plumping her pillow on the floor at my feet and looks up at me. Her mouth is even with my cock. She closes her eyes and licks her lips, and my body responds as predicted. A knowing grin tugs at her lips. Fuck.

Her fingers run up my right inner thigh. I brace for her onslaught, which comes with remarkable speed. Her hand closes around me and she squeezes, eliciting a moan from me.

"Are you okay, Chase?"

With my eyes closed, I step back from the temptress on her knees and respond to Thomas. "Yeah." Think quick. "Trying to get into character, you know?"

"Oh, all right. I'll leave you to that." He consults his notebook. "I have enough to keep me busy." He clicks his pen several times. "Catch you later, Chase. Melody."

The door closes behind him, and Melody lets out a howl of laughter.

"Not funny, Goldie."

She laughs so hard that tears stream down her face. "Getting hot and bothered there, Char—Chase?"

My restraint breaks. Bending down, I reach under her arms and yank her upright and slam my mouth onto her willing one. I mold her body against mine.

The trailer door opens and we spring apart. "Hey, Chasey, how are you feeling?" Jessa's voice precedes her into the trailer.

I do a one-eighty and give her my back, all the while trying to calm my body down. For her part, Melody jumps in front of me.

"Hi, Jessa," Melody says. "Is this your costume for today?"

"Oh, no. I thought I'd stop by and check in on Chasey here before heading to wardrobe."

While I futz at the refrigerator, Melody approaches Jessa. "Well, I've finished up one leg of his costume and need his undivided attention to get the other one done for call time. Perhaps you could stop by when you're done with your clothes. And makeup." She hustles her toward the door. "Your hair looks great, though."

"Well, all right. I'll check back in when I'm ready for the shoot. Bye, Chasey!" The door closes behind her.

I applaud my girlfriend's ingenuity. "Well played, Goldie."

She bows. "Thanks. I didn't think you wanted to talk with her right this second." Her eyes drift downward, then she pouts. "She ruined all my hard work."

I chuckle. "*Your* hard work? Felt like it was my hardness." I rub my crotch.

"Letch!"

I glance at the clock and grimace. "As much as I'd love to pick up where we left off, you really need to get me into this costume. No more wandering hands." I slant her a piercing glare.

She lifts her pinky to mine. "Pinky swear."

I lock my little finger with hers and she gets back on her knees and starts in on my right leg. "So, are you okay with going to Chicago after we wrap? Will it be cool for me to stay at your family's?"

Melody continues the intricate stitches. "Yeah, I'm fine with going to Chicago. My parents won't ever let me stay in a hotel. As for you . .

." Her shoulders raise, then lower. "Never done that before, but there's a first time for everything."

"I'm honored. If your parents have an issue with it, I can stay with my folks, no problem. Although, we'll have to find time to sneak in a few quickies." I wink at her.

She continues to sew me in my costume and, in much less time than before, she finishes. "There. Try that out."

As I walk around the trailer, she stands and shakes out her legs, grimacing with the movements. "Are your legs bothering you?"

"It's not the easiest position, but I'm good."

Dropping to my knees in front of her, I let my fingers trail down both of her legs, massaging them. She moans. "That feels so good." I end my impromptu massage with kisses behind both of her knees.

She laughs. Carefree and happy. Which, in turn, lifts my spirits. After putting on the now infamous gloves, we spend the next minutes wrangling me into the top part of the costume. "I'll get your boots while you snap in," she directs.

I open my legs and let the material hang. "I don't think so."

"What?"

I look down toward my cock and then back to her. "As my dresser, I think you need to do your job."

"Oh you do, do you?"

"Yep."

My boots clatter to the floor as she stands in front of me. "I guess I can't shirk my responsibilities."

"Nope." I let the "P" sound pop off my tongue, prompting a giggle from her. Drawing her in, I kiss her lips. "Now, go do your duty."

She mock salutes me and falls to her knees. Again. I widen my stance. She grabs for the snaps.

"Easy. You're dealing with some pretty important cargo."

In a husky voice, she replies, "Very true."

She traces my dick over the underwear and I reconsider whether this is a good idea. Before my body gets too aroused, I snap my fingers. "Eyes on the prize."

"Oh, they are." Without moving her head, she looks up at me and snaps the top of my costume closed. "Done," she breathes.

"I might be."

She giggles and stands up, then her face turns serious as she makes minor adjustments to my costume. Satisfied, she orders me to put on the socks and boots.

"The price is a kiss."

She beams at me. "Gladly." Wrapping her arms around my neck, she gives me one, complete with her tongue.

"Damn. I wish I wasn't sewn into this outfit. I'd like to—"

"Shhh. Save your creativity for later, Charles. Now it's time to turn into the good doctor."

I wish I could argue with her, but I can't. Instead, I shove my feet into the boots and pick up the mask. "How do I look?"

She appraises me, making additional adjustments. "Great. I'm happy with your outfit. Are you?"

I steal one final kiss. "I am because you did it for me."

"Judith designed it."

I shrug. "Whatever. You make this Doctor very happy."

The trailer door opens again, and Judith herself walks in, carrying a tissue. She's still a bit green around the edges. "How are you feeling, Judith?"

"Been better, been worse. I wanted to come and check out the costume before you head out to the set."

I stand still while she walks around, assessing Melody's handiwork.

"Looks good."

Judith picks up my hand and studies the gloves. "These are expertly done. Form a fist, please." I comply. "Yes, very good."

Melody's blushing, this time from her boss's praise. I let her bask for a few moments. "Am I ready for the cameras, ladies?"

Judith nods. "Yes."

She motions for Melody to leave the trailer first. My eyes don't wander farther than her delectable ass.

MELODY

Today's shoot went well, with no problems with wardrobe. To my eyes, Charles gave his best performance to date. Hopefully, I've had a hand in that. During the shoot, Judith pulled me and Helene aside to refine wardrobe issues for the extras in tomorrow's shoot, which we figured out. I like to think my ideas were more innovative than Helene's. Assuming Judith gets the job on Noble's next movies, I send up one more prayer that the lead costume designer position becomes mine.

With light footsteps, I skip toward Charles's trailer. When I enter, it's filled with people. Jessa is there, sniffing around my man again. Seriously? Plus, Mark and of course, Thomas. I stifle the frustration overcoming me, wanting to be alone with my boyfriend. He's a big star and has many obligations.

I go to my design suitcase and remove the scissors and other things I need to get Charles out of the costume.

Charles mocks, "Uh-oh, folks, shit's getting real. The scissors are out."

I open and close them a few times in rapid succession. Mark claps him on the back, "We'll leave you to it." He passes me and stops. I freeze. Has he figured out about Charles and me? He turns his head.

"Hey, Chase, want to go out on a yacht tonight? A friend of a friend is in Positano and invited me."

"Sounds cool, man," Charles says while looking at me. "Let me get out of this suit and I'll let you know. I have to go over the lines for tomorrow."

Mark addresses Thomas. "Want to join me?"

The PA clicks his pen. "Thanks for the invite. I'd love to."

Mark nods and heads toward the door. On his way, he does a two-step with Jessa, whispering something in her ear that makes her tap his chest. Holding the door handle, he tosses, "Melody, you're welcome to come as well. Bring your friend, Sophia."

Jessa appears at Charles's side, and I snap the scissors harder. When she kisses him, I almost break them into two.

"See ya later," Charles calls as Jessa walks down the aisle toward the door, his gaze never straying from mine communicating the kiss was an act. *Of her making.*

When Thomas takes a seat and pulls out his clipboard, Charles reaches between his legs and unsnaps the bodysuit. I help him get out of it and throw away the soaked undershirt. No matter how breathable we tried to make it for him, the suit still makes him sweat.

Charles sits next to his PA and removes his boots, tossing the socks into the garbage as well. The two men refine the details for tomorrow's shoot and longer-range plans.

I motion for Charles to stand so I can cut him out of the leggings. Because Thomas is still here, I try to be as quick as possible for my boyfriend. After I free Charles's left leg, Thomas stands.

"I think I'm good here. Will I see you on the yacht tonight?"

Charles's knee bounces, the material flapping. "Not sure yet."

Thomas clicks his pen, says goodbye to us, and leaves. Finally alone, Charles opens his arms and I fly right into them. My head resting against his chiseled pecs, I let my fingers wander over the muscled expanse of his back.

"I've been wanting to do this all day," he murmurs in my ear before kissing me senseless.

Stepping back, I look into his passion-laden eyes. "Let's get you out of the rest of the costume." He rolls his hips and I get back to work, which doesn't take long.

Soon, Charles stands before me in only the black boxer briefs, and his hand goes to his waistband. My mouth waters as he slowly—oh, so slowly—teases me by pulling down one side, and then the other, until he stands naked in front of me.

I place my index finger to my lips and walk around him, examining every square inch of his sculpted body. "Damn, Mr. Wainwright," I drawl as if from the South, "you're a mighty fine specimen."

He throws his head back and laughs, then reaches out and grabs me around my waist. "You, my dear Goldie, are my Aurumite." His lips descend on mine. I let my hand roam lower, cupping his hard ass. I pinch.

"Did you just goose me?"

"Yep. But it wasn't satisfying 'cause it's so hard."

He rubs against me. "Not the only thing on me that way." He kisses me again.

Hyperaware we shouldn't be doing this in his unlocked trailer, which seems to have no privacy, I take a step back. "Charles, I'm not feeling safe in here, if you know what I mean." I cast my eyes toward the door.

His face turns from teasing to understanding. "I get it. Let's take this back to my hotel."

"That's an idea I can get behind." I slap him on the butt as he selects a pair of workout shorts and puts them on, commando.

I'm fixing up my design suitcase when a knock sounds. "Geez."

Charles shouts over me, "Come in."

I busy myself with finishing my task when the new intruder makes herself known. In a very big way. "Charles! So good to see you!"

The hemming tape slips from my fingers. It can't be.

"Lindsay!"

Oh God. His sister is here. All the feelings of insecurity that plagued my childhood rush to the fore. She made my life a living hell. I figured I'd have to see her sometime, but thought it would be back in Chicago, not here. In Italy. The most romantic place on earth just got ruined. I slam my design suitcase closed and grasp the overnight bag Charles had stashed behind it.

Aware of how I feel toward his sister, Charles licks his lips. In a forced upbeat tone, he introduces us. Again. "Lindsay, I believe you know our assistant costume designer, Melody Hunte. Melody, my sister Lindsay."

I place the overnight bag at my feet and draw to my full height. Lindsay Wainwright, in the flesh, stands before me. My back goes straight and my chin rises. "Lindsay. What brings you here?"

For her part, Lindsay's eyes travel down my body, but I refuse to be cowed. I'm no longer a child and she can't do anything to demean me. "Melody. I'm surprised to see you." She shakes her head, then looks at Charles. "I came to see my big brother, of course."

Mimicking her response, I repeat, "Of course." I look between the two of them. Both tall, dark-haired, and blue-eyed. Only she sports deep wrinkles around her mouth. At least I don't have wrinkles. "Well, I should be going. I will see you back here tomorrow at six a.m., Chase."

"Wait." He grabs my arm.

I look at his hand, then at his sister and back up at him. "Looks like you have a big evening ahead. A yacht cruise with your sister," I whisper.

His eyes plead with me, but I'm not going to let Lindsay get her hooks back into me. Of all people, she can't find out about our relationship. Not yet. I gentle my voice. "You'll have a nice visit." I fake a yawn. "Besides, I'm sort of tired. It's been a long few days and I hardly got any sleep."

My last words bring a grin to his face. "Yeah, I hear you on that score." In a louder voice, he says, "I'm thinking of skipping the yacht to have dinner with the little runt." He nods toward his sister.

"Hey." Lindsay punches his arm. "Who are you calling a runt, Godzilla?"

He chuckles. While I'm happy to see he has a good relationship with his sister, I don't need to witness it up close and personal. I pick up the bag again. "I'll leave you to it."

When I'm almost at the door, Charles says, "I'm thinking we should meet up here more like five a.m. tomorrow. Distractions can slow us down."

Despite his sister being here, his words make my core clench. "Okay. Have a good evening, Chase. Lindsay." I escape the confines of the trailer and stumble back to my hotel.

～

"Why the hell did she have to come here?" I'm whining and I know it.

Sophia sighs. "Well, she *is* his sister." She takes another sip of her Cosmo. "So, tell me, how are things between you and Charles?"

Still fuming over Lindsay's appearance, I grab a piece of bread from the breadbasket and dip it into olive oil. "Good. I mean, real good." I take a bite and the deliciousness eases my annoyance somewhat. "He's wonderful, you know?"

She laughs. "No, I don't 'know.' Care to enlighten me?"

With a dreamy expression, I tell her about our weekend. Not all the details, of course, but she's a smart girl.

The server brings us our meals as we look out to the water. A huge yacht lumbers by, to which I point with my fork. "That must be Mark's friend's yacht. You really should've gone, you know. Thomas is on it."

She tastes her pomodoro sauce and moans. "And miss this amazing meal with my bestie?"

I steal a taste and agree. "Wow." Digging into my own chicken dish —not broiled, thank you very much—I ask, "Aren't you interested in Thomas anymore?"

"I am, but Mark's a, a distraction. He's everywhere I am, and it's kinda weird. When I was sick, so was he, and yet he left me chicken soup every day outside my door."

"That was nice of him."

"Thomas saw me once, across the street from the drug store, and gave me a half-hearted wave."

"I'm sorry, girl. I know you were into him. But Mark seems to be a nice guy."

She busies herself with her pasta. "He's a manwhore."

"So was Charles."

My bestie shovels some food into her mouth. "Mark's always looking for his next score. I've heard he has one conquest per movie he works on, and leaves her in the dust when it wraps. I want no part of that."

"I could talk with Charles about him."

"No way!" Her finger roams around the rim of her glass. "Mark is who he is. He's not for me."

"If it makes you feel any better, Thomas doesn't have much time for anything but a meaningless fling. Charles keeps him very busy." With silly stuff that he should be doing for himself, like booking his own flights.

She taps her fork against the side of her dish. "Really?"

I nod. "I tried to work your name into their conversation today, but I couldn't get a word in edgewise. He has a full plate. But you know, Mark did specifically ask me to invite you onto the yacht. In front of everyone in the trailer—Charles, Thomas, and Jessa."

"Jessa was there?"

I cut a piece of chicken. "Yup."

Sophia eats a few forkfuls. "Okay, enough about me and my dismal love life. What are your plans with Charles?"

I like the fact she uses his real name even if it is a deflection. "We're going to go to Chicago after we wrap here. Then, I'll have to return to New York City, while he has to go to LA for the red carpet for *I Was Made for Her*."

"Why don't you go with him? I don't think you're needed at HBO so soon."

I shake my head. "Only you know we're dating. If I walked the red carpet with him, it would be everywhere."

"And that would be bad because?"

"Can't you read the headlines now? 'Daughter of Braxton Hunte Dating Hollywood's Heartthrob.' No, thank you."

"Now, Mel, you're going to have to get over that. You *are* his daughter. Charles *is* Hollywood's heartthrob. So what? You're an amazing costume designer. No matter who he dates, the gossip columns are going to have a field day. Ignore them."

If only it were that easy. "I know I'll get there, Sophia, but not yet. I need more time."

"How does Charles feel about sneaking around?"

"We're not sneaking." I drop my fork. "Not really."

Sophia reaches across the table and places her hand on top of mine. "I know, honey. It's hard because he's the lead. I also know you don't want to be seen as going from being Braxton's daughter to Chase's girlfriend."

My eyes land on the white tablecloth and I smooth out a nonexistent wrinkle.

She presses, "Am I right?"

"Yes," I whisper. I force my gaze to lock with hers. "Can you blame me? I love my dad so much, but I need to be valued for my own skills. And . . ."

She waits for me to continue. "And what?"

My boyfriend elbows everything out of his way, taking over all space in my brain. I'm overwhelmed by the rush of emotions, as my stomach performs major backflips, all my limbs tingle, and heat bathes my entire body. I glance at my bestie, who's leaning forward in her seat urging me to spill.

I gulp. "And, I think I'm in love with Charles." Hearing the words out loud makes my heart beat erratically. "I haven't told him yet," I whisper.

"You will when the time is right." She leans back in her chair and beams at me. "I'm so happy for you. Try not to overthink all of this. At the same time, don't push him away from you, either."

I brush my palms together, wiping away the dampness. That's it. I need a break from all things Charles. When the waiter takes away our dirty dishes, I ask, "Want to get a gelato?"

"Now you're talking."

We make our way deeper into the town until we end up at my favorite gelato shop. The woman behind the counter recognizes me and reaches for a cup without asking my flavors.

Sophia elbows my torso. "Come here much?"

"Basically every day after filming." I rub my stomach. "This will end once I'm back in New York."

"I get it. There's nothing like real Italian gelato."

I take my cup from the clerk and Sophia places her order. Once she gets hers, we start walking back to our hotel. "Charles never eats anything as decadent as this."

"Must be tough being so in shape."

I giggle. "There isn't any fat on his body, that's for sure."

"Not even a jiggle?"

I savor the hazelnut gelato before responding. "Nope. Could bounce a euro off his ass."

Laughing, we toss our empty cups into a garbage can and continue walking beside the water to our hotel. I leave her at her door and continue into mine, and flop down onto the bed. The very empty bed. Against my better judgment, I grab my phone and send a text to Charles.

> Had a great dinner with Sophia. Hope you are enjoying your visit with your sister.

I keep my personal thoughts about Lindsay out of the text and drop the phone onto the bed. He doesn't respond.

Sighing, I get up, brush my teeth, and wash my face. I pull out a pair of pajamas and get myself into bed. Turning my head, I look at the empty pillow. "Good night, my love." I turn off the lamp and my eyes close.

Until a knock drives them open.

CHASE

I stand in the empty hallway in front of Melody's door. Pulling my fist back, I rap. It's only nine thirty, so she still could be out on Mark's friend's yacht. I mask my probable disappointment. While she was at a luxurious party, I was eating in the hotel's restaurant with my sister. It was an unexpected surprise to see her, and I'm glad we caught up. I know Melody told me she treated her terribly growing up, but that's ages old. Lindsay's been through so much. My guilt hasn't subsided, no matter how well she's recovering.

My thoughts scatter when the door opens and a drowsy Melody stands before me in the cutest pajamas I've ever seen. Not that I've seen too many, actually. Usually women wear sexy lingerie. Not one of them were as sexy as her.

My brain escapes me, all my finesse lost. "Hi."

"Charles." She plays with her long, loose hair, which hangs past her shoulders. She startles and jumps back into the room. "Come in."

"Thanks." I join her inside and she closes the door.

She looks like a jumpy cat. Where did this weirdness between us come from? "I won't stay if you don't want me to."

"No. I mean, yes, I do want you to stay."

Relief rushes through me. "I'm glad, because I definitely want to stay with you. Were you sleeping?"

"Not really. I had my eyes closed, but couldn't relax."

She's a bad liar, but I go with it. "Oh." I reach out and rub her shoulders. "Need a massage?"

"Mmmm, feels good."

"Let's get on the bed so I can give you a proper one." I turn her body toward the bed and tap her ass. "Now get on your stomach."

Obediently, she lies down as instructed and I straddle her. Leaving her shirt on, I run my fingers beneath the soft fabric and focus my attention on making her relax. Given her satisfied moans, I'm doing a good job.

"Charles, if you continue this, I'll be asleep in no time."

I lean down and kiss the back of her neck. In her ear, I reply, "Then I'll cover you up with the blanket so you can get your rest."

She twists so she now faces me, her hands landing on my shoulders. "Stay. Please."

My cheeks inflate. "Since you asked so nicely."

I toss my shirt over my head. Then I discard my pants and shoes. Wearing only my underwear, I slide next to her.

"I pictured you here with me, you know."

"You did?"

She nods. "And here you are."

I raise one eyebrow. "What was I doing? In your fantasy, I mean."

"Sleeping."

"I can do that." I close my eyes and pretend to forget the warm woman lying next to me. And the insistence of my lower half.

Her hand lands on my cheek, and her finger traces my lips. Without opening my eyes, I snag the digit and suck it into my mouth. "I thought you said sleep."

"I may have been mistaken. You must've fallen asleep after I wore you out."

My eyelids pop open. "Just how did such a slip of a woman do that to big old me?"

She giggles. "It started like this." Her hands drift down my abdomen, caressing the definition of my ab muscles, causing them to jump and my breathing to hitch.

"Then I did this." She pinches the waistband of my underwear.

I grab her wrist. "Uh-oh." Her quizzical look makes me drape my leg over hers. "I think it's my turn." I unbutton her top and peel it open, my eyes zeroing in on her nipples, which come to points. I lean over and suckle, her back arching against me.

"Charles."

Moving between the two peaks, I wait for her to do the thing she does in the back of her throat that lets me know she's ready for more. I want to give her more. So much more.

"Oh, yeah." Her arms wrap around my neck and then she makes *the* noise.

I rear back, my eyes now fixated on her pajama bottoms. With a quick motion, I slide them off her body so she's naked before me. "Goldie, you're so beautiful." I position myself between her open legs. My tongue circles her clit.

Melody's head thrashes against the pillows, and her body contracts. Inserting my index finger into her channel, her body's slickness welcomes me.

"Yes, please!"

I continue my assault until her core clenches around my now two fingers, and she cries out in pleasure. Pleased at the orgasm I gave her, I make quick work of my underwear and toss them over the side of the bed.

"Charles." Her hand to the center of my stomach stops me.

"Melody," I reply, kissing her lips and tangling our tongues.

Her hand drops lower and encircles my straining cock. She rubs over my head and brings my pre-cum to her mouth. Those movements are my undoing. Grabbing her arms, I toss them over her head, line up, and enter her body with my own. On my first thrust, I'm overwhelmed with how wet and tight she feels around me. Sensation after sensation rocks my body, unlike anything I've experienced before.

I've never felt this before.

I thrust again.

Bareback.

"Shit. Condom."

Her head whips against the pillow as I try to drag my unwilling body out of hers. "Can you pull out at the last second?"

Inside her body, I try to consider her question. I've never done this before. "Guess there's a first time for everything."

"I trust you."

Her words, coupled with her crossing her ankles around my back, makes me want to make her see stars. She trusts me. *Me.* And she knows more about the real Charles than anyone else. I circle my hips, hitting her in the spot that guarantees her another explosive climax. I don't have to wait long before she screams out again.

Enflamed, I piston in and out of her body. A tingle runs up my spine. Using all my concentration, I pull out of her warm pussy. Holding my throbbing erection, I come all over the tits I had cherished earlier. With effort, I collapse to her side.

She flings her arm over her face. "Wow."

"Agreed."

I wait a minute for my gasping to drop to a mere pant and roll off the bed. In the bathroom, I grab a towel and wet it. Returning to the bedroom, I wipe my seed off her body, ending with a nibble on both nipples. Tossing the towel on the floor, I return to her bed.

Eyes like liquid amber meet mine as her hands encircle my neck. "How can this get better every time we do it?"

I kiss the tip of her nose. "Because of you."

She rests her head on my shoulder and I hold her tight. I've never once considered myself a cuddler, but with her, I love it. I squeeze her naked back, inhaling her fresh scent. "Go to sleep, Goldie."

Her breathing evens out, and I follow her into slumber.

All too soon, my alarm goes off. Turning to shut off my cell before Melody awakens, I slip out of her bed and gather my clothes. I need to get back to my hotel and work out before meeting up with her in my trailer.

I gaze down at the sleeping beauty who pushes me to do more. To be better. To be myself. Like she does. Bending down, I kiss her cheek and whisper, "See you soon." She doesn't move.

Gathering my clothes, I put them on and return to my hotel. Given the ungodly hour, no one else is up and about. After a pit stop in my room to change into workout clothes, I head to the gym. For the first time, I'm not alone.

"Hey there, Doc."

"Mark! Surprised to see you here, dude." I shake his hand and make my way to an elliptical.

"Yeah, figured I should do something to eradicate last night's debauchery."

I chuckle as I start on the machine. "How was the yacht?"

"It was fucking amazing. Too much to eat and drink. The pasta!" He rubs his belly before hitting the weight bench. "Only thing that sucked was Sophia wasn't there. And where were you? I thought you were going to go?"

"My sister showed up unexpectedly, so I went out to dinner with her." I keep the rest of my night to myself, honoring Melody's wishes.

"Sweet."

He does his reps while the incline pushes me harder. Deciding twenty minutes of cardio is enough for today, I do the cool down and head toward the pull-up bar. Mark's now at the rower.

"You didn't happen to see Sophia while you were out, did you?"

I shake my head.

"I don't know what it is about her, but she has all my attention. I turned down a couple of women last night. What's wrong with me?"

Resting between sets, I reply, "Sounds like you got it bad."

"It's probably because she's been dissing me. If she deigned to talk with me, I'd be on to another woman by now."

Hand on the bar, I reply, "I don't know. She might be the one for you." I begin this round while stifled outrage comes from the rower.

"Exactly what would you know about finding 'the one'?" He heads over to some boxes and jumps.

Dropping from the bar, I consider my words carefully. I know a ton about it now, all because of Goldie. "Oh, I don't know, Mark.

Seems to me it happens when you least expect it." I shrug. "From what I've observed, you know."

He huffs, and not simply from exertion. "Whatever. Are you ready for today's shoot?"

In between exercising, we discuss the upcoming scene and make a few minor changes to our approaches. We're starting to film the movie's climax, where I'm going to manipulate his DNA so it attacks itself and kills Mr. A. We're both more than eager to wrap up and get back to our real lives.

I clap his back. "I'll see you on set. Need to shower and get over to my trailer for costuming."

He smirks. "Put in a good word with Melody for me. She's Sophia's best friend and the only shot I have at getting to her."

"I'll try."

Returning to my room, I shower and dress in record time. Soon, I'm in my trailer grabbing a specialty water. The door opens and a grin crosses my face to welcome my dresser. A brunette walks in instead of the gold I was expecting.

"Lindsay," falls out of my mouth.

"Hey there. I wanted to spend as much time as possible with you today before I have to head back to Switzerland bright and early tomorrow morning."

Tamping down my disappointment that Melody isn't here, I invite my sister in and offer her a water. She holds up her coffee cup.

"So, this is where you're transformed into Doctor Manipul8?"

"Yeah. Melody does a great job, even if it takes two hours to get me into the suit."

"Two hours is a crazy-long time." She wanders around the trailer, touching the bottom half of the costume draped over a chair. "It seems weird that they couldn't have made the leggings like normal pants. No one else I know ever has to get their pants sewn on them."

I chuckle at her words, which resemble my initial griping. "I know what you mean. But these fit me like second skin yet don't look like women's tights."

She smiles. "I guess there's something to be said for that." She wanders to the back and opens the closet door where the bodysuit part hangs. She takes out the hanger. "This is some fine workmanship, Charles."

From my vantage point, she studies the torso part, then turns it around. The door opens again, and my blond beauty ascends. Needing to warn her of Lindsay's presence, I rush to the front.

"Just so you know, Lindsay's here," I whisper.

She stiffens, then throws her shoulders back. "Thanks for telling me."

I need to get these two together so they can air out their differences—they both have so much to say. If Melody is going to be a part of my family—which I'm hoping she will be—they need to get along. Not now. We haven't come out as a couple to anyone besides Sophia and I don't think Lindsay is at the top of Goldie's list. Melody brushes by me and heads for her work-station.

Swallowing a sigh, I return to her side and take the boxer briefs from her hand. Nodding toward the bathroom, I say, "I'll go change." Damn my sister. I had high hopes for this session.

Melody busies herself with setting up the area for me to get sewn into the leggings. On my way to the bathroom, I stop next to my sister, who straightens from her inspection of the bodysuit.

"Hey, I'm getting into costume now. Do you want to stick around here, or catch up later?"

Her eyes trail to the front area when Melody drops her pillow to the ground. Lindsay's mouth tightens. "I can see we won't get any quality time together now. How about lunch on set?"

"Sounds good, runt."

She swats my arm. "Go get 'em, Godzilla. I'll catch you later."

I enter the bathroom, clicking the door shut. Lindsay's footsteps lead her toward the exit and, against my better judgment, I open the door a crack. The two women say each other's names, then Lindsay exits the trailer. Expelling my pent-up breath, I close the door with a snick and change into the boxer briefs. Airing of grievances will have to happen at a later time.

On bare feet, I stride back into the trailer and approach my woman, who's muttering something. "What'd I miss, Goldie?"

She twirls around to face me. "What?"

She scans my body. I can't help myself and flex. Her eyes widen.

I prompt, "You were saying?"

"Oh! Nothing. Nothing at all." She glances at the clock. "We really should get going on your costume, Charles. No matter how scrumptious you look right now."

I puff up. "I like the sound of that."

She giggles. "I bet you do."

The door to the trailer opens again and she rushes to grab the open-seamed leggings. I pull the waistband up and she's adjusting the material around my legs when Thomas appears.

"Hey, Chase. Missed you last night."

"My sister showed up, and we went out to dinner."

At my words, Melody falls to the pillow on the floor at my feet. She goes about stretching the fabric around my left thigh.

Thomas clicks his pen and starts in on today's schedule. Time flies and soon I'm clad from the waist down. "Excuse me, Char—Chase, can you please walk around so I can ensure the fit?"

"Of course."

I obey her command, and she makes a few more adjustments. "Looks good. Now put on your gloves while I get the bodysuit."

Thomas brings me the silk material, which I slide onto my hands and up my arm. "I'm going to leave you to finish up in here. I'll take care of everything we discussed." He turns to walk away but stops. "Oh, I almost forgot to ask, who are you taking with you to the red carpet for *I Was Made for Her*? I need to let the studio know."

Melody. I want to show her off. Hell, I want to scream our relationship from the rooftops. But I can't. "I haven't given much thought to it. Why don't you select someone for me?"

My PA nods. "What about Lindsay? Being with your sister will guarantee positive press."

From the back of the trailer, Melody drops something, causing both of our heads to swivel. I call out, "You okay back there?"

"Yeah."

I really need to get my sister and my girlfriend together. Their childhood rivalry isn't good for either of them. I return my attention to Thomas, sideswiping his question. "She'll be in Switzerland for a bit."

"Oh, okay." His pen clicks a few times. "Want to run a contest from your social media fans? Winner gets a date?"

"What am I? Eighteen? No. Just pick someone."

"Fine. The studio wants a name soon." With that parting shot, he leaves.

Exhaling, I stalk toward the back of the trailer and grab the body-suit out of Melody's hands. "I know you want to keep our relationship a secret, but it's tougher than I thought it would be. I want to take you to the premiere."

I start to step into the costume but, at the last minute, change my mind and put it over my head. Maybe this peace offering will break the ice?

Her lips widen into a beautiful smile. "I know," she replies in a softer tone, helping me with the tight material. Which does slip down my body with much more ease than feet first. "I need more time to wrap my head around all this."

"Don't take too long."

Her lips purse. Once I'm situated in the suit, she directs me to do the snaps. Guess my olive branch fractured. Despite having done this countless times, I have a tough time with the damn things. Finally sorted, I put on the socks and boots, pick up my mask, and head toward the front of the trailer.

Before I reach the door, I say, "See you on set."

Quick steps race down the hallway, and a kiss lands on my cheek. "Break a leg."

With her lips still sizzling on my face, I make my way to Noble and we begin shooting. Things are moving fast now, as everyone seems to feel the electricity in the air. The movie's almost done and everything's running smoothly.

In the middle of a take, I run down the cobblestoned street toward where Jessa's character is being held hostage. I shout, "Aurelia!"

As I run, something feels funny.

A breeze where there shouldn't be any.

My bodysuit flies open from between my legs and bunches at my torso.

MELODY

Noble calls "action," and the actors hit their marks. Judith, who sits next to me, whispers, "I was told I'm on the short list."

"Oh, Judith, that's wonderful!"

On her other side, Helene agrees. "Yes, I have no doubts that you'll be chosen. Then you'll have to name your successor on the show."

As filming progressed, Helene has been more and more pushy about taking over Judith's job. I've been quiet about my ambition, rather proving my worth by my work. However, since Judith's promotion seems more likely than before, I chime in, "Will you make that decision, or will the execs at HBO?"

Judith's eyes trail the actors. "It's basically my call, with their final blessing. I have to say, I've been impressed with both of your work, on the set and here. Maybe I should withdraw my name from Noble's list so I won't have to make this decision."

I smile at her joke. No way would she turn this offer down. Helene, however, puts her hand on Judith's forearm. "Don't do that, Judith. You've worked too hard to turn back now."

"Don't worry, Helene. I was only kidding."

I watch as Charles runs through the street, screaming for his "girlfriend" who's being held by Mark. Frowning, I lean forward. Something's not exactly right with his costume.

He runs and the bodysuit unsnaps, giving the whole set a peek at his fine ass, even if it's covered by the boxer briefs.

"Oh my God," I mutter and jump out of my seat. I rush to his side while chaos erupts. Judith and Helene are hard on my heels.

I grab the material around Charles's abdomen, which should have been securely held in place by the snaps. "Let me look at this!"

Before I can examine it, Helene pushes in and runs her fingers over the snaps.

In a brusque voice, Judith demands, "What happened?" Noble mirrors her sentiment, using more colorful descriptors.

I stand, helpless, while Helene points to something on the bodysuit and Judith ducks her head to inspect it.

My eyes go to Charles, who's surrounded by women prodding his body. The part that belongs to *me*. He removes the mask, which I take from him, and stormy blue eyes meet mine. "Another wardrobe malfunction?"

"I don't know what happened yet," I whisper, still unable to see whatever they're prodding.

He clears his throat. "Ladies, if you wouldn't mind, can I get out of this thing?"

Feeling embarrassed for him, I nod. "Yes, let's get you to your trailer."

He shrugs. "I can strip out of this damn costume right here. Just don't feel like having my junk poked when you really only need the bodysuit."

Heap my own embarrassment on top of me now. I shoo the hands away and reach for the bottom of the costume. Together, Charles and I pull it up his body.

Noble yells, "Everyone, take a lunch break." Turning back to us, he levels me with a withering stare. "Get this fixed. I want to know what happened."

"Yes, sir," I reply, redoubling my efforts to get Charles out of the bodysuit. His furious reaction when his glove got tangled in the boy's hair replays in my head, making me less effective.

"Step aside, Melody," Judith demands. She takes over the removal process while I'm relegated to onlooker again. Within minutes, she has my boyfriend out of the costume and takes a long look at the snaps.

What happened to that bodysuit? I checked everything so carefully today, like all days. Nothing was wrong.

Judith holds up the material and moves the snaps, which somehow are loose. "How did this happen, Melody?"

My stomach tightens. "I don't know. It looked fine in the trailer."

Charles pipes up. "I had a little trouble snapping them today."

Shit. This is what my career needed right now. I look at him. "Why didn't you tell me?"

"I thought everything was okay, since I was able to snap them."

Judith lowers the bodysuit. "Looks like regular wear and tear."

I step over and lock my gaze with the woman for whose HBO job I'm vying. "May I see it?"

She passes the bodysuit to me. "Is the other suit wearable?"

"Yes." Thank God I thought to get the other one cleaned and asked Sophia to pick it up for me. With only two suits made, I didn't want to take a chance of a spill. Of course, I never considered this could be a possibility.

Behind me, Helene snarks, "That's lucky."

Ignoring her, I examine the bodysuit. The material around the snaps looks worn. But something's not right. The snaps themselves are loose as well. How could this have happened? It's almost as if someone did something to them, the dissolution is so perfect. How could that be?

Lindsay comes up to our pow-wow. "Is everything going to be okay?"

Today's events rearrange in my head. White-hot heat sears through me. "You!"

All eyes turn to me. I hold up the bodysuit. "This wasn't any regular wear and tear. I shake the bodysuit. "This was pushed along somehow. Maybe by a solvent of some sort." I give my childhood nemesis the evil eye. "What did you do?"

Judith is the first to speak. "Melody, the material simply wore out. As you said, you have the other bodysuit all ready for Chase to put on. Switch it out."

Judith's final words are drowned out by Lindsay's screech. "What do you mean, what did I do? You're his dresser. Seems to me any problems fall at your doorstep."

My body tenses as if to spring.

Noble ends the escalating melee. "All right. You"—he points to me —"go get Chase into the other bodysuit. Don't take more than thirty minutes. Time is money, and this is the second time we're being held up by wardrobe."

In a tense tone, Charles says, "Come on. Let's get this done." He stalks toward his trailer, and I trail behind like a stupid chastised schoolgirl.

Which I'm not. I *know* the bodysuit was tampered with. No doubt in my mind that his sister did it. She was in the back of the trailer with it, all alone, for a while this morning. She knew it would make me look bad. Motive and opportunity.

Without saying a word, Sophia grabs my hand and diverts me to her locker. I take the other bodysuit and head to the trailer, passing Thomas on the way.

Stomping up the steps, I'm greeted by Charles raking his hand through his hair. "What the fuck did you do out there?"

Still fueled by righteous anger at what his saintly sister did to me, I don't temper my response. "What *I* did? Are you nuts? Your sister put something on the snaps to make the material disintegrate."

"How could you say such a thing?"

Indignation races through my blood. "You have absolutely no idea exactly what your sainted sister is capable of. I hold no illusions." I do a thorough inspection of the replacement bodysuit.

"You need to get this out of your head. Whatever slights you believe Lindsay did to you as a child, you're both grown ass women now. Well, at least I know she is."

I pause in my inspection. "Good to know, asshole." I triple-check the snaps and surrounding material, all of which appear fine. I shake the garment.

He takes a deep breath. "Listen, Melody, I know my sister. No way would she do this."

Trying to mimic his stance and lower the temperature in here, I reply, "I know her, too. Better than you."

"She's been—" he cuts himself off. Brow furrowed, he directs, "Get me in this damned costume."

I hold it out for him and together we make quick work of getting him into it. He bends down to snap it, but I stop him. "Let me do it. I want to be sure everything's okay."

Stance wide, hands on hips, he glares at me. Ignoring the anger rolling off him in waves, I snap the costume and do one last inspection. All the while overlooking the fact his dick is almost in my face.

"There. I think you're fine. Walk and check it out."

He takes a few steps. Everything looks good from here. "How's it feel?"

"Good."

"Fine."

Without another word, he storms out of the trailer. How could Lindsay have put the solvent on without my noticing? Gotta hand it to her, she's good.

However, I'm better. I'm not going to let her get away with this sabotage. My fingers find the rubber band around my wrist and I pluck it several times.

Back on set, Noble talks with Charles. No, he's *Chase.* I take my seat next to Judith and Helene.

In a terse voice, my boss asks, "Is he all set now?"

"Yes. This suit's fine, as far as I can tell."

Judith nods and Noble calls for quiet on the set. My eyes find Sophia behind a nearby camera, and I send her a silent thanks. She makes the universal motion for "what happened?" I skim the crowd and find Lindsay and point. Sophia dips her head. The clapper comes down on the take, and Sophia focuses her attention to the camera.

The rest of the day's shooting goes off without a hitch. Throughout, I try to come up with a scenario where I can confront Lindsay. She will *not* get the better of me now.

When Noble calls it quits for the night and summons the actors for a meeting, I make my way toward Chase's trailer. To confront my no-good, unsupportive boyfriend. The dammed jerk.

I set up my things to get him out of the costume. Thomas is here and, even though I'm still hopping mad, I remember Sophia wants to get to know him better. I modulate my anger out of my voice. "Hey, Thomas. Chase should be here shortly."

"Thanks." He pauses. "Hey, good job earlier."

I incline my head.

"Well, there's nothing much going on now, so I'll be out of your hair in no time."

This is for Sophia. "What are you doing tonight?"

"Going back to that club we went to when we first got to Amalfi. You?"

"Sounds fun. Would it be okay if Sophia and I joined you?"

He clicks his pen. "The more the merrier. A few others from the crew will be there."

All discussion ceases when Charles enters the trailer. Thomas intercepts him to sign some documents. Before he leaves, Thomas invites him to the club.

Charles says, "Not tonight. I'm beat and need to get a good night's sleep. Tomorrow's the last shoot."

Alone in the trailer, I focus on my job. With efficient movements, I cut him out of the leggings. Before I can instruct him to unsnap the bodysuit, it's already halfway up his torso. We don't exchange more than ten words. He goes into the bathroom to change into his own clothes, while I clean up my stuff.

Dressed in street clothes, he looks even more delicious. Damn him. Grabbing a fizzy water from the fridge, his clipped tenor reaches my ears. "I think it's best if we spend the night apart. I'm sorry you hate my sister so much, but I know she didn't do anything to my costume. She never would do anything to hurt me on purpose."

I shove the last items into my tote. "See you tomorrow, Mr. Movie Star," I huff.

We part ways and my anger dissipates, leaving a wake of hurt and betrayal. He wouldn't even let me talk. Defended his sister at all costs. What about me, his girlfriend? I stop as if I was the one being sewn into a costume. Am I still his girlfriend? What sort of couple doesn't talk things out? My parents always have open lines of communication. Maybe I was wrong about Charles.

Chase.

My heart drops and I slam my hand over my mouth to prevent a wrenching sob from spilling out.

The trudge to my hotel takes forever. When I reach my floor, Sophia's sitting outside my door. "Hey, Mel," she says as she stands. "You look like you could use a drink."

I unlock the door and we enter. "You're right. I know just the place. Thomas invited us to that club we went to before."

She smiles. "He did?"

At least one of us might have a good night. "Yup. So let's get changed and head over."

"Do you want to talk about what happened today?"

"No."

She sighs. "Fine. I'll meet you here in an hour." She leaves me alone.

Without any interest in going out tonight, I shower and put on the hot pink dress Charles—Chase—bought for me in Positano. I'll show that stupid Doctor Manipul8. I'm applying my lipstick when Sophia knocks. You can tell we're besties, since she's wearing the violet dress, also from Positano.

Filled with people from the movie, the club is packed. After getting our Cosmos, Sophia spies Thomas across the dance floor and passes me her drink. Alone, I watch as she approaches him. Mark materializes out of thin air and grabs her hand, twirling her around. He leads her two left-feet in a Latin rhythm.

Holding both drinks, I sip mine, alone, feeling *his* defection with every swallow. A couple of minutes later, Sophia rejoins me.

"Why aren't you out there dancing? You were near Thomas."

"Yeah, but Mark came up and then Thomas went off with Tina from makeup." She reclaims her Cosmo and gulps it down in one swallow.

I wrap my arm around her. "Stupid men."

A new voice intrudes in our conversation. "I'm glad you're here."

I turn around and Lindsay, holding a glass of what appears to be water, half-smiles. My entire body tenses.

She starts, "I wanted to talk with you. Both."

Sophia and I exchange glances, then focus on our schoolgirl tormentor. Lindsay was as awful to Sophia as she was to me growing up.

I lift my chin. "I can't imagine what you want to talk about."

She tips her glass, leaving a sheen on her lips. "I bet you can't. Listen, I've made a list of people I need to talk to. It must be serendipity because you're both on it, and you're both here."

Sophia's hand lands on her hip. "Yay. Serendipity."

Charles's sister takes a deep breath. "Let me talk for five minutes without interrupting me, okay. This is hard."

I cross my arms over my chest.

Sophia looks at her watch. "Fine. Start."

Lindsay bends down and leaves her glass on a nearby table, then stands and rubs her right hand up and down her left arm. She clasps her hands in front of her. For someone who wanted to talk with us, she's not saying a word.

Sophia prompts, "Four minutes, thirty seconds."

Lindsay fists her right hand, and her knuckles turn white. "Well, I want to first apologize to you. I was a terrible child and I did awful things to you growing up. I am sorry. This is no excuse, but I've had some issues. Big ones. You see, I . . ." She plays with her dark brown hair. So like her brother's.

"We all had problems," I note.

Sophia rolls her eyes.

"Yeah, well, I'm sure yours didn't land you in the hospital with alcohol poisoning. And then in rehab for six months. Both, twice." Her leg bounces. "Some people take a little longer to learn."

Sophia's eyes widen and I absorb her meaning. Neither one of us knew she was battling alcoholism.

"I've just finished a six-month stint in rehab in Switzerland. I have a sponsor, who's really helped me. I made a list of people to whom I owe apologies. You two were at the top of it. I am so very sorry for how I treated you growing up. I was wrong to say you were riding on your father's coattails, Melody. I was wrong to insinuate you didn't belong at our school because you were on scholarship, Sophia. You don't have to accept my apologies, and I do understand if you don't. I wanted you to know some background about me, and I feel awful about how I treated you back then." She bows her head.

Well, shoot. She seems contrite. Doesn't erase what she did to us, though. Sophia and I lock eyes, and my bestie starts, "Lindsay—"

Her head pops up.

"When did you start drinking?"

"I was ten. Charles—Chase—was drinking with his friends then, and I emulated him. Beer at first. Then vodka became my liquor of choice."

Sophia continues, "How did you get your hands on that when you were only a kid?"

"I stole leftovers from my brother and his friends. I appropriated from my parents. I became quite creative."

Her confession clicks things into place for me. She was my major tormenter since we were ten. When she started drinking. "I can't even imagine drinking at that age."

For the first time, Lindsay's lips twist into a slight smile. "When you're raising yourself, practically, you'd be surprised at what you can get into."

I remember Charles telling me their parents were absentee, both partners at a large law firm in Chicago. Not mean, simply not around much. Which gave Lindsay room to get into a lot of trouble. Clearly.

Still, she needs to hear this. "You were the ringleader of the mean girls. You made our lives a living hell."

Sophia adds, "We couldn't go to school functions without you and your friends making us feel like pariahs."

"I know. I'm so sorry. I can't go back in time, but please believe me when I say I wish I could."

We let her confession hang for a moment. I reach for the knitting needles usually in my hair, only to drop my arms when I realize it's loose. "I believe your disease made you do and say those awful things when we were growing up. I'm not speaking for Sophia here, but I accept your apology. I can't forget what you did, though."

Sophia says, "I'm with Mel. I appreciate your apology, but you caused quite a lot of damage."

"I, I can't expect anything more."

I study her expression. Since we're going for honesty here, I push, "And Char—Chase's costume today. Did you have anything to do with the snaps?"

She places her right hand over her heart. "No. I swear to you, I would never do that to Charles."

Her brother's the actor of the family—no way could she feign such innocence. My stomach flips as I lean into Sophia's ear. "Do you believe her?"

After a moment, she nods.

A buzzing starts in my head having nothing to do with the club's music. Ignorant of my inner turmoil, Lindsay holds out her left hand, where a diamond sits. "I'm turning my life around. I'm engaged now. My, my fiancé is finishing up his rehab in Switzerland in a month, which is where I'm headed tomorrow. He's wonderful."

Sophia answers for us. "Congratulations."

Lindsay plays with her engagement ring. "Well, I'm going to go now. I only came to this club because I heard you were here. I don't make it a habit of going into places like this. Not anymore. Goodbye." With a wave, she disappears toward the exit.

Two things hit me at once. One, Lindsay was as tormented as us growing up. The pity for her that emerged when Charles and I were in Ravello reappears. However, it in no way excuses the awful way she tormented Sophia and me. The painful scars she left behind run way too deep.

Two, I need to figure out who really ruined his costume. If not Lindsay, then who? Who hates Charles so much?

As I'm puzzling through this mystery, one more thing clobbers me over the head. I owe Charles a big apology.

CHASE

I shovel the last bit of broiled fish into my mouth. Thank God shooting ends tomorrow. Not a day too soon. Well, yesterday would've been better.

My fork clatters to the plate.

What the fuck happened with my costume today? I know Lindsay wouldn't have done anything to it, but she did have access. Clearly Melody convicted her already. Losing my appetite, I leave my half-eaten dinner on the dining room table and flop onto the sofa. An ad for a musical runs on the TV.

"Fuck you," I yell at the screen and hit the power button.

Flinging my arm onto my forehead, I study the ceiling and focus on Lindsay. If only I could explain my sister's life better to Melody. Maybe she would've given her a break today. Although, I did tell her we basically raised ourselves with the help of some half-assed nannies our parents employed, more to keep up with the Joneses rather than provide us with any true guidance.

No, that's my sister's story to tell if and when she feels ready. The fact she got hooked on booze when she was a kid still tears me up inside. To think I contributed to her downfall . . . I pick up my phone and text her an encouraging note. She has so much strength to over-come the addiction.

Now she's getting married. She showed me the rock last night. I'm happy she's found someone who fits her so well, and definitely need to meet him once he gets out of rehab.

My smile turns downward when thoughts about my own personal life surface. Melody seemed to be perfect for me. Until she called me "Movie Star" today. She's like the rest of them.

I sit upright and stare blankly around the hotel room. My one-hundred-fiftieth such room this year, but who's counting?

Rage and disgust and frustration roil through me.

I jump to my feet.

Tossing my shirt onto the floor, I head into the bedroom. Might as well try to get some shut eye so I'll be ready for the big day of shooting tomorrow. If only I didn't have to meet up with *her* at the ass crack of dawn to get sewn into my fucking costume. One more day. That's it. I'll never have to see her again.

The doorbell rings. One of the perks of being in the hotel's presi-dential suite is a doorbell rather than a knocker. Must be the wait staff coming to clean up from my dinner. Without bothering to put my shirt back on—why should I since my physique is honed to perfection, plus it's what's expected of me—I yank open the door and turn my back.

"The meal's on the table."

"Did you eat it?"

Melody's voice halts me in my tracks. I pivot toward the door to verify I didn't mishear. Nope. She stands in the hot pink dress I bought for her in Positano, her hair loose around her shoulders, wearing a pair of five-inch stilettos.

My hands contract into fists at my side. "What are you doing here?"

She stares at the floor. In a small voice, she asks, "Can I come in?"

"Why? Want to see how a movie star spends his evenings?"

She raises her gaze to mine. "Charles, no. I want to talk with you."

The pleading in her amber-hazel eyes beckons to me. My heart pounds, but my brain refuses to agree. Pushing down the surging hope at her use of my given name, I reply, "You've said enough."

She looks down the hallway and her chest expands. I shove my hands into my back pockets to stop them from reaching out to her.

"Charles," she tries again, "I owe you a big apology."

Out of everything that could've come out of her mouth, such a line would've rated a nine on the Rotten Tomatoes scale. Perhaps a ten? My pulse accelerates. Without moving, the words "Come in" are wrenched from my mouth.

The door shuts with a barely audible snick, and I close my eyes. Not ready to look at the one woman on earth who I thought was different, I spin around. Her next words suck the air right out of my body.

"I was wrong about your sister. I'm very sorry."

I cross my arms, my gaze landing on the carpet.

"She told us about her drinking problem."

"Problem?" I clench my jaw. "She almost died. Twice." That I know of.

Her quiet voice is closer to me. "She told us."

I step toward the balcony, trying to keep some distance between her and me. Each step I take is more difficult than the last. My resolve wavers. "Us?"

"Yes. Sophia and me."

Her reflection in the sliding glass door becomes clearer as she approaches. My body stiffens. "Oh."

Her image disappears as she stands directly behind my body. I move to the side and her reflection reappears. Her face is contorted in anguish.

My resolve falters.

She reaches out and touches my forearm, which tenses. My head turns to look at her fingers. Long, capable, and filled with talent.

"I had no idea, and I understand why you kept her story to yourself. Even when I told you some of what she doled out to me growing up." She remains still. "I'm sorry I accused her today."

I dip my head.

She blurts, "I was blinded by fury. At her for being my childhood tormentor. At you for defending your sister." She inhales. "I lashed out, and I was wrong."

One shred of hostility remains. Is she also sorry for throwing the title of Movie Star at me? I remain motionless. Waiting.

When she doesn't say another word, pain lances through my body and I step away from her touch. In a strangled voice, I reply, "Thank you."

"What more can I say?"

My hand rubs against my mouth. She's apologized for so much, but still not *that*. I whisper, "I guess goodbye."

Her harsh intake of air reaches my ears, but I don't move. She takes a step away, and another, and another. With every footfall, I stifle my urge to beg her to repent for calling me a "movie star."

She stops in front of the door. "Charles, you're the best man I've ever met. You're kind and funny and sweet and talented. I have no doubt you'll achieve all the success you desire."

Those are not the words of someone who only views me as a movie star. The door opens and I turn around. "Wait!"

Her eyes meet mine.

Her regret. Her sorrow.

They quell my pain.

She whispers, "I love you."

My feet propel my body across the room and I spin her around in my arms, closing the door and pushing her against it. She's never said those words to me. Given my upbringing, I've still never uttered them to any woman outside a sound studio. Ever.

Bracing myself away from her on the doorframe, I rasp, "You don't think of me as some movie star?"

Her face squinches. "No. You're so much more. You're a real actor. A truly wonderful man."

At her description of me, my heart expands. A sense of connection to this woman fills my being. Yet I can't utter those three words. Not yet. Instead, I close my arms around her. "Oh God, Goldie." I bury my face in her hair—the locks that first caught my attention.

Her palm caresses my cheek. "I'm so sorry."

I grab her lips with my own. "Stop saying that. I forgive you. I'll always forgive you."

"I promise not to ever jump to conclusions again."

"Yeah?"

"Yes." She closes the gap between us, and all talking ceases.

Later, I stroke her bare arm across my equally naked torso. Her leg tangles with mine. "I was so scared I'd never be here again."

"You belong here. I couldn't imagine sleeping without you."

She giggles. "Then it's a good thing that I came here tonight."

I roll her onto her back and settle myself on top of her. "A very good thing."

I return from my early morning workout—I won't miss these early morning call times, that's for sure. "Are you ready to sew me into that damn Doctor Manipul8 outfit one last time?"

"I'm going to miss it," she replies, standing in front of the kitchen's island.

"Are you serious?" At her nod, I continue, "You can always put a pillow on the floor and kneel before me any time you'd like."

She rolls her eyes. "In your dreams."

I hold up my phone. "Better take a few photos today then."

She giggles, but her face turns serious. "I've been thinking. We know your sister didn't touch your bodysuit." She inhales. "But who did?"

"You're sure someone tampered with it, and it wasn't simple wear and tear?"

"Yes, I'm positive. It was too perfect not to have been tampered with."

"I really don't know. My trailer always has a bunch of people in it."

She sighs. "Who would do it, though? Do you have any enemies on set?"

I consider everyone in the movie. "I can't think of anyone here. If we were in LA, I'd say some actors aren't too happy with me because I snagged a role from them."

She plays with her hair. "Lindsay showed up unexpectedly—did anyone else?" At my frustrated head shake, she implores, "Well, keep your thinking cap on. Maybe someone will come to mind."

"Will do. This is my third time playing Troy Oro, you know. If someone was angry about losing the role to me, they would've done something earlier."

"I was thinking that, too. However, the damage to the bodysuit didn't happen by itself. I'm positive of it."

At her determined look, I caress her cheek. "I believe you."

She tilts her head into my palm. "Okay, stud. I'm running back to my hotel room to change and I'll meet you in your trailer in thirty minutes."

"If I didn't say so before, I'm mad as hell you wore that dress out without me."

She rises to her tiptoes and kisses me. My hands land on her waist and slide down to her ass. After a minute, she steps back. "I'll model it, with a couple others, for your private pleasure."

"That's what a man wants to hear from his girlfriend."

She beams and slips into her stilettos. "I'll see you there soon. You need to take a shower, though. You stink from your workout."

"Actors don't stink."

"Ha! And rock stars don't sweat."

I capture the sassy woman and wrap her in my stinky body, kissing her thoroughly. When we part, we're both breathing hard. I slap her ass. "See you there."

When she leaves, I hop into the shower and get dressed. Beating her to the trailer, I chug my specialty water. The door opens and, instead of my girlfriend, Thomas enters.

"Hi, Chase. Are you ready for your final shoot as Doctor Manipul8?"

"I'm so ready to be done with this costume, that's for sure." We high five.

"I wanted to catch you before all hell broke loose once the shoot is done." He clicks his pen. "I've arranged for you to bring Cherie Adams to the red carpet."

He looks at me expectantly, wanting praise for scoring one of the hottest young actresses as my date. I fail to applaud. I want to bring Melody, now more than ever.

"Did you hear what I just said? *The* Cherie Adams will be on your arm."

"I heard you. Whatever."

"Dude. Cherie Adams is not a 'whatever.' She's the ultimate."

No one compares with Goldie. "Yeah." I finger the bodysuit hanging up. "Fine." I double-check the snaps.

Thomas's eyebrows disappear into his hairline. Behind him, the trailer door opens and Melody jumps in.

"I'm so sorry it took me longer than I thought to shower and get here, Charles!" She stops dead when she realizes we're not alone. "I mean, Chase, I apologize for getting here late."

"That's okay, Melody. I haven't been here long. Thomas and I were wrapping up some details."

Thomas's eyes take on a calculating beam. He looks between Melody and me several times and clicks his pen. "I just told him I scored Hollywood's hottest star to be on his arm for the *I Was Made for Her* red carpet. The media will go crazy."

"Oh." Melody drops her tote bag next to her design suitcase and opens the top level. "Who, exactly, is that?"

Thomas straightens. "Cherie Adams."

Goldie's face takes on a decidedly green hue. "Wow. Yes, she is quite the score, Thomas."

The pen's clicking is the trailer's only noise. Until Melody gives me the boxer briefs. "I need to get sewing."

Before I move, Thomas says, "I've got tons to do for tonight's wrap party. It's the end of an era. Gonna be a blast."

"Great. I'll see you back here later."

While he ambles down the hall, I rush into the bathroom and change into Troy Oro's underwear. Nearly naked, I stride into the main area and grab the leggings. Sliding them up my body, I say, "I want to walk the red carpet with you."

"I know you do. But even if I had changed my mind, Thomas already has lined up your date for the evening."

"No one but you is my type."

"After this red carpet's over, we'll come out as a couple, okay? I promise."

Elation overcomes me for a moment. "I wish we could do it now."

She drops the pillow to the floor, needle in hand. "Not too much longer."

Bending down, I kiss her lips. "I'm holding you to that, Miss Hunte."

She giggles as she sews me into the costume.

MELODY

I pass Charles the mask and give him one last go-over. Adjusting his gloves, I say, "Perfect. You're ready for your close-up, Mr. Wright."

He puts the mask over his face and becomes the superhero. "The only up close and personal I want is with you. Between the sheets." He reaches for my breasts. "Or on the dining room table. Or on the balcony. In the shower."

"You!" I swat his hands away and finish cleaning up from the two-hour process. Even though he hasn't said the words, I'm sure he loves me. I can be patient.

Our banter is cut off when the trailer door swings open. My best friend walks in, lugging one of her cameras. She appears confused.

I approach her. "Sophia?"

She starts, "After you left last night, I got to thinking. I've been doing some extra camerawork unrelated to the movie while we've been here."

I nod, but Charles takes off the mask and cocks his head. "She's been refining her camera skills with an online course, specializing in night-time shoots," I clarify.

Sophia waves her hand. "Right. Anyway, once I got over the shock of what Lindsay told us last night, I went back to my room and was playing around with what I've shot over the past week. I think I found something interesting."

Did she uncover who ruined the costume? I can't control my excitement. "What?"

With a small smile, she sets up her monitor and presses play. "Watch this right here."

The camera's pointed at the entire trailer area, not only to Charles's. The time stamp shows it's 10:00 p.m., and several people mill around. I focus on his trailer as people wander about, but no one enters. A couple minutes pass and still this trailer remains empty.

I turn to my bestie. "Sophia, I don't think there's anything."

Next to me, Charles stills. He bends and gets closer to the monitor. "Shit. Rewind that part, Sophia, please."

With a satisfied smirk, she does. "I stopped watching right here and ran over to show you."

I direct my attention to what's captivated my boyfriend and best friend. A shadowy figure wearing dark clothes and a beanie lurks around the area. He bypasses several other trailers and slinks over right to Charles's, careful not to get caught in any light. His head swivels as if to confirm no one saw him, and the figure pulls something out of his pocket.

My breathing accelerates. "It's a key!"

"It is," Sophia confirms.

He slips into the trailer and doesn't reappear for ten minutes, during which time none of us move an inch. When the door reopens, the figure slips out and walks away from the camera. I'm about to say something when he stops and turns around, a light catching on his face for a split second.

Charles commands, "Freeze it right there."

Sophia rewinds the video and stops it. Even with the light, it's still hard to discern facial features.

The height and build are hard to discern without something to compare them to. I say who I think it is, ready to be disproven. "No way is that Thomas."

Charles's brows form a V. "I'm praying it isn't."

Was I right?

A knock sounds and we all jump back as if we were doing something wrong. The man himself enters. "Are you ready? Noble's getting antsy."

Sophia turns off the screen.

Charles's cheek twitches. "I'll be right there. Just doing a final test of the suit."

Thomas crosses his arms over his chest. Next to me, Charles walks toward the back of the trailer and returns. "It feels fine."

"Great." I force my voice to remain steady. "You're ready for your last outing as Doctor Manipul8."

Without giving away his feelings, Charles passes by us and leads the way toward the set. Leaving her equipment in the trailer, Sophia and I follow. Walking with us, Thomas asks, "Did he seem funny to you?"

"Chase? No, he's fine. Must be last shoot jitters." I've never heard of such a thing, but it's the best I could do as I may be walking next to the man who deep-sixed my career. Well, almost. Not if I have anything to say about it. But why would he embarrass Charles? Is he jealous?

When we get to the shoot, Sophia leaves to take up her position at the camera. I nod to Thomas and sit next to Judith, never letting him out of my sight. The actors huddle off to the side.

Judith asks, "Is everything all right with the costume today?"

"Yes. I triple-checked everything. Thank God this is the last day."

Helene takes the seat on the other side of Judith. "Has Noble made a decision about his next movie? Have you gotten the job?"

Our boss shakes her head. "Haven't heard yet. Although, given the mishaps on the set, I'm not too confident."

Guilt races through me. "I really hope they don't reflect on you, Judith. Your designs were amazing. Any problems were fixed quickly."

Helene leans back. "You'll get it. I'm sure." She pauses. "All you'll have to do is decide on your successor on *Ladies of the Abbey*."

Which better be me, I finish the thought in my head.

The actors break up and take their places. Quiet is called and silence descends.

Hours later, they break for lunch. During the entire shoot, I've been mentally replaying the video Sophia showed us. If only there was better lighting. The clothes he wore were dark and ill-fitting, as if he was trying to hide every last piece of himself. Skull cap included.

Wanting to be alone with my thoughts, I find a quiet corner to eat my very last Kraft services focaccia sandwich. I will *not* miss the same old boring food on set, that's for sure. At least HBO switches the menu up. Although, the dinners in Italy do rock.

I eat what I originally deemed the most delicious sandwich ever without tasting it. Charles sits with the cast across the way, laughing at something Mark said. Why would Thomas do this? What's he hoping to gain?

Sophia's tray lands next to mine. "I want to watch the tape again, Mel. That's all I've been able to focus on today, despite the high action we're filming."

"Yeah, me too. We could go back to Charles's trailer when you're done and see if we can pick up any more clues."

She bites her sandwich. "Yeah, I'd like that. I can't believe Thomas did this. Why would he?"

"I was thinking the very same thing."

She tosses the remainder of her sandwich onto the plate and stands. "Come on, let's go. We need to get to the bottom of this."

Without a word, I trail her as we skirt around the boisterous group and head to Charles's trailer. Inside, we boot up the monitor again and watch what we saw before, still without any further clarity. This time, however, we let the tape roll a little longer, hoping to catch another glimpse of the intruder.

Our patience is rewarded five minutes later.

The dark figure reemerges underneath another light in the background. I point. "There! There he is again!"

"Ahead of you, girlfriend," she replies as she presses a bunch of buttons.

The figure is now much closer, the foreground cut out. We watch as he takes the hat off his head and a shock of short, red hair comes into focus. Our gasps ring out.

Turning to each other, we both say in unison, "Helene."

My hand flies to my mouth. "I can't believe it!"

Sophia packs up her equipment. "I can. She wants the lead costume designer job on HBO when Judith gets named to do Noble's new movies. She'd stoop to nothing to get it. She knows her work isn't up to your standards, so she decided to make you look bad." She zips up the case. "Only she didn't. She didn't count on you to have had the first bodysuit cleaned. She certainly didn't count on *me* to rat her out."

I give her a huge hug. "Which means Thomas is innocent."

"It does." She passes me a camera bag and we leave the trailer, desperate to get back to set and expose the saboteur.

When we arrive, I catch Charles's eye and he excuses himself from the table. To my shock, Mark joins him as he approaches us. Sophia turns her attention to putting her equipment down on the table, taking the bag I was carrying from me.

My boyfriend comes right to the point. "Did you find something?"

"A picture is worth a thousand words, don't they say?" Sophia pulls out the monitor. She starts the video from the moment Helene turns into the light and walks away.

Charles says, "We already saw this part."

I reply, "But not the next."

When Helene goes to toss the beanie away, Sophia stops the video and enlarges it on her as the red bob is exposed. Both men have the same reaction as we did.

Charles whispers, "Why didn't I think of her sooner?"

Mark locks eyes with Sophia. "You deserve an Academy Award for this footage."

Sophia blushes under his praise. I wrap my arm around her shoulders. "You do."

Charles rises to his feet. "Let's go. Hand me the monitor, Sophia. We need to talk with Noble."

The four of us head to the director. I separate from them and ask Judith and Helene to join us. Keeping my eye on the traitor in our midst, we stop behind the table where Sophia has her equipment spread out.

Charles says, "Sophia here is the true genius."

Mark places his hand on my bestie's shoulder. My attention diverts from their interesting interaction when Noble speaks, "Judith. I'm glad your entire team is here. Sophia was moonlighting to improve her camera skills and caught something she wants us to see about the last wardrobe mishap."

Sophia turns on the video and the newcomers have the same reactions as we did when we first saw it. Helene's hand covers her mouth when she first shows up on screen, then her shoulders drop when her subterfuge isn't uncovered.

Noble notes, "Nice angle. Too bad the person is so well-disguised."

Pride on Sophia's behalf surges. I say, "Just wait."

Helene's arm drops to her side and she scans the area. As if she's looking for an escape route. Charles moves his position to be on her right, and Mark to her left. I slide back to be behind her. *Gotcha.*

Before we get to the part where she takes off her hat, Sophia once again enlarges the video on Helene. When her red hair is uncovered, Noble swings to face the culprit. For her part, Helene turns to run and realizes she's surrounded.

Judith's steel-laden icy voice freezes everyone in place. "Helene!"

Noble's not so restrained. He bellows, "Security!"

Helene doesn't remain silent. She shoves her finger into my chest. "You! You're getting everything that's mine. What I've worked for all my life. All you had to do was be born to that rock star, and doors opened for you. You waltzed onto our show, while I struggled for years at every turn."

Her words lance through me. I take a step back to dislodge her finger, and words stumble from my mouth. "That's not true. None of it is."

Judith raises her hand. "Cease, Helene."

Two men wearing "security" T-shirts join our group. Noble points to Helene. "Get her out of my sight. I want her prosecuted for tampering with my costumes." He wheels around to my former colleague. "I intend to make sure you never work another day in this business. You'll consider yourself lucky to get a job as a department store's window merchandiser once you get out of prison."

Helene blanches but doesn't resist as one of the security team pulls her away from us. Sophia turns over a thumb drive to the other man, who follows his partner.

Noble takes a few moments for his breath to calm. "Sophia, I'm more than impressed."

She bows her head. "Thank you."

He nods and addresses Judith, "If it wasn't for you and"—he looks at me—"you, this film wouldn't have stayed on track. Hell, I wonder if she imported whatever germ it was that made us all sick."

Judith begins, "Noble, I'm so very sorry. I had no idea she was so unhinged."

Noble raises his hand. "I believe you. You told me she'd worked with your team for years. I'm confident nothing like this happened before."

My boss licks her lips. "No."

He plows through. "Right. That all being said, and weighing all the equities, I've decided to bring you along with me on my new films. Despite all this, I admire how you handled all setbacks. You were prepared to change course on a dime and came up with solutions rather than excuses. I need that on my team."

Judith inhales. "I'm honored." She pauses. "I accept."

Charles and I exchange glances. Noble continues, "I'll have the contract drawn up. Now, if all this unpleasantness is behind us, I'd like to finish up *Doctor Manipul8*." He claps as if to say "break," and stalks toward the director chair.

The rest of us remain in place, speechless. I stop myself from flinging into Charles's arms. It's over. Helene's been exposed. She's gone.

Sophia starts to collect her equipment, and Mark jumps in to help her. Charles takes a couple of steps backward and I follow. He whispers, "I want to fuck you so hard right now."

His crude words bring a smile to my face. "Looks like that will have to wait. Right now, the hot Doctor has a movie to finish."

"You better be ready."

"Oh, I am."

We part ways. Returning to my seat, I take a deep breath. I can't believe Helene would go to such terrible lengths to hurt me and boost her own career. Still, I can't shake her comment that I only got the job because of my dad.

Judith sits down. "I haven't missed how hard you work, Melody. Thank you for always being ten steps ahead."

I incline my head.

"I want to offer you a choice. I can't imagine doing a movie without you at my side. Yet I know the HBO show needs a steady, capable hand. So, it's up to you. Which position do you prefer?"

This is the moment about which I've been dreaming for years. The lead costume designer on *Ladies of the Abbey* or Judith's assistant on Noble's next films? For me, the choice has already been made. I should be feeling joy, but old insecurities about my dad have resurfaced. They're never far away.

I lick my lips. Instead of answering her question, I ask my own. "Are you asking Braxton Hunte's daughter for the notoriety it'll bring, or are you asking Melody Hunte?"

I hold my breath.

"You've never been anyone else to me except for Melody." She leans forward. "Your parentage never figured into my equation."

Tears well up. "The press release when I was hired said—"

"Was done by HBO's PR team. No, Melody. I never would've hired you if you weren't qualified. I'd say a degree from NYU made you eminently qualified."

Air rushes out of my body. I earned my position all on my own. Still. "And now, you're asking because Helene is gone and there's no one else?"

Judith shakes my shoulders. "Listen to me, young lady. Do you know how many costume designers there are? I could snap my fingers and have a stack of qualified résumés on my desk in the morning. No, this is not some pity ask, if that's what you're thinking. You've proven yourself time and again. Even here, when Helene tried to ruin the Doctor Manipul8 costume, you had a backup all ready to go. Only an experienced designer would've thought so many steps ahead."

Her words warm my heart. Before I can respond, she continues, "And another thing. Before all this came out, right when I was put in the running for Noble's movies, I *knew* I wanted you to be my right-hand. My only real issue was figuring out a way to tell Helene. You're young, yes, but you have a great head on your shoulders, killer instincts, and fantastic work ethic. I haven't seen such a combination in a designer since, well, me." She grins.

I blink. "Really?"

She removes her hands. "Yes. Really. Now the question remains. Do you want to stay in television, or do you want to join me in this exciting world of movies?"

This is happening. I made it so. "You know I love you, right, Judith?"

"What's not to love?"

I huff a laugh at her attempt to interject levity into the situation. "Nothing. I admire your career and the steps you've taken. I've learned so much from you. As between your two amazing offers, though, I have a clear preference." I wave to the set. "While all this is challenging, I much prefer the family we've created on the show. I'd love to take over your position on HBO."

She snaps. "Done. I will recommend to the brass you become the lead costume designer on *Ladies of the Abbey*. Although, I admit I'll miss working with you."

Inside I scream, "I got the job." Outwardly, I beam at my almost-former boss. "And I you."

Noble yells, "Quiet on the set! This is the last scene to be shot, and before we start, I want to say thank you for all of your hard work. This hasn't been an easy time for any of us, and I appreciate everything you all have done to wrap up the Doctor Manipul8 trilogy. Now, let's get rolling."

While they film several takes of the scene during which Doctor Manipul8 kills Mr. A—poor Mark dies over and over again—I squirm in my seat, hardly able to contain my excitement. I want to tell Charles, my parents, Sophia, and everyone on the show. I start plans about certain changes I've been contemplating.

Lost in my thoughts, I'm shocked when Noble yells, "CUT! That's a wrap!!"

I, together with everyone in the cast and crew, jump to our feet and clap. I have only one job left, and that's cutting Charles out of the costume. Bursting with excitement, I hug both my soon-to-be former boss, then my best friend, and everyone in the cast. Finally, I make my way to the trailer.

"Mel, wait up!"

I spin in the direction of Sophia's voice, and she rushes toward me. Her flushed face indicates she has big news. Before she reaches me, I ask, "What's up?"

"Noble pulled me aside and he complimented me, again, on my camera skills. Then he asked me. No, not really asked, more like *told* me I was going to be working with him on his next movies! He's giving me a promotion to camera operator!"

"Oh, honey, I'm so proud of you!" We jump up and down in each other's arms.

When we part, she looks down to the ground. "Mark gave me a hug, too."

"Mark? What about Thomas?"

Her cheeks tinge pink. "Mark's kinda hot, you know."

I laugh at her admission. "I'm so excited for you! You deserve this promotion and working with Noble will do wonders for you professionally." I bite my bottom lip. "I only wish I could be working with you, but I took Judith's job on the TV show."

"You got it?"

I nod and she engulfs me for another hug. When we break apart this time, we both have tears in our eyes. "I'll come visit you in New York."

"You better." I hug her again.

Charles interrupts our celebration. "Is this a private party, or can anyone join in?"

My best friend and I open our arms and he embraces us both.

CHASE

I wipe my mouth with my napkin while tension releases throughout my body. The past few days have been perfect. The wrap party. Melody's promotion on the HBO series. My own feeling of accomplishment at having played Troy Oro, aka Doctor Manipul8, for the final time.

Melody and Lindsay having a short, yet civil, conversation on the phone yesterday.

Her father inviting me to stay in their house and to call him Brax.

The possibilities ahead are endless. Those three important words I've never spoken without a script are at the tip of my tongue.

I beam at the people around the table. Ma and Dad seem to be getting along well with Brax and Sara—especially since Sara's the band's accountant. Which is relatively close to being a lawyer.

"After working less than a year as partner, though, I couldn't take it. It was too hard being away from Brax, and my heart wasn't in the firm's work anymore. I admire what you both have accomplished with your firm. Especially you." She directs her attention toward Ma. "Being a woman partner can be its own form of torture."

Ma laughs. "Can't argue with you there."

"How did you manage? I mean, you had not one, but two children to raise as well as juggling your career."

I jump into this conversation. "My parents worked a lot, so they hired nannies for us." Wanting to divert this discussion, I add, "We went to the same schools as Melody, although I was too old to attend the same one as your daughter at the same time."

Melody puts down her wine glass. "That's true. Your reputation preceded you, even to my year. Your playing the lead in *Fiddler on the Roof* in the high school play was legendary."

My father says, "Goodness, he practiced that piece on the violin for hours. I swear, he played it in his bed."

Everyone laughs. I squeeze Melody's thigh to convey my appreciation at her diversionary tactics. "I wanted to be sure I got it right."

"And you did, honey," Ma supplies. "I can't say we weren't happy when it was over, though."

More chuckles. Melody and I stand to clear the table. In the kitchen, I pull her close for a kiss. "Good work out there."

"Thanks. I didn't want to get too deep into your childhood, including Lindsay, this being our first meeting and all."

I kiss her nose. "It seems like everyone's getting along really well."

"I'm so happy." She wraps her arms around my neck.

"You know something else, Goldie?" She quirks her eyebrow. "I actually miss being sewn into my costume every morning. Is there something you can do about that?"

She grabs my head and kisses my lips. "Tonight I can cut you out of your jeans."

I hoot a laugh. "I'd let you."

She steals another kiss. "Come on, let's get this cleaned up."

We load the dishwasher and return to the dining room, where a game has been set up. Her father says, "Good thing you came out when you did. Otherwise, I was going to have to send in a search party." His wink at Melody lessens the impact of his words.

I rub my hands together. "What do we have here?"

Sara responds, "Cards Against Humanity."

"Oh fun," Melody replies. "I love this game. We play it on set when we have a break." She pauses. "On the TV show, I mean."

Brax swells. "I'm so damn proud of you, Princess. Getting named the lead costume designer on the show is a big accomplishment."

Her cheeks redden. "Thanks, Daddy."

Not to be outdone by her father, I say, "It really is a big deal, especially since Judith gave her the choice to stay with her on Noble's next movies." I wrap my arm around her slim shoulders, which have carried so many hurts. "She's special."

Melody looks at me, all the love in the world shining in her eyes.

"All right, let's get to playing this game," Dad says. "What do we do first?"

After Sara gives a quick rundown of the rules, we start dealing the cards. The first two rounds go to Brax, but Melody wins the third.

Ma says, "I caught your son on the real estate show follow-up show. Congratulations are in order. Angie seems to be a lovely girl."

Melody's father sits taller. "King's very lucky to have found someone as wonderful as Angie. They make a great team."

My girlfriend says, "I've heard great reviews for *Battle of the Real Estate Matchmakers*. Since I've only been home two days, I haven't seen it yet."

Ma replies, "You're going to love it, Melody. King does a great job. And the houses they feature are amazing. It's set out in the Hamptons, where people like my son live."

Ma has to brag about her actor son, with access to all the people she and Dad have tried to woo all these years. Still. "Ma, Brax's career is much more storied than mine."

His eyes—so much like his daughter's—crinkle. "I'm shocked to hear you say that, Chase." Melody taps her card on the table, and he amends, "Charles. Usually actors think very highly of themselves."

"Rock stars usually don't have an ego problem either," I note.

"Touché." His fist reaches across and we bump.

Melody says, "Well, I am looking forward to seeing the show. I haven't had too much contact with King through the years."

Brax sighs. "I know you haven't. But he's changed quite a bit.

When you get back to New York City, I'd love it if you could get to know him now. I think you'll really like him."

Sara places her hand on her husband's forearm but addresses the table. "We had dinner with him and Angie when they were in town not that long ago. They're a lovely couple, and I do believe we're finding our way back to each other. As a family."

Brax swallows. As if by tacit agreement, the game resumes, punctuated with much laughter.

Dad says, "So, Melody, you're going to be working in New York City. How's it going to work between you two, since my son lives in LA?"

If I have my way, I'll be on Broadway soon. I can buy a place in New York. Or move in with Melody. Still, I haven't heard back from *Hamlet 2.0*. With each passing day, my hope diminishes. Melody fiddles with the knitting needles in her hair. "We'll see what time brings. I have a good feeling our locations will be aligned in the very near future."

Brax clears his throat. "Maybe not in the *very* near future."

All eyes swing to him. He clenches and unclenches his fists. "Listen, I know you told me not to talk with you about the movie, Princess, but I can't take it anymore."

My breath freezes.

"What do you mean, Daddy?"

His gaze swings to me. "I think you two will have to be separated for a couple of months in the near future. Sitting here, with you, it's like I'm looking at my younger self." He looks directly at me.

I swallow. Dread crawls up my spine, hitting a discordant note at each vertebra.

"We made the decision this afternoon and I can't contain it. Congratulations, Chase. Charles. You got the role! You're going to be playing me in the Hunte movie. Isn't that great?"

It's as if everything in the room moves in slow motion.

Ma and Dad, for their part, appear elated. He says, "That's wonderful!" She says, "How great is this!"

Then it speeds up.

Melody yells, "What?" She pushes away from the table and jumps to her feet. She leans forward. Not toward me, but at her father. "What. Did. You. Just. Say?"

I can't move. I try to catch my breath, but it comes in shallower pants. Trembling fingers reach toward Melody. She swerves away.

With deliberate movements, I rise. I swing my gaze to the man I've been tapped to play. "I, what?"

"You got the part!"

I turn toward my girlfriend. My arm reaches out.

Huge, hurt amber eyes land on me.

She explodes. "Don't you dare touch me ever again!"

MELODY

My dad's words rush over me. Charles is going to play *him* in the movie.

Charles.

My Charles.

Chase.

He was using me this whole time.

Summoning all my strength, I add, my tone clipped, "You never told me you were going for that part."

"Goldie—"

"Don't! Don't use that name for me."

He flinches as if my words struck him. Good. I hope they did. "All right," he begins again. "I auditioned for the role before our movie started filming. Before we met."

This enflames me more. "So that makes it okay? You didn't audition when we knew each other?"

"No, I didn't."

"You never think to mention this 'little fact' to me? Not once. Not once since we—" I break off mid-sentence, aware of noises around me.

My mother walks behind me. "Melody, honey, why don't you stop

for a moment and listen. I'm sure Charles has a reasonable explanation for all of this."

I move away from her. "No. I won't stop. This, this, *movie star—*"

Chase winces. "Listen, Melody, you told me you didn't want to be a
part of the Hunte movie. You said—"

I throw my arms in the air. "Since when did you ever listen to what
I said? You auditioned to play my dad." I stop. Within me, hurt and
betrayal war with the fact I was used. Again. "I thought you were
different!" I advance on the object of my wrath.

My dad steps between us. "Now, now, Princess. Charles said you
told him you weren't interested in the movie, like you told me. It's not
fair for you to be mad at him now."

I whirl on my dad. "Not fair? That's rich. Can't you see him for
what he is? He's a scheming, conniving *movie star* who used me to get
this part."

Chase erupts. "I did no such thing."

I give him a derisive laugh. "Yeah, right. You can't deny you auditioned for the part?"

"Well, no."

A chain-link fence forms around my heart. "You also can't deny
you never told me."

"No, but—"

I hold up my hand, imagining a piece of black silk, like what I used
to make Doctor Manipul8's gloves, lands on top of the fence. Silk is
strong. Impenetrable. Nothing can get through it.

My mother whispers, "Let's give them some privacy."

I ignore the four people shuffling out of the dining room and
continue, "You saw the opportunity to get close to Braxton Hunte's
daughter and you took it. You knew I was talking with my parents,
that I told them about us. You knew, didn't you, they would be predis-
posed to like you. Was this your idea, or did Sam put you up to it?"

Chase strides next to me. "No, dammit. You have it all wrong."

"Really? 'Cause it looks right to me."

His arm comes toward me, and I step out of his reach. "Melody,
you have to stop and listen to me."

"No, I don't." I tip my chin.

His arm drops to his side and his cheek clenches. "You promised me you would stop jumping to conclusions when you apologized about Lindsay."

He scores a direct hit by throwing my own words at my face, and my breathing hitches. A split second later, all the blood in my body rushes through my limbs, my fingers forming a fist. "There are no conclusions being jumped here. You auditioned for the role. You never told me."

His eyes widen and he looks from side to side. "I love you."

Those three words. The damn words I've been dying to hear from his lips land like final stitches in the silk material around my heart. I shake my head and take several steps backward. "You love what I can do for your career. You love I'm the daughter of the man you want to portray. You love how easily I was to manipulate."

"Stop it." His voice is now as frigid as mine.

My body goes rigid. My voice lowers to ice. "Christ, I gave you my virginity. You must've loved that, too."

His hands land on my shoulders. "What is it going to take for you to understand? You have this all wrong! I love you, for fuck's sake." He shakes me.

I jump away from his touch. "You used my body, you used my status as Braxton Hunte's daughter, you used my desire to keep our relationship secret to hide your scheming." I clap. "Bravo! You truly are a much better actor than even I thought you were."

He takes a deep breath. "How many times do I have to tell you this? I never was my real self until I met you. I always was acting. You, *you* made me drop the mask. You saw me for who I really am."

"A lying manipulator."

"No, a *real* man with *real* feelings. And they're all for you. Yes, I should've told you about the audition, but you were so decisive about not having anything to do with your father's movie that I figured I would tell you if there was something to tell."

"Whatever."

His jaw flexes. "Be reasonable about this, Melody."

An icy calm surrounds me. "I am calm. So calm, in fact, I think I should ensure you receive an Academy Award for this performance. Best Manipulator of All Time."

The color drains from his face.

"Get your shit out of my room and go home with your parents. Or fly back to LA. Enjoy your red carpet walk with Cherie." I spin to face the back wall. "Enjoy your life."

I wrap my arms around my middle as his footsteps recede. How dare he exploit me like that. He took all my confessions and used them against me. I gave him my *virginity*, dammit. Yet tears don't flow.

I'm not sure how much time passes. I don't move an inch, but rather focus on bringing air through the silk material covering my heart. My mother walks back into the dining room and places something on the table. "Melody, sweetie, they're gone."

"Good."

"We all, ah, heard your fight. Want to talk about it?"

I flinch. "No."

"All right." She pulls out a chair. "How about we have a hot chocolate? I made you one. With the marshmallows you like."

Growing up, Mom always made hot chocolate whenever I was down about something at school, usually brought on by Lindsay. I force myself to take a seat at the table, next to her. My fingers clutch the mug's handle.

"I'm sorry things ended like that."

I flick the rubber band around my wrist. All I feel is utter betrayal by the man I thought I loved.

Wisely, she changes the subject. "Have you thought about what you're going to do now that you're the lead costume designer?"

Her words bring me back to what's important in my life. I can control my job, which isn't using me for my family connections. I blow on my drink. "I have a few changes in mind."

Nodding, she asks, "When are you going back to New York?"

I had planned on staying here for a couple of weeks. Now the idea of remaining in the same hometown as Chase makes my skin crawl. "I think I'm going to head back tomorrow."

"So soon?"

Nothing's keeping me here and being around my parents isn't appealing. They're too much in love. I need the anonymity of the City. "Yeah. I have to hire a couple of new designers and since I've never done that before, it might take me a while."

"I understand."

My dad enters the room. "Princess," he begins, but I raise my hand.

"I can't right now."

He looks at my mother and addresses me. "All right. Your room is ready for you." Translation—all Chase's shit is gone.

"I'd like to sleep in the guest room, if you don't mind."

"That's fine, honey," Mom says.

Leaving my untouched hot chocolate on the table, I stand. "I'm going to bed. I'll see you in the morning before I head out to the airport."

I don't wait for them to respond but trudge up the stairs to my bedroom. Making quick work of selecting my clothes for tomorrow as well as a nightshirt for tonight and toiletries, I leave the room I had shared with Chase and trek down the hall. In minutes, I'm staring at the guest room's ceiling, knowing sleep won't come.

I refuse to shed a single tear for that man. *Movie star.* Instead, I replay our entire relationship, finding numerous times he could've told me about the audition. It's clear he set his sights on me once he realized who I was, and what a connection to me could do for his career. Before I had to sew him into that damn costume, he didn't speak more than ten words to me. He was just another arrogant actor.

Then I was assigned to spend hours a day with him.

I bet he had Thomas research me. I can only imagine his elation when he realized I was his "in" to Braxton Hunte. A small voice reminds me he knew who I was from growing up here. I shake my head. No. Chase is a cool customer. I remember the way he peppered me for information about my family life, obviously trying to gather more details he could use for himself. He probably passed the intel along to Sam, who used it to his advantage.

I turn over and smack my pillow. He fed me all that bullshit about my talent, and how he saw me as separate and apart from other costume designers. And I fell for it like a thread to a needle. Bet he laughed with Mark about how gullible I was.

He succeeded where Grant could not. I actually *slept* with the bastard. How he lowered himself to have sex with plain old me pushes the imagination. I remember our conversation when I confessed I felt outclassed by the women he's been with, and he lied to me by saying I was beautiful and different. Yeah, I was different. Stupid and naïve.

An easy mark.

I flip over. He used me worse than anyone else ever has in my life. He pursued me, got inside my head and heart and body, then was rewarded with the role he always wanted. All that crap about wanting to perform on Broadway! Have to hand it to Chase, he really is a method actor.

One thing is certain. I will never again lower my shields and let someone else into my life. No one is to be trusted. Except Sophia. She's the exception who proves the rule. I will create an efficient department at HBO, but not get too attached to anyone. I have a friend circle so I can get out, but there's no reason to encourage any one-on-one time with them, especially the men. Groups are fine. I can disappear into them. Never again will anyone get so close to me.

I toss and turn all night, haunted by Chase's betrayal.

MELODY

A week passed since the fateful dinner at my parents' house, and I'm back where I belong in New York City. My first agenda item was to clean my condo from top to bottom. Everything's scrubbed clean, with no traces that anyone but me has been here.

All of my attention has been focused on *Ladies of the Abbey*. As soon as HBO officially offered me Judith's job, I set out to hire two new members of my costume design team. It's been surprisingly difficult.

Becca, an assistant producer for the show, enters Judith's office. My office. "Your next interview is here."

"Thanks, Becca," I say while picking up the résumé and reviewing it one final time.

"I hope you like him."

"Me too." I place his résumé on the top of my desk. "I want to get this right."

She nods. "I understand. Let me bring him in."

Why did I decide to interview a man for this job? I take a deep, cleansing breath. Because his background is great, he went to my alma mater, and he's had more years of experience in the field than I have, only at smaller networks. Man or woman, it doesn't matter so long as they're competent. Right? Not like I'd ever sleep with him.

A tall, muscular man with dark brown hair worn in an undercut enters my office. My body tenses as the thirtyish man crosses the threshold and offers his hand. His eyes aren't blue, thank God. I force a smile and we shake.

Thirty minutes later, I know he's the right fit for the job. His attitude, his outlook, and his positivity are contagious. Well, the combination will be contagious to the rest of the team. Not to me. But I can fake it.

"It was a pleasure meeting you. I really enjoyed hearing your views about costume design on the small screen."

"Thanks." He rubs his hands on his thighs. "The pleasure was all mine. I appreciate how hard you work on the show, and all of your efforts have been showcased so well over the past seasons. I hope to be added to your team."

I stand. No use keeping him in suspense. "No need to hope. I think you'll be a perfect fit around here and would like to offer you the job."

He rises to his full height, causing me to tip my head backward to meet his gaze. Like I used to have to do with Charles. Chase. He diverts my thoughts with a broad smile. "Thank you so much. You won't be disappointed." Thank God he doesn't have a cleft in his chin.

I force my cheeks to inflate. "I'm sure I won't. Do you have time now to meet with HR and go through all the required paperwork? You can start on Monday."

"Thank you, again, Miss Hunte. I promise to give you my all."

I escort my new hire to human resources and lean against the closed door. I hope I didn't make a mistake. He looks sort of like the movie star, but that's it. He's qualified. He has a winning personality. He'll do a good job. So what if I want to hurl when I look at him? That'll subside. It has to.

Blowing out a breath, I stop at the kitchenette and make a coffee. As I doctor it with creamer and stir, my mind flies halfway across the globe. Drinking coffee in Amalfi while Charles drank his stupid fizzy water. I shove the memory away and return to my office.

One hire down, one more to go. I sort through the résumés and invite three more people to come in to interview. With that chore completed, I turn to more exciting tasks. Like designs for the opening episode, which starts filming in a month.

After I've been working and reworking the lead actor's dress for hours, I'm satisfied with the result. Hers was the final costume needed. Accomplishment courses through my blood.

I did it. I created all the designs for the first episode. Only twelve more to go.

I twirl around in my seat and look out over the now dark New York City. Becca raps on my office door. "I'm heading out. Want to grab a bite to eat?"

Becca's asked me to join her for dinner every day since I returned to the City. And every day, I give her the same answer. "Not tonight. I'm still trying to get my arms around things."

Similarly, her reply is the same as well, "Okay. Maybe tomorrow?"

Sometime later, I pack my tote and head out, saying goodbye to the security guards at the front. I take advantage of the nice evening by walking the twenty minutes to my condo. The fresh air does not soothe my soul, though. Nothing ever will.

Along the way, I stop by a salad bar and pick up dinner. The only thing, besides coffee, I'll eat today. Not hungry anymore.

In my condo, I plop down on the sofa, take-out container on my lap. It's time for me to redecorate in here. I need new furniture, something untainted by where others have sat.

Without thought, I direct Alexa to turn on the TV as I start to eat the lettuce. The music for *Entertainment This Evening* starts. I don't want to watch anything about the business. Before I can formulate the command to change the channel, the voice-over says, "Last night was the ladies' turn, but tonight it's the men's. Let's check out the red carpet from last weekend to see 'Who Rocked the Premiere'!" Flashes of several men walking the red carpet follow her announcement. Chase Wright among them.

My fork, forgotten in my cold hand, lands in the Styrofoam.

The package rolls, where each man is asked who he's wearing and then the cameras roam up and down their bodies. When it comes time for Chase's turn, I mouth "Versace" as he says it out loud.

I watch, transfixed, as he does a slow twirl, showing off the black three-piece suit with a skinny blue tie that matches his eyes. The piece moves on to another actor and I exhale. I was wrong. Our new hire looks nothing like him.

I set my uneaten salad down onto the coffee table and lean back, my mind reeling over seeing him again. This was bound to happen. He is a superstar and on the cover of at least two magazines a month. Not to mention coverage by such shows as *Entertainment This Evening.*

Memories of the first blow job I ever gave, right here in this very room, fight to surface. How he responded to my touch. The silk around my heart slips a fraction. With ruthless determination, I shore it back up and shove the thoughts away.

My attention is once again drawn to the television when the host announces they're going to play an interview with the stars of *I Was Made for Her*, the nation's number one movie, after the break. I spend the next two minutes trying to force myself to tell Alexa to change the channel. And lose.

The interview rolls.

A scene from the premiere is first, with Cherie Adams on Chase's arm. He's smiling down at something witty she said. I'm sure it was clever, as he never smiles like that for something stupid. My stomach churns.

After several scenes from the red carpet, the interview starts. All three lead actors are in a room, talking with the reporter. They laugh at each other's jokes. I'm fixated on Chase's features. He looks tanned and happy and carefree. My stomach lurches again.

The reporter asks Chase what he enjoyed the most about filming the movie. He looks directly into the camera and replies, "We all got along so well, like a family. You don't get that too often in movies, where you can simply relax and be yourself. There were no hidden agendas. That's what I appreciated the most about this shoot."

It's like he's mocking me. I shift in my seat, pain welling from deep within. I force my eyes to remain on the television.

Before the interview ends, the reporter returns to Chase. "I see you brought Cherie Adams with you to the premiere." She leans in. "Do you want to share any news with us?"

He mirrors her position. So do I. His eyes take on a mischievous glint. "She's very special to me." Then he sits back.

I collapse into my sofa, my hand on my clenched stomach.

"I would be remiss if I didn't ask you about the rumors that you've been tapped to play Braxton Hunte in the upcoming movie about his band. Are the rumors true?"

"Yes," I respond for him, my voice wobbly over the single syllable.

Chase swallows, his Adam's apple bobbing. "I've heard them as well." He chuckles. His fellow actors join in his mirth.

The reporter wraps up the interview, clearly disappointed she didn't get the scoop she wanted.

When the commercial starts, I finally find my voice. "Alexa, turn off the TV." The screen goes dark.

My chest hurts. Chase looks like he's having the time of his life, without a care in the world. And why shouldn't he? He got an evening with Cherie Adams, in all her blond-haired beauty. Her bright blue dress was cut almost down to her navel, with a slit up to her upper thigh, which I'm sure he liked taking off. Not to mention he's in the number one movie in the country.

I refuse to let his fucking coups get the better of me. My chin rises. I got what I wanted, too. I'm the lead costume designer on my show. Judith told me I earned it all by myself, not because of who my dad is. I choose to believe her. Besides, now that I'm making all the decisions, the top brass will have to see my worth.

Yes. We both got what we wanted. Only his triumphs come with a sex kitten on his arm and TV hostesses fawning all over him. My stomach flips at the way he was doting on Cherie . . .

When my eyes start to swim, I leap to my feet, swallowing over a hard lump. I haven't shed a single tear for him, and I don't intend to start now. My cell rings.

"Hi, Daddy," I inhale.

"Hi, Princess. I haven't spoken with you since you left. How are you?"

Not going there with him. Or anyone else. "I'm fine."

Clearly understanding I'm not going to talk about what went down, he asks, "How's your new job going?"

"Oh, it's great." I divert my thoughts by launching into a conversation about what I've been doing for the show, and he praises me for my hard work. *He* recognizes my talent.

"Sounds like you have your hands full."

"I do."

"That's great. Before I let you go, I wanted to ask if you've reached out to King and Angie?"

"Yeah, we made plans to go to dinner tomorrow night."

"I'm sure you're going to enjoy getting to know both him and his fiancée." He pauses. For the first time, our conversation's awkward. When I don't fill the silence, he says, "Well, I should go, your mother will be back here soon. I love you, Princess."

"Love you too, Daddy."

Tossing the phone next to the uneaten salad, I decide it's time for bed. Not that sleep ever comes.

The next night, I enter the restaurant late and King's already seated. We never got to know each other growing up, and this is our first try at reconnecting. Joining the table, I give my big brother a hug and shake his fiancée's hand. "Sorry I'm late. I got caught up with a design in the office."

"I can imagine how busy you must be, Miss Lead Costume Designer." He smiles, the corner of his hazel eyes—so much like mine—crinkling. I explain about my hiring process and what I've been up to with the designs.

"Please, tell me about yourselves. I had no idea you were into real estate." I glance at my brother.

"That's because I wasn't." He laughs. "Angie, here, is a great teacher. And motivator. And co-star." He leans over and kisses her cheek.

Ignoring the shot of jealousy racing through my veins, I look at Angie for clarification— her diamond ring blinking at me. She tells me about how they were brought together by their reality show and how she hated him on sight.

"The feeling was mutual," King says, reaching for his bourbon.

"And then it wasn't," Angie continues with their story, including their attending one of Hunte's concerts at Jones Beach this past summer.

King picks up the narrative. "We saw him and Sara a couple of weeks ago in Chicago, when we were there for a real estate convention. We had a nice time. It's really great to have reconnected with him. And now you. Family means a lot."

His sincerity sends warmth through every part of my body. "I like getting to know you, as well. I'm so very sorry I wasn't around this summer when you were in the hospital."

He waves his hand. "I'm fine now. Everything's been taken care of by the cops. Now we're planning our wedding and looking for a house out in the Hamptons."

"It took me a long time to convince your brother we needed to stay within our means and not buy a multimillion-dollar house."

They gaze at each other and move in for a kiss. The love radiating between the two of them causes me to fix the napkin on my lap. "I'm happy for you two."

King smiles at me, his white teeth almost sparkling with happiness. "So tell me, sis, what's up with your personal life? I know all about your job, but what do you do outside it? Do you have a special someone?"

"No." I bet our parents put them up to asking me.

King confirms my suspicions. "Dad mentioned what happened at dinner."

They look at each other. Angie affirms, "We don't mean to pry."

I play with the knitting needles in my hair. "I know you don't," I say, because it's what's expected. We sit in uncomfortable silence for a few minutes.

Angie tries to rekindle our conversation, "Your brother and I go to the beach to clear our heads. What do you do here in the City to relax?"

Her question brings me up short. "Well, I go out with my friends." That sounded normal.

She breaks off a piece of bread for her and King, and offers the basket to me. After pouring olive oil onto my plate, I dip the warm bread into it. So reminiscent of Italy. I drop the bread, uneaten.

Angie continues, "The City is so busy all the time. While it must be nice to go to new restaurants, do you find all this bustle relaxing as well?"

I consider her query. "Not really. But it's fun. I wouldn't have suggested this place if I hadn't found it with my friends before the movie shoot."

The waiter brings our entrees. King salts his without tasting it, and Angie rebukes him. I like her. He needs a woman's hand, since he's always seemed so hard to me. She's softened him around the edges. I take a bite of my beef Wellington. While I've enjoyed this dish before, tonight it's tasteless. I'm sure it has everything to do with my current emotional state, and not a reflection on the chef's culinary talents.

Angie takes a bite of her steak and exclaims, "Well, I'm certainly glad you found this place. It's great."

I force my face to reflect her excitement and try my dish again. Still unappetizing. I cut up several pieces of the beef, moving them around my plate. King finishes his meal first and I push mine away from me. Angie takes her time, savoring every last bit.

King lifts his bourbon to his mouth, eyeing me speculatively. "How did you enjoy working on the movie? Was it much different from your job on the show?"

I sip my Cosmo, the only thing with any taste. "It was, in a sense. Of course, shooting over in Italy is much different from what I do here in the City." I chuckle.

"I've enjoyed several trips to Italy. Angie and I are thinking of going there for our honeymoon."

"Oh, you'll really enjoy it there. It's very romantic. Florence has the most amazing vibe and gorgeous countryside. There are so many bridges there." I sigh.

"I agree," King says. "I loved the Lake Como region. But my favorite place was the Amalfi Coast. Did you get to Positano?"

I choke on my last sip of my Cosmo. "Yes." I wheeze. "I went there with a bunch of people from the set. It's nice."

"I can't eat another bite." Angie lays her fork on her plate. "I've read about a place in the Amalfi Coast called Ravello." She leans her head on King's shoulder. "It's supposed to be one of the most romantic towns in the whole world."

I push away from the table. "Please excuse me. I need to use the restroom." Without looking back, I seek the only viable escape.

At the sink, I turn on the cold water. Fight the memories. Trying to regulate my breathing, I cup my hands and catch the water. The bathroom door opens, but I ignore it as water splashes over my face.

"I'm so sorry."

I tense at Angie's words, which shred me from the inside. As water drips into the sink, I tamp down my tumultuous feelings. "I'm fine." My voice sounds strangled to my own ears.

She tears off a couple of pieces of paper towels and offers them to me, which I put over my wet face. When I can't hide anymore, I crumple the paper and walk over to the garbage can.

"Have you talked with anyone about what happened?"

There's no use pretending she doesn't know everything from my parents. "Nothing happened. Chase was exposed as a fraud and a user. A *movie star*." I keep my eyes averted from her, studying my manicure instead.

"I'm so sorry he broke your heart. Please, don't close up. Take it from me. I know what I'm talking about. I owe everything to your brother, who brought me out of the hibernation I had consigned myself to after I lost my first husband."

"Thank you for your kind words. I'll be fine."

"You'll survive your broken heart. It'll mend. You'll find your real smile again." She steps closer to me, placing her hand on my shoulder. "You're going to be my sister, and I want to let you know I'm here for you."

"Angie," I say, turning my face away from the woman. "I just can't."

"I understand." She worms her arm through mine. "Come on. Raise your gorgeous head up and let's go back to our table. Dessert awaits."

I force a reluctant chuckle. "I thought you were full?"

"Never too full for something sweet." She gives me a sideways glance. "Plus, we have to celebrate your birthday."

Her words jolt my system. Explains all the calls I sent to voicemail today. "It is, isn't it?"

"You only turn twenty-five once!"

As we walk back to our seats, I bury my feelings over Chase once again. Yet, not even a family birthday celebration can ease this heartache.

Someday I'll smile again. Today's not the day.

CHASE

homas flutters around me like a feeding bird. The clicking of his pen makes me want to crawl out of my Versace suit and wrap my tie around his throat. With supreme effort, I maintain the mask I've been hiding behind for the past several days.

"What time am I picking Cherie up?"

"The limo's going to arrive here in thirty minutes, then you'll go to her house and head over to the red carpet. She's been prepped with info about all the actors in the cast and will look amazing on your arm. She's wearing a bright blue dress, which matches your tie. And your eyes, of course."

I roll my "matching eyes."

"Also," my PA continues, "we need to discuss the next several weeks until you start filming your next movie. Have you decided what role you're going to take?"

I shake my head. "I'm meeting with Sam next week and will let you know."

"Okay." Five more pen clicks. "I've got you down for the party tonight, plus the one at Jessa's in the Hills this weekend. Then there's a club opening on the fifteenth, and . . ."

My mind wanders. I want to sit in my dark bedroom and disappear. It feels like my heart's been half beating since that awful day at the Hunte's house. When he finishes, I shrug. "Set up what you think is best."

"Okay, I'll take care of it." He consults his watch. "The limo's going to be here soon, so let's make sure you're all set." He runs through the names of the designers I have on, which makes me think of a certain costume designer.

The one who refused to believe me when I told her the truth. I *had* forgotten about the audition. Well, mainly. I was honoring her wishes not to involve her with her father's movie.

Damn Braxton Hunte anyway. Why couldn't he have kept his big mouth shut?

I shove those thoughts to the side when the front gate intercom blares. Thomas answers it. "Limo's here."

He offers me a pair of sunglasses, and I double-check the arm. Prada. I'm sure he told me this before, but nothing's staying in my brain. "See you tomorrow."

Alone in the limo, I pour myself a glass of scotch and welcome the burn. All the while replaying Melody's words.

". . . a scheming, conniving *movie star* who used me to get this part."

"I think I should ensure you receive an Academy Award for this performance. Best Manipulator of All Time."

It's the last one that scores the deepest cut. I told her I loved her, and this was her response?

Having to explain everything to my parents was beyond humiliating. Of course, they felt it would all blow over and began calling their friends to ramp up their standing in the community by having dinner at the Huntes'.

I take another swig of the scotch. Well, I'm done. If she thinks I deserve an Academy Award, then by damn, I'm going to show her. I'm going to walk—no, own—this fucking red carpet.

My co-stars will laugh at my jokes.

The press will adore me.

Because I *know* she'll see it, I'll make sure Cherie hangs off my every word. Every delectable inch of the actress's body will be putty in my hands.

I'll show *her*.

~

It's just after one, and the after party is in full swing. Booze flows like the lines from writers, and everyone is either half-drunk, half-stoned, or both. Stunning starlets mingle. Hook-ups disappear in discrete rooms in the producer's mansion.

Next to me, Cherie smiles and flutters her eyelashes. Which brings me right back to the time Melody did the same act, making Cherie's attempt seem like a pathetic replica. I bite my tongue and brush her blond hair off her forehead. It's the wrong shade. My arm drops.

"You seem to be a million miles away, Chase."

I force my lips upward. "I was thinking about what's coming up for me next. I'm sorry if I'm not paying you the attention you deserve."

"Do you have any roles lined up?"

She's asking about Braxton Hunte. I shrug. "There's some parts in the hopper, but nothing's been signed yet." Not a lie. "How about you? What's up next on your docket?"

Being in the business, she gets it. Sucking in her breath, she says, "I've been looking at a script. It's very hush-hush." She lowers her voice and I lean in closer. "They asked me to play Marilyn Monroe in a story about her glory days."

My eyes widen. "Holy shit. That sounds like the role of a lifetime."

Her eyes search mine. "It's an opportunity, that's for sure. My agent's been pushing me to take it. But . . ." Her voice trails off.

"What's holding you back?"

She takes a sip from her champagne. "Do I really want to take on such an iconic role? Everyone adores Marilyn Monroe. What if I can't do her justice?"

I take her by the shoulders. "Cherie, they wouldn't have offered the part to you if they didn't think you'd be a perfect fit."

"I guess. If I take it, though, I'd always be compared against the original. I'm sure I'd be found wanting."

Her fear over the role is understandable. These things can fall flat or soar to new heights. "And you don't want to be known as the actress who played her. You want to be known for your own talents."

She nods. "You get it. I want to forge my own path and not be remembered as an imitation."

"Have you told your agent this?"

"He'd just think I was a stupid blonde."

I tip her chin upward. "No. He wouldn't. If he does, you need to fire him. This is your career, and only you can direct it. Your agent works for you and not the other way around."

Tears well behind her expressive eyes. "I know you're right, but it doesn't feel that way."

I thumb the tears off her cheeks. "You have to choose the parts you want to take because they feel right to you. And if you think you can bring them to life unlike how anyone else could. If this movie does that for your soul, take it. If not, pass. Other actresses will line up to take this one, and other movies will be there for you."

"You make it all sound so easy, Chase."

I step backward. "Believe me, I know it's not." I sip my second scotch.

Her eyes rivet to my drink, and her nose wrinkles. "How can you drink that stuff?"

I set my barely touched glass down on a table. "I have absolutely no idea."

She bursts into peals of laughter, causing me to join in. Her vibrant personality is refreshing here in Hollywood. Maybe what I need in my life.

The music changes to a slow song and Cherie places her hand in mine. "Enough shop. Come dance with me."

I let her lead me onto the dance floor. The last time I danced was in the small Italian town on the road to Ravello. Closing my eyes, I clear my head and pull Cherie into a proper position. We move effortlessly, and she rests her head on my shoulder.

She's too boney.

She's too tall.

She's not . . . Goldie.

I step on her toe, causing her to wince. "I'm so sorry," I murmur.

"I'm happy you did. It proves you are a fallible human after all. For a while there, I was thinking you didn't have any flaws."

Her words bring me up short. "Hardly." The music changes to another slow song, but I can't stomach staying here any longer.

"I think I've hit the wall. It's been a big day for me, with the premiere and crush of the press. Would you like me to take you back to your house, or would you prefer I sent the limo back for you?"

"I'm ready to go."

We make our way through the still packed room, saying our good-byes. I text the limo driver so he's waiting for us when we finally escape the mansion. Letting her precede me into the vehicle, I instruct the driver to drop her off first, then take me home.

Sitting next to me, she leans her head against my shoulder. "I had a lovely time tonight, Chase. Thanks for thinking of me."

"You're welcome. I enjoyed tonight with you as well."

She bites her lip. My stomach flips. I've been here before and now all I want to do is forestall her offer. "I'm exhausted, though. Jet lag this time has really been a bitch."

Her eyes drop to her lap. "I understand all about jet lag. Directors expect us to be some sort of machines and disregard all the crazy time changes."

"Yeah. At least *Doctor Manipul8* filmed all in Italy, so once we got started, we didn't have to worry." Except for the one day I flew back to New York City to audition.

"You're lucky! In my last shoot, we went from Vancouver to Miami without a break in shooting."

"That must've been rough."

She laughs. "You have no idea. I had coffee inserted via IV."

I chuckle at her exasperated tone, and shortly we arrive at her house. I tuck some stray hair behind her ear. "Please let me know what you decide about the Marilyn Monroe film. Make sure it's the decision that's right for you."

She nods and leans forward, kissing me gently. "Thanks for the advice. I'll see you around, Chase."

When she leaves, a twinge of guilt at not accompanying her into her home hits me. I shake my head. No. First, I don't need any photos posted of us, and the concomitant issues they would bring. Second, I'm no longer interested in her beyond friendship. Third, Melody—I cut my thought process off and instruct the driver to take me home.

The next day, Mark's in town for some business meetings so I hook up with him in a small café in Malibu, overlooking the water. We scored a private room, thanks to Thomas, who stops by.

"Appreciate your setting this up for us, man," I say to my PA.

He gives me a salute. "Just doing my job. Do you need anything else from me before I head out?"

Mark speaks up, "Do you have a brother? I need someone like you in my life."

Thomas preens under Mark's compliment. "Sorry, just a sister."

"She married?"

Thomas punches Mark in the shoulder. "I'd never let you near her, you slut!" He turns his attention to me. "Remember, you're meeting with Sam in his office next Tuesday. The other stuff can wait."

"Thanks, Thomas."

He clicks his pen.

The slut next to me offers, "Give your sister a big wet kiss from me."

"Asshole," he mutters and excuses himself.

When I order a personal pizza, Mark's eyebrows lift to his hairline. "Nice to be on break, huh?"

"Definitely," I reply, drinking my pinot noir. "Although, I still hit the gym three times a week and swim in my pool daily."

Soon, our meals come, and I dig into the pizza. Since the end of filming, I've been allowing myself to enjoy carb-laden foods. I'm starting to feel human again, but know my strict regimen will be picked back up as soon as Sam and I settle on my next role.

I'm in the middle of swallowing the crust when my phone rings. Wiping my hands on my napkin, I raise my finger to Mark and check the screen. It's a New York City number. Could this be about my audition? My heart rate picks up. Turning to face the windows, I answer, "Chase Wright."

"Hello, Mr. Wright. This is Athena Davis with *Hamlet 2.0*. I don't normally make personal calls to the actors who auditioned for us, but I wanted to make an exception for you."

I can't catch my breath. They wouldn't call me unless they had positive news. "Thanks for calling, Ms. Davis."

"You see, your audition was excellent. You had the lines down, but more than that, you nailed the character."

I can't keep still, so I stand and walk to the side of the room.

"However—"

I pause mid-stride.

"We've decided to go with another, more seasoned Broadway actor for the part. We felt he would be able to bring experience to the role. I hope you understand."

My entire body slumps. I wanted that part more than I even let myself believe. Knowing a response is expected, I force my voice to remain steady and reply, "Of course. Thanks for calling me to let me know."

"I'll keep you in mind for any future plays I'm involved with."

"Thank you." I disconnect the call and hold on to the back of a chair, staring out the window without seeing the boats or the waves.

Mark's hand lands on my shoulder. "Everything all right?"

I swallow. "Yeah." Like a second-string actor, I follow him back to our table.

The rest of my pizza remains untouched, but I order another glass of wine. Mark puts his fork down and circles the rim of his glass with his finger. "Care to tell me what that call was about?"

"I didn't get a part." I finish the wine and motion for the server to bring me another.

"Sucks, dude." He sips from his glass. "Was it the Hunte movie?"

My breath catches at the mention of Melody's father's gig. I shake my head. "No. It was a part I really wanted."

"Well, if rumor means anything around here, your name is the one on everyone's lips to play Braxton Hunte. You know what happened to Rami Malek when he played Freddie Mercury."

"Yeah."

"Maybe your not getting this role was a sign that things are lining up for you with the Hunte movie. Hell, I'd love to be in that one myself. Just don't see me playing a rock star." He chuckles. "You, on the other hand, would be an excellent Braxton. I've seen videos of him when he was younger. With makeup and a wig, you'd be a dead ringer."

I finish my wine.

Seeing that he's getting nowhere with me, he wisely changes the subject. Although the new topic isn't better. "I don't think, though, the Hunte movie will be filmed in any place as wonderful as Italy. Probably on a sound stage."

"I guess."

"Now, Italy, was amazing. Even though I caught whatever that bug was. God, that was awful."

"Yeah, it delayed shooting for quite a few days."

He chuckles. "Believe me, you didn't want me on set when I was so sick. I'm guessing most of us were in the same boat."

I nod.

"By the way, did you hear Noble selected Sophia to be the camera operator on his next movies? He was impressed with how she uncovered what Helene had done to your costume."

"Yes. She was very excited." Pulling my head out of my ass for a second, I ask, "Anything going on between you two? Sophia seemed to be warming up to you near the end of filming."

He fiddles with the napkin. "If only I had another week, you know?" I wave, my mind returning to my dismissal from *Hamlet 2.0.* His words don't register as he continues, "I texted her a couple of times since we've been back to the States, but her replies have been lukewarm at best."

Mark continues talking, but my mind's back on losing out on the part.

His eyebrows bounce. When I don't respond, he implores, "Did you hear what I said?" Rapidly blinking, I refocus on Mark, who's wriggling in his seat. "Noble tapped me to play the villain in his next movies."

His excitement penetrates through my disappointment. "Really? Congratulations." I hold out my fist, which he bumps.

"Yeah." His gray eyes shine. "That's why I'm out here. Sorry I blurted it out right then, though."

I shake my head. "No, don't be. I am truly excited for you. Another villain?"

Mark holds his hands up. "Guess I'm good at them. It's a really juicy part." He tells me the story and about his role. I have to agree, this is a wonderful opportunity for him.

"You know the best part, right?"

At my perplexed expression, he answers his own question. "Sophia's going to be on the set!"

His answer forces a chuckle out of me. "You got it bad for her, don't you?"

"Dude. She only started to give me the time of day near the end of *Doctor Manipul8*, and then we parted ways. I'm going to change that when we start filming."

"I wish you luck. Although, love is overrated. Keep it superficial, and you'll be good." I finish my wine.

"That's not the tune you were singing on set."

With a twist of my lips, I note, "I should have."

He looks as if he's going to mention my costume designer, but wisely changes course. "Well, I'm going to take that as bad advice from someone who's never been in love before. I think Sophia might be right for me. Just you wait, Chase." He pats my forearm. "When the lightning in the bottle hits you, you'll change your tune."

I doubt that.

CHASE

I park in the lot and take the elevator up to the top floor. Passing through the glass door with "Kirkland Management" etched on it, I'm ushered into a conference room overlooking downtown LA. A bottle of my favorite sparkling water is given to me by the efficient receptionist.

"Thank you."

Within moments, Sam strolls through the doors, accompanied by a younger man and woman, presumably associates. The woman places a stack of papers down on the table, while the guy distributes an agenda for today.

"Why so formal, Sam?"

Instead of answering me, he introduces his interns.

Realization dawns. I needle my agent, "Ah, need to show the interns how things are supposed to be done, huh? When they're not around, it's like a quick phone call here and there."

Sam's eyes slant. "No," he says with a sarcastic tone. "This is how I conduct business when my clients actually deign to come into the office. Which you haven't in what, three years?"

I shrug. My mood hasn't improved since I got the news I was passed over for *Hamlet 2.0*. Which was compounded by the fact I had exactly one person I wanted to discuss it with, and she's strictly off-limits. Her words "movie star" sound on repeat in my mind.

Sam nods to the young lady, who pulls out a piece of paper. Her gaze darts to mine for an instant and refocuses on the words in front of her. Her chin lifts. "So, uhm, Chase, your role as Doctor Manipul8 has ended, and the franchise has been very successful. The prior two movies grossed, on average, over two billion dollars worldwide, with six hundred thousand right here in the United States."

The numbers flow right over me. The movies were successful. But didn't tax me acting-wise. Since it seems she's waiting for me to say something, I oblige, "That's great."

She continues, "Which puts them on par with *The Avengers* movies." Her eyes snap to mine. "The top grossing superhero movies of all time."

I fake a smile and hold up my still-closed bottle of water. "Hope we beat them."

"Well, this movie won't release until next year, so I bet you're going to break the record! Noble's already boasting it's his best work ever."

"I read the interview in *Variety*."

Sam points at the young man, who takes over the meeting. "According to your contracts, you earned one million for the first movie, and an extra half-mil above that for your second. Not including your box office and merchandise cuts."

"And Sam here took his share off the top."

My agent smiles. "Of course. Who do you think negotiated your contracts?"

His words bring a reluctant chuckle from me. "Someone did a good job."

Following his boss's chuckle, Sam's intern continues, "Well, your pay for this movie was a flat two million, plus an increased share of the profits and merch." He flips the page. "For *I Was Made for Her*, your payday was another million."

All of these recitations mean I never have to work another day in my life. I'll never live long enough to spend the profits from even one of the films. This realization clears my head. I'm free to do whatever I want to do. Even Broadway.

"Very good summary of Chase's recent work." Sam retakes control of the meeting. "I heard about *Hamlet 2.0.* I'm sorry you didn't get the part."

"I'm sure," I reply dryly. I open the bottle of sparkling water and take a sip.

Sam places a stack of papers before me, titled CONTRACT. "This should help you get over losing the play. You're set to star as Braxton Hunte in the Hunte movie, tentatively titled *Out of the Red.*"

My hand reaches for my bottle again, but I pull it back. The two interns study me as if I were a specimen under a microscope bleeding money. Sam points to the staggering salary. My palm lands on my forehead.

"Brax told me I was selected . . . I'm surprised you got the contract so quickly."

"Brax, is it?"

My throat constricts. "He told me to call him that."

"Nice" He pauses. "Thank you for being impressed with my nego-tiating skills." Three people in the room laugh. I smile because it's expected. "Take a look at this contract and let me know if you have any questions."

Without much interest, I skim through the document. The amount of money they're going to pay me is astronomical. The shooting schedule will take up the next four months, between rehearsals, voice lessons, and going to various locations. I can use a four-month hiatus from being Charles Wainwright, that's for sure.

But this isn't Broadway. And it's about *her* father. Remaining seated, I push back from the table.

Sam seizes the moment. "Chase, I haven't read the script yet, but I have high hopes for this movie. They've hired the writers from *Bohemian Rhapsody*, so you know this is going to be big. Not that *Doctor Manipul8* isn't a huge franchise, but this one movie could rede-fine your career."

His last words stump me. "Redefine it?"

"Yes. You've played leading man roles, from romantic comedies to a superhero. This part will rocket you into superstar status. Your paydays will more than double. More. Than. Double."

My heart skips a beat. "It's all about the money with you, isn't it?"

"You know that isn't true, Chase. I want what's best for you, for all of my clients." His eyes dart from me to his interns, and back to me. "I want your career to continue to grow."

I rub my hands together. Here's my chance. "I've lost several movie roles lately to younger actors."

He picks up a pen. "That's true. But don't you see? Playing Braxton Hunte will give you what you've been looking for. Respectability."

"Respect," I choke out.

"Don't think I don't know why you wanted that role on Broadway. You lost a couple of roles and were seeing the end of your career in front of you. You naturally thought if you got a job on Broadway, you'd be able to extend that. This movie will do that for you without having to deal with the grind of Broadway. Believe me, I've had several clients go that route, only to come back to me begging for a movie. I don't want to see that happen to you."

Absorbing what he said, I grab my water and take a sip. And another. "You've had clients do Broadway, only to return to movies?"

"I didn't say that. What I said was I had clients go off to do a play or a musical or something and come back looking for a movie. I succeeded about half the time, and most only got supporting roles moving forward."

"But you have had exceptions?"

He scribbles something down onto his notepad. "I have." He sighs. "But they had gotten their start on Broadway before hitting it big in the movies. They are the ones who can switch between the two genres without taking a hit."

"And I started in movies."

"Exactly."

My hand clenches around the water bottle. This role is going to be amazing, and it could launch my career in a different direction, the way I thought going to Broadway would. "Do you really think playing Brax would open more doors for me?"

"I can't say for certain, as I'm sure you're aware. You can never truly predict how things shake out in this business. But if past is prologue, the movie will be a huge hit and will propel you to even bigger and better roles."

I roll my chair back under the table. Movies. I know how to make them. I'm comfortable in front of the cameras. CGI is my friend. I can act in an ensemble or with only one other person on the screen. It takes me away from home for months at a time, but that's not an issue for me. I can hook up with whoever on set and leave her when it's over. My life yawns ahead of me.

"What about Netflix? I've been hearing good things about that studio."

"So have I. In fact, I've been getting info from them and Amazon Prime Video. Those roles usually have more meat to them."

I nod. Picking up the contract again, I read it more thoroughly.

Sam's intern interrupts. "I think this role will be great for you, Chase. I've Googled Hunte and read about their career. I bet the script will be fantastic."

I tip my head at her enthusiasm. "I do have one major problem, though. I can't sing like him."

Sam waves his hand. "They'll overdub your voice. No one really can sing like Braxton."

My head slams against the back of my chair. He's addressed all of my possible objections. All except one. How do I feel about playing my ex-girlfriend's father? My stomach constricts.

I look at the young woman. "If you'll please excuse me, I need to use the restroom."

As I make my way to the men's room, my heart rate picks up. Thankfully, I'm the only one in here. It takes me a few deep breaths to get my breathing back to normal.

Can I do this? Can I play him, knowing that he's Melody's father? My *ex*-girlfriend. Who I desperately want back, but know she'd rather design an entire wardrobe for my sister than spare one word for me. I stare into the mirror. *Get a grip, man.* She's just one woman in a long string of them.

So what that I let my guard down with her? Fat lot of good that gave me. She turned my innermost feelings against me.

So what that I laid bare my soul to her? I'm still me. Better, in fact. By letting my thoughts out, I exposed them for the stupidity they are.

So what that we had explosive chemistry, unlike anything I've felt before? Another woman will take her place. All I have to do is snap my fingers and a line will form.

My stomach calms down. My pulse returns to normal. I need to get back on the horse. Take this "role of a lifetime" and make it my bitch. Dare the Academy Awards *not* to give it to me. In the mirror, I watch as the cleft in my chin rises.

I can do this.

I will do this.

Determined, I return to the conference room. Six eyes follow me as I return to my seat. Sam asks, "Any additional thoughts?"

I keep my mind blank. "No. I'm good."

He smiles, obviously calculating the zeros on his upcoming check.

I pick up a pen.

MELODY

I tie my cross-trainers, tuck some cash into my sports bra, and head out to meet up with Sophia in Central Park. She's in town for a few meetings with Noble to do some post-production things for *Doctor Manipul8*, discuss her role in his upcoming movies, and will be heading to Chicago tonight.

"There you are!" Sophia rushes to give me a hug. "I'm so glad you were able to get away from work today."

I play with the knitting needles securing my ponytail. "Yeah, well, it is Sunday."

"I guess even *lead* costume designers need a day off."

I stand taller at the mention of my new title. "I'm still not used to being called that."

"Don't you dare doubt for one second you got the job due to anything other than your mad skills." Sun beating down on us, we approach the jogging path. "I'm returning to Chicago tonight. I wish we'd had more time to hang out."

"Me too. But you were so busy with Noble."

We start walking at a brisk clip. "And when I was free, you were at HBO."

Because I needed to escape my own memories. "It's become my second home."

"More like your first home."

We round a bend, all the while her comment festers. After a few more steps, the need to explain myself becomes overwhelming. "HBO's much more involved than I thought. I've had to hire two new people to replace Helene and myself, plus I have been in several rounds of meetings with the network. Quite eye-opening, actually."

"Sounds challenging. Professionally, you're proving yourself."

"I'm trying to. As with any change, people are nervous. I'm keeping everyone on the same page, though."

"I have no doubt."

We round a corner and thread our way through the throngs of tourists. As we near the large building housing the Metropolitan Museum of Art, Sophia points to a kiosk. "Want a drink?"

Today's summer heat is typical for New York. Swiping my arm across my sweaty forehead, I nod. We get a couple of fruit smoothies and take a seat at a nearby bench.

"I wish I lived here."

I bump my shoulder against hers. "One simple answer to that. Move."

She stirs her drink with the straw. "I would if I wasn't flying all over the world all the time. Nobel's next movies, which start pre-pre-production next month, are going to be shot in various locations, but based in LA. It doesn't make sense for me to get an apartment here when I won't be around to live in it."

I let the strawberry banana smoothie cool my body from the inside out. "I guess you're right."

"Things never change." She giggles.

Her positivity almost succeeds in infecting my body, but not quite. I freeze the smile on my face, even though it wants to slide away. I won't let the precious time we have together be ruined by my broken heart. Which will mend. Someday.

"I do hope you'll be able to get out and see the amazing country-side you're going to be shooting in."

"Me too. But for that damn bug in Italy, I would've been able to explore the Amalfi Coast more." She sips her drink. "Like you and Charles did."

Boom.

My mouth tightens around the paper straw. She knows all about how he used me to get the part in my dad's movie. "Maybe you got the better end of that stick."

"Sorry, Mel. I didn't—"

"No worries." I cut her off as I sip the final bits of my smoothie.

She slurps the last part of her drink. Standing, she collects my empty cup and walks over to a trash can. I use the few moments to calm my speeding heart. Chase belongs in the past. I shunt all memories of him as far away as possible as she approaches. Standing up, I join her on the jogging path.

As we finish, she mentions that Mark's texted her a couple of times. "Really?"

She toys with her collar. "Yeah."

"Are you two going to go out?"

"He's in Florida."

"He'll be in LA soon, though." I take a few more steps. "Have you heard from Thomas?" My use of Chase's PA's name causes a pain to slice through me. Because she was so into him on set, I maintain control of my neutral expression. By a thread.

"No." Sophia points to an outdoor café. "Want to grab a bite?"

I sigh. "I'd love to, you know that, but I'm not up to it. I'm so sorry."

Walking next to me, she says, "I get it. I'm sorry, too. If I could get five minutes alone with that Charles, I'd give him a huge piece of my mind."

Her defense makes me tip my lips upward. "He's not worth it," I say softly.

She stops and turns to me. "When I'm back in town, I'm not going to be giving you any more breaks. We're going to hang out for hours. Do each other's hair. Go out. Get drunk."

"That sounds like fun."

"Pinky swear?" She holds up her little finger, into which I hook mine.

I give her a heartfelt hug and we part. On my way back to my condo, I pass a magazine stand where a photo of Chase stares at me. Before I can stop myself, the magazine's in my hand. In my condo, I toss my keys and the magazine on the kitchen island. His stupid, smiling face stares back at me. Taunts me. I reach over to crumple it, but step away. Removing my knitting needles from my hair, I head to the bathroom for a shower.

Back in my kitchen, I make a snack of crackers and cheese and sit down. Next to the magazine. "You're an asshole!"

I plunk my plate on top of his lying face. Laying a piece of cheese on top of a cracker, I take a bite. And chew.

I take another bite. And chew.

I finish the cracker.

I look down at the rest of the items on my plate and push away from the table. Standing up, I walk around my kitchen and then the rest of the condo. I find myself standing in front of the violin. Annoyed at the world, I turn and end up at the island where I move the plate and pick up the magazine.

Above Chase's head is the headline, "What's Next for Chase Wright?"

"Jerk!"

Despite my knuckles turning white, I flip the pages to the article. I'm greeted by a photo of Chase standing in front of a pool, soaking wet, wearing an equally wet white, button-down shirt that's molded to his defined torso. My heart stutters. "Fuck."

My eyes bounce from the photo to the article. I try to stop myself from reading it, but my damned eyes betray me. The article talks about his wrapping up his role as Doctor Manipul8 and shows a promo photo of him in the new superhero costume. I sewed him into that outfit. Objectively, the suit looks good. Subjectively, though . . .

I force myself to look at the rest of the photos, which show him out with Cherie Adams, after the red carpet premiere of *I Was Made for Her*. God, they look so good together. With her gorgeous figure and perfect blond hair, she's his exact opposite—his perfect compliment. It's like *he* was made for *her*.

Drowning a tortured sob, I give up and skim the rest of the article, which concludes with a discussion of his next role. Playing Braxton Hunte in the upcoming rockumentary.

My stomach lurches. "He did it. He took the role." Of course he did.

Tears threaten, but I slam my eyes shut. "I haven't shed a tear for you yet, and I'm not going to now." I take several deep breaths, which are interrupted by a knocking at my door.

Without thought, I fling open the door.

Chase stands before me.

Everything freezes.

The air.

My breath.

Time.

When he clears his throat, I push the door forward.

He moves his foot over the threshold to block the door's closing. His achingly familiar tenor voice reaches out, "Melody. Please."

The door bounces off his foot. I regulate my voice downward. "Go. Away."

He pushes, and I press back. "Please. I need to talk with you." His voice contains a timbre I've never heard from him. Desperation?

Perhaps it's the pleading note in his voice. Maybe it's my own traitorous body wanting to give him a better put down than I just did. Whatever the reason, I let the door go and step to the side, causing him to fall forward, fueled by his own momentum. He catches himself before he face plants. Unfortunately.

Standing behind the door, I give him the evil eye. My brain yells for him to die. DIE!

Clearly he doesn't hear me, because he continues breathing. With precise movements, he turns to face me.

I cross my arms.

His head motions toward the living room. "Can we talk in there?"

"No."

He swallows and tugs his hand through his hair, ending on his forehead. Then he draws to his full height.

I don't move. Not an inch.

"You look thin."

I point to the open door. "You can leave if you're here to comment on my weight."

He licks his lips. "No. I'm not here for that."

I force a breath to go in. And out.

"God, you're so beautiful."

Out of all the things I expected him to say, this was not one of them. My hands land on my hips. "Still a great movie star reciting lines, I see."

He flinches. "Melody, please, I'm not acting. You *are* beautiful. You have hair like spun gold and a royal profile."

I throw my head back and force a harsh laugh. "You're much better when someone else writes your words."

His jaw tightens. "They're not lines."

"Fine. They're not. Since that's all you have to say, you may go. Now." I point at the open door.

"No."

I flick the rubber band around my wrist. "Why are you here, Chase?"

His gaze bounces from my wrist to my eyes. "Charles."

"Spit out what you came to say and leave."

He strides toward the kitchen island and stops on a dime. Picking up the stupid magazine I was reading, he brings it back to me. "You were reading about me?"

"Don't get a swelled head. Someone left it down by the mailboxes and I brought it up here because I needed the newsprint to, to pack up a few things," I prevaricate.

His eyebrow rises, but he doesn't comment. Skimming the article, he points to the final paragraph where it says he's going to play Braxton Hunte. I raise my chin. "It says my next role is of your father."

I turn my head.

"Lies. It's all lies."

I swing toward him. "What?"

He whacks the magazine against his thigh. "Not your father. He was telling the truth at the dinner table back in Chicago. I was offered the role. I turned it down." His cheeks turn a light shade of pink. "Sam's not happy with me."

He turned down the role? "You did? Why? It's a great part."

"I haven't seen the script, so I can't agree or disagree with you. It was pitched as the next *Bohemian Rhapsody*. I was practically promised an Oscar."

My brain tries to get up to speed. "You didn't take it?"

"No. I didn't." His hand lands on his forehead. "I have you to thank for my decision."

"What did I have to do with any of this?" Cramming down an unusual buzzing in my chest, I add *why are we having this bizarre conversation?*

Chase walks toward me, stopping about three feet away. His voice drops. "Everything. You sewed me into the Doctor Manipul8 costume every day for two weeks and turned my life upside down. You let me dream big. You let me simply be *me*."

For the first time in ages, I take hold of the rubber band around my wrist, but leave it unplucked. His words don't make any sense. "Okay?"

His hands land on my shoulders, and he squeezes. My body goes rigid. "I turned down the 'role of a lifetime,' as Sam described it to me, because you showed me who I want to be. I want to act in front of a live audience, and not be behind a camera. I want to hear applause, and laughter, and crying. I want the emotions I'm portraying amplified back at me."

I don't move a muscle, his hands remaining on my person. "Oh."

"I want to do all that here. In New York City. Because I want to breathe the same air as you, celebrate our successes together, and share the bad times with you." His chest expands. "Because I love you, Melody."

The air stills.

He's said that before. In Chicago. "Practice those lines much?"

A smile reaches his blue eyes. "I had the best teacher. You."

His hands haven't moved. Neither have I. I search his face for traces that he's lying. Yet his handsome face remains open. Heat rises behind my eyelids.

He shakes me a little. "You taught me all about love. About pursuing your passion. I finally believe in my own talent because you modeled how it's done."

My limbs gain twenty extra pounds. I don't believe him. I can't. "You used me. I bet you couldn't believe your good luck when I offered myself to you like an idiot."

He tucks my hair behind my ear, causing me to bite my inner cheek. "No, I never used you. Not for a moment. I was honored you chose me as your first. *Am* honored."

Why is he saying this to me? "What do you have to gain from telling me all this?"

"The only thing that matters to me in the world. You."

My breathing hitches. I rub my palms on my hips, trying to process the past few minutes. "Did you really turn my dad down?"

"Yes." His eyes drop to my mouth, then bounce up to my eyes. "I want to cut my chops on Broadway, not doing more movies."

He told me that in Amalfi. That's why we flew here for his audition. "Did you get the part in *Hamlet 2.0*?"

Air expels through his mouth. "No. They went with a more established Broadway actor."

"It doesn't matter." I gulp in air. "You're just like the rest of the world, Chase. You wanted me for what I could do for your career. For my connection to my dad."

"Think about what you're saying, Goldie."

I spasm at the nickname.

"Remember what happened. True, I auditioned for the part before filming of *Doctor Manipul8* began filming in Italy, and I'm guilty of not telling you right away. That's it. I got to know you as my dresser, and then we went to Positano and everything changed. I think I fell in love with you on the ferry ride back to Amalfi, even though it took my brain a little longer to catch up with my heart."

I swallow.

"Everything between us was real. I never gave a second thought to your father's movie, truth be told. You helped me focus on my career in a strategic manner, a destiny only I could steer. I started out wanting to be on stage and sort of fell into movies. And success. Which bred more movies. I've put an end to that vicious cycle now. I turned down the movie role. I don't want it. I don't want any of those roles."

"You're crazy. It's going to be an epic film."

He shrugs. "Maybe. For someone else. I do wish your father and the crew all the best. But it's not what I want for me. I want to live here in New York City and work eight performances a week in front of different audiences." His hands slide down my slack arms. "More than anything, though, I *need* you in my life. Today, tomorrow, and forever."

My heart lurches. My blood moves faster through my system. Is he telling the truth? Can I believe him? "Chase—"

He cuts me off. "Charles."

I force myself to utter the forbidden name. "Charles." My voice cracks. I lick my lips. "How can I believe you?'

"Because I'm telling you the truth. I have no job, no place to live. All I have is me, wanting to be with you. I love you, Melody Annabel Hunte. I've never said these words to any woman outside of a movie script. If you'll let me, I'll say them to you every single day as long as we both shall live."

I suck in my breath. He's baring his soul, and it's fresh and clean and honest. And *mine*. Still. "What about Cherie?"

He winces. "What about her? We're friends." He steps back and I mourn his heat. "We had a fling before I met you, but now we see each other from time to time as friends only."

I close my eyes. He's been living the Hollywood high life for a decade and has countless notches on his bedpost. Yet, he could've lied just now and he didn't. I open my eyes. "Thank you for telling me the truth. However, you did take her to the premiere. I saw pictures in the magazine." My eyes go to the table.

"I did. You know Thomas set it up. But believe me, nothing happened." He pauses. "I didn't do anything with her because she's not you. She's too tall. Her hair's the wrong shade. She doesn't have your smile or wit or talent with a needle."

My upper lip worries my bottom. "I guess I'm going to have to accept the fact you've slept with a ton of women."

"Not a ton." He steps forward and puts his finger under my chin, coaxing it up. "They didn't mean anything but sex. I've never made love with anyone but you."

I search his eyes for a hint of deceit and come up empty. As I inhale, all my molecules jump over each other, rearranging themselves into a new order. One where Charles Wainwright is my leading man. Still, years of life lessons can't be undone with one pretty speech.

My chest tingles. "I want to believe you."

His thumb catches the tear rolling down my cheek. "How about this? Why don't you close the door and let me start proving myself to you?" He reaches into his back pocket and produces a copy of *Backstage*. "You can help me select my next auditions."

I laugh because that was not what I had expected. I thought he would try to seduce me and make me forget all the hurt. This overture, however, means more to me. I close the door. We spend the next several hours poring through the magazine, selecting three parts he'd like to try for. Two plays and, at my urging, one musical.

Charles presses a button on his cell. "Last audition submitted! All that's left is the waiting."

Excited for him, I throw my arms around his neck and give him a hug. Realizing what I've done, I start to pull back.

"Don't," he whispers.

His tone sends my nerve endings scattering in all directions. He doesn't reach for me, though. He's offering himself *to* me.

I gaze into his magnetic eyes. Charles turned my life inside out and upside down, all the while making me a better person for it. A better designer. A better friend and daughter and even sister. More than anything else, he's made me believe in myself and my talents. Not because of an accident of birth, but for what I bring to the table.

Standing, I hold out my hand. "Take me to bed, Charles. I want to share everything I am with you, my love."

His expressive eyes darken. "You'll never regret this decision, Goldie."

"I know."

CHASE

The beautiful woman under me giggles. "Charles, you're going to make me late!"

I bring her arms over her head and secure them with my hands, all the while raining kisses over her expressive face. Life with Melody is never dull. She sees the world differently from me, and I love that about her. I love every single thing about her.

"You're the boss. You set the hours. Besides, filming doesn't start for another two weeks." I nuzzle her neck.

She tilts her head onto the pillow in order to give me better access. That's my girl. *My* girl. Mine.

My hands leave her wrists and they skim down her naked body. Even though it's been two weeks since we reconciled—well, I groveled and she let me back into her life—nothing about sharing our bodies gets old. It only improves.

Letting her nipple slip from my mouth, I gaze up at her amber, hooded eyes, filled with so much passion. I slide up her body and rest my weight on my arms, bracketing her face.

"Charles." She arches her back.

I kiss her lips. "I'll never get tired of hearing you say my name."

"And I'll never get tired of this." Her legs rub against mine as she fits her softness against my straining body. "I have a lot of catching up to do."

"Not as much as me, Goldie. You've taught me what it means to give yourself over to someone else, body and soul." I kiss her mouth, my tongue entering hers. Pulling away, I gaze into her passionate eyes.

Her nails scrape down my back, ushering in a shiver of desire.

My fingers enter her core and I work her into a frenzy, but deny her release. Instead, I splay her wide-open and position my mouth right above her clit. I lick her swollen bud. "Like this?"

Her head swivels from side to side on the pillow while her lower body moves in time with my licks. Her body clenches, then she screams her release.

Sitting on my haunches, I wipe her juices off my mouth, a satisfied smirk playing around my lips. She lies, limp. "You're mighty talented with that tongue."

I cup my hard cock in my hand. "That's not the only thing I'm talented with." I give myself a tug.

She sits up. "Need a hand with that?"

"That'll be a start."

Her fingers close around me, causing my breath to cease for a second, then rush through my body. When her tongue swipes at my tip, I grab her hair and direct her closer. She looks up at me, my cock still in her mouth.

Is there any more amazing sight?

"I want to come inside your body. Because I can. Because you're mine."

At my use of the word "mine" her eyes widen, and her mouth slackens. "How?"

Because I'm feeling selfless, I roll my hips. "However you want."

Fast as a clapperboard, she rolls a condom on me and pushes against my pecs, sending me sprawling onto my back. She climbs on top of me, her delicious thighs straddling me. "I want it this way." She kisses my mouth.

Wrapping my arms around her, I pull her down and deepen the kiss.

Her fingers find my erection and hold it upright while she seats herself on me. My eyelids flutter closed at the welcoming feeling. Forcing my lids back open, I watch as she takes her bottom lip between her teeth.

Thrusting upward to her downward strokes, our bodies wrestle in the most amazing way. Her tits sway in front of me, and I latch onto one nipple, sucking hard. Her hips jolt forward.

"Charles. God."

"Just Charles will do. I'm a man, not a deity."

"You're my divinity," she breathes. She increases her tempo, causing all sorts of friction between us.

Her body stiffens and she screams again. With her core flexing around my cock, I take a shallow breath, my balls starting to tingle. Roaring, I let myself go.

She collapses on top of me, my hands landing on her ass to keep her in place. Next to my ear, her breathing comes in increasingly deeper pants until it evens out.

Not wanting her to move, I flex my fingers. "I love you so much, Melody."

Her head lifts a fraction. "And I love you, too."

"This isn't how I had planned this, but I can't hold back anymore." I slip some of her gorgeous blond hair behind her ear. "Melody." Words desert me.

"Yes?" Against my will, she slides off my body and sprawls on the bed next to me. A wanton nymph. *My* wanton nymph.

With the sudden freedom from her body, I sit up and dispose of the condom, then reach into the drawer of the side table. With the velvet box in my hand, I face my future with all the determination to secure the most important role of my lifetime. Which this is.

I land on my side next to her, the box hidden in my hand that's supporting my head. "Melody," I begin again. "I can't imagine my life without you in it. I lived that way for what? A few weeks? I was the most miserable SOB ever."

She giggles at my accurate characterization.

Undeterred, I continue, "I never intend to go through that ever again. Whatever happens, I want you at my side. Only then I know everything will turn out the way it should." I open the box.

Her eyes go round.

"Melody, will you be my wife?"

A surprised giggle bursts through her lips. "Like this? You're asking me while I'm naked and still euphoric from the two orgasms you gave me?"

I quirk my eyebrow. "Looks like it."

She sits up, and I join her. My confidence dips a fraction.

"What will I tell my parents about how you proposed?"

A smile quirks. "I guess it depends on what your answer is." I shake the box in front of her.

"But I'm naked!"

"So am I." I kiss her mouth. "Say yes and we'll come up with a better story."

"You're incorrigible," she complains. "But I guess that's why I love you so much. Of course I'll marry you!" She throws her arms around my neck, her lips fusing to mine.

With supreme effort, I pull back and put the four-carat emerald cut diamond on her left hand. "Perfect fit." I kiss the inside of her palm.

"Like you," she whispers, stroking my already hard cock.

I toss the box over my shoulder and bring her thigh up to my hip. "Forever."

After Melody went to work, I worked out, cleaned the condo, and went to my acting class. Following another stimulating session with my fellow actors, I stop at the mailbox and retrieve Melody's copy of *Variety*. Walking into our condo, I toss the magazine on the dinette. A headline grabs my attention, and I flip to the article. Smiling, I put the magazine under my arm and head over to her office.

"Knock, knock," I say as I enter her space. I'm always awed at the amount of fabrics, mannequins, and notebooks strewn all over in here. My fiancée seems to know exactly where everything is.

I stroll over to her and kiss her forehead. "I've missed you," I murmur.

"You're a sight for sore eyes. I've been holed up in this office all day, trying to get through some of this paperwork and finish up the prototypes." She drops her pen on top of her notebook. "I thought we were meeting at the restaurant for dinner?"

"I couldn't wait that long to see you again." My fingers trail down her cheek to her left arm, and I close them around her hand. Bringing it up, I stare at my engagement ring perched there. "It looks so good on you."

She dons an adorable smirk. "You should be happy I said yes. After all, I'm doing all the heavy lifting around here. *One* of us has to work while the other one sits around eating bonbons all day."

I chuckle at the traditional role reversal. Tugging her to her feet, I place her open palms on my tight stomach. "Really? Bonbons?"

She giggles as she traces my muscles through my shirt. "Okay. That might have been a slight exaggeration."

I suck in my stomach, making my abs more pronounced. "I demand tribute as restitution!"

She rolls her eyes, but the smile on her lips tells another story. In a husky voice, she asks, "What do you have in mind?"

I scan her office for a flat surface, but everything's covered with either paper or fabric. But not her chair. "I'd like to have a repeat performance of this morning's activities." Turning, I bring us to her chair and sit down so she's on top of me.

"I can see that." Her head swivels toward the open door. "I think we need to do this show in private."

She's right. But I'm not giving up without a fight. I stroke her hair. "A kiss then. From my fiancée."

"That I can do."

Her lips pucker and she leans forward. As soon as our mouths meet, the kiss explodes. After a long while, we pull back, each breathing hard.

Our foreheads touch. "What you do to me, Goldie."

"Right back at 'ya."

With slow moves, she climbs off my lap and I stand, reaching into my back pocket and producing her copy of *Variety*. "I actually came over here to show you this."

Her eyes bounce from me to the magazine. "What's in it?"

"Thought you'd never ask. I mean, you were so busy kissing me and all," I tease, a large part of me still disbelieving she's actually mine. I double-check her left hand, and my heart swells at the confirmation.

She shakes her head. I open the magazine to the small article and point. "Let me do the honors."

I shake the magazine. "Headline—'*Ladies of the Abbey* Gets Hunted.'"

Melody's eyebrows rise, and she bites her bottom lip.

I start reading, "The hit HBO drama has undergone some changes during this hiatus. Judith Harris led her team from the show to the set of *Doctor Manipul8*, and she emerged with a new title. That of the newest lead costume designer for Ned Nobleman—better known to all as simply Noble.

"'I was so impressed with Judith's work ethic and ability to be prepared for any eventuality, not to mention her extremely creative designs. When my next movies were greenlit, I knew she had to head up my team.'

"Noble's gain was HBO's loss. Moreover, it was discovered on the movie set that one of Judith's assistant costume designers, Helene Parker, was undermining the film in order to get ahead. Parker is now awaiting trial in California for her efforts of sabotage.

"Which left Judith's other assistant, Melody Hunte, 25, as the sole remaining option for HBO if they wanted to stay in-house. HBO is known, however, for bringing in new talent under such circumstances.

"Not in this case, however. Hunte was named as the new lead costume designer for the HBO series and word on the street has it that she's very hands-on. She's already hired two assistants and is busy at work creating new designs for this season.

"'We're thrilled to have such a young and vibrant talent with us, leading *Ladies of the Abbey* forward. Ms. Hunte offers a unique perspective and brings an exciting eye to the design. She is going to make a very big splash here on the set, and we can't wait to showcase her work,' an HBO spokeswoman said.

"Hunte is the daughter of the legendary rock star Braxton Hunte, of the band of the same last name, about whose career a movie is in the early stages of production now."

I finish the article and set it down on her desk. Melody slams her mouth shut. "Wow. That was some article."

I point to the part about Helene. "I wish they had done a better job of describing all the bullshit she put you through." I tap on the magazine. "You know, I have only one unanswered question when it comes to Helene. How on earth did she manage to pull the stunt about my gloves?"

Melody swallows. "I've thought about that for a long time. I don't think she did anything. I believe the buckle somehow got caught in that boy's curls, and everything unraveled from there. Although, Helene was prepared with the silk material we finally used."

"Accident then?"

She nods. "I think so. When she realized how easy it would be to foster more accidents like it, I think that's when she went over the edge." Melody picks up the magazine and repeats the last line. Big, expressive hazel eyes meet mine. "I'm being recognized for my own work. Not for being someone's daughter."

I drop to my knee in front of her. Grabbing her hands, I say, "You're your own talent, Melody Hunte. You bring wit and creativity and vibrancy to any set you're on. Your creations are clever and fit with the aesthetic the director is trying to convey. Yes, Brax is your father, but you are a formidable woman in your own right. I bet you, one day, there will be a movie made about you." I kiss her fingertips.

"Oh, excuse me!" Melody's new assistant stands in the doorway. "I didn't mean to interrupt."

Melody stands up and waves her left hand. "No worries. What's up?"

The assistant's mouth flies open. Her eyes bounce from Melody's hand to her face and then to posture on one knee. "Oh my God. Did you just get engaged?"

Melody starts to stammer a reply when I jump to my feet. "Guilty! Melody always said she wanted to have a romantic proposal, one she could share with her parents and, someday, our kids. I'm proud to say she agreed to be my wife." I bring her hand to my lips, a smile dancing around my mouth.

Melody bursts out laughing. "I never thought being surrounded by my work would be a romantic setting, but leave it to Charles to turn anything into a memorable occasion."

Her assistant turns and yells, "Melody got engaged!" She rushes in and hugs us both.

We spend the next hour accepting congratulations from everyone on the show, and even the network. Melody exalts under their excitement, at being accepted as a talent in her own right. Even better, for being loved as the amazing woman she is.

Finally, I escort her out of the building and toward a new restaurant opened by one of the premiere chefs in the world. I offer her my arm and escort her inside. Right to a table where her family awaits.

"Mom! Daddy! King! Angie! I can't believe you're here!" She gives them each huge hugs and then thrusts her left hand in front of them. "Charles proposed today!"

Brax walks over to me and shakes my hand. "Son, we're so happy to welcome you into the family, even if you turned down the role playing me."

"Thanks, sir," I reply. We've cleared the air between us over the movie. I'm actually a bit excited to see the premiere, without being a part of it. He breaks into a broad smile and wraps me in a bear hug.

After hellos and congratulations are shared—as well as how I romantically proposed this afternoon in Melody's office, which causes my fiancée and me to share a conspiratorial wink—I bring up the *Variety* article. Everyone is excited to see Melody blossoming. No one more than me.

I place my arm around the back of Melody's chair and raise my champagne. "To my future wife, the woman who resides in my heart. She taught me to trust in my secret desires, and I'm here following them. Because of her. I'm humbled to be welcomed into your family and promise to allow Melody's light to shine brighter than she even believes possible."

I raise my glass. "To my fiancée. Who shares her golden light with everyone she touches. I love you."

EPILOGUE – MELODY

Time has passed in a blur. I'm taking our engagement slow, enjoying the process as much as possible. I toss a copy of *Bride's* onto the coffee table and rest my head on my fiancé's wide, muscular shoulder.

"What's next on our to-do list?"

Charles has been so supportive in planning, having definite ideas on our décor. Especially the flowers, which he's insisted all be shades of yellow. To match my hair. I fiddle with a long lock of it.

"I think we need to plan our honeymoon."

He turns toward me. "Now you're talking." He kisses me, and all thoughts of wedding plans scatter.

My finger traces his cheek, ending in the dent in his chin. "You're so hot."

His eyes sparkle. "That's what a man likes to hear from his woman." He kisses the tip of my nose. "Although your beauty eclipses mine."

I accept his exquisitely-worded lie. I know I'm not special in the looks department, but Charles sees me this way, and I'm not about to argue. I rest my head on his shoulder. "I think we've gotten a lot of the major stuff taken care of for the wedding for a while. We'll figure out a super-awesome honeymoon in a while." I trace a heart on his upper chest. "I was thinking we could work on something a bit different."

"Uh-oh. What are you thinking?" He taps my forehead.

"Nothing bad. I was thinking I'd like to move. I love this condo, but my parents bought it for me when I went to college. I'd like to get something only for us."

"I like the sound of that, Goldie. Our place."

I nod, my head bouncing on his body. "In the City, right?"

"Since I'm now a bona fide Broadway actor, I totally agree. I have my house out in LA that I can sell. We'll never live out there."

"Are you sure?"

Charles shrugs. "Yeah. We can use the profit as a down payment." Not that we need any help in that area.

Blood races through my body and I kiss his cheek. "I'll let Daddy know he's getting this place back."

His hands close around my body, and he rubs them up and down my back. "Our place. I like the sound of that. Stay in the Upper East?"

"Yeah. I like it up here. Maybe a couple of blocks down on Central Park?"

He hugs me closer, his nose breathing in the vanilla from my shampoo. "I'm down with that."

"Do you think we could hire King and Angie to find it for us?"

He pulls back. "That sounds like a great idea. I know they're set up out in the Hamptons, but I trust them to find us something perfect."

"Great." I text my brother. We've spent more time together than ever, and he's a pretty great guy. The fact Angie will be my sister-in-law rocks. "I can't wait to see what they have to show us."

My phone dings with an incoming text. "King says he's on board."

"Great."

"He wants to know if we want to be featured on his reality TV show."

Charles removes his body from mine. "Not great."

I cock my head. "Why not? Having us on their show might help out their already high ratings. He is my brother, after all."

He combs his hand through his hair. "I know King's your brother.

But I'm acting on Broadway now. I'm not looking to boost my next movie."

"I know that. You're still a big movie star though—"

He winces at my use of the term. "Exactly why I don't want to be on the show."

A new text arrives. "Angie just texted me. She's saying she understands if we don't want to be on the show. She says Let's Do It!, her network, wanted to put her wedding planning and ceremony on TV, and she overruled it."

"See." He crosses his arms in front of his chest. "She gets it. No cameras."

My cell dings. "This is from King. He says there's a difference between being on the show and having their wedding exploited." I drop my phone onto the coffee table. "He's right, you know. Their wedding is private, while if we decide to go on their show about our real estate hunt, we'll be doing exactly what the show was designed to do."

"I hear you. However, don't they advertise addresses on their show? Everyone and their mother will know where we're living."

"You have a point. If we decide to go on the show, we'll have to negotiate how they do that." My finger traces my cell, and I return my head to his shoulder.

Slowly, his hard physique relaxes, and I move my left hand to over his heart. My engagement ring refracts so much light. "How much longer do we have before you have to get to the show?"

He caresses his ring. "Two more hours."

I look into his eyes. "Whatever shall we do to pass the time?"

He doesn't respond with words. Instead, he places his hands under my legs and stands with me in his arms. "I'm not sure. I think if we go to the bedroom, something will come up."

I link my arms around his neck. "I'm betting on it."

An hour later, we lie together in bed, sweat lingering on our skin. I trace the cuts of his abdominal muscles. "How many murderers have bodies like you?"

He rumbles a laugh. "Every time I walk onto the stage without my shirt, we have to wait for the audience to settle down. My friends all make fun of me."

I kiss his stomach. "I think it was a stroke of genius for the producers to cast you as the villain. No one expects it of you."

He puffs up. "Athena Davis wanted me to audition for the lead. Thanks to you, I stuck to my guns and refused. I think it adds to the enjoyment of the play."

"'And Chase Wright's first turn on Broadway is a smashing success. He brings an aura of unpredictability to this delightful murder-mystery.'"

He smiles. "My favorite review ever."

I turn onto my stomach. "Even better than their enthusiasm over your playing *Doctor Manipul8.*"

"Yes. However, being sewn into that costume during the last part of the trilogy was a highlight for me."

"That's because you had an amazing dresser."

He smacks my naked ass. "True!" He gets out of bed and heads to the bathroom. Shortly, the water in the shower starts.

I check the clock. Charles still has enough time before he needs to head out to the theater. I pad into the bathroom behind him and slip into the shower. "I think you might need some help getting clean."

"Getting dirty, you mean?"

"Trying to do my fiancée duties." I squeeze around him, my hand landing on his semi-erect cock. "I think he needs a little help."

One eyebrow rises. "You do?"

I school my expression to show feigned concentration. "Yes." I glide my hand up and down, back and forth, cupping his balls ever so often.

He swallows and widens his stance. His erection grows larger under my ministrations. "Seems like you're doing a damn fine job, Goldie."

The water rolls down our backs. I rub my thumb over the pre-cum at his tip, which formed already even though we made love not thirty minutes ago. His eyes close when I bend and take him in my mouth. I let my tongue lick over his hardness, then take him as deep as possible into the back of my throat.

"Melody, I'm close."

Instead of moving back, I suck harder and swallow everything he has to give me. I stand, a satisfied smile on my face.

"I want to make you come, but I'm not sure we have enough time."

"I trust you'll make it up to me later."

"Without a doubt."

I let my fingers roam over his hard muscles. Muscles he works hard to maintain, both in exercise and diet. He's very disciplined in all aspects of his life. Except when it comes to me. With me, he's carefree and loving.

"I love you so much, Charles," I say, wrapping a fluffy white towel around my body.

"Right back at you."

My heart swells. "I'll let you get dressed and I'll meet you in the living room." I kiss him once more.

Exchanging the towel for a breezy navy blue dress, and sans shoes, I walk into the kitchen to put together a power snack for Charles before he heads out to work. I understand his worry over being on *Battle of the Real Estate Matchmakers*, but I think it could be fun. However, he does have a valid point about everyone knowing our new address. I pause from cutting up his apple—I'm feeling very domestic at the moment, plus I'm taking advantage of it being Sunday and don't have to work—and text this idea to King and Angie.

Setting the table with his apple and a jar of peanut butter, I begin making his protein shake. My eyes land on the spoon rest boasting "Positano" resting on the oven, a grin tugging at my lips.

Clad in a pair of jeans and a long-sleeved T-shirt, Charles strolls into the kitchen. "A man could get used to this treatment."

"Don't get too used to it, Big Boy." I pour his shake into a glass. "Tomorrow's Monday, and you're back to being on your own."

He slumps into a chair. "I hate Mondays the most. You have to work, and I get to mope around all day."

I steal a piece of apple. "You have your acting classes on Mondays."

"True." He slurps down the shake. "That is the bright spot until you get home."

"I'll try to leave the office earlier. We're in the middle of shooting, though, so you know how that goes."

He spreads some peanut butter on his apple. "I do. Which is why I'm in the 'theatre' now."

I laugh at the affected way he pronounces *theater*. "I'm sure you'll survive one day without me. How about what I have to endure as the fiancée of a man of the *theatre*." I use his same affected pronunciation.

"What? All the fans throwing themselves at me?"

I frown. "I wasn't thinking of that until you brought it up." I grab another slice of apple from his plate and chomp down while he chuckles.

"No," I continue. "I was thinking of how my Wednesday nights and Saturdays suck. You have doubles those days."

"We'll work it out, Goldie."

My cell beeps with an incoming text. "King says we could give an oblique neighborhood versus the actual addresses of the places we go visit. Or the address of places we don't buy. If we decide to go on the show."

He crunches the last bit of his apple. "You really want to be on the show?"

"Not really," I admit. "However, I do want to support my brother. You're such a big star," I bat my eyelashes at him.

Charles's jaw tenses. Then a wolfish grin overtakes his face. "I'm sure you can think of a way to make up the shoots to me. Something along the lines of what you just did in the shower would be a good start."

I step back. "Are you sexually propositioning me to be on the show?"

"I wouldn't say that exactly. More like offering you a way to sweeten the pot." His phone alarm sounds. "This conversation isn't over."

He steps into the kitchen and embraces me, kissing me with all the passion we shared this morning. Will share again tonight. "I love you, Goldie."

He opens the fridge and grabs a fizzy water before striding across the room. As his hand lands on the doorknob, I yell, "Break a leg!"

Charles smiles and disappears into the hallway.

Alone in the condo, I plop down on the sofa. Do I want to be on King's show? I'm torn personally, but I do know I want to support my brother. This feeling overrides my misgivings.

Because I can't give King the go-ahead without getting Charles one hundred percent on board, I call my parents. "Princess! How's life treating you in the Big Apple?"

My gaze lands on the remnants of Charles's snack and pull myself out of the sofa. Walking to the dinette, I begin to clean up, starting by closing up the peanut butter jar.

"It's good here, Daddy. Charles and I decided that we'd like to move." I place the peanut butter into the pantry and add, "We love your condo, of course. But we'd like to have a place that we pick, if you know what I mean."

"I get it. Finding a home is something very personal. Your mom and I will happily stay in the condo when we visit our kids, who both seem to be growing roots in the Empire State." He chuckles.

I stack the dirty dishes in the sink and toss the debris into the garbage can. "Thanks. What do you think if we show our home search on King and Angie's show?"

My dad takes a moment to respond. "I never thought my two kids would be together on a TV show," he says in a thick voice. "Personally, I think it would make for some amazing television."

"Charles and I are trying to decide what to do."

Noise in the background from my dad's side comes through my receiver. "Your mother just got home. Hold on." In muffled tones, I hear a kiss followed by him telling her about the show. "I'm putting you on speaker."

My mother's voice comes through. "Hi, Melody. How's wedding planning?"

"It's coming along well, Mom. Got the major vendors locked down."

"That's great. Now your dad tells me you're looking for a new place?"

"We made that decision today."

"I trust you to make the right choice for you."

"Thanks, Mom." We get caught up on the local gossip about my job, her role as Hunte's tour accountant that has expanded with the movie, and my dad's excitement over said movie.

"Oh, one thing before you go, Princess."

"Yes, Daddy?"

"Hunte is performing next month at Madison Square Garden. We'd love it if you and Charles could be there. King and Angie are coming."

A smile crosses my face. "Of course I'll be there. It depends on what day for Charles, though, as he's working on Broadway."

"Oh right. Sara, what day of the week is the Hunte concert?"

She replies, "Monday."

"Oh great. Charles is off on Mondays, so we'll definitely be there."

We hang up and I decide to sneak into the theater tonight to watch my kickass fiancée perform. Returning to our bedroom, I stride to my jewelry box. My life has come such a long way since I took a movie job with Judith during the HBO show's hiatus.

I got my dream promotion on HBO.

My talent is finally being recognized.

And the most important thing in the world to me—the love I share with Charles.

I select a pair of earrings and pick up a rubber band I had discarded ages ago. Charles helped me realize I don't need it any longer. I've learned how to navigate challenges with a positive outlook, just like he's allowing his true self to shine.

Whatever life brings from this moment forward, I have confidence we'll tackle it all. Together.

∾

Wondering what's going to happen at the Madison Square Garden concert? You're not going to believe it!! The Hunte Family Series concludes with the last book in the series, OUT OF THE BLUE, up next.

In the meantime, turn the page for a glimpse into Melody and Charles's life ~ four years in the future!

BONUS EPILOGUE: MELODY

"Rafe, come to Mommy."

My blond-haired baby—his name a derivative of Ravello and an homage to Charles's favorite artist—toddles toward me and flings his arms around my neck. His hazel eyes—identical to all of the Huntes'—bore into my soul. Which he owns. "I go with you and Daddy!"

I hug my son tighter. "I know you want to come with us, Little Man, but it's going to be a late night, filled with all sorts of grown-up stuff that won't be fun for you. Not even Elmo will be there." Unless you count some of the crazies who may walk outside the ceremony.

Rafe steps back, wearing a distressed facial expression. "Cookie Monster?"

I shake my head.

He deflates. "With no Elmo or Cookie, no fun."

I smile at his logic. "You're right. You'll get to play with Danielle, though."

At the mention of his cousin, who was named after Angie's first husband, my son's face lights up. "She have my Elmo."

"Now that's quite the noble gesture," Charles says from behind me, not bothering to correct Rafe's grammar.

I stand and turn to see my husband all decked out in his tux. I walk over to him and straighten his already straight skinny tie, simply because I want to have my hands on him. "You look nice."

His piercing blue eyes skim over my body, clad in a Vera Wang ensemble in turquoise. "With you wearing that, I bet no one will give me a second glance."

I walk into my husband's arms and we share a kiss.

"Yucky!"

Pulling away from his warm embrace, we both look down at our son. Charles raises his eyebrow. "Just wait, Little Man. In fifteen years, you're going to have a change of heart."

I laugh. "Let's not rush him, okay? He needs to learn how to speak in full sentences first."

The doorbell grabs our attention, and I walk over to the intercom. "Hi, Geordie," I reply to the doorman. "Is Ellen here?"

"Yes, ma'am, with your parents. Your brother and his family are walking across the lobby."

"Please send them all up."

A noise from down the hall announces Charles's parents and Lindsay and her husband have made it out of the guest bedrooms. Over the years, Lindsay and I have forged a delicate truce, although it doesn't hurt that she lives clear across the pond in Switzerland.

"You all look wonderful," I remark.

On legs that get steadier by the day, Rafe approaches his grandparents. "Pretty!" They laugh and pick up my son.

Lindsay's holding him when the elevator door opens. "G'Mom! Pop-Pop!!" Rafe squirms away from his aunt and toddles to his other set of grandparents, throwing himself at them with abandon.

My dad scoops Rafe up and tosses him in the air, to his elated squeals. My mom admonishes him not to be so reckless, but he grins at her and tosses my son again.

King and his family walk in through the door left open by my parents. Angie holds Danielle's hand and rests her free hand on her growing belly. She's due in four months and is radiant. I rush to greet them.

"You're glowing, Angie. You're going to outshine everyone tonight."

She lets Danielle go, and the little girl heads directly to my son, who presents her with his Elmo. Ellen, the babysitter, ushers them over to the side of the living room while King helps her set up the playpen and all the other assorted paraphernalia.

Charles distributes champagne to everyone—sparkling cider for Angie, of course. Clearing his throat, he says, "I want to thank you all for coming to the Tony's tonight. Brax, hopefully tonight we'll do you proud."

My dad lifts his glass. "You already have. You and Princess turned the mediocre movie about Hunte into a spectacular event on Broadway. No matter what happens tonight, I couldn't be prouder of all your hard work."

"Thank you, Daddy."

We all sip the Dom. I can't believe where my life has taken me over the past four years. Moving into this great condo. King and Angie's wedding. My unforgettable marriage to Charles. Bringing new children into the Hunte fold. The end of my HBO show and joining the brand-new Broadway production of the Hunte movie, *Hunted*. Charles helped me get over my nepotism fears, and I joined the crew as the lead costume designer. Of course, Charles is playing my dad. He definitely deserves a Tony for his amazing portrayal.

King continues the toast. "The production is amazing, and I'm sending you all positive vibes! I have a feeling tonight's going to be wonderful."

"Let's hope so," my mother says. "We should be heading over so we're not late. Plus, we all have to walk the red carpet."

I swivel my head. "Wait. Where's Trent?"

"He's meeting us there. He had a rehearsal," Daddy replies.

I nod and then rush over to Rafe. I hate leaving him every night, and tonight's no exception. I kiss his head. "Now be good for Miss Ellen, Little Man."

Without lifting his head from the Muppets, he answers, "Yes, Mommy."

Charles stands behind me. "Rafael Braxton Wainwright. Give Mommy and me a proper kiss."

My husband always demands a kiss from his son. While I would've let him continue to play, I do appreciate Charles's mandate. Rafe drops the doll and races over to me, kissing my cheek. "Bye, Mommy!"

I stand up with him in my arms, hugging his little body to mine. After kissing the tip of his nose, I hand him over to his father. Charles says, "I love you," and kisses his entire face, eliciting an excited shriek from him. Next to us, Danielle emits a similar sound in her parents' arms.

The grandparents demand their share of kisses from the kids, and my heart expands in the way they adore them. Charles's parents and Lindsay and her husband also give kisses to both of them.

Laughing, Angie says, "Come on. We better leave before we never make it out of here. The limo's waiting."

After final kisses to both kids, we pile into the elevator. My dad presses the button for the lobby, and the ride down is quiet as we transition from family fun into our professional appearance mode.

We travel across the lobby and get into the limo the show provided for us. My dad immediately goes for the Bud at the bar, while Charles opts for his pinot noir. The rest of us share another bottle of Dom Perignon, except for Angie, who settles for a seltzer.

"Tell me, sis, do you miss working on a television show?"

I consider King's question. "Honestly, I don't. Working on the musical has a similar feel, in that the crew is very tight-knit. Probably even more so than on TV because we're leaner. And creating the costumes for everyone was so much fun. Who knew going all the way back to the nineties would be so satisfying?"

Charles's eyes meet mine. Before he can speak, my dad grumbles, "You don't have to talk like it's the eighteen-nineties. It wasn't that long ago."

I bring my champagne to my lips in order to hide my grin. My mother settles her hand on his sleeve and whispers something into his ear. Whatever she said brings a huge smile to his face, and he places his lips on her cheek.

"Yucky," I repeat Rafe's comment, drawing chuckles from everyone in the limo.

Soon we arrive at the world-famous Radio City Music Hall, teeming with people and lights and a red carpet. Charles asks, "Are you all ready?"

We all take fortifying sips of our drinks, then place the empty glasses on the bar. Charles motions for King and Angie to leave first, followed by Lindsay and her husband, our parents, and then he slides out. I take a deep breath and join him on the sidewalk. The early June air settles into my lungs, and I link my arm with my husband's.

Screams come into focus as we walk the red carpet, being pulled over by various reporters for quick interviews. So many well-wishes make me even more nervous than before. By the time we enter the Art Deco building, my body's almost vibrating.

"Don't worry, Goldie. No matter what happens tonight, you're always my shining star."

Then my husband says something like that, and my nerves dissipate. I place my palm on his stubbled cheek. "And you're always mine." I give him a kiss that, even though brief, promises much more. Hooded eyes hold mine for a moment.

"Let's go find our seats," my mother suggests.

We file into the iconic room. My parents are seated right behind us, and their row is filled in with the rest of Hunte—Colton and his new wife, Amy, Ricky and his girlfriend, Lex and Whitney, plus their manager Keith with his date. I give each one a kiss, and they all wish me good luck.

Our remaining family passed by us, with Charles sitting at the end. He grabs my hand and squeezes. In his eyes, I see anticipation, excitement, and hope. I try to reflect his feelings back at him. His stage portrayal has been a great transformation. After intense vocal lessons, Charles's singing voice is nearly as good as my dad's, plus his violin playing gave him some degree of confidence playing guitar. He doesn't turn into my dad, but rather portrays his essence with grace and power. I have no doubt he'll win Best Performance by a Leading Actor in a Musical.

As for my chances of winning for the costumes, my stomach turns. I would love to win a statue, but all the costumes by the nominees are amazing. In my case, simply being nominated was enough. I don't think we'll win my category. The night belongs to Charles.

The lights dim and conversations die down. Then, the host comes on stage and gives his monologue, but I can't concentrate. My hands fly to the back of my head several times, only to be reminded my knitting needles are sitting on my nightstand.

When Best Costume Design for a Musical is announced, my leg bounces. Charles places his large hand on my knee and looks at me with so much love I almost forget I'm seated at the Tony's. Almost.

"And the winner is . . . Melody Hunte-Wainwright, lead costume designer for *Hunted*!"

Tears spring to my eyes, and Charles places his warm hands on my cheeks, bringing my lips to his. Breaking apart, I jump to my feet and hug everyone before joining the rest of my crew on stage. I have no idea what my speech was, other than I offered all my love to Charles for his portrayal of my dad. In a daze, I walk off stage and go to the reporter area to answer their questions.

A murmur runs through the crowd back here, and someone nudges me. "It's your father's category."

I rush backstage to watch, holding my breath while the announcer opens the envelope.

"And the winner for Best Original Score Written for the Theater is . . . Braxton Hunte, Colton Frontage, Lex Hibbard, and Ricky Jones for *Hunted*."

I jump and scream as Daddy and his bandmates rush the stage, high-fiving each other.

My dad takes the mic. "I want to thank everyone behind the musical, especially my wife, Sara, who teaches me what love means every day. Congratulations to my daughter Melody, who won her Tony a little while ago. And, of course, to her husband, Chase Wright, who I hope wins his." He holds the statue up in the air to applause. The four of them make their way toward me, and I'm caught in my dad's embrace. He swings me around like he used to do when I was a kid, my legs flying akimbo.

"I'm so proud of you, Daddy!"

He kisses me. "And I of you." Eyes, identical to mine, glance toward his friends.

"I'll let you go do your press."

He nods and disappears backstage, while I return to my seat. Charles gives me a huge kiss, and King removes the Tony from my grasp. My brother nudges his shoulder against mine. "I never had any doubts." Angie leans forward and blows me a kiss, while Lindsay offers her palm for a high-five, Trent and Cordelia give me the thumbs-up, and Mom rubs my shoulder.

My happiness is cut short when the next category is announced, and it's Charles's. It's my turn to offer him support, although I harbor no doubts. The announcers take their time reading the list of nominees, and I beam at my husband when his nomination finally is spoken. His hold on my hand gets tighter.

"And the winner is"—they open the envelope—"Chase Wright!"

He expels all the air in his lungs before lunging at me. His kiss empties my mind. "Congrats, my love."

We share an intimate smile before he gets to his feet and bounds to the stage. I admire the way his tux shows off his amazing body, especially the way his ass looks in it. Remembering when his body fat went from almost zero to five to ten, and how distressed he was, I stifle a smirk. He still looks beyond amazing to me, even with an extra couple of pounds. Perhaps because of them.

Up at the podium, my husband beams into the audience, but his eyes remain locked on mine. A tear falls down my cheek as he begins to speak.

"Thank you so much for this." He raises the Tony. "I want to thank the Academy for your support of *Hunted*. I also want to thank my father-in-law, Braxton Hunte, for trusting me to do him justice every night on stage. And twice on Wednesdays and Saturdays."

The audience laughs.

"I've gotten to know the members of Hunte very well since we started this project, and I mean this from the bottom of my heart, they are the most badass guys you'll ever know. Brax, Colton, Lex, and Ricky, thank you so much for entrusting me with your story. And, Brax, for allowing me to share my life with your daughter, the love of my life, the mother of my son, Melody. Who is a Tony winner in her own right."

Even though I can't see it, I know cameras are focused on me. For once, I don't care. I'm so proud of my husband, it's taking everything out of me to remain seated.

Charles leans toward the microphone. "I'm honored that my parents together with my sister and her husband are here and able to share in this honor with me. As is my brother-in-law King Hunte and his wife Angie, plus Trent and Cordelia." The audience claps while I'm sure the cameras zoom down our row.

King places his hand on my arm. I want to look at him, but I refuse to take my eyes off my husband as he walks off stage. When I can't see him any longer, I hug my brother. My dad taps my shoulder, and I grab his and my mother's hands. Leaning forward, I wave at the others in my row. What a night! I'll never forget this amazing evening.

Hours later, after the drinks and the parties and the limo ride back home, after tucking in my baby boy and his cute little cousin, after bidding good night to my family, I snuggle into Charles's side.

"You're gorgeous and talented and wonderful." I kiss his naked chest and walk my fingers to his equally naked hip.

His hand stops mine, and he brings it out from under the covers and kisses it. "You're beautiful and creative and amazing."

"Seems like we've cornered the market on superlatives."

He winks. "Maybe not all of them. Yet." He rolls over, pinning me under his hard, hot body.

I buck my hips, cradling the part of him I want most. "I've got another one for you. How about sexy?"

Charles pushes my hair off my face. "I have another one for you. How about mommy times two?"

My breath stills. "As in?" I can't form a coherent thought.

"As in I think Rafe needs a baby brother or sister. What do you think?"

A tingle starts at the base of my spine and works its way upward. "I'd have to take a leave of absence."

Charles nods. "You did it before."

He's right. I did. "You're such a great father, Charles. This baby will have a super big brother, and you'll be great with him or her."

He kisses me, his tongue dancing with mine. "Not to mention the best mother ever, Goldie."

I burst into happiness. My hand slides down his naked body and wraps around his hard erection. Gripping him, I ask, "What are you waiting for?"

He brings my arms over my head and kisses me breathless. "You've made me the happiest man on this planet. The awards from others are nice, but you mean more to me than anything."

I kiss him again and again, because I can. I nip his earlobe and whisper, "Let's get to the making the baby part."

"Have at it, Goldie. I'm all yours. Forever."

A NOTE FROM ARELL

Dear Fabulous Reader,

Thank you so much for reading Out of the GOLD: Imagine Being Braxton Hunte's Daughter, the third standalone novel in The Hunte Family Series!

This is the story of Brax's daughter, Melody. Like her brother, King, she deals with the challenges that many rock star's children face ~ namely, forging their own identity in the wake of such an uber successful parent.

Costume designer Melody fought to stand on her own two feet separate and apart from her father's shadow. I deeply felt how hard she was hurt by Lindsay and Grant, and rooted so hard for her beautiful soul to soar. I hope you did as well.

Like Melody, Chase had it all ~ or did he? Goldie, as he came to think of Melody, helped him uncover his deepest desires and supported him in his hard road to realize them. I think we all can understand how hard his struggle was, and hope you cheered from the sidelines throughout his journey!

As usual, I've inserted a few parts of my own life throughout the book ~

• For our twentieth wedding anniversary, Big Mike and I took an amazing trip to Italy, and we spent a good amount of time on the Amalfi Coast. Scenes from Amalfi, Positano, and Ravello are directly taken from our trip. Reliving them in these pages brought a Mediterranean caress to my face, as I hope it did to yours! Please put this gorgeous part of the world on your bucket list ~ or visit it virtually!

• Charles and Goldie stop at a small restaurant on the road back to Ravello after their quick jaunt to New York City, and are waited on by Cush. Well, when Big Mike and I visited Florence, we were served by Cush in a restaurant across the street from the museum housing *The David*. He was so personable that I knew he'd have to make an appearance in one of my books!

• The spoon rest from Positano that Melody purchased, and now has a place of pride in her kitchen? Yup, you guessed it! I did purchase one during our Italy trip ~ only mine says "Amalfi" ~ and I always feel good vibes when my eyes land on it!

• I've lived in and around New York City for most of my adult life, and have had the pleasure of attending so many shows on Broadway. While I've never performed, I do understand the amazing feeling of being swept up in the story with my fellow audience members. I can only imagine that's how Charles would feel!

• I've devoured the relatively new "rockumentary" craze, having enjoyed both *Bohemian Rhapsody* and *Rocketman*. As my mind started piecing together Melody and Chase's story, I thought how awesome would it be for there to be a similar movie about Hunte. And so it was born! And now I want to see it, lol!!

Thanks for devoting your precious time to Out of the Gold: Imagine Being Braxton Hunte's Daughter. I hope got as sucked into Melody and Chase's story as I did!

All my love,
   Arell

GRATITUDE

Out of the Gold: Imagine Being Braxton Hunte's Daughter couldn't have happened without so many awesome people!

The book is dedicated to Big Mike's stepdad, Joel Gutterman. He suffered through so many complications following a "routine" triple bypass that resulted in a massive heart attack. After seven months, he finally found his rest when I was writing this book. To this "Gentle Giant," I wish you Godspeed.

My husband, Big Mike, is my support system and reality check. He roots for me to succeed and was excited when I told him this is my best book ever ~ even if he'll never read it!

To my Mom, you're my biggest cheerleader! Thanks for signing up for my e-newsletter, buying my paperbacks (even though I tell you all the time not to do that!), and being proud of my new career.

I'm so lucky to have been referred to Trenda Lundin of It's Your Story Content Editing. She really did a deep developmental dive into this book, and I'm forever grateful for her insights and suggestions.

Emily A. Lawrence did a great job with my edits, offering great ways to tighten up my prose and be much more effective in my storytelling.

Proofreaders Angel Nyx and Roxanne Blouin took their time and caught all my stupid errors. Big huge, virtual hugs!!

Cassy Roop of Pink Ink Designs is simply fabulous! Her cover took my breath away, and her formatting is second-to-none!

Anna Taylor Sweringen, Sophia Henry, and Jessa York are three amazing women I've met during my publishing journey. Anna took her time with me during the 2019 NJ Romance Writers Conference to help me flesh out how Charles gives up everything for love. Sophia and Jessa both helped me hash out some sticking points in outlining the book, and Sophia even read a very early draft to give me additional pointers. I'm forever grateful to them and promise to return the favor!

A big thanks to Noella Phillips, who suffered along with me as I made change after change to the outline so long ago, and kept pushing me to do better. I hope I nailed it!

Shout out to Kim Herman and Maria Dema who named the movie Chase was in! My initial thought was *The Twisted Ladder*, but during an e-newsletter competition, they came up with what has become *Doctor Manipul8* ~ so much better! Thank you to these creative ladies!!

To my alphas ~ Maria Dema, Sophia Dema, Joslyn Westbrook, Rebecca Berland, Gwyn Novak, and Dana Fernandez ~ and beta ~ Freddie Bonaire ~ you ladies rocked it!! Your comments improved this book a million times over.

Big love to my ARC Team!! Your enthusiasm over Melody and Chase's story never diminished, even though it was a long wait. Thank you for taking the time to read, review and share Out of the Gold: Imagine Being Braxton Hunte's Daughter!!!

My Facebook reader's group, Arell's Angels, is where I go to let loose! Shout out to my group of "Insiders" ~ Carmen Richter, Kerri Curtis, Tina Evans Atkinson, Ash Adams, Karen Hoffman, Nese Gordon, Debbie Kolins, and Nikki Lynn Archambault ~ your daily posts keep the group rockin'. Also, to Dana Fernandez, Laurie Gamble, Denise Shields, and all the Angels who participate in our Hotties of the Month, daily games, my weekly Facebook Lives, sneak peeks, collaborative stories, and author takeover Sundays ~ you're the best!

I'm so lucky to have the support of so many wonderful people in my life, especially Lilly Wilde, Dwight Lissenden, Joslyn Westbrook, and the amazing sprinters in The Virtual Write-In Group ~ Isabelle Peterson, Taylor Delong, Libby Waterford, DeLisa Smith, and Randy Wuske, all of whom make this journey so wonderful.

And to everyone who picks up this book, *I hope Melody and Charles light up your soul.* And if you enjoyed Out of the Gold: Imagine Being Braxton Hunte's Daughter, please share it with your friends and write a review.

Blessings,
   Arell

ABOUT THE AUTHOR

For as long as Arell Rivers can remember, she has been lost in a book. During her senior year in college, she picked up a romance novel … and instantly was hooked!

Arell started writing her first book because the characters were screaming at her to do so. The story came out in her dreams and attacked her in the shower, so she took to the computer to shut them up. But they kept talking.

Born and raised in New Jersey, Arell has what some may call a "checkered past." Prior to discovering her passion for writing romance, she practiced law, was a wedding and event planner and even dabbled in marketing. Arell lives with two adorable cats and a very supportive husband who doesn't care that the bed isn't made or dinner isn't on the table. When not in her writing cave, Arell is found cooking in the InstantPot, working out with Shaun T, or hitting the beach.

CONNECT WITH ARELL

- Subscribe to Arell's newsletter: geni.us/HunteSubscribe
- Join Arell's Facebook Group, "Arell's Angels":
  www.facebook.com/groups/arellsangels
- Like Arell's Facebook Page: www.facebook.com/arellrivers
- Follow Arell on Instagram:
  www.instagram.com/authorarell
- Hang out with Arell on Amazon: geni.us/ArellRivers
- Check out Arell on Goodreads: geni.us/ARGoodReads
- Follow Arell on BookBub: geni.us/BookBubFollow
- Head over to Arell's website: www.ArellRivers.com
- Email Arell: Arell@ArellRivers.com

ALSO BY ARELL RIVERS

The Hunte Family Series

An enemies-to-lovers series about the dynasty created by rocker Braxon Hunte

Book #1: Out of the Red (Brax and Sara, set in the mid 90s)

Book #2: Out of the Shadow (King and Angie)

Book #3: Out of the Gold (Melody and Chase)

Book #4: Out of the Blue (Trent and Cordelia)

Book #5: Out of the Box (box set of books 1-4 plus a bonus novella)

The Hold Series

A second chances series about rock star Cole Manchester, his publicist Rose Morgan, and their friends

Book #6: Hold On (prequel novella for Cole and Rose)

Book #1: No One to Hold (Cole and Rose trilogy, book 1)

Book #2: Hard to Hold (Cole and Rose trilogy, book 2)

Book #3: To Have and to Hold (Cole and Rose trilogy, book 3)

Book #4: Take Hold of Me (Wills and Emilie)

Book #5: Hold Still (Ozzy and McKenna)

Book #7: Hold Me (box set of books 1-3, 6, plus a bonus novella)

Sins of the Fathers

A billionaire series about the children of 3 notorious businessmen

Book #1: VICE (short story, originally published as "Tinsel Bomb" in the 2021 anthology TINSEL AND TATAS)

Book #2: ANGER (Theo and Amelia)

Book #3: PRIDE (Xander and Madison)

Book #4: IDLE (Paige and Jesse)

Untamed Coaster

A found family series following the rock band of the same name

Book #1: SINFUL BEATS (Quinn and Callum) (crossover from Sins of the Fathers)

OUT OF THE BLUE

Ready to learn about a mysterious new addition to the Hunte family?

Read on to enjoy the first chapter of OUT OF THE BLUE, *Book #4 in The Hunte Family Series!*

~

Trent

I never expected to see her again.

I *certainly* never thought my record label would hire her to be my band's social media manager.

But now, here we are, on a tour that could make or break my career—me with a massively dark secret that could ruin everything, and her with enough emotional baggage to fill a stadium. I should leave her alone.

Too bad I've never been good at doing what I *should*...

Cordelia

I've worked too hard, come too far, overcome too much, to get screwed over by something as frivolous and fleeting as *love*. So, I absolutely will *not* be giving in to my attraction to Trent.

Well, not *again*, anyway. That anonymous one-night stand is all he'll get out of me. My heart can never be part of the deal.

No matter how much he makes me wish things could be different for us…

∽

Out of the Blue
The Hunte Family Series, Book 4

Arell Rivers
©2020 Tarnished Halo Publishing LLC

Chapter 1 - Trent

I raise my mug, foam sloshing over the rim of the cold glass. "To The Light Rail. First we'll be an opening band, next stop world domination!"

As if they rehearsed it, Dwight, Joey, and Maurice chorus, "Here, here!"

Our glasses clink and the cool effervescence of Budweiser, my favorite beer, bounces down my throat. Even my Bud celebrates I'm on the cusp of achieving my dreams. Finally.

We're at our favorite Mexican restaurant in Jersey City, celebrating our impending big break, hopefully for the last time as unknowns. Sitting outside on this warm September day, we scarf down a variety of appetizers. All my bandmates put in for an extended leave from their day jobs today, since we'll be touring for at least the next few months. With everything that went down with Mom, I'm still on leave from mine. For a minute, I clasp the cross necklace she gave me ages ago. Using a jalapeño popper, I stuff down my grief over what happened. Not. Now.

Maurice pushes his thick rims up his face—the deep black frames a good complement to his skin tone. "We've been here before, guys, so we shouldn't get too ahead of ourselves."

Joey, our bassist, punches his shoulder. "Shut it, piano boy. No negative talk allowed." For emphasis, he shakes his head, his mass of dark brown hair swishing over his light brown skin.

Maurice takes a swig of his drink—his signature, a Cuba Libre. His glass thuds onto the table. "Don't get me wrong. I *am* pumped. I only wanted to bring us all back to reality."

"Fine. What can we do to change your mind?" interjects Dwight, our kickass drummer. "The radio station already called and said we won. We're opening for Hunte at Madison Square Garden in two weeks. *Fourteen days.* Then we'll be their opening band for the Eastern seaboard part of their tour. We're going to be huge!" As he speaks, his voice raises with eagerness.

Reaching over to my best friend, I put up my fist, which he bumps. "Yeah, this is it. I can feel it." And I can. This is so different from the other times we were supposedly "on the cusp." Excitement courses through my veins. If only my mother were here to experience our success with us. I stifle a sigh.

"I don't want to be a wet blanket, guys. We've been here before and it's always fizzled. I can't take another disappointment." Maurice sips his drink. "Neither can Fee. She said this is our last shot and if it doesn't work out, I'm going to have to step back."

Maurice and Fee got married three years ago, and they've been talking about having kids soon. Guess I can see her point, but fuck. This is our big break. "C'mon, Maurice. We won the radio station's contest fair and square. This time is different from all the others." I almost believe my own words.

His shoulders rise then fall. "We still haven't heard from Apex."

He's right. Hunte's label hasn't contacted us yet. "We will, man.

How about this?" I toss my cell on the table. "Will you feel better when they call?"

Maurice stares at my silent phone. "Well, yeah."

"Okay. While we wait, you can coddle your Cuba Libre. The rest of us will more than cover for your pussy ass." My bandmates grin at our banter. As if by unwritten agreement, we finish our drinks—including Maurice—and the server delivers another round together with our meals.

Munching on some of the remaining nachos, Dwight turns to me. "Wish your mom were here to cheer us on." He offers me a chip.

Automatically, I pop the tortilla into my mouth. Unlike when I *thought* about her, his *speaking* about my mother does dampen my spirits. The pain of her loss, only four months ago, is still raw. I rub my arm, over the tattoo I got in her honor. "Thanks. Me, too."

"I'm sure she's looking down on us, proud as all get out. I bet she even had her finger on the pulse of the contest, if I know her." Dwight spreads his own hands wide over the table.

His words are like a balm. "I can see her now, directing everyone from the Pearly Gates." I smile at my closest friends—for all intents and purposes, my only remaining family. "She's probably taking a victory lap with her harp and halo right now." I picture her doing just that. Telling everyone up in heaven her boy won this contest.

I'm jolted out of my pleasant musings when my phone bounces. Four pairs of eyes land on the phone jumping on the table. It's an unknown number from New York City.

Clearing my throat, I scoop it up. "Hello?"

A woman's voice floats through the line. "Is this Trent Washington?"

"Yes."

"I'm Cordelia Hernandez, and I work for Apex Hits. I've been instructed to call and give you the logistics for your performance at Madison Square Garden, opening for Hunte in two weeks."

Although I'd tossed out the phone to pacify Maurice, I never thought this call would come through now. "Okay. Good. Great." I fumble to put my phone on speaker. "Is it alright if I put you on speaker? I'm with my band now."

"Sure. Are you ready?"

"For?"

She sighs. "For the details about the concert?"

"Oh, right. Yeah. I mean, no. I need to get some paper." *Way to play it cool.* My bandmates pass me a napkin and a borrowed pen. "Got it. Shoot." I write down her detailed instructions. When the call concludes, I hold up the napkin toward Maurice. "Proof enough for you?"

Through his thick glasses, he squints as he reads my chicken scratch. Looking up at me, his face sports a wide smile. "It's real."

We all ride the high of winning. I haven't felt this good in ages. And I'm sure Mom had a hand in our good fortune.

When all the food has been eaten, and more celebratory drinks downed, our meal wraps. I knock on the table. "Guys, I wouldn't want to be on this journey with any other group. This is it. We're on our way. Remember when Maroon 5 wasn't known at all and then they opened for The Rolling Stones? We're the next Maroon 5!"

"I think they already had won some Grammys before they landed the gig," Maurice corrects me. Joey pops him on the back of his head, and we laugh.

As we walk out of the restaurant, Dwight slaps my back. "Okay, Adam Levine. See you tomorrow at rehearsal." He hops on his beloved Harley, straps on his helmet, and revs the engine. Twice.

I grin all the way home. Unlocking the door to Mom's townhouse —now mine—I enter the empty space and my lips compress. My excitement at our win turns down to simmer. After tossing my keys into the bowl on the entry table as Mom always chided me to do, I stride into the living room.

"We're going to be big!" I scream to no one as I sink into my recliner. The puffy black one Mom thought was ugly but still allowed me to buy.

Everyone in the band, minus me, is now married. Dwight got hitched only three months ago—it was his wedding Mom was buying a present for when she was killed in the mall shooting. The pain surrounding her death rears. His guilt. My agony.

I pack those memories away and shunt them into the darkest recesses of my mind. Today is only about happy thoughts. A new beginning.

Restless, I stand and go into the kitchen for a bottle of water. After I down it and flip through all the channels on my television, three times, I leave the clicker on the coffee table. Drifting through the house, I soak in the details my mother used to make our thirteen hundred square-foot Jersey City townhouse a home. The curtains from Target that looked like those on an HGTV show. A rug Mom picked up at a flea market as it reminded her of one she saw at a hotel. The mismatched china, collected from thrift stores, I haven't had the heart to throw away.

Her touch is still all around me, even if she's not.

I find myself loitering at the threshold of her room, which contains her desk. It's the last piece of furniture I still need to go through. I wander inside and my hand alights on her closet's door pull. I slide the door open. Lilac, faint, reaches my nose from the couple of blouses still on hangers. My eyes squeeze shut and I inhale Mom's scent.

After a few beats, I open my eyes and face her desk. Buoyed by my band's good fortune, and supported by her spirit around me, I shut the closet door and sit on her chair.

I wet my lips and lift the rolltop.

Post-its, in all different colors, greet me. Her precise handwriting wraps around my heart and throat, constricting both. Slowly, I gather each sticky note and throw them away. It's not like she needs to be reminded about friends' birthdays or events anymore. The heart-shaped one with "Dwight + Denice" on it makes my heart race.

Dwight blamed himself for her death until I was able to let him off the hook. Which was only thanks to my therapist's help. After all, Dwight didn't make her go to the mall to pick up their wedding present on that fateful day. A horrible coincidence, but he's not responsible. No. That honor belongs to the mall shooter alone. The mantra my therapist gave me replays in my mind several times—*Her death wasn't his fault, he didn't send the shooter there*—until my breathing gets under control and I accept it as true. Again. Grace flows through my body. For her. For them. For me.

However, my grace never will extend to the fucking shooter. No, he left ten people dead before he turned the gun on himself. Police told me he was some white supremacist pig who targeted the mall because it's in a "Black neighborhood." I refuse to even *think* his name. Only pray he burns for eternity.

Shaking my head, I focus on my task and go through the rest of the items on her desk, then move on to the top drawer. It's surprisingly easy to process her things. Papers she thought were important no longer hold any sway. Except for her tax forms, which I carefully put into a pile with contracts for her house. My house, I correct myself.

I go to open the middle drawer but it refuses to budge. Figuring something got stuck, I try shimmying it with no luck. As I don't want to break anything, I continue to the bottom drawer where several files brim with my report cards, which are ages old. I flip through some, remembering milestones from second grade and even high school.

Poor Mom. She really tried to keep me focused, but my attention always diverted to the guitar. I would practice for hours in my room and delay doing my homework until she bugged me enough. But I still managed to get into Jersey City State and major in music production. My degree has helped the band several times, so I don't think of it as wasted years. Even though all I wanted to do was perform.

Here I am over a decade later, poised to make our mark on the music world. Finally. Overnight success, we are not. I know deep inside, though, this truly is our big break. We're going to become household names.

I'll make Mom proud. She always believed in me. Now it's my time to shine. I just wish like hell she were here to experience it with me.

Sighing, I throw away the last of her useless papers and return to the stuck drawer. As I'm studying it, I realize there's a keyhole. Hmmm. Why would Mom lock a drawer in her own bedroom?

Intrigued, I paw around for a key but come up empty. Wait! Didn't she keep some keys in a little ceramic cup on her dresser? I stride over there, and sure enough, several keys remain inside. Taking the whole cup back to the desk, I try each until one fits inside. Turning it, the drawer pops open.

"Success!"

I can't wait to see what she felt was so important. When I rip open the drawer, I'm greeted by several hardback books. Some have floral covers, others have stripes, while others have world maps.

Frowning, I pick up one that simply says "Diary," and my mind immediately drifts back in time to when I was a kid, maybe six or seven years old. Mom sat with one of these books in her rocking chair —which I've moved into the living room beside my recliner. Curled up, she had a pen in her hand and wet cheeks.

I remember asking her what was wrong. She smiled through her tears and said she wished my father could have seen how big and strong I'm becoming. How he would've celebrated with me as I picked up my first guitar and started playing like I was born to do.

I ran over and gave her a big hug. Sometimes she would look so sad, and I'd leave her alone to mourn. My dad, her only true love, was a Marine killed in Operation Desert Storm in the Gulf War before he even found out about my existence. They definitely would've gotten married if he'd returned from the war. She never dated after him. At least they're reunited now.

Dare I read her most private words?

I debate with myself for ten full minutes before cracking open her diary.

"How dare you?" I scream at the tombstone. "You had no right!"

I read the inscription aloud. "Lorinda Washington. Beloved mother, daughter, sister. Dancing with the angels." Yanking on my short dreadlocks, I sneer, "You were beloved by them only because your parents predeceased you. And why did I feel it necessary to add in about my aunt? Not like you talked with her for over a decade."

Kicking the ground next to her grave, I offer a derisive laugh. "Should've only said one word. 'Liar.'"

I turn my back and take two steps away, only to spin around and stare down once again at my mother's final resting place. "You know what? This is *your* cross to bear. You did this. It's all on you. Hope you rot in Hell!"

My hands form fists. "Don't ever expect to see me back here again. I'm never coming back."

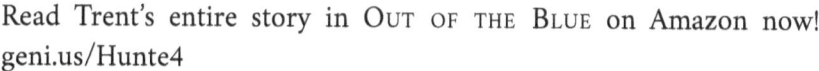

Read Trent's entire story in OUT OF THE BLUE on Amazon now! geni.us/Hunte4